BENEATH BLACK ICE

A NEW YORK CITY TALE

By BlackkIce Smooth

BENEATH BLACK ICE

Cover Art Design Credit: Mat Yan

Cover Art Design Vision: BlackkIce Smooth

Edited By: Trenton D. Munson, Natasha Counts, Carlton Clayton & Author

Beneath Black Ice ®™

Published By: BlackkIce Productions

Library of Congress Control Number: 2016953031

ISBN:978-0-9980810-0-7 (pbk)

ISBN:978-0-9980810-1-4 (ebook)

WARNING: This novel contains explicit dialogue.

The views expressed in this work are solely those of the author.

Manufactured in the United States of America

10987654321

BlackkIce Productions

DEDICATION

I dedicate this book to my Father and all my loved ones that have passed on, whether family or close friends.

BROOKLYN, WE DID IT!

ACKNOWLEDGEMENT

First, I would like to thank the almighty creator, for all the blessings brought into my life. My parents: Dorothy and James (May he continue to Rest in Peace) for giving me life, support and guidance. My sister Dorothy for support. My two children: Shanequa and Jaden. Both the Mothers of my children: Lisa and Sharon, for the gift of my children. All my Aunts, Uncles, Nieces and Nephews. All my cousins. Audrey Hawkins aka GaGa and extended Marcelle family.

My uncle Carlton Clayton, for always looking out for me, my mom and sister. Welcoming me into your home, when I visit your state to take my daughter off to College. Advise, and contributing some editing in regard to this novel. The entire Boyd family, Clayton family, Lewis family, McIntiosh family, McRae family, Singleton family, Bell family, Battle family, Bryant family, Isom family, Marcelle family, Hawkins family.

I would like to thank whomever was the lady in my life in the mist of the creation of this novel, for the years of listening and supporting my ideas. I would like to thank Val Carey, for inspiring me to write a novel, once she released her first edition of TOTM.

Natasha Counts, for giving advice and contributing to some editing in regard to this novel. You can now wipe off the dust on that manuscript I sent you (Sheesh). You know the one, that you barely touched.

Hakim Riddick and the entire 290 family, for all the great years we all shared together as one big happy family. The entire Brownsville Brooklyn Section. The entire PS175, PS156, JHS263(Marcus), and Wingate HS family (85-89")

The entire HB4 and SEQI family. Last but not least, All the Haters and Doubters for keeping me in your thoughts for failure as I succeed.

Table of Contents

SURPRISE

The evening of April 19, 2003 was a warm Saturday, it was the day before Easter Sunday in the Brownsville section of Brooklyn and the local shopping district of Pitkin and Belmont Avenues were packed with shoppers and thieves making last minute holiday run.

The sounds of church choirs filled the air with early jubilation as they rehearsed their spirituals for the next morning services. The local barbershops and beauty salons were packed with customers wanting to look their best for the special holiday.

Back in the days, especially in 1980's to mid 1990s, Easter was a big thing in New York City urban communities. It was a welcoming of spring among being a festival and holiday celebrating the resurrection of Jesus Christ. Families prepared themselves the day before for the next day's big show, where they will be all dressed up in new clothes, some adorned in fancy hats and chic hairstyles. The neighborhoods burst in a rainbow of colors.

Not only were the churches packed on Easter Sunday (mostly by those whom only attended church on Easter, Christmas, funerals and weddings), but Time Square (the Forty Deuce) was crawling with people; locals and tourist alike.

Amusement parks, movie theatres, skating rinks and bowling alleys were very popular places to attend too.

Barbershops and hair salons made a killing in cash during Easter weekend, as customers lined up during the early hours of the day outside waiting for the shops to open. It was simply a weekend of making money and spending it.

Career criminal, Hakim Gamble sat inside a parked vehicle just of the corner of Blake and Rockaways Avenue in the heart of Brownsville. Hakim was known on the streets as "Demon" due to his unusually gray eyes and very dark complexion. He focused his attention on MUSTAFA'S, a local barbershop he frequented for a few months, to get a haircut.

He sat there intently and patiently, watching customers enter and leave the shop, until he received a text message on his cellphone. After receiving the message, he quickly exited his vehicle.

MUSTAFA'S, a popular shop with a small beauty salon section inside. There were eight work stations in all. Six were barbers; the beauticians used the other two. The waiting area easily accommodated twenty customers and there were four large screen televisions connected to an elaborate home theatre system to keep everyone entertained. A front reception desk made of marble with a small display hair products. African artifacts, framed posters of hometown hero's athletes like Mike Tyson, Riddick Bowe, Shannon Briggs, Dwayne" Pearl" Washington, Zab Judah decorated the walls throughout the establishment. Mustafa's beauticians and barbers were the best in Brooklyn and well known throughout the city.

The shop was situated between a Spanish restaurant and a bodega. For many years, during the late 1970's and early 1990's it had been a laundromat it was purchased and converted it into a barbershop.

"Everybody shut the fuck up and don't move!" Demon shouted as he burst his way through the entrance panning his shotgun across the room. The door crashed hard into the front counter, knocking over items on display. In one motion he slammed it shut, flipped the OPEN sign to CLOSED and pulled down the curtain. He positioned himself in front of the door, blocking the only exit.

Before he arrived, the shop was buzzing; all the waiting area seats were all occupied and the work stations were full. Raucous chit chat and gossip filled the room, as each person tried to talk over the next. Now the place was under siege; patrons were motionless as if they were in a freeze frame on a movie set. Despite the confusion, no one dared to make the slightest move.

The dirty oversized tan trench coat he wore concealed his weapon as he stood at the front door waiting to be buzzed in by King, one of the shops barbers, who often sat at the front desk.

Unlike his prior visits, Demon wasn't well dressed in a suit and tie. Under the coat he wore a black T shirt, dark jeans, and worn-down tan construction boots. He had on a black baseball cap, that was pulled down, just above his eyes.

Demon towered over everyone; his head was just inches from the top of the door frame. Even the oversized trench coat couldn't conceal his broad shoulders and herculean arms. His light gray eyes, so unusual for his dark complexion glowed deep in their sockets, like a Gladiator. It wasn't necessary to state his intentions, everyone knew not to test him.

"If you got a cell phone, you better drop that shit on the floor right now!" Demon demanded as he scanned the room. "Because if I find one on you later, your dead!" Demon continued to warn his victims. The buzzing of the hair clippers and snipping of scissors silenced; replaced by the clatter of the phones hitting the floor, some with their batteries dislodged and skittered across the tile.

Actor Denzel Washington, whom was portraying Malcom X in the film X, was preaching on the four wall mounted television screens. The volume was now uncomfortably loud now that the shop was quiet and still. The loud televisions seemed to annoy Demon, as well as the sermon. The smell of the hair relaxing products and heated hair pressing equipment seem more intense now, almost palpable, as they hung in the still air. Demon directed his main attention to Mustafa, whom stood at the far end of the shop at his work station next to his customer, with his clippers still in his hand and raised the barrel of his shotgun and aimed it in Mustafa's direction, causing customers sitting in the barber's and beauticians chair within the path to naturally duck.

Everyone's heart skipped a beat, as they all thought the gunman was about to start firing his weapon. Mustafa's eyes widened like a deer in a headlight as he stayed still and alert, he did not move his eyes from the barrel of the gun that was pointed in him from across the room.

Mustafa was the owner of the shop, whom was also a very skilled barber with a large and loyal clientele of customers throughout the city. He was well connected in the music industry, professional athletes and well-known drug kingpins that visited his shop on a regular basis. He attended to them personally.

The years had been good to the young handsome entrepreneur, whom maintained his athletic stamina he had back in his college football days. He was polished, well-groomed and disciplined, looking much younger than his 30 years of age.

Women would crowd the shop every weekend to get their hair done by the beauticians that worked there, bring their children to get a fresh hairdo, but mainly to get a glimpse of Mustafa's chiseled biceps or just to drool at his T-shirt that stretched over his massive chest, wide back and eight-pack. They wanted to see him, smell him, be near him. He also had personal visitors, women like those in the shop, both married and single, who visited him in between appointments on a weekly basis. These visitors were there for personal business that took place in the office, for reasons unlike the other business that took place there.

"Mustafa! Turn that shit off, before I blast them off the fucking wall!" Demon said forcefully, referring to the TV's. "And after you do that, bring the key to this door and get the fuck over here!" Demon continued.

Mustafa quickly shut down the TV's, picked up some keys from his work station counter and walked toward Demon through the stillness in the shop, deliberately keeping the keys in the sight of Demon. Mustafa could feel the weight of the customers eyes heavy on his back as he got closer to the barrel of Demon weapon. While up closer, Mustafa got a good look at the gunman. *Demon* he thought to himself, as the gray eyes and very dark skin was all it took to recognize the gunman. At first Mustafa didn't indicate any sign of recognition, but figured since him and Demon had many friendly conversations while he sat in his chair in the past, maybe he could talk the gunman out of the robbery. "You don't have to do this, Demon. There's kids and women in here man. You got everybody scared in here," Mustafa said.

"Shut the fuck up!" Demon boldly cut him off.

"You know what the fuck this is! I don't give a fuck who's in here nigga!" Demon continued as Mustafa stood there speechless, while recognizing Demon was all business.

"Which one of them keys lock this door?" Demon asked just before someone on the outside started banging on the door to get in. The person banging on the door, then put his face to the window on the side where the front desk was and peeked in.

Oh Shit! Demon thought to himself as he looked at Mustafa and then King, whom was still sitting at the front desk. King wisely stood up and signaled to the guy who was looking in, that the shop wasn't taking any more customers, so the guy jokingly put up his middle finger and walked away.

"The keys, nigga! Which one is for this door?" Demon asked after being interrupted by the guy who was knocking.

"This one," Mustafa responded as he sorted out the keys and showed Demon which one.

"Give them up and get your ass out there and pull down them side window gates!" Demon continued as he grabbed the key out Mustafa hand. Due to the door being operated by an electronic buzzer, and buzzer buttons being located at the front desk and every workstation in the shop, Demon wanted the door locked by key. Locking the door by key pretty much bolted the door and gave him total control of the only exit, if he became somehow distracted and avoiding someone quickly hitting a buzzer button to escape.

It was now clear to everyone in the shop, that the gunman and Mustafa knew each other. Mustafa thought back to Demon's prior visits to the shop, when he posed as a normal customer. Demon first visit, he requested Mustafa over the other barbers, and patiently waited until he finished with numerous clients that had appointments. After a few visits, he became a regular and booked appointments himself. Once in his chair, he would always converse with Mustafa, the other barbers and beauticians on a friendly basis, gaining their friendship and trust. He wore dress suits and carried a brief case as if he worked on Wall Street.

The conversation between Mustafa and Demon always leaned toward compliments on Mustafa's expensive taste in clothing, the jewelry he wore, the vehicles he drove, where he lived, the women that visited him at the shop and his exceptional skills at building custom motorcycles. Mustafa whom started building motorcycles as a hobby for himself, now built motorcycles for selected customers, meaning those whom could offered to pay for them. There was often one of his creations on display in the shop.

It never dawned on Mustafa during Demon's prior visits, that the guy he considered to be a friend, was staking him out and lining him up for the kill.

This muthafucka, did his homework on me. From the first day, he walked in my shop and requested me, He knew damn well he was gonna rob me. I should've seen it coming and did my own homework on this muthafucka, before getting cool with this thirsty nigga Mustafa thought to himself as he handed over the keys to Demon. Demon then placed the cold barrel of his shotgun against Mustafa's forehead. Mustafa thought it was just talk when he would hear people say, that their life flashed before their eyes. In a way, he still thought it was bullshit as his own life now seemed like a movie rewind and fast forwarded over and over again.

The look in Demon's eyes, was nothing less than a hungry panther in a darkened jungle, that was ready to feed on its prey flesh. Mustafa then closed his eyes, as they began to seep with tears. The barrel became unsteady against his now moistened forehead, sliding down a bit towards his eyes and nose.

"Open your fucking eyes and stop acting like a little bitch, Mustafa. Get your shit together nigga," Demon said, not taking his eyes off of him. "The streets been talking, my nigga. You know the name of the game. It's time you start paying hood taxes," Demon continued, hinting to Mustafa that he knows a little more about his business beyond the shop and motorcycles. Mustafa then opened his eyes, realizing what Demon was really after. Demon smirked at Mustafa's reaction, then tapped the barrel on his forehead.

"Yeah, nigga. I know your little secret," Demon said, while nodding his head. "You got three minutes to get your ass outside and pull down the gates covering the windows down and get your ass back in here!" Demon continued as he tapped the barrel on Mustafa's forehead a little harder.

"Okay," Mustafa replied.

"If you come across any other customers asking you to come in, you better tell them the shop is closed and ain't taking any more customers for the day. If you bring another muthafucka in here, try to run, signal for help or even blink fucking funny, I'm gonna kill you and the rest of theses muthafuckas in here!" Demon warned Mustafa. Don't test me nigga! Don't test me!" Demon continued to warn Mustafa as he nudged his head with the barrel of his gun.

Mustafa acknowledged Demon by nodding his head and wished to himself that he had his forty-four magnum on him instead of it being inside of the desk in the back office.

All types of thoughts entered Mustafa's mind all at the same time. *Who put Demon on to my hustle and lined me up? Should I take a chance and grab his gun or just run once I get outside? If I run, will he really try and shoot me and kill everybody else in the shop or would he have a lookout outside gun me down if I attempted to cut out or tell passerby what was going on inside the shop?*

Were the thoughts than ran ramped in Mustafa's mind. He wasn't sure if Demon was working alone and was very cautious about acting on his thoughts. Demon then ordered King to buzz the door and stepped aside allowing Mustafa to pass him, but kept his weapon trained on him as if he was a moving target while Mustafa went to open the door so he could pull down the gates.

Once outside, Mustafa wanted to run. The sun rays beat down on his head, the sky still bright and hot for this time of day. He looked to his left towards Sutter Avenue and then to his right at Blake Avenue. He figured if he pulled down the gate in front of the door quickly, it would trap Demon and give him time to make it around the corner of Blake Avenue. There were too many people milling about for Demon to pop outside and take a chance of shooting at him. But he didn't know if Demon was acting alone or had any lookouts.

Fuck this shit! I'm getting the fuck out of here! Mustafa thought to himself as he turned around to take off running and bumped into one of King's regular customers, that was trying to enter the shop.

"Damn, Mustafa! You almost ran me over like you Bo Jackson!" The customer looking to gain entry jokingly said as Mustafa almost put him on his ass.

"Sorry about that, my brother. I was just rushing to pull down the gates, my mind is somewhere else," Mustafa responded.

"Pull down the gates? You shutting down the shop already? But it's still early," The customer disputed, while checking his watch for the time.

"We've been open since six in the morning, we get tired too you know," Mustafa continued as he pulled down the gate that revealed the front desk, where King was sitting.

"Look at all them heads, sitting in there. Can you squeeze me in, for a cut?" The customer asked, while placing his face to the window and seeing everyone look at him strangely.

"Nah, man. Come through early tomorrow, I'll make sure you get a cut first," Mustafa answered as he began to close the other gate.

"That's fucked up, Mustafa. Is this how you treat your regulars now?" The customer asked as he started to back up and walk away.

"Nah, man. I'm just honoring my staff wishes. Don't take it personal," Mustafa responded. "How about this? If you come through bright and early tomorrow, I will personally give cut your hair for free," Mustafa continued.

"A free cut?" The passerby asked.

"Yep," Mustafa quickly responded, hoping the passerby would hurry up and leave.

"Say no more. I'm not turning down a free cut, I'll see you tomorrow then," The passerby replied before walking off.

After King's customer walked off, Mustafa then made his way over to the next gate and notice the barrel of the shotgun trained on him through the curtain. Mustafa's eyes widened in surprise and he nearly pissed on himself, he wondered if Demon have been watching and listening the whole time. Once again, Mustafa was looking down the barrel of a shotgun that quickly erased his chain of thought about escaping.

Reality started to kick in and he realized that his life and the lives of everyone in the shop would be at great risk, if Demon meant everything he said, if he didn't follow his instructions. He quickly pulled down the other gate, that took away all the visibility to the inside of the salon and returned inside.

Once back inside the shop, Demon locked the door as Mustafa stood near him. Demon then placed the shotgun barrel up under Mustafa's chin as if he was going to blow his brain right out of his skull. Demon's eyes pierced Mustafa's soul as he stared at him. He could read Mustafa's fear yet for some unknown reason hesitated to pull the trigger, and removed his weapon from under Mustafa's shaking chin. He then gave Mustafa a head signal to move toward his work station.

As Mustafa turned around to walk away as instructed, he was struck on the back of the head with the shotgun. Mustafa drop lifelessly to the floor. He laid there motionless for a few seconds then started to move. When he gathered himself, and attempted to rise back to his feet. Demon kicked him in the gut, lifting him off the floor and then viciously stomped back down to the floor.

"Nigga, did you think I didn't see you about to take off running, muthafucka?!" Demon shouted while pressing his boot harder onto Mustafa's back. "You think I'm a fucking joke? I told you not to test me nigga! You lucky the only reason you still breathing right now, is because I know what you got in that safe back there," Demon continued to shout as he trained his weapon on Mustafa as if he was ready to take his life. He scanned the room. So, if you and the rest of these muthafuckas in here want to live! Yall better do what the fuck I say! When I say it!" the enraged Demon continued to shout.

Mustafa was still on the floor and dizzy from the attack. Once again, he struggled to get to his feet, but was stomped down and pressed to the floor again. Everyone watched on as things started to spiral out of control. Blood was now leaking from Mustafa's head, staining the white tile crimson of the floor. The gun was trained on Mustafa's head and it seemed as if Demon was going to pull the trigger.

"Chill Big Man! I think he gets the point already! So, chill," The customer whom was sitting in Mustafa's chair, whom was now standing shouted.

"Oh my God, no," A female customer whispered, cradling her hands over her mouth, as the brave customer started to walk towards Demon. The brave customer, a local of the neighborhood that went by the name of Curly, then pulled out a .357 Magnum pistol from his waistband and stared at Demon until he gained his attention.

Demon then looked over at Curly and they both began to smile. Everyone became very tense and were afraid that all hell was about to break loose.

"Get your punk ass up muthafucka," Demon ordered Mustafa, whom struggled to get on his feet.

"You better be lucky my man stepped in when he did. Now, take your stupid ass over there to my boy, before I change my mind and put a bullet in your head," Demon ordered him on with a barrel tap on the back. Mustafa slowly got up and staggered to held his bleeding skull. He slowly walked towards the accomplice holding the back of his head trying to contain the bleeding. The blood leaked through his fingertips onto the floor.

"Yo! Take this nigga into his office and get the coke and cash out the safe, so we can get the fuck out of here," Demon instructed Curly. "And make sure you shut down the surveillance camera and take the tapes out of the recorder," Demon continued.

Curly acknowledged Demon, then aimed his weapon at Mustafa's head as he approached him. Once Mustafa was near him, he ordered him to turn around then frisked him for any hidden weapons. He then removed Mustafa's gold Rolex watch from his wrist and took his wallet that was filled with Benjamin's from his pants pocket. Curly then stuffed Mustafa's belongings into his own pocket and then grabbed Mustafa by the arm and pressed his weapon into the salon owner's side.

Mustafa's head continued to leak blood as Curly pushed him into the office, and closed the door behind them. Once inside the office, the accomplice turned on the radio that was located on Mustafa's desk and turned up the volume to the maximum.

Demon decided to kick over a large waste basket that was located near the front door. He then dumped all the garbage out of it onto the floor. He then started to stare at King, whom was still sitting at the front desk.

Oh Shit! I hope this fool don't bust upside my head, like he did Mustafa King thought to himself as Demon started to stare at him. He knew it was basically his fault for not paying attention when he let Demon in, because he was caught up gambling, playing poker on the internet.

King wore a large gold Cuban link necklace that held a large gold boxing gloves medallion studded with diamonds around his neck.

The diamonds sparkled under the florescent lights of the shop as well as the diamond rings he wore on his fingers. He also wore a pair of big diamond stud earrings, resembling the ones that R&B singer R. Kelly and athletes like NBA Star Allen Iverson would be seen wearing.

"King, you already know my nigga. Take all that shit off," Demon said, as he instructed him to remove his jewelry. As a matter of fact. I'll take that laptop too, nigga. I don't give a fuck if you were once a two-time Golden Glove champ. Anybody could get it! And if you even think about trying that boxing shit with me, I'll blow your fucking chest out!" Demon shouted as he aimed his weapon at King. King, a product of the streets, wanted to flex on Demon and hesitated to Demon's instructions at first, until Demon moved in a little closer on him. He then thought about how Mustafa almost got his brains blown out.

So, he wisely closed his laptop and placed it on the counter along with all of his jewelry. The gunman removed King's jewelry and laptop from the counter and tossed it into the empty waste basket. He then ordered King to come from behind the front desk.

Demon then looked over at a customer that was sitting in the waiting area near the door.

"Okay, it's show time, Homie. Dig King's and the rest of these muthfuckas pockets out and let's get this money," Demon said.

Everyone was confused at the command until another accomplice whom was posing as an awaiting customer, got up and pulled out a 9mm handgun, aiming it at King. King recognized the accomplice to be Bow, a local thug that was in and out of jail for all types of shit.

"Alright, listen up muthafuckas. Take everything out of your pockets, I want them nice and empty. Now!" Bow yelled out as he dug into King's pockets and checked him for a weapon. "Everything means everything. Don't even think about bullshitting me. I don't have a problem with putting a bullet in your ass," Bow continued as he removed King's wallet and loose cash from his pockets and tossed it into the waste basket as Demon swept the room with the aim of his shotgun.

After removing King's property from his pockets, He then ordered the remaining employees of the shop to remove their property from their pockets and to toss it into the waste basket also. He then ordered them to get face down on the floor and tied up their hands and feet with large plastic zip ties. Doubting that the employees gave up everything, He gave each individual a more complete search, by checking inside of socks, shoes and the female's bras for that hidden treasure.

"Jack pot!" Bow shouted as he spotted a large lump in King's sock. The large lump, turned out to be just over two thousand dollars in cash, he removed it and tossed it into the waste basket.

Bow then slugged King in the back of the head for attempting to hold out on such a large sum of money, then he continued to give the rest of the employees a second search for hidden cash and valuables. Bow was able to come up with a few more dollars than voluntarily given.

Demon started to look at his watch as if he was working within a time frame. He then looked towards the rear office door, as if he was anticipating Curly to emerge from the rear office with the drugs and cash from the safe at any giving second. He realized that the robbery was falling behind schedule and needed the pace to be picked up.

"Hurry up with them niggas already! You got to hit all these customers pockets too. By the time our homie come from the back, we should be ready to get the fuck out of here!" Demon instructed Bow, referring to the customers sitting in the waiting area, and letting his partner know he wasn't working fast enough.

After giving the employees a good search, bow then walked over to the customers whom were sitting in the waiting area with the waste basket as each person dropped their property into it, including their cellular phones they previously dropped to the floor.

"Now take off your clothes, boys and girls. I don't want to see nothing but drawers, panties and bras. And if you don't have on any drawers or panties, don't worry, your already ass out!" Bow said as he instructed the customers in the waiting area to take off their shit. "Strip down and pass everything to the front," Bow continued to instruct. Once everyone in that area had their clothes off and tossed their clothes forward.

"Now get down on the floor and place your hands behind your head," Demon then instructed. The customers in the waiting area did as they were told.

Yo! Did you clear them yet? If not, then hurry the fuck up and hit them customers sitting over there in those chairs," Demon said referring to the customers sitting in the barbers and beautician's chairs as he looked back at his watch. "And when you finish with them, check on our boy in the back, because he is taking too long," Demon continued. Bow started working on the customers sitting in the barber and beautician chairs. He was down to one last customer. Everyone else that was sitting in a chair, has giving up their valuables, stripped off their clothes and laid down on floor.

"Oh shit!" Bow yelled out in disbelief. "Yo, Big man, check this muthafucka out," Bow said while pointing at a customer sleeping in one of the barber's chair.

Demon then looked over at Bow to see what was going on, and noticed the guy sleeping then looked back at Bow whom had a smirk on his face as if he was entertained by the sleeping customer.

"Use your brain, nigga. There's no way with all this commotion that he could be asleep. This not a game nigga, wake his punk ass up and take his shit. Then go see what the fuck is taking Mustafa so long with giving up what we came here for," Demon whom was growing impatient said as he started to place the key in the door cylinder. Bow hit the sleeper hard across the face, forward then back slapped him with his gun, waking him into delirium.

The customer eyes popped open fast as he nearly fell out the chair from the vicious blows. He naturally jumped up from the chair, but stumbled back into it due to being dazed from the blows to the face. He rubbed his eyes to clear his vision and suddenly noticed the Bow holding a gun to his face. He nervously looked around and noticed that all the shop employees were laying on the floor tied up. He also noticed that all the other customers were grief stricken from the event at hand.

"Rise and shine muthafucka. That dream you was having, just turned into a fucking nightmare, nigga," Bow said as he pointed his weapon at the much taller customer. The customer finally gathered his senses and started to size up the man holding the gun in his face. He then cut his eye towards Demon then back at the gunman standing before him.

"Sit your punk-ass down muthafucka and take everything out of your fucking pockets, put it in this basket then strip," Bow ordered the customer as he slid near the customer with his foot. The customer whom was still wearing the barber's apron around his neck fell backwards onto the chair and started to nervously fumble through his pants pocket. He pulled out his wallet and went to place it in the waste basket, but dropped it and it slid across the floor.

Bow looked at the customer in disbelief as the wallet slid across the floor. He figured the customer was either nervous or was being an asshole. He leaned toward the customer as if he was going to strike him for dropping the wallet on the floor and then. A loud banging against the office door erupted as struggle ensued between Mustafa and Curly behind it.

The struggle could be heard very clearly over the loud music that was playing in there by everyone in the shop. Demon and Bow looked at each other in search of an answer.

Demon grew nervous and now became more and more anxious to finish the robbery and get the hell out the shop once he heard the ruckus going on in the back. He placed the key in the door cylinder for a quick exit when it was time for him and his two accomplices were ready to escape and then suddenly.

"BANG! A loud gun shot rang out from behind the closed office door that was quickly followed by two more shots. Demon and Bow grew more tense as everyone else were now really scared for their life.

"Oh my God, Mustafa! Mustafa are you okay? He killed Mustafa!" One of the beauticians screamed frantically as she struggled with the zip ties. Demon knew her screams would cause chaos and knew he better take control of the situation before more blood needed to be shed. He quickly walked over to her and stood over her.

"Shut the fuck up, bitch! Fuck Mustafa! I already warned that nigga not to test my man. If you yell out again bitch, I'm gonna shove my dick, down your fucking throat!" Demon yelled as he viciously stomped her in the back a few times just before he kneeled down and leaned over and grabbed her hair and snap her head back causing her to jerk violently. Her scream was like the sputter of a balloon that was suddenly untied. He then laid his shotgun beside her.

A woman screaming or moaning was Demon's idea of a hot date. The young woman screams and moans aroused him unexpectedly. He began to feel on her ass and breast. She wore tight denim leggings that gripped her body perfectly.

On his previous visits, Demon admired her body and always wanted a piece of her.

"Now that you got my dick hard, I should drag you in the bathroom and make you fix it or maybe I'll just help myself right here," Demon threaten as he started to unfasten his pants. He then began to pull on her pants, attempting to bring them down to her knees. The young woman started to scream louder and squirm her body, hoping someone in the shop would help her. Onlookers watched helplessly in horror, as Demon lived up to his name.

"I like it when a bitch scream! It makes my dick harder than a muthafucka! I know your man gotta be loving this fat soft ass!"

Demon said as he continued to fondle the young woman bottom. The sleeping customer jumped up and motioned to help the young woman, but Bow pressed his gun up against his forehead, and pushed him back into the chair. Bow then looked at Demon. He grew more and more frustrated with Demon's attack on the helpless female and no longer focused on the customer sitting in front of him. He lowered his weapon and simply stared at the assault taking place in disbelief. Their initial plan was to rob Mustafa of his drugs and money, not to Rape anybody.

"Yo, Big Man! What the fuck you think you doing? Get the fuck off that bitch. You should be checking on our homeboy, and see what's taking him so long to come out that office, instead of trying to get your dick wet!" The now angry Bow shouted over to Demon, just before the out of control Demon tried to pull the young lady pants completely down. Demon, whom was so eager to violate the woman then stopped his unsuccessful attack and looked up at Bow and the onlookers whom watched him in disgust. He was still kneeled on one knee as began fastening his pants as his partner continued to watch him.

The customer who was still sitting in the barber's chair now had the attention drawn off of him and decided to make his move. He reached beneath his barber apron and pulled out a gun and began to fire it into the unsuspecting Bow that stood in front of him.

Bow was struck in the face, neck and chest, causing him to drop instantly as his weapon still remained in his hand once he hit the floor. Frantic screams rang out in the shop as customers started to scramble for cover while they watched the unsuspecting accomplice drop lifelessly to floor.

The armed customer quickly jumped up out the barber's chair and rushed towards Demon whom was temporarily paralyzed from seeing his partner gunned down. Demon then reached for his shotgun and quickly fired it at the armed customer whom was charging towards him. The customer dove to the floor avoiding the blast from the shotgun as the slug struck a barber chair and spun it around. The armed customer landed on the floor and returned fire, hitting Demon twice in the neck and once in the head killing him instantly.

Once Demon was down, a customer whom was in the waiting area next to the door then jumped up and helped the heroic customer to his feet. He then warned the heroic customer to watch out for the other perpetrator in the back office. The heroic customer then instructed the customer that helped him up to quickly unlock the door and pull the gate up so the rest of the customers could make an escape before Curly exits the office to see what's going on.

The helpful customer followed his instruction and frantically fled the shop along with other customers whom were all yelling and screaming in their underwear as they exited the shop into the street. The heroic customer knew there wasn't enough time to untie the employees before Curly would appear from the office, so he focused all his attention on the rear office door. The door finally opens and Curly was in his sights.

Oh Shit! It's that nigga Curly The brave customer thought to himself as he recognized Curly from his past, that robbed him.

"What the Fuck!" Curly screamed out as he emerged from the back office with a large black garbage bag in one hand and his weapon drawn in the other. He observed both Bow and Demon lying in a pool of their own blood, nearly naked customers fleeing the shop, and the shop employees screaming and crying while tied up on the floor. He knew he heard the gunfire beyond the door while he was emptying the safe in the back, but thought his partners were in control of that whole situation.

Thoughts of going to jail for a very long time quickly entered his mind. If caught, he knew he would go down for killing Mustafa whom he shot to death as the owner of the shop reached for a gun he had hidden inside of the safe. Now, he was alone and needed to escape before the police arrived.

He then noticed the heroic customer, who was kneeling down on one knee, behind a barber's chair aiming a smoking gun at him. He recognized his face and smirked. *I know this nigga* He thought to himself. It didn't take him to long to realize that the only thing that stood between him and his freedom was the armed customer that possibly took his partners out.

He boldly aimed his gun at the armed customer, gripped the garbage bag that was filled with bricks of cocaine, cash and the surveillance tape tightly.

"Remember me, nigga?" Curly asked, as he pulled the trigger. The heroic customer ducked behind the chair, as the shot struck a mirror, causing it shatter. The fearless customer, wasted no time and opened fire and continued to fire until his weapon was empty, as Curly went crashing into the rear office door and onto the floor, landing right next to Mustafa's lifeless body.

The heroic customer quickly reloaded and cautiously approached Curly at gunpoint to see if he was dead. Once the heroic customer determined that Curly was dead, He then removed the powerful handgun from Curly's hand and walked out of the office to a barber chair and sat down. He leaned his head back and took a deep breath. He then reached into the collar of his shirt and pulled out a gold beaded chain that had a golden shield hanging on it like a medallion.

"I'm a cop," The heroic customer said as he looked down at the employees, whom were still tied up, He then reached into his pants pocket and pulled out his cellular phone and started dialing.

"911, state your emergency," Answered a young lady on the other end of the phone.

"10-13! SHOTS FIRED! OFF DUTY OFFICER REQUESTNG BACKUP! AT THE BARBERSHOP ON THE CORNER OF ROCKAWAY AND BLAKE! ROCKAWAY AND BLAKE! THREE PERPS DOWN! SEND A BUS! I REPEAT! OFF DUTY OFFICER INVOLVED REQUESTING ASSISTANCE CENTRAL!"

CHAPTER 1

CONNECTIVE LIFE UPGRADE

DeVonte, **A native of Brooklyn New York,** was now the proud owner of a small estate firmly planted in the suburban county of Northampton, located in the commonwealth State of Pennsylvania.

The home was legally purchased and built by a business associate of his, who then sold it to him a few months after its construction. DeVonte and his business associate devised the plan to have the estate built in the location under the associate corporation for various reasons. The estate was designed to meet DeVonte's desires to his associates expense to the very lease. DeVonte previously put in tireless for this business associate as well as others he was connected to.

Basically, all of DeVonte's associates were wealthy, powerful and well connected. They all were very grateful for his loyalty and the services he did for them. They paid him well and showered him as with expensive gifts.

One business associate in particular was a well-known entrepreneur that owned a string of supermarkets, shopping malls and gas stations within the United States and possessed all types of legal and underground connections around the world.

DeVonte's business associate proposed business plans to a particular township within the county of Northampton in regard to building and opening a supermarket to expand his enterprise. He also proposed to donate a recreation center for the community and to build a home there all in good faith of the township.

This plan was devised because DeVonte conducted an investigation within the township in regards the purchasing of property within it. It was revealed that this particular town was not too keen on new comers as well as big businesses invading the area. The township didn't want to attract unnecessary traffic through their quiet suburban neighborhood.

It was logically necessary to have the estate built from the ground up, by DeVonte's associate's corporation to avoid attention from his 9 to 5 job with the city and the IRS. The cost of the home was above his legal pay grade, and the money he earned from moonlighting was not legal. The township was unaware of DeVonte and gave his business associate no problem in obtaining the permits to build the estate and recreation center. Once the legal issues and permits were in, the construction of DeVonte's estate was up and running.

After months of smooth construction, the estate and recreation center were completed. His business associate spared no expense to furnish the estate to DeVonte's approval. In addition, the associate supplied the recreation center with the proper equipment and supplies to get it up and running for the community.

DeVonte was then introduced to the township as a representative associate who would permanently oversee the recreation center as CEO and program director. He was also introduced as the primly caretaker of the estate, as long as business talks for the supermarket were still in process. As predicted by DeVonte and his business associate, the deal to open up a supermarket in the area flopped. The township asked for way more than what it was worth.

After a few more months went by, DeVonte's associate arranged that legal papers were drawn up to sell the estate to DeVonte for one hundred dollars. A under the table deal was already made for the associate to obtain the grandfather law rates for the land purchased for DeVonte's estate. As a result, DeVonte's property tax would be very low and affordable.

The exterior construction of his brick two story home was tastefully and expensively designed as well as exquisitely furnished interior. The estate possessed an aura living an expensive and extravagant lifestyle. The seventy-five hundred square foot home stood on a hill and was structured with grey brick and firestone. The home sat on two and a half of pleasantly landscaped acres of thick green lawns and luxurious stone pavements that matched the seven-foot stone wall that guarded his property line.

The entrance to the driveway leading to his home was secured by a heavy-duty steel gate that was controlled by a remote control and accompanied by a surveillance camera including a voice intercom. The grey stone paved driveway stretched from the entrance to his establishment and circled around a huge outdoor floor fountain that was located in front of the house. The driveway continued down a decline path to the rear of the house towards the brick four car garage.

The entire interior first and second floor level of the home, were from the paint on the wall down to the marble tiles were white and gold. Walls of the home were white and the molding were similar to gold marbled like granite. Giving it an elegant appearance with an exception for the huge finished basement there consisted of a multiplex movie theater, a bar, a state of the art works out gym complete with showers and bathroom. The floors on the first and second level of the house were white marbled tile except for the bedroom floors, which had plush expensive black carpet that would make your feet sink into natural comfort.

A 14-karat gold and crystal chandelier hung from the cathedral like two-story foyer that twinkled and sparkled as if it was in a ballroom. The double staircase had white marble steps with a white strip of carpet to avoid someone busting their asses. The railing and molding were made of white granite to match the color of the black marble tiles.

DeVonte equipped each bedroom with an entire wall grey charcoal grey/mortar fieldstone that contained a propane fueledfireplace. He also had one in the entertainment room and his office. In the family room, there was a huge wood burning fireplace.

DeVonte's small suburban town and its whole surroundings were far different from the hard streets of Brooklyn, New York where he was once raised. It was truly like day and night when you compared the atmosphere and way of life among the values of the people whom lived within the area.

For decades, Brooklyn, was one of the most notoriously violent and dangerous borough within New York City. The crime meter was off the charts and basically ran neck and neck with the Bronx as one of the worst boroughs the city has ever come to know.

Dating back to the 1930s through 1940s, the leaders of the early organized crime groups of the Jewish, Italian, American and Irish mafia called upon a group of Jewish killers from Brownsville, Ocean Hill and the East New York section of Brooklyn, New York. These killers were used by the early mafia as enforcement within New York City. The Brooklyn gangsters also accepted murder contracts from other mob bosses throughout the United States.

This group of assassins went by the name of THE BROWNSVILLE BOYS, MURDER INCORPORATE and was known in the syndicate circles as THE COMBINATION. The mere mention of Brownsville Brooklyn rang many bells within New York City as well as other major cities within the United States, coining the phrase of the hard knock life.

The legacy of violent crimes continued for decades as the neighborhoods still remain one of the most notorious for its crime and violence. As history would reflect and have repeated itself, Brownsville, Brooklyn goes hard and a mere change of scenery could be a definite upgrade.

The new peaceful setting in the heart of Pennsylvania was a perfect place for him to relax his mind and enjoy the atmosphere of good family living. His new atmosphere consisted of all the activities he was deprived of as a child.

Hiking, bike riding, fishing, boat sailing, hunting and skiing would be his new pastime. The fresh aroma of barbecues surrounding him and he admired the quiet nights with the stars shining brightly as they lit the sky were welcomed breath of fresh air. DeVonte's previous days of living in the city among the tall skyscrapers, apartment buildings and air pollution cheated him of the beauty of peaceful nights that consist of the stars and moonlight glowing from the dark sky above him.

Friends and family would visit him to get a taste of fresh air and relaxation. He had no problem sharing the peace that the world had to offer outside the city that never sleeps.

It was Friday and DeVonte had a group of friends over for the weekend. His girlfriend and her female friends were expected to arrive later that day. DeVonte was exhausted after returning home from his short business trip to El Paso, Texas earlier that day. He frequently traveled to Texas on to connect with one of his associates to handle business. He had a regular routine of catching a commercial flight to El Paso, Texas then rent a vehicle once he landed to go meet up with his partner.

Once DeVonte's business was handled, he would go check into a local five-star hotel that he booked in advance rest for a few hours. He would later head out for a nice quiet dinner out on the town with a few friends. By morning, DeVonte would order room service for breakfast then head to the hotel's gym to work out. Once his workout was complete, he would return to his suite and take a shower then head out to do a little shopping.

The flight home was also routine and was sponsored by his associate who would charter flights for DeVonte at the price of fifty grand a flight. DeVonte would check out of his hotel, drop off his rental and take a cab to the private airport where he would load up his baggage and aboard a private jet. He would land at a private airport located in New Jersey, rent a car and travel to New York City to meet another business partner before heading home. The business was great and money was no shortage.

Four of DeVonte's closest friends were already present in his home and were all lounging in the entertainment room for the moment. The room contained a custom made all white pool table with white marble and gold trimming with his initials embossed in gold in the center of it and near every pocket. The balls where made of clear transparent marble and had the number and color embossed on each ball with exception of the eight ball which was made of black marble.

DeVonte's lawyer, Rick also known as Ricky a longtime friend from his old neighborhood was a very handsome man. He had a light, hazel eyes, curly hair and an athletic build. Rick stood very tall and was on many occasion mistaken for being the former NBA player turned actor Rick Fox. He was DeVonte's best friend and in many ways a brother to him.

Back in the days, Rick was an All-American basketball player whom had incredible leaping ability as well as one of the most wicked jump shots in the history of high school and college basketball. Rick's basketball skills helped his high school win two state championships. He also had the opportunity to participate in the McDonald's All-American Games, once he became a senior in High School back in the late 1980's.

The McDonald's All-American Games began in 1977 when the All Americans and All Stars played a game against a group of High School Stars from the Washington D.C. Area. A year later competition between the East against West began setting rivalries on which coast could play ball the best.

Rick, an honor student the entire time he attended his high school, was an elite athlete and received a full academic and athletic scholarship to play Basketball at Harvard University out in Cambridge, Massachusetts with law as his major.

Rick's first three years at Harvard, he led his division, as well as the National Collegiate Athletic Association in scoring. Averaging 30 point per game, as a junior, he was recognized as a potential first round draft pick in the NBA.

During his senior year, Rick fell to a career ending injury during a regular season basketball game just before the playoffs. He dislocated his knee, tore his ACL and PCL causing him to be out injured the remainder of the season and playoffs.

Rick's parents always lectured him on getting his education and not to place all his eggs in one basket in regard to a career in the NBA. Reality set in, as Rick attempted to rehabilitate himself back to the athlete he once was, before his injury. His body did not recover as quick as he thought it would, which caused him to realize his chances of getting picked up in the draft by a NBA team would be second to none.

Naturally, he was disappointed about not having a future in the NBA, but he was not discouraged about life without basketball. Rick decided to move forward with his studies in law and graduated from the University with honors. He passed his first bar exam on the first try and worked for years at the Manhattan District Attorney's Office, prior to opening up his own firm.

Rick sat on a stool near the bar, located in DeVonte's entertainment room. He was using DeVonte's IMAC to conducted an internet search on the large screen wireless computer, while Devonte rested upstairs. The other guys were entertaining themselves by either playing a game of pool or watching television. Rick got a little thirsty and decided to walk behind the bar counter to the custom made white marble gold trimmed refrigerator that was filled with assorted domestic beers, soft drinks and champagne located right next to a wine cooler.

"Who wants something to drink?" Rick asked loud enough for everyone in the room to hear. At first, no one paid him any attention. He removed an ice-cold bottle of beer from the refrigerator and popped the top off the bottle. He grabbed himself a slice of lime and wiped the frost off the bottle. He took a sip of his beer, then began to head back to the stool he was sitting on.

"Rick! Before you sit down, pass me blue bottle of wine; You know, the Moscato. And also let me get glass," Jason requested as he called out from across the room, while relaxing on one of the many white theatre reclining chairs. Rick after taking another sip of his cold beer looked over at Jason and thought to himself. *Why this fool, didn't say anything when I first asked and was up? He waits until I'm about sit down*

Jason, was a very handsome, muscular, dark complexion male that stood about 5'11 tall. He formally played football as a running back for his high school and college team. He was once an All-American hopeful, but acquired a non-career ending injury during a college All-Star game in his sophomore year. The injury caused him to fall off the charts in the draft his senior year.

After graduating from college, and receiving his bachelor's degree in sciences. Jason teamed up with DeVonte to open up a rehabilitation center for athletes, where he manages during the off season of his semi-pro team he plays for. Jason remains determined to enter the NFL and continue to train hard to reach his goal of getting there.

"Why do you want a glass? Take that shit to the head," Rick asked with a puzzled look on his face as he walked behind the bar and removed a nice chilled blue bottle of Moscato from the wine cooler. He unscrewed the cork out the bottle then walked towards Jason.

"I don't want to hear DeVonte mouth, about me drinking that shit straight out the bottle. You already know, how he gets on my case for that type of shit," Jason continued. Rick facial expression remained puzzled.

"Man, the fuck up! If you don't take this damn bottle and stop acting like a chump, I'm gonna hit you upside the head with it," Rick jokingly said. "Listen to me Jason, DeVonte is way too tired to give a shit how you sip this! He's been sleeping ever since he got back into town, I doubt he will see you," Rick continued as he awaited Jason to take the bottle.

Jason then took possession of the bottle Rick handed him and leaned his head back to take a gulp of the chilled wine. He then looked up and noticed a shirtless DeVonte wearing white lounging pants standing on the balcony, looking down. DeVonte overheard their conversation and just watched Jason as he took a drink from the bottle, but said nothing.

DeVonte was like a mentor to Jason and always tried to keep him focused on school and sports. He did his best to keep Jason away from the bullshit that was going on in the urban streets of New York City. Jason was smart and a pretty good football player for both high school and college. DeVonte refused to see another good athlete follow down the wrong path, like many other players from the urban communities before him. He didn't want to see Jason get caught up in drugs nor any other criminal activities.

As DeVonte, stood on the balcony looking down with a glass of his favorite cognac, he took in the view of the entertainment room and replayed the hectic events transpired earlier in New York City prior he arrival home, DeVonte attempted to sleep, but remained very restless in bed. He woke in a cold sweat and immediately got up to make himself a drink at the bar located in his bedroom. Since he couldn't fall back to sleep, he decided to check on his friends.

Jason seemed to be the only one in the room whom noticed that DeVonte was standing there, as he adjusted his seat back to the upright seating position, and he held his bottle of sparkling wine in his hand.

"What's Up Dee?" Jason yelled up to DeVonte while giving him a military type salute. "You know peer pressure is a muthafucka," Jason continued while feeling stupid for letting DeVonte observe him not sticking to his own decision, on not drinking straight out the bottle. DeVonte took a sip of his cognac and lift his glass up to acknowledge Jason.

"Your boy Rick, said it was cool for me to drink this wine straight from the bottle. I told him to pass me a glass but he shut me down on that," Jason explained to DeVonte, who remained silent and started to look at Rick as if he was a fool. Rick looked at Jason in amazement, as Jason snitched him out to DeVonte.

"Somebody call 911! Because this snitching ass muthafucka right here just threw me under the bus with the quickness!" Rick said as everybody in the room started to laugh. Rick then looked up towards DeVonte and smiled.

"How was your trip to Texas my brother?" Rick continued while taking a sip of his beer.

"Texas was nice and everything went smooth as always! But once I got back in the city, I ran into a little static in Chelsea with a client. I ended up canceling the business arraignment with him permanently, But I will fill you in about that situation later." DeVonte responded just before placing his glass to his lips to sip on his cognac. From the tone in his voice and the look in his eyes. Everybody in the room knew just what he meant by that and decided to quickly change the conversation.

"Anyway, Big Brotha Almighty. What time will Erica and her friends be getting here? I heard she is bringing some fine ass bitches with her, and they are staying here the whole weekend too. The room got silent for a minute. "You know I gotta prepare myself so I could get my pimp on player" he continued just before taking another sip of his wine. DeVonte didn't say a word. He just stared down at Jason as if he was a disobedient child who didn't know any better.

"Bitches?! I thought you was the bitch. The way you are choking and sucking on that bottle, just to swallow something sweet and smooth." Dennis yelled out. "You appear to be a big bad football player, yet you in here sipping on wine and got your pinky finger sticking out?" Dennis jokingly continued as he simulated Jason with an imaginary bottle in his hand.

Dennis, was no athlete. He was just a work out fanatic that stood at 6'4 tall, with a solid muscular build. He had thick eyebrows like Tupac and a shiny 360-degree wave pattern hairstyle. He had a caramel complexion and was constantly confused for someone that was of Latino decent. Dennis for his size was more of a comedian than enforcer. His body physique was similar and as intimidating as Kimbo Slice, except he was a teddy bear not a street brawler.

DeVonte couldn't help it, but to crack a smile in regard to Dennis comments on Jason, as he began to shake his head in disbelief. He then glanced at his gold Rolex watch and took another sip of his cognac.

"How long have I known you Jason?" DeVonte asked once he took a sip of his drink.

"Since, I was a young and dumb," Jason responded as he felt an unwanted lecture coming. DeVonte took another sip of his glass before responding.

"Well, you're way too intelligent to be talking like an idiot," DeVonte responded as everybody started to laugh, including Jason while knowing he had it coming.

"I don't invest my time in bitches or hoes. So, you will never see one enter my home. Not today, not tomorrow, never. I suggest you chill on that shit this weekend, especially when the ladies get here. Please don't kill the weekend vibe," DeVonte continued. Rick wanted to nip the shit in the bud, before Jason mouth gets him in trouble.

"With all that being said, and getting off the subject of Jason once again saying dumb shit. DeVonte has something very special planned for Erica, tomorrow night. It's a surprise engagement party and he should know, He could count on all of us to make it even more special with our help. She's been his ride or die for a minute now, and I guess it's time for him to take it to a higher level, by putting a ring on her finger," Rick said as he started to hand out a sheet of paper to Jason, Dennis and Mike.

"What you're looking at, is a list of assignments DeVonte need us all to take care of. If anybody has any questions, ask them now before Erica and her friends get here. Rick continued.

No one seemed to have any questions at the time.

"I will appreciate if all my boys, treat Erica's friends like the beautiful women that they are. I don't want anyone to disrespect them by calling them bitches, chicken heads, birds, because that type of female ain't welcome in my Castle," DeVonte said as he headed down the long corridor on the second level. He then stopped in his tracks.

"Oh Yeah fellas! I need everybody in here to keep my plans for tomorrow night on the low from the ladies. I don't need my homies to snitch me out because you smell the scent of pussy or feel you got to pillow talk, because you get some ass. Rick will fill Yall in on it later," DeVonte continued to yell out as he turned back around and disappeared from everyone sight.

Jason watched and stared harshly at DeVonte as he walked away and out of site. He then reclined his chair and began to sip on his bottle. He began to think to himself.

This muthafucka DeVonte, think just because he got a nice crib, cars and a fat bankroll. He could talk to us, like we his flunkeys and shit. These chumps in here be riding his dick, like he really the muthafuckin man. I must be the only one in here whom knows what time it is with this dude! And, how he really be getting his money and shit. I should be his right-hand man, not this Pretty Ricky muthafucka. I swear if he didn't look out for me in the past, I would line this nigga up, for all his shit! or snitch his ass out to the FEDS. His thoughts were soon interrupted.

"You Big Dummy!" Mike shouted out, while doing his best impersonation of Fred Sanford for the 1970's comedy show Sanford and Son. Everyone in the room started to laugh including Jason whom was boiling hot inside.

"Jason! When you gonna learn brotha?! You've been under DeVonte's wing for a minute now, so you should know better than more than anyone else in this room. DeVonte be on that Smooth Operator Denzel Washington type of shit. He even hit you with the deep Barry White Voice" Mike continued to say while laughing. Mike sensed that Jason may have felt like he just got scorned by one of his parents for saying something stupid. So, he decided to smooth it out with a little comedy.

"I forgot how DeVonte changed his playa style up and be out there respecting these hoes now. I remember when he was on some real fuck a bitch shit! And was shitting on hoes like they were toilets" Jason responded. Deep inside Jason was like

Fuck your long ass speech DeVonte! Yo ass has been shitting on bitches for years! Now you captain save a hoe?! Get the fuck out of here with that bullshit! I'm my own boss!

"See Jason! That's your problem right there! You don't know how to control your mouth sometimes" Rick said adding his two cents into the conversation. Jason took another sip of his bottle as he turned his attention to Rick whom was standing near him and looked him up and down.

"I knew it would be a matter of time before DeVonte's number one dick rider would have something to say!" Jason said as he stared at Rick with a devilish grin on his face. He could see Rick's whole facial expression change, as he turned his grin into laughter.

Rick gave Jason the I should kick your fucking ass look as he stared him down. He could never figure out why DeVonte had any interest to be Jason's mentor. Jason's mouth was reckless. To avoid knocking in his teeth, Rick chose to ignore him as he redirected his energy towards the rest of the fellas. He started a quick briefing of what he knows of what's planned for the weekend as he said the following:

Check this out fellas! DeVonte plans on asking Erica to marry him, tomorrow night during dinner at MAJOR SOUL's. I don't know if you guys ever heard of the place, but MAJOR SOUL's is a four-star club/grill with a serious southern cuisine out in New Jersey, New York, Georgia and North Carolina. DeVonte, has a real close connect with the owner.

This spot has all types of live entertainment. Bands, singers, and comedians that be doing their thing there. The food is off the chain. The dinner reservations and limo transportation have already been booked and we are all attending. If anybody need to get some gear, we can handle that shit all early tomorrow at the mall.

Erica and her home girls have no clue, what's in store for tonight. As far as they know, it's just a regular night on the town dinner party. DeVonte's needs everybody word, to keep it on the low, because if you leak the plan to one of these young ladies, you might as well tell all of them. And that would fuck up the whole night, if Erica gets word of it. Anyway, I've already met one of the young ladies coming through today named Stacy a few times, and she's fine like a muthafucka. So, believe me when

I tell you, if these Ladies are coming here to DeVonte's crib, and they are rolling with fine ass Erica and Stacey. You best believe they ain't gonna be no needy, bum ass, chicken heads, pecking at your broke ass pockets Rick continued.

"Rick, any big girls? If so, I want first crack at the thickest bitch on the menu tonight!" Mike jokingly said, informing his buddies on what he wanted. "Big girls, like to get their fuck on and they flexible too!" Mike continued to say with a grin on his face. The whole entertainment room burst into laughter.

"Nigga! What did we just say about calling them bitches?" Rick said while laughing.

"Nigga? Oh, it's okay to say nigga all the time? But Yall have a problem with me saying bitch? Plus, the only bitch that could hear me say bitch is Jason, who's over there deep throating that blue bottle like a five-dollar hoe," Mike said while pointing at Jason with a smile on his face. Jason stopped drinking his wine and looked at Mike.

"Mike, I learned how to suck like a five-dollar hoe from Yo momma! Back in the days, she sucked a mean one for them blue and red tops vial of get high," Jason snapped back with the quickness. "Yo momma, sucked dick so much, her lips still got stretch marks," Jason continued as everyone started to laugh including Mike whom laughed the hardest.

Mike whom was a sort of slim guy who was muscularly ripped and had that retarded strength. Dude only weight about 195 pounds and stood 6'o tall, but was benching 345 pounds and squatting 420 pounds free weights. He would always find time to do calisthenics, by doing pull ups, pushups and abdominal curls to keep his body ripped. Back in the days when he was a young kid, his dad once told him.

"Son! You're one skinny little son of a gun. Your gonna have to build your body up and get strong to compete against the bigger kids". He then brought Mike a set of cast iron weights and gave him some little instructions on how to use them to develop his muscle. Mike followed his father instructions in weight lifting and started doing calisthenics after seeing so many young men who just returned home from prison flood the public parks working out on the bars. That's where he met DeVonte, when the two both decided to work out in the park the same day.

Mike and DeVonte became workout buddies and coached each other during their strength training. Unlike DeVonte, Mike chose to keep his strength and ripped body concealed under baggy clothing. He trained basically for his health and to kick trouble makers asses that fucked with him whenever the time came. Mike was a bully's worst nightmare, he would lure his victims to believe he would fall victim to their aggression, just to use his amazing physical strength and exceptional fighting skills to teach them a lesson.

Mike started a career in the department of sanitation as soon as he reached the age of 21. After a few years of riding around in the big ole funky garbage truck, he planned on getting promoted to the Sanitation Police supervisory position one day. He was a hard worker that put in many long overtime hours during the winter months in regard to snow removal. He also drove the street sweeper around any chance he got to earn some extra paper. Mike was a smart guy whom saved his regular salary along with extra income earned from overtime so that one day he could make a good investment with it.

After years on the job with the Department of Sanitation, He got an idea of starting his own private security company, that would supply armed security for high ranking executives of businesses and celebrities within the states, of New York and New Jersey. The idea came to him one day when he was approached by an upcoming female R&B singer whom was scheduled to perform at a ALL BLACK event he attended in Midtown Manhattan. Mike whom rarely wore fitted clothing, was wearing an all-black designer suit. The young female singer couldn't help but notice him as he stood outside at the front entrance.

"Excuse me, I was just wondering," a female voice gently said from behind Mike. "What security agency do you work for?" The female voice continued to ask as she appreciated seeing the sexy chocolate dipped in all black man whose stance expressed authority. Mike turned around and came eye to eye with the vision of beauty. The question took Mike by surprise as he gracefully informed her he was just a guest at the event and wasn't security at all. She was now embarrassed and cracked a smile. The aroma of his cologne and the well fitted designer suit and shoes attracted her. She looked him up and down from head to toe while admiring his physique just before saying.

"Oh! I'm so sorry if I offended you in any way! You just look so strong and sharp in that suit, that you could pass for someone in the secret service for the President of the United States. But, since I'm wrong, I guess I better learn not to stereotype people based on their appearance so easily next time." She said as she looked at him with her bright hazel eyes and bright smile, that sent a warm feeling thru his body. My just stared at her and was temporarily speechless

"You know you're the third person that asked me who I worked for in the last ten minutes, since I have been standing out here. You know, maybe I should start getting paid to stand out here like them guys standing over there, "Mike replied as he as he pointed over to the real security personal whom were working at the event. A little voice in his head screamed *You vain ass muthafucka! You didn't return the complement to her, yet you continue to talk about yourself. What a dick!*

"You are looking quite spectacular yourself. For some reason, I feel like I should be asking you for your autograph or something." Mike said not trying to sound corny as he adored her pretty face and coke bottle shape that was all wrapped in an all-black long sequins evening gown. Her dress looked like it was painted on, yet it was still very classy.

She started to blush, as her caramel cheek bones started to turn red. Her hand purse began to vibrate just before the cell phone inside of it began to ring. She reached inside of it and answered the phone while excusing herself from her conversation with Mike as she took a few steps away from him. Mike stared at her and absorbed all the beauty she had. He forgot all about the event he was there to attend for the moment. He was glad he was standing outside, because if he didn't, he would've never had met this young lady.

Once she was finished with her brief telephone conversation, she then walked back over to him.

"Sorry about that Um! Dang man! Here we are both out here having a conversation and neither one of us seized the moment to introduce ourselves properly with a name" The young lady said with a smile on her face. Mike cracked a smile revealing his pearly white teeth, basically because he knew she was right and he felt every man should introduce himself when he comes in contact with a woman.

"My name is Mike" He responded as he extended his hand for a formal handshake.

"Nice to meet you Mike! My name is Meka. Sorry for the brief interruption, but that was a business call," Meka said as she looked at her watch. Mike for some reason thought he was about to be brushed off by her, and figured she was trying to do it nicely.

"I was informed by my peoples that it's almost time to handle my business, so I have to get inside and get ready for work" She said as she started to walk away and head into the entrance. Mike was puzzled for a minute and watched her walk away from him.

"Wait a minute, Meka. You work here?" Mike asked just before she walked through the corridor. Meka then turned around once she reached the entrance and looked at Mike. She then waved him to come closer to her as she kept looking at her watch as if her time outside was short. He walked towards her as she requested. He hoped for some reason that she called him over to give him her phone number. Once he stood in front of her, she signaled for him to bend over and place his ear next to her soft lips.

"Yes! I have gig here tonight! I'm what you can call a up and coming artist, and you my handsome fellow will have the pleasure of seeing me perform at this event tonight. Wish me luck on my journey of taking the R&B world by storm," she whispered in his ear as her soft lips touched his earlobe. Mike was hypnotized by her minty warm breath. He was at a loss for words, as he wished her soft lips would had touch his. He had no idea that she was a singing artist.

"Oh, I hear that lady! Maybe I will take heed to going into the security business for the stars and become the head security of the newest R&B Diva named Meka. Mike said with a bright smile on his face.

"Mike, my stage name is ADORE! Only old and new close friends call me Meka," Were Meka's last words as she winked at him. Her manager tapped her on the shoulder, she turned around and was greeted by her manager and the event promoter who was patiently awaiting her arrival in the lobby. After a brief conversation, both her manager and the promoter escorted her to the backstage area to prepare her for performance. Mike then made his way back into the venue and awaited Meka's, now known to him as ADORE performance.

ADORE's voice was above incredible and her performance was captivating. Mike couldn't help but have thoughts of starting his own agency, while watching ADORE perform under the bright spotlight. After the event was over, Mike stood outside in hopes he would get to see Meka again and maybe get her phone number.

But after a half an hour, Meka emerged from the building accompanied by a large entourage of people that merely prevented him any close-range contact. She was escorted into a large stretch limo that was parked out front.

Once Meka was inside of the limo, it quickly drove off as Mike watched it disappear into the night. He was so inspired about starting a security business after meeting Meka, that he went home and did some research in regard to operating his own agency. He knew that DeVonte was someone he could count on, once he could present a proper business proposition for him to invest in the agency.

He also knew DeVonte could come through with some needed connects, that would put him in the right direction as well as help him pull in some good clientele. He put together a plan and created a business proposal to present DeVonte who was all for the business investing.

After a year, He already had a reliable staff of about ten guys, who were all certified and licensed internationally to carry a weapon and to perform duties as private security in different parts of the world. The guys he employed into his agency were either former law enforcement or former military personnel. They all possessed muscular physiques and attended physical combat courses every three months. Mike himself also had to update his certification and licensing as well.

Mike's shift at the Department of Sanitation was convenient enough for him to appear at certain events and supervise his staff whenever requested. He continued to remain in top physical shape. He never imagined that his intimidating physique could become a money maker for him. He ran a business proposition by DeVonte who seemed to have a good ear for starting new investments.

A well-constructed pool house was built in the rear of DeVonte's home on his 3 acres of land. It was located on the rear lower level along with a picnic area, Tiki bar, basketball and tennis courts. It was structure with the same brick and stone as the house and also the same color. Inside it contained a male and female locker room both equipped with a shower area, A large in ground pool as well as a separate hot tub and Jacuzzi located a distance from the pool. It looked like something you would see at a resort, with beach chairs and the works. DeVonte reasoning for the pool house was simple and to the point.

All year pool parties and unlimited swimming recreation for himself and his guest. No matter the weather you were able to enjoy a swim at his house.

What better privacy to have, than to have a pool house he thought. He had the pool house equipped with waterproof moist resistant speakers embedded into the walls for the surround sound effect, as well as in every room located in his house in which the speakers where located in the ceiling. Next to the pool house he had a picnic area that consisted of two large brick Barbecue Pits that where large enough to load enough food for a football team.

The basketball and tennis court were both the official size as used by professionals. He also had a mini half-court basketball gym inside his home, that was fully ventilated located on his first floor.

The **STREET BALLING** screen print was labeled on the court as well as the fiberglass backboard and chairs on both sides of the Basketball courts. There were spotlights posted to shine down and keep the court bright if needed as well as having a score board and score keepers table on the outside court. Recreation for his buddies was always available and a must because he was a single bachelor.

DeVonte didn't care too much for gas/propane grills so his barbecue pits were for charcoal and wood chips. He had exclusive patio sets, located on his stone paved deck and another located next to a Caribbean island style Tiki bar filled with the best of top shelf liquors and wines. Under the Tiki bar was a stainless-steel refrigerator and wine chiller that contained an ice making machine.

"Yo Rick! Do me a favor and get them trays with the rib eye steaks, chicken and racks of ribs I marinated last night out the fridge. And could you also check and see if them fools want any sausage links and burgers for appetizers?"

"Mike, I need your expertise on the grill baby! I know you probably want to lay low and chill, but I really need you on deck to Chef tonight to impress the ladies," DeVonte yelled out from somewhere from the second level.

"Whatever boss man!" Rick yelled out. Mike, you heard the man fool, you on deck to chef tonight so get that charcoal out the garage with your strong ass," Rick said jokingly as he jumped up and headed out the entertainment room towards the kitchen. Mike looked over at Jason and Dennis whom wasn't giving any responsibility for the night.

"You two lazy muthafuckas don't never have to do shit when yall come here!" Mike said looking at both Dennis and Jason whom were both leaned back watching the Boondocks on the 70-inch screen high definition television. Jason looked over at Mike whom was standing there. "Don't forget your apron sweetie and make sure you don't get no tears on the grill boo boo," Jason said while he and Dennis both laughed while they enjoyed their show and sipped on their drinks.

Mike just shook his head at the two with disgust and exited through the side door and walked around to the front of the house. The weather felt good outside as the sun shined bright. Mike made his way to the front of the house and was temporary blinded.

He couldn't help but to stare at DeVonte's truck and two Rolls Royce parked in the circular driveway in front of the house. The platinum colored Escalade ESV DeVonte owned was chromed out with 26inch rims was parked right next to his two fully loaded Rolls Royce.

The Platinum colored SUV sparkled under the sunlight as well as the White Phantom and Black Dawn. Damn, DeVonte got the whips on crazy display, my dude be straight ballin for real Mike thought to himself as he also wondered his boy DeVonte hasn't put him on to whatever he was doing to afford all the shit he owned and was his numerous investments. Mike wasn't hating on his friend, he himself just recently purchased a brand-new Yukon Denali XL fully loaded with 26inch chrome rims. Mike just looked at the two luxury vehicles and day dreamed that someday he too would possess the same as his friend.

He snapped out of his trance and continued to walk towards the side of the house leading to the rear of it. He entered the three-car garage that DeVonte kept like a stock and storage. It was filled up with cases of top shelf liquor, wine, beers and bottled water. Sacks of charcoal, hickory wood chips, firewood, fireworks and everything else needed to entertain his company. This storage kept him from having to make unnecessary trips to the market and warehouse for supplies.

This damn garage looks like BJs and Costcos warehouse in here," Mike said out loud soon as he walked in the door. *I'm going to need about two big sacks of you (referring to the large sacks of match light charcoal) so I don't have to make another trip, and I can't forget about you too (referring to the apron and chef hat)* Mike thought to himself, as he collected all the needed items before exiting the garage. *Damn! I might have to double back later, because I forgot the Hickory chips*

He continued to think to himself as he headed to the grill pits.

"Yo Dennis! How many chic's do you think are coming through today?" Jason asked as if Dennis knew the answer.

"How the fuck would I know?" Dennis answered.

"Do you think they gonna be fine?" Jason continued to ask after Dennis already informed him that he knew nothing.

"Dude, you are asking questions like you the police! I don't have a fucking clue to none of the shit you are asking fool. My guess is, DeVonte's girl already know it's four brothers here. With that being said, I guess it should at least be a chick for every dude here," Dennis said while informing Jason of his thoughts.

"Plus! DeVonte's girl Erica, she fine as hell. And, you know in most cases, Fine chicks only roll with other fine chicks," Dennis said without removing his eyes from the television set.

Erica, the love of DeVonte's life was a true dime piece if there was ever one created. Her coco brown smooth skin complexion, long dark thick curly shoulder length hair, hazel brownish green eyes and her set of full soft lips were a mere sample of her fine attributes. God and her mother blessed her with a set of 44 DD breast, a thin waste, thick strong thighs and calves that supported one of the thickest apple bottom that the Lord could ever bless on a woman. DeVonte always loved his women thick, but well-toned. He had a talent it seemed to find dime pieces when he was in search of romance.

"Yo, You two dudes want to keep dick wishing all day, or are you going to help Mike and Rick out" DeVonte yelled down from the balcony that overlooked the below room, while scarring the shit out of the two who were still hanging out in the entertainment room.

"Oh shit," said Jason as he looked upward and observed DeVonte looking over the railing.

"Man, you just scarred the shit out of me barking like a drill sergeant" Jason continued. DeVonte started to smile after realizing that the two biggest dudes in the house where acting like two punk asses.

"I need you two NFL looking brothers to help the other brothers out. The ladies are enroute, and I want to get shit up to speed before they get here," DeVonte said attempting to camouflage his smile.

"All I know is, I better be getting some pussy tonight Dee.

If I gotta put in work to entertain these chicks my brotha!," Jason said with a smile on his face as he rose up from his seat. Dennis just shook his head at Jason.

"Don't worry Dee, we got you on this! We gonna work hard now and play later Playboy," Dennis said as he hopped up to his feet and saluted DeVonte. DeVonte then returned the salute and stepped away from the railing, heading down the long corridor on the second level.

"Come on! Let's get this shit over with already," Dennis said as he and Jason exited the entertainment room and headed outside. Once outside, Jason headed over to the BBQ pit to give Mike a helping hand by loading up the grill pits with charcoal and placed the soaking hickory wood chips on the aside until the grill was lit and charcoal glowed. The sun started to shine brightly on the picnic area. After Mike and Jason finished loading both pits with charcoal. Mike lit both grills while Jason took a seat at the picnic table.

"Is DeVonte still holding onto that pimped out Ford Hoopty?" Jason asked Mike, whom was sorting out the lit charcoal in the pits with a large stick.

"Yep, and you know it! That shit is parked in his garage. I think he drives that shit to work to keep everybody out his business. You know he bought that shit to weed out the gold digging, thirsty ass, needy ass hoes that be on that materialistic shit," Mike jokingly said while shaking his head.

Before all of the fancy cars and big house, DeVonte didn't always have the money to back it up. Back in the days he purchased a decent hoopty. A hoppty is an urban term for a piece of shit car, that got you from A to B. DeVonte hooked his up, with tinted out windows, chrome rims and a loud stereo system.

He always felt if he met a woman and she was still interested in him after seeing his ride. She was on the real. He still drove this car to work due to all the hating mother fuckers at his job whom would probably key up a nice ride in a heartbeat. His co-worker would roll up in the newest whips and throw a few snaps in his direction.

"Damn! Yo Granddaddy let you hold his pimped out shagging wagon today?" Yelled out James, one of DeVonte's co-worker whom one day was looking out the window and saw DeVonte parked his car in the lot.

"Yeah, He told me Yo grandma just finished paying it off after all them years of shaking her ass for him on the Forty Deuce," DeVonte replied with a smile as he entered the entrance to the job.

James started to laugh. "Not my granny! She would've got him a Cadillac! Not a bullshit station wagon, brotha!" James replied as he continued to laugh. There was a *No Thin Skin Policy* at DeVonte's job. If you had thin skin you wouldn't survive, because nobody gave a shit if you were sensitive.

"DeVonte marinated this meat, just right! So, please don't burn this shit up dude," Rick said as he brought out the trays of steak, ribs, chicken and shrimp with the help of Dennis who was assisting him towards the picnic tables. As they placed the trays of uncooked food on the picnic table, Mike stood up straight after loading up the hickory wood chips on the hot glowing coals.

"Burn shit up!? Man, you must have bumped your pretty little head playboy! I'm the Barbecue King out this bitch you feel me" Mike replied as he beat his chest with his fist as if he was King Kong. "Why you think I'm always on deck to chef these pits every time we all hook up?!" Mike continued.

"Shit! Man, I thought it was just because you look the cutest in an apron," Ricky replied with a silly smirk on his face. Mike just smiled and threw his middle finger up just before he turned around and began to light up the grill.

WELCOME TO BROWNSVILLE

IN THE LATE 1970's a young Denzel along with his mother and sister moved to the Brownsville Projects located in Brooklyn New York. His mother Adrianne gave birth to him in Kings County Hospital in the early 1970's and he lived his infant years in the Bedford-Stuyvesant section of Brooklyn, until he was about four years old. His father was a known hustler and gambler that frequent Lafayette Street, and went by the name of June Bug. June Bug worked many odd jobs but continued to hustle on the streets.

June Bug occasionally sold marijuana and promoted illegal gambling, to earn a little extra money to make ends meet.

Unfortunately, that money went towards gambling, alcohol, and late nights out at the local underground night clubs.

By the time Denzel was approximately five years old, his parents decided it was time to separate. The separation was due to his father's constant gambling and fucking up the money to support his family. Denzel's mother found an apartment for herself and her two children and moved out of the apartment she once shared with his father. The apartment building was located on Saratoga Avenue near East 98th Street, just a few blocks away from Brookdale Hospital in Brownsville.

Denzel's great-grandmother lived just around the corner from their new building and occasionally stopped by to check on them.

Their time residing in Brownsville was short lived, when his mom found a bigger apartment in the Crown Heights section of Brooklyn. The new apartment was located in a building located on Crown Street. The building was shaped like a castle and was just off the corner of Bedford Avenue. A Popular bowling alley was located right across the street as well as a little night club on the opposite side of the building. Today the Bowling Alley is now a facility for Medgar Evers College.

Denzel's great-grandparents, moved to Brownsville Projects, and his mom took him and his sister over there to visit them all the time. Denzel mom submitted an application with the New York City Housing Authority for an apartment. After a few years in Crown Heights, housing accepted Denzel's mother application and his family was on the move again. It was a big transition in their lives by moving from the quiet neighborhood of Crown Heights to the hard-core area of Brownsville Houses. The life in Crown Heights was very simple back then in the early to Mid-Seventies. Denzel teachers lived in his neighborhood, Some just door steps away in his building.

It was a common thing for a teacher to stop by and have a talk with the parents of the students attending Public School 161. There were many brownstone homes located on Crown Street owned by both Caucasian and African American Families.

The innocents of children ignoring their difference in skin color filled the community as both black and white children played together, in harmony.

The transition and change of lifestyle was decided by Denzel's Mom whom apartment was targeted in multiple burglaries. Having a low income, then receiving an increase in rent also helped aid her in her decision to apply and later move into the housing projects.

The Crown Height apartment was located on the first floor and windows where located in the rear of the building along with an alley way. It took nothing for a theft to climb into the window and gain entry into the apartment. The security gates on the window were easily bent back, as the burglars took their time, while knowing the family wasn't home.

It had gotten so bad at one time, that the burglars would bring stolen merchandise from other homes they hit to Denzel's family apartment as a stash house. It was rumored that someone in the building, whom knew the coming and goings of the family was setting them up for the hits. Color TVs, Stereo Systems, Bicycles and even children toys where taking on every hit became draining to Denzel and his family.

Denzel's father was called on upon many times to respond to their apartment to show a male's presence at their home on many occasions. He would show up with about five to six heavily armed males, whom were ready to handle anybody that tried to break in while they were there.

June Bug would send Denzel along with his mom and sister off to stay with a relative, while he and his crew sat in the dark in the apartment waiting to unleash all hell. He always made mention to Denzel mom, that someone had to be setting her up, because no one never tried to break in when he was present.

Denzel began to have nightmares of intruders breaking in their home, while everyone slept and it became the beginning of his hate for a thief. The constant screams of "GET OUT OF MY HOUSE," by a young Denzel in the middle of the night worried his mom, so she figured it was time to move on to somewhere else to relax her children minds. The move to Brownsville housing project, only brought the realness of what goes down in the hood as the lessons began from the beginning of a new year.

It was now early January of 1979, and the move from Crown Heights area to Brownsville section of Brooklyn was complete and official. The soft mellow streets of Crown Heights, did not prepare a young Denzel for what he was about to experience in Brownsville Projects, as the sounds of gun-fire, echoed in the air throughout the late hours of the night. Their new apartment building was located right across the street from his great grandmother. A six-story building that contained a total of thirty-six apartments in it. There were six apartments on each floor with a door separating three apartments on each side. Denzel's apartment was located in the middle of two apartments on the fourth floor.

The apartment next door to the left of them, was basically a party house. It consists of a middle-aged woman, her boyfriend, with three pretty teenage daughters and one teenage son. The woman, next door, also had other members of her family staying there also. Their apartment door remained open, all day and all night during the week. Music playing and loud talking was the normal.

On the weekend, it was like a non-stop party. The first night after moving in. The woman who went by the name of Donna, knocked on the door and introduced herself to Denzel and his family. His mother and the lady next door, soon became close friends. Now the apartment on the left was totally opposite. It contained a woman, who was quietly raising five children.

Everyone living in the building seemed pleasant, and the hallways stayed full of noise with the children of the building running in it rampant. Unlike the apartment building on Crown Street, there was no superintendent over watching the conditions and behavior of its tenants.

Growing up in Crown Heights, Denzel was not familiar with or had no idea of the word mental retardation, nor has he been around anyone whom suffered from the disorder, well at least not to his knowledge. When he visited his great-grandmother in Brownsville projects before moving there, both him and his sister would always visit some friends whom lived next door to her. The friends were like play cousins to him and his sister, because his great-grandmother and their grandmother were very close, like sisters.

During birthday parties at his friend's apartment in his great-grandmother's building, the kid's grandmother would invite over a young male who suffered from the disorder of retardation, who lived in an apartment two doors away. While at the parties this young male would dance along with the other children, flapping his hands and making weird noises.

Denzel, while not having any knowledge of the young male condition, would start laughing out loud, on how the young male was dancing and acting. He would be scrutinized for his comments, but no one never informed him of the disease or condition the young male was in. It wasn't until, he actually moved to Brownsville Houses, that he became aware of the illness.

Denzel's first day of school, in his new neighborhood came in the month of January. It was winter semester, and he was in second grade. His mom went to register him in Public School 175, located just two blocks away on Blake Avenue and Bristol Street and directly across the street from a notoriously bad Junior High School formerly known as 263 called "MARCUS".

The Elementary School is now currently a High School, but back when Denzel finished the fourth Grade by the Year of 1981 the Board of Education transferred all of its students out as it reformed the school into a Re-Direction School for dropouts who wanted to get their GED.

Once the administrative part of enrolling Denzel at the 175 admissions offices was over, Denzel was escorted along with his mom by a school staff member to his classroom.

They reached the third floor, and could hear sounds of children laughing loudly throughout the hallway. The school staff member then knocked on one of the classroom doors and started shaking her head in disbelief. A young male, later known to Denzel as Henry opened the door widely. The school staff member then walked away, as Denzel and his mom walked into the classroom. A short older woman who was the teacher walked over to approach Denzel and his mom. As the teacher got closer, one of the male students ran up behind her and snatched the wig off of the woman's head.

Denzel and his mom were temporary stunned by what had just taken place in front of their very eyes.

"Oh Shit!" The woman shouted as she took off behind the kid that snatched her wig off.

Denzel and his mom then realized the woman wasn't as fragile as they thought, as she gave chase of the young student. The teacher was quick on her feet and leaped over a desk and caught the student. She placed the student in a choke hold, while the classroom roared with laughter from the amused students.

Denzel then looked at his mom as if he wanted to say *What the fuck have you done got me into!*

The caught student gave up the wig to the teacher, whom then released her choke hold on him. After retrieving her wig, the teacher tossed the student down to the floor and gave a soft little stomp to the back of the head. She then wiped the dust off her wig then placed it back on her head. She walked over to a mirror that was mounted on a wall near her desk and adjusted her wig to the way she wanted. The spunky teacher then walked over to Denzel and his mom to introduce herself as the teacher of the class.

"Hello, I'm Miss Ramos," The short teacher said as she extended her hand out to Denzel's mother. Miss Ramos spoke very fast and possessed a raspy voice. It was also possible she was from Panama or Cuba due to her accent. *Welcome to the Jungle!* Denzel thought to himself as he looked around the classroom, while his mother and new teacher exchanged greetings. The disorderly students in the class continued to run around and talk very loudly while the teacher and Denzel mom engaged in conversation. After the teacher and his mom's brief conversation, Denzel's mom told him she would see him later and left the classroom.

The teacher then yelled out for the students to be quiet as she pulled Denzel out in front of the classroom for an introduction of him being a new student in the class. In the middle of her announcement she observed two students not paying attention as they talked among themselves. She quickly walked over to the bulletin board and removed a very chalky eraser.

She stared in the direction of the two students whom wasn't paying her any attention and lined them up in her sights, as they continued to hold their private conversation.

Suddenly at the blink of an eye, she tossed the chalky eraser across the classroom like a professional quarterback, striking one of the kids in back of the head. The impact caused a cloud of dusty white smoke, that resulted in the rest of the children in the classroom to becoming completely silent just before they all burst into laughter. Denzel also started to laugh, as he glanced at the two children whom where all whitened out from the dusty eraser.

Denzel was amazed at the action taken place by the teacher in his new classroom, because nothing like that had ever happen in his former school. The most action Denzel ever witness in his former school, was a student getting his ass whipped by his mom for acting a fool in class.

The classic ass whipping had taken place when Denzel was in first grade, And the memory stuck in his young mind for many years, Because the kid ran around the classroom with his mother chasing him as she swung the belt. The highly upset mother nearly hit innocent children as she swung wildly, while her son crawled under desk and jumped over some also to flee her. The teacher pleaded for her to stop, Once the student ran behind her, and the mother nearly popped the teacher with the belt by mistake.

Miss Ramos then walked over to the sink located in the classroom and proceeded to wash her hands clean. She then wiped her wet hands on her knee length trench coat she wore as if it was a normal event in her classroom. She cleared her raspy voice and proceeded to introduce Denzel to the class as one of their new classmate, while all the children just stared at him. Once the introducing was over, Denzel stood there scanning the entire class room until he came across a familiar face. He recognized a young male sitting in the back of the class, as someone whom attended his previous school in Crown Heights.

Rodney Smalls, a light complexion male was a former classmate of Denzel, in kindergarten as well as the first grade, back in his former school 161. Once Denzel reach the second grade, he notice Rodney was no longer in the school, and figured he moved away. Miss Ramos then looked at Denzel whom was still standing there facing the class, like he was gonna make a speech or something. The teacher then walked over to Denzel and leaned over to whisper in his ear.

"You look like a nice quiet kid, and you better keep it that way. Because if you don't, I'm gonna treat you like the rest of these little fucka's in here. Do you understand me?" She asked while Denzel acknowledged with a head nod.

"I'm glad we understand one another, so unless you plan on singing, dancing or telling the class a good story. Find an empty seat in here, and go sit your ass down," Ms. Ramos said as she walked away towards her desk and sat down. Denzel quickly found an empty seat in the back of the classroom, near his ex-classmate and sat down.

Once it was time for lunch recess, Denzel walked over to Rodney just before the class lined up, to be escorted to the cafeteria.

"What's up Rodney?" Denzel as he went to slap Rodney five.

"What's up Denzel? I see you moved out here too huh?" Rodney replied as the both headed out the classroom to the cafeteria downstairs.

"Yeah man, my mom wanted to move closer to my great grandmother," Denzel said as he looked around at all the new faces.

"Well, me and my family moved out here last summer. Denzel, Brownsville is not a joke. This neighborhood and school, has a lot of trouble makers. So be ready to fight. Because if you don't fight back, everybody's gonna fuck with you," Rodney warned his friend as they both stood in the lunch line with their classmates. Rodney pointed out a few of the bullies that was in their class and some other classes, while they sat in the cafeteria eating their lunch.

The word trouble makers were an understatement for some of the students who attended that school. It was almost like a mini Spartford (A Correctional Facility for Juvenile Offenders) in there. The fourth up to the six graders thought they owned the school, as they took advantage of their age difference with the younger kids. They were known to remove food off the younger kid's lunch tray and dared the younger kids to say anything.

The playground affiliated with the school was located across the street in Bristol Park. The younger students would have to evacuate from the swings and slides, once the fourth to six graders were let out for recess. Their where no school yard monitors assigned in the playground like they have today to monitor and secure the safety of the children.

It was normal to see a second, third grader getting threaten, slapped or punched to give up a swing or a slide they were using. The only ones untouched, were the younger siblings of the fourth, fifth and six grade bullies. To avoid the unnecessary harassment, many of the students went to the gymnasium during recess. In the gymnasium, there was at least one teacher assigned to monitor the children.

Rodney's warning of trouble makers in the school and neighborhood, was very accurate. Unknown to him he was about to be tested, soon enough.

Tyrone, a young husky male whom outweighed Denzel by at least twenty pounds. Decided he was going to test his new classmate heart, on his first day. During the lunch recess, he walked over to Denzel whom was standing next to Rodney in the gymnasium after they both finished eating. Without any words exchanged or warning, he punched Denzel right in the center of his chest and awaited a response.

Denzel stood there in shock and didn't retaliate at first, he thought it was some type of ruff house game the kids played at the school. The blow barely faded him, and he smiled as others watched on. It wasn't until after Tyrone stomped onto his foot and pushed him, he began to realize he was being attack as Rodney warned him prior.

Denzel, whom already planned on not falling victim to any bully fury shoved Tyrone with tremendous force causing the bully to fall down to the gymnasium floor and slid a few feet on his back, until he banged his head on a beam. A small crowd started to gather, as they formed a circle around the two in hope to see a fight. Tyrone then jumped up and got into Denzel's face. A kid in the crowd shouted.

"Oh shit! Tyrone! I know you not gonna let that new kid floor you like that!" Tyrone then balled up his fist, and stared into Denzel's eyes. Denzel was way slimmer than Tyrone and was about three inches taller than the trouble maker.

"Who told you, that you can hit me back?! Punk!" Tyrone asked in a forceful voice tone, in an attempt to intimate Denzel, whom pretty much was showing no fear. Tyrone looked over Denzel's shoulder and spotted his trouble making buddies mixed in the crowd. He felt he was invincible, knowing if things didn't go his way, they would jump in.

The crowd started to grow eager to see action, as the two just stared each other down. The onlookers knew the possible fight could be interrupted before it even gets started if the schools staff got wind of it. One of Tyrone's buddies became frustrated with the stare down and quickly instigated the fight, by pushing Tyrone into Denzel. Rodney previously warned Denzel that certain kids at the school liked to jump people, especially if one of their buddies was getting their ass kicked. Denzel kept that thought in mind as he scanned the crowd in the gym, looking for his on back up. That back up would be Reggie, whom also attended the school.

Reggie and his family were very close friends with Denzel and his family. Denzel's great grandmother and Reggie's grandmother were very close, and considered each other as sisters. Reggie was about a year older than Denzel and was crazy as hell. He was the type of kid that always found himself in all types of trouble and thought it was fun.

As crazy as Reggie was, he was also as protective of Denzel and his little brother Phillip. There was no sight of Reggie, so all hopes of back up went out the window. The look on the onlooker's face told him that, no one was willing to interfere and stop the fight that was about to happen. Tyrone then pushed Denzel off balance with both hands, causing the crowd to re-act with chants and all types of noise. Denzel quickly responded by striking Tyrone in the jaw stunning him, for a moment. He then followed that punch with numerous blows to the body and face. Tyrone began to back pedal until he stumbled into the crowd.

Tyrone had no idea that Denzel was so quick with his hand speed and strength. He was so used to having his victims run away or back down, that he wasn't prepared for a real fight. Tyrone's buddies watch closely as the new kid started to embarrass their friend, by kicking his ass. Tyrone became very frustrated and started swinging his arms wildly like a mad man. He practically missed every punch he threw, as Denzel bobbed and weaved to avoid Tyrone's punches like he was trying to mimic Muhammad Ali.

Tyrone friends started to taunt him, causing him to charge Denzel in an attempt to grab him and wrestle him down to the floor. He knew he had a weight advantage over the much slimmer Denzel and wanted to put it to good use. But every time he attempted to grab Denzel, he was met with a closed fist to the face and body. The numerous blows Denzel hit him with, started to show on his face as swelling to the eyes and speed knots to the forehead began to form on his face.

"STOP! DON'T MOVE! DON'T MOVE!" Shouted a mature male voice over a bull horn, that caused the crowd to scatter. It was the assistant principle Mr. Edstein whom was walking so fast that his toupee was flapping in the air. Denzel took off running to avoid a trip to the principal's office on his first day at his new school. A suspension or minor discipline would've looked bad on his part and definitely would've earned him an ass whooping when he got home from his mom.

Denzel returned back to his classroom after recess with a brand-new respect from his new classmates after the fight with Tyrone. He chose to remain humble and remained quiet in class as he focused on his school work. The young thugs in his class now knew not to fuck with him, unless they wanted to take a chance in having Denzel ruining their reputation as tuff guys. Rodney was glad that Denzel kicked Tyrone's ass and his new friend Henry whom was a little comedian, all stuck together and no longer fell prey to their class bullies.

It was a busy first week of school for Denzel whom practically was falling victim to a lot of events happening in P.S. 175. The second day of school Denzel arrived early and sat in the cafeteria at a table awaiting the time to go line up inside the gym. While waiting, he heard two females having a loud argument as they sat at a table behind him, he turned around and notice to large females and figured they had to be six graders due to their size. He thought nothing of it and turned back around watching the other girls at the school as they walked by. The argument grew louder and before anyone knew it the two females were fighting, while Denzel continued to day dream.

Suddenly without warning, the two oversized females came crashing down on him, smashing his face into the table as they fought-on top of him. His screams for them to get off him went unheard as he tried to wiggle his small frame from under the two Amazons. Two special Education staff members whom where monitoring their students in the cafeteria at the time broke up the fight and pulled the two big girls off of the smashed Denzel. The loud laughter of children exploded through the cafeteria as Denzel laid stuck on the table like a smashed roach and someone screamed out.

"Somebody Call 911! He dead!"

Mr. Sabb, a very large muscular black male who was one of the Special Education teachers lifted Denzel off the table. He held in his laugh, as he could see the weird expression on the young male face, and could only imagine how it felt to be pinned down like that.

"Hey little man, are you okay?" The hulking teacher asked as he checked Denzel for visible injuries.

"I'm okay sir," Denzel responded as he looked over the teacher's shoulder and stared at some of the teacher's students. Denzel couldn't help but notice some of the male students had full mustaches and beards like grown men. He still didn't understand the seriousness of mental and physical retardation.

"Sir, why does some of those kids have mustaches like their adults and are funny looking? Denzel asked in a non-disrespectful manner with true innocents. Mr. Sabbs couldn't believe that the first thing this young kid would do is ask about his student, when he should've been more concerned about just having two big bitches fighting on top of him. But the teacher just explained to Denzel the differences of his students and that they require special attention and needs.

The school bell sounded off in the cafeteria, letting the students know it was time to line up in the gym to be escorted up to their classroom by their teachers. Denzel then thanked the teacher again for helping him get from under the two big girls and headed to the gym along with the other students.

"I tried to tell you to watch out, but you were too busy looking at them other girls That's why you got smashed out on the table!" Sabrina, one of Denzel female classmates said as she laughed at Denzel once he got to the area where his class was lined up in the gym.

"You were buried alive under all that fat meat!" Henry jokingly said as he laughed out loud as he turned around while he stood in front of the line.

"They were so heavy on my back, I couldn't even move," Denzel said as he shook his head in disbelief.

"Boy you are having a heck of a first week, first you get in a fight on your first day at this school, then someone has a fight on top of you like you wasn't even there," Rodney said as he joined the line and got word of what happened in the cafeteria.

"Man, you are telling me, I really wonder what's next for me in this dang on school," Denzel stated as he felt vulnerable to the unexpected. Mr. Edstein started to walk around the gym with his bull horn in his hand, instructing students to line up and quietly await their teachers. In his other hand, he had a handful of Charms lollipops, that he called Merits. He would walk around and hand out Merits to the students whom he believed was standing quietly and at full attention on their class line while they awaited their teacher. He would shout over the bull horn "A MERIT" when he hands a student a Lollipop, as he gained everyone's attention.

Denzel and the rest of his classmates tried to earn themselves a Merit, but was bypassed a few times because they kept making jokes on what happen to Denzel in the cafeteria that day. Miss Ramos soon came to get her class and escorted them to their classroom.

A few weeks went by, and Denzel began to adjust to his new surroundings at school. His new buddy Henry showed him the ins and outs of the school as they played in the hallways, while out the classroom with a bathroom pass. Back in the days the young children would get a bathroom pass from their teacher so they could go hand out in the halls, staircase and sometimes sneak to the store. Some of the older males and even younger males would meet up with the females at the school to hump and kiss while out on the bathroom passes on the regular. All it took was the passing of a note for the girls to get a pass and meet at a designated location in the school to hook up.

One day Denzel and Henry got the bathroom pass with plans on sneaking outside to go to the penny candy store, located up the street from the school. Before they headed outside, they both decided to use the rest room located on the second floor, right next to one of the Special Education classes. As they walked in the boy's bathroom they noticed two females in there, one of the females was bent over throwing up in the urinal, while the other rubbed her back. Denzel and Henry both looked at one another confused to why these two special education females were in the boy's bathroom.

"Hey, what Y'all doing in here? This is the boy's bathroom," Denzel shouted, while thinking the girls were confused to where they were at. Suddenly a tall male jumped out from the bathroom stall and began to stare at the two second graders violently. The male was a special education student whom had a mustache and was crossed eyed. He appeared as if he belonged in High School. Before Denzel and Henry could say another word, the male punched Denzel in the chest very hard sending him back into the wall.

"Oh Shit!" Denzel yelled out, after receiving the hard blow. Both him and Henry took off running out of the bathroom and down the corridor, as the male gave chase. The male was screaming out like a mad man as he attempted to catch the much quicker Denzel and Henry.

"Help! Help!" Henry shouted as the male caught up and almost grabbed him. Denzel and Henry then made it up to the stairwell and darted up the stair case to the third floor, where two males sixth graders where hanging out.

"Yo! What's wrong with you two little niggas?" Asked one of the six graders.

"Some retarded nigga is chasing us! He trying to beat us up!" Henry said as him, and Denzel zoomed past the two like two jack rabbits. The two six grader students started to laugh at them, until the special education student exited the stairwell in pursuit of them.

"Yo! What the fuck are you doing up here?!" Yelled out one of the six grade students, catching the special education student out there off guard. The male then stopped in his tracks and looked at the older kids hanging in the hallway.

"Man! Get Yo retarded ass out of here! Before we fuck you up!" The other six graders said as they showed no fear of the special education student. Denzel and Henry continued running nonstop until they reached the stairwell on the other end of the corridor and darted down the staircase, while the six graders distracted the male chasing them. The special education didn't want any part of the two six graders and disappeared back into the stairwell, while Denzel and Henry made it safely back to class.

"Denzel, why you and Henry sweating and breathing so hard for?" Rodney asked as the two returned to their seats.

"Some retarded nigga punched Denzel in the chest in the bathroom, then started chasing us.

"Chasing you? For what?! He wanted some candy?" Rodney asked.

"He was trying to beat our ass! What you think?" Henry said with a smile on his face. Rodney started to laugh, but quickly stopped because Miss Ramos turned around and reached for an eraser.

"Y'all didn't sneak outside and hit the penny candy store?" Rodney asked.

"Nope, we didn't get a chance to go to the store. Once I got punched in the chest, I forgot all about sneaking out to the penny candy spot, when that nigga was chasing us. Rodney started to laugh again. "Damn! That nigga was strong!" Denzel said as he rubbed his chest, still feeling the effects of the hard blow.

"Yeah, some of those special education kids be real strong, that's why Mr. Sabbs has all those muscles to hold them down, when they go off," Rodney said as he remembered seeing one of the special education students flipping out in the cafeteria once, knocking staff on their asses.

It was later said that the two female special students where in the boy's bathroom, because one of them was very sick and the boy's bathroom was the closest bathroom to their classroom. The male special education was in the bathroom to protect the two girls. When Denzel and Henry entered the bathroom, the special education male must've thought the two females were in danger and sprang into action on the two younger kids. That blow to the chest helped Denzel realize the strength of some of the mentally retarded people where extremely strong and that they could get violent at any given time, whether provoked or not.

Neither the less, Denzel wanted to seek revenge for being struck by the special education student, it was an anger that was growing from within, but he chooses not to act on it and focused on the rest of the school bullies to come his way to try him. That blow to chest, stayed in his mental rolodex throughout his two years at the school. Henry and Denzel always joked around about it, and laughed at who ran the fastest and who was screaming in the halls for help.

Trouble in his new school was the least of Denzel's worries, he also had to deal with the bullies and trouble makers of the streets of Brownsville Projects. The Projects are typically full of five types of young males who live in it. First, you have the trouble makers whom 90% of the time grow older to be career criminals, as most of them inherit the trait of being a menace to society from their fathers, brothers and cousins whom have been in and out of the system throughout their life. These young males are taught by their career criminal relatives to be hard and to be aggressive towards others, and if they didn't live by this rule, some were abused by the same relatives if they thought they were soft on the streets.

The projects also had young males that where the total opposite of the Bad Boys, whom just enjoyed being kids and showed respect toward their elders and each other. They were the good quite students who paid attention in class and excelled in the studies. These are the young males whom grew up to have some type of success in their life by becoming doctors, lawyers, teachers, members of law enforcement and the list goes on and on.

The third type of male developed in the projects where known as the suckers. These young males where called soft and remained passive as they fell victim to the Bad Boys aggression, as they refused to fight back and stand up for themselves. These are the males whom later in their life put themselves in the position of some type of power, whether it through their careers or became body builders. The demand for dominance they never had as a youngster was being lived through their new way of life.

A fourth type of developing in the hood where the young males who converted from being a good kid into a Bad Boy basically, because it seemed as if good guys finish last in the hood. These males realized that many women loved having a ruff neck, thug, rude boy in their life.

The Fifth and last but not least, you had the silent but deadly young males, whom had certified fighting skills. These males didn't bother anyone nor did they looked for trouble to get into. When trouble came their way, they simply welcomed it by dominating whomever tested them.

Big Daddy, Denzel's grand-father, came to check on his two grandchildren in their new neighborhood after they got settled in for about two months. He would occasionally visit them after a hard day of work, just before heading home to Bedford-Stuyvesant to deal with Denzel grandmother who was a piece of work. Big Daddy was a very tall and husky man, whom had the hands the size of a boxing glove.

Big Daddy was old school. He was very protective and didn't let anybody fuck with his family. He kept a wallet full of cash and a big gun tucked in his waistband at all times. It was like a well-known trademark for Big Daddy to have amongst his children and grandchildren. Once when asked by one of Denzel older cousins at a family function, why did he carry a big gun? Big Daddy responded.

"This is for the bad people who don't want to see Big Daddy feed his family." No one understood what that meant until they all got older.

During Big Daddy's first visit to Denzel's home in Brownville projects, he brought in some Chinese food he ordered from the restaurant on Livonia Avenue. Prior to picking up the food, he had spoken to Denzel's mother on the telephone asking her what he should bring her and the kids to eat. As soon as he walked into the door, he was embraced by both Denzel and his sister whom always loved to be in the presence of their grandfather. The two happy grandchildren knew by the end of the night, Big Daddy would give them at least ten to twenty dollars apiece to put in their pockets.

It was a cool Friday night and approximately eight o'clock, when Big Daddy finished his food and wanted to smoke a cigarette. He realized he was fresh out and didn't care for the brand Newport's that Denzel mom smoked. The need for nicotine was real, and he wanted a new pack of his favorite cigarette from the store, like it was a desert of some sort.

Now back in the days, before the big hype of cancer. A person under the age of twenty-one years of age, could purchase a pack of cigarettes with no problem. All you needed was money and it was a quick transaction. The rules have changed and today many stores are fined for selling to a minor if caught.

"Which one of you kids want to go to the store for Big Daddy? I need some cigarettes," Big Daddy asked as he reached into his back pocket and pulled out his fat wallet full of cash.

"I'll go Big Daddy" Denzel quickly responded, knowing that he would probably get a nice tip for going.

"Okay, Get me one pack of Winston's. Now, Denzel, I'm going to give you enough money so you can buy you and you sister some snacks," Big Daddy said as he removed a twenty-dollar bill from his wallet and handed it to Denzel.

Denzel took the money into his hand and stared at the bill, as if he admired the crisp new bill.

"Adrianne, does this boy know how to count money yet? Does he know how to count change from a big bill?" Big Daddy said while laughing at the expression on Denzel's face.

"Yeah, he should, He's in the second grade now. He goes to the store for me all the time and never had a problem with bringing back the right change," Denzel's mom responded. "He just has a crazy thing for bills over then dollars, that's all" Denzel mother continued.

"Denzel, you look at that twenty like it's a hundred-dollar bill. If you think that's a big bill, take a look at this," Big Daddy said as started pulling out a few hundred dollar bills out his wallet. "Snap out of it boy, and go get my cigarettes," Big Daddy continued.

Denzel then placed the twenty-dollar bill in his pants pocket and asked his mom did she needed anything from the store also. Once she told him no, she then walked over to the front door, looked out the peek hole and opened it for Denzel to exit. Denzel then headed down the stair case and bumped into an older kid whom went by the name of Belly.

Belly was a husky kid who lived upstairs on the top floor of the building. He was carrying a very large ham and cheese sandwich in his hand, That Denzel nearly knocked down to the floor as they collided.

"You almost knocked my fucking sandwich out my hand asshole, you better be lucky you didn't!" The older kid said as he continued up the stair case.

"Sorry, I didn't see you when I came out," Denzel responded as he stared at the large sandwich that Belly was eating.

"Oh, You the new little nigga that just moved in here huh?" The husky teenager asked. Denzel shook his head up and down to acknowledge yes.

"How old are you shorty?" Belly asked

"I'm eight," Denzel responded.

"You got any brothers?" Belly continued to ask as he leaned against the wall on the staircase to take a large bite out his sandwich.

"Nope, it's just me and my sister," Denzel informed his new neighbor.

"Damn! You don't have any brothers to back you up or teach you how to fight?" Belly asked once he finished chewing the mouth full of sandwich he had in his mouth. Denzel shook his head to say no.

"Don't worry shorty; It's enough niggas in this building to teach you how to fight. I don't know if you know about the ville shorty, but out here you better know how to fight and fight niggas back that fuck with you. Because if you don't, you're going to get your ass kicked all the time," Belly said as he continued up the staircase to his apartment.

Why the hell did she move us to Brownsville projects, out of all the places in Brooklyn?! Denzel thought to himself, referring to his mother as he continued to head down the staircase. He then exited the building and headed to the local grocery store that people in the neighborhood called MANNY'S. It was located on Rockaway Avenue just off the corner of Blake Avenue. There was a Pizza shop, located at the corner a few doors over from the store that was closed for business at that time of night, But Denzel could still see the workers cleaning up through the steamy glass windows.

The aroma of pizza being cooked all day, still existed in the air. It traveled through a cracked window they left open for ventilation. The owner Gino, A short muscular Italian refused to keep his shop doors open for business past eight o'clock at night. It wasn't because he was in the hood, it was based on the three-past robbery attempts within the last two months.

Denzel continued to walk past the Pizza shop, and took a quick glance into the Laundry Mat that was open for business and located in the middle of the Pizza Shop and MANNY'S grocery on Rockaway Avenue. He observed the young black males whom were managing the laundry mat. The word on the street was, these same males were hustling marijuana as well as narcotics out of that location. They were sitting around, watching television and playing cards, while a few customers were in there washing and drying their clothes. Unknown to Denzel at the time, these young men were gangsters whom were known to be armed and very dangerous. They frequent MANNY's store, and seemed to be some type of security for the young owner of the grocery store.

The grocery store owner Manuel was a short chubby Cuban guy, with a very hot temper. It was rumored that he once beat a man to death with a baseball bat in the back of his store, just for stealing a can of beer. Nothing was every confirmed on that case, but the rumor spread like wild fire. Manuel connection with the local thugs in the neighborhood, made his store untouchable against the stick-up men whom terrorized the rest of the businesses in the area.

After gathering a few snacks for himself and his sister from the aisle, Denzel walked over to the register and placed his items on the counter. He observes a tall male teenager with a large curly afro approximately thirteen years old standing there as if he was waiting to make a purchase of something of some sort. The heavyset male Hispanic behind the counter looked at Denzel and asked.

"Is that it? Poppy?"

"Nope, let me get a pack of Marlboro cigarettes and five packs of Now and Laters," Denzel responded as he reached into his pocket and removed the twenty-dollar bill that Big Daddy have given him. The curly head pre-teen took notice of the bill that Denzel handed to the man behind the counter, as well as the change giving back to Denzel whom placed the money in his right pocket.

"Hey shorty, can I get a quarter?" The curly head teenager asked as he leaned against the counter looking down on the shorter Denzel. The free hearted Denzel looked up at the taller male, then reached into his pocket and handed him fifty cents.

"Thanks, shorty! Good looking out!" The teenager said as Denzel collected his bag containing his snacks and his grandfather's cigarettes. Denzel then exited the store. The teenager waited a few seconds at the counter, then exited the store without making any type purchase.

Denzel crossed Rockaway Avenue then quickly walked in the street on Blake Avenue to avoid the rats that ran around the now abandoned Public School 125. As he walked home, he then noticed the teenager he gave money, walking beside him closely.

"Hey, shorty! You new around here?" The teenager asked as he looked around suspiciously.

"Yeah, I just moved around here," Denzel answered just before the older male punched him in the stomach without warning causing Denzel then bent over from the impact of the blow and before he knew it, he was surrounded by five more teenagers whom started to repeatedly push and punch him. The group of pre-teen thugs pushed Denzel up against a parked car, while they all took turns punching him in the body.

One of the thugs must have been watching too many kung Fu flicks, because he backed up and started running toward Denzel with a flying kick. Denzel avoided the flying kick to the head by ducking, as the young thug almost sailed thru the car's front windshield.

"Welcome to Brownsville, little nigga. Now give us all your fucking money!" Shouted the curly hair pre-teen Denzel previously and generously have giving fifty cents to in the store.

"I gave you some money already!" Denzel replied as he struggled to get away. The curly head pre-teen then slapped Denzel in the face, causing Denzel eyes to water up.

"Shut the fuck up, punk! That was coins; you got dollar bills in your pocket," The curly head pre-teen responded as he attempted to place his hand in Denzel pocket, but couldn't because Denzel continued to scuffle.

"That's my grandfather's money, not mine!" Denzel shouted as if the young thugs even cared.

"Fuck your grandfather, nigga! You better give up that money before we really start beating your ass," One of the young thugs yelled as he balled his fist and placed it in Denzel's face.

Denzel started to look around and focus on all of the young thugs who surrounded him, with tears in his eyes caused by his inner rage. This was the first time in his life that he has been jumped, and he knew he had no wins against all of the older young thugs. He could only hope somebody would come to his rescue.

"That's right little nigga, cry like a little bitch." Another thug shouted in Denzel's ear, as the tears in Denzel eyes made him feel as if he was more superior over his younger victim.

"If you take my grandfather's money, he's gonna kill you and that bitch mother of yours, that shitted you out!" Denzel yelled in rage as he grew angrier by the minute.

"Your grand-daddy ain't gonna do shit, but get killed out here nigga," The curly male said as he went to stick his hand into pocket, where he observed his victim previously placed it inside of the store. Denzel quickly pushed the curly hair thug with all his strength, causing the thug to fall backward into oncoming traffic. The thug was almost struck by a vehicle as he landed on his back.

Denzel struggled to get free as he saw the ring leader hit the deck, but was quickly grabbed by two of the other thugs, just as he started to take off running.

"Yo! This little muthafucka just tried to get you hit by a car. What you gonna do with his ass?" Asked one of the thugs who was holding onto Denzel as he laughed out loudly at his friend. The curly hair thug jumped up, just before getting hit by a passing car.

"I'm gonna cut this little nigga up!" The curly head thug shouted as he walked over to a garbage can and removed an empty bottle from it. He then broke the base of the bottle and then walked over towards Denzel.

Two of the thugs attempted to hold the struggling Denzel still, as the curly head thug raised the bottle up, ready to strike his young victim with it.

"Yo! What the fuck are your knuckleheads doing over here? Leave that little kid alone!" A deep older male voice shouted as he grabbed the bottle out of the young thug's hand, just before he began to slash Denzel with it. The other thugs took off running at the sight of the hulking light complexion male whom towered over them. The curly hair ring leader remained on the scene as if he wasn't intimidated by the older male.

"Don't eye ball me like that little nigga! I will fuck you up and bring you home to your parents," The older male said, while the curly hair thug looked at him.

"Yeah, you little punk. I know both your parents. I remember when you were shitting in your pampers. You better get your fucking ass in the house, before I let them know what the fuck you out here doing at night" The older male warned.

"We were only playing with the kid," The curly head thug responded wants he realized the hulking male and his father were good buddies.

"Playing! You must take me for a sucker; I could see what the fuck you and your little bad ass friends were about to do to this kid," The hulking male said.

"We were just playing manhunt with him. Ain't that right shorty?" The curly head thug asked Denzel as he stared at Denzel hard, while attempting to intimidate his victim to agree with what he was saying.

"Nope! I gave this punk fifty cents in the store, then him and his friends jumped me. They said if I didn't give them the rest of my money, they were gonna beat me up bad" Denzel boldly said as he stared the curly hair kid dead in the eye. The curly head kid looked at Denzel as if he wanted to slap the shit out of him again, but he knew the older male wouldn't allow it. So, the curly head thug just took off running in the direction his friends headed in.

"Are you okay kid?" The older male asked Denzel whom was still standing there a little teary eyed.

"I'm okay; I guess mister. Thanks for stopping them punks from killing me." Denzel said as he picked up his plastic grocery bag containing his snacks and grandfather's cigarettes off the ground from where he dropped it, once he was attacked.

"No problem shorty, just be more careful out here in the streets. It's a dog eat dog world out here in Brownsville, you hear me?" The older male asked as Denzel whom shook his head up and down to acknowledge yes.

"If anybody fucks with you, you let them know you know Moose," The older male instructed Denzel.

"Thanks, Moose, I better get upstairs before I get in trouble." Denzel said as he started to walk off towards his building.

Once Denzel turned the corner and got closer to his building, he observed his grandfather walking towards him.

"Boy, what the hell took you so long?" Big Daddy asked just before noticing Denzel's eyes were glassy, and he had dried tears on his cheek. Before Denzel could answer his grandfather, he observed the young thugs that tried to rob him hanging out near the chain basketball courts located in the middle of the projects in front of building 295 and 294 Osborne Street. The Chain Court was a nick name for the basketball court basically because the nets on the hoops were made of small metal chains unlike the normal cotton/polyester nets.

"Those boys down there, beat me up and tried to rob me of the money you gave me, once I came out the store" Denzel informed his grandfather as he pointed in the thug's direction.

"What! Tell me what they did to you boy" The now angry grandfather asked his grandson, while being shocked of what he just heard.

"They punched and kicked me, and that one with the big curly afro was gonna cut me with a broken bottle," Denzel quickly said.

"Cut you with a bottle, huh?" Big Daddy asked as he grew even angrier.

"Yep, until a man stopped them," Denzel said as he started to get a little hyped up as tears started to flow down his face again. Big Daddy wiped the tears from his grandson's eyes.

"Stop crying boy!" Big Daddy instructed Denzel asked as he looked into his teary-eyed grandson, just before he pulled out his large .38 Caliber Saturday night special.

"We gonna send them little muthafuckas a message right now!" Big Daddy stated as he aimed his gun towards the group of thugs whom were shooting hoops on the chain courts.

"Hey, you little bastards!" Big Daddy yelled out as he gained the little thugs attention.

"This is for fucking with my grandson!" Big Daddy shouted as he pulled the trigger. The loud shot, shook the night air as the first bullet struck the flag pole on the chain court and the young thugs began to scramble out of the way. Big Daddy continued to squeeze the trigger until his pistol was empty as he took out a light pole. All the young thugs fled the area, as well as people just hanging out on the benches.

"I think they got the message now, what you think boy?" Big Daddy asked an amazed Denzel who nodded his head yes.

"Let's get back upstairs, before your mother gets worried after hearing them shots and the cops come lock Ole Big Daddy up," Big Daddy said as he patted Denzel on top of his head with one hand as he tucked his smoking pistol back in his waist line with the other. They both entered the building. Big Daddy then dumped his empty shells into the incinerator and returned to the apartment, where Denzel mother waited until they both returned.

Denzel's welcome to Brownsville, was an eye opener for him at the tender age of eight years old. He began to develop an unnatural rage towards those whom violated him in any way or fashion. The hunger for revenge began to eat away at his young soul, but he was way too young and not physically capable of acting out his plots of revenge. As he grew older he has had a few more encounters with the negative element in his neighborhood, and he stored the faces of all who violated him in the back of his mind, until that final incident that made him reach his turning point.

CHAPTER 3

MEET AND GREET

Erica entered her car and started the engine. She activated her car's Bluetooth connection to her cell phone and began to start dialing.

"Hello" a female voice answered.

"What's up Stacey?" Erica responded.

"Nothing much, just waiting to finish this shift." Stacey informed her.

"Well, I hope everybody packed for this weekend," Erica said. "Remember I told you, DeVonte is taking everyone out to dinner at Major Souls Bar and Grill," Erica reminded Stacey.

"Yeah, I remember. Saturday night, right?" Stacey asked.

"Yes," Erica quickly responded.

"I think I inform all the Divas already, if not, I will let them know to wear something for the occasion," Stacey informed her friend.

Stacey was Erica close friend whom was very attractive and had a chocolate brown complexion with skin that was silky smooth. She possessed a figure that could turn many heads as soon as she stepped into a room without trying. Even though she was slim, she was very plump where it counted.

Erica and Stacey have been friends since the second grade. Stacey, along with her three other friends, were coming along as guests of Erica, for a weekend stay at DeVonte's house. Stacey and her three friends were registered nurses at a local hospital in New York City.

Doreen, Alexis and Chantel, along with Stacey were four of the finest nurses to have ever worked in the same hospital at the same time, in the United States. The four of them were previously featured on the front cover of Ebony and Essence magazines as the hottest nurses in America.

Doreen, a full figured black female possessed a light clear complexion which enhanced her gorgeous face. To be a big beautiful woman, Doreen had a very thin waist. She was blessed with a large round breast and a very large perfectly shaped bottom. Her eyes were almond shaped. Even her belly ring that hung from her navel was sexy, because her belly was so flat and did not hang over for a full-figured woman and no love handles where present. The best way to describe Doreen was fine ass amazon.

Now, Alexis and Chantel who were sisters, and where born a year apart, both were Cooley chicks from Trinidad. When I say Cooley's for those who don't know, coolies are of Caribbean Indian decent. Some may even look African American but possess Indian features, like coco skin and straight or curly long dark hair. When it came to both of these sisters, they were fine and had bodies shaped like an hour glass. They both spoke with slight light Caribbean accents and could make any two-piece bathing suit look like a work of art.

"Okay, I'll meet you girls out front or do you want me to meet you Divas in the parking lot?" Erica asked.

"We will meet you in the front. Everybody will be jumping in my brand new White Infinity Q54 truck. The girls are goanna leave their cars here in the job parking lot," replied Stacey before they both ended their conversation and hung up the phone. As the four ladies jumped into the Q54, Stacey drove out of the hospital's employee parking lot. Stacey and her three passengers couldn't help but hear the song "ALL YOU GOTTA DO IS SAY YES" by Floetry blasting from Erica's White on Black BMW 650 stereo.

Stacey pulled up closely beside the beamer and rolled down the front passenger window where Doreen was sitting. Doreen knocked on Erica's window to get her attention. Erica looked over and rolled down her window.

"Damn, I'm loving the sounds of that stereo. It sounds so crisp and clear" Stacey yelled out so Erica could hear her over the loud music blasting. Erica then lowered the volume of her stereo and instructed Stacey to pull her car up in front of hers. Once Stacey pulled up and parked in front of her, she exited her vehicle and approached the expensive SUV.

"Okay! Okay! Okay! Nice ride Baby girl," Erica said as she complemented Stacey on her new ride.

"Thank You baby girl, I figured it was time I treated myself to something nice after putting in so many hours of overtime at work," Stacey responded with a smile on her face.

"I feel you on that girl. You have to treat yourself to something nice" Erica quickly responded. Erica then greeted everybody sitting in Stacey's SUV with Hello.

"Who's ready to party and get white girl wasted this weekend?" Erica shouted while asking as she was leaning on the front passenger side window.

"I don't know about these bitches girl, but I'm ready to party like a naughty little school girl" Doreen responded with a smile on her face. A horny bitch like me haven't had no dick in a while. So, I plan on getting my drink and fuck on I hope there's some good prospects that can handle all of this," Doreen continued as the SUV erupted into laughter.

"Damn! You a nasty bitch," Erica said while laughing at Doreen's wild statement.

"She's not only nasty! She's two kinds of crazy" Chantel said as she shook her head with a broad girlish grin on her face. Doreen calmly reached into her large Gucci bag and pulled out a thick 13-inch dildo, one rabbit vibrator and two bullet vibrators all newly packaged along with packs of batteries and placed it on the dashboard. She then turned to Erica whom at the time was staring at all the gadgets on the dash board in amazement.

"Erica! A bitch brought backup, just in case none of your beau's friends are lucky enough to experience some of Doreen okay" Doreen said with a serious expression on her face.

Alexis laughed harshly before saying "Freak, you better have an extra one of them fuck toys for me if I strike out tonight, believe me you ain't the only bitch hot and horny for real," while she fanned herself with her hand. All the women began to laugh loudly like a bunch of school girls.

"Okay, we outer here girl follow me." Erica said as she jumped into her beamer and sped off with the Q54 in pursuit.

DeVonte entered his very large kitchen and started to prepare a large tossed salad, tuna salad and ears of corn. The walls where painted white and trimmed with black. The cabinets and island where black and the counters where black marble granite to match the black marble tile. All his appliances where stainless steel.

Jason got up out of his chair and made his way to the kitchen to grab a bag of chips for him and Dennis to munch on. He saw DeVonte doing his thing making the salads and attempted to slip away unnoticed

"Jason! Do me a favor player and take this key to get into my office so you can turn on the music?" DeVonte asked as he reached in his back pocket and removed a card that was actually a key and handed to Jason. Jason took the key and as DeVonte gave more instructions.

"Just swipe the key over the bar code scanner to gain entry. The remote looks like an iPad and it should be on my desk. When you get a hold of the remote just make sure you pick the selection SURROUND SOUND so it will play through every speaker I have set up okay" DeVonte said. Jason acknowledged as he looked up at the ceiling to glance at the speakers installed in it. He noticed the speakers were no longer the BOSE speakers DeVonte previously had installed, He noticed the insignia for the speakers were BEATS by Dr Dre.

"Damn Dee! I see you done made the power switch to the BEATS system? I heard they surround sound is off the fucking charts!" Jason said as if he was amazed that DeVonte got the latest sensation in home entertainment.

"I had it installed last week" DeVonte responded as he looked up himself admiring his new investment.

"So, what you wanna hear first? Will it be Biggie? Jigga?, Nas?, Luda?, 50 Cents?, Kanye?, Wayne?, Ricky Ross? or Do wanna go old school with your boys Big Daddy Kane or Kool G Rap?" Jason asked as he started to head out the kitchen and down the corridor towards Deon's Office.

"Put on that joint REAL NIGGAZ DO REAL THINGS by my man B.I.G. first, followed with a little Jigga and MOS DEF to set that Brooklyn vibe," DeVonte replied while taking a quick sip of cognac. Once Jason made it down the corridor he scanned the key and entered the office in which he believed DeVonte had designed to copy the office of the Cuban drug lord in the movie Scarface.

The room was the splitting image of the office in the movie with a little of DeVonte's touch. He had a black throne- like chair with his full initials embroidered in the leather with gold framing. A statue of a large panther with crystal eyes stood guard in attack position in front of his large black desk.

A 32-inch TV Monitor with surveillance of his property was mounted on the wall. Jason wasted no time as he walked over to DeVonte desk and picked up a large remote the resembled a IPad. He took a seat in luxurious chair and created a play list of assorted songs selected music and scrolled over to the song of his choice. Jason then selected the surround sound mode and hit play.

The sounds of the Notorious BIG flowed through all the speakers DeVonte had installed in the house, picnic area as well as the pool house. As the music started to thump, Jason twirled around in the chair and faced the large cabinet containing an arsenal of high power weapons. Jason then placed the remote back in place and headed back towards the kitchen. All the fella's heads were bopping to the beat. "Yo! BIG freaked that Dr. Dre beat that him and Snoop did on that DEEP COVER sound track 187," Jason said as he entered the kitchen. Jason started to recite Biggies lyrics from the REAL NIGGAZ DO REAL THINGS track as if he created it himself.

"You know I'm Brooklyn all day! Big Daddy Kane, Chubb Rock, B.I.G. and that nigga that goes by the name of Jigga," Rick said.

"Don't forget about my man Chubb Rock, he represented the Brooklyn movement also at one time," DeVonte said before reaching for his cell phone to place a call to Erica.

"Hello Babe. Are you on your way yet?" DeVonte asked while looking at his yacht-master gold Rolex watch.

"Who is this? And who are you looking for?" Erica replied while holding in her laugh.

"You can call me GOD! You know like you do every time I fill your body up with this ten inch fat pipe. You scream out oh my GOD!!!," DeVonte jokingly responded.

"Oh, I know who this is now, You're the guy that brings me 10" to heaven." Erica said after bursting into laughter.

"Yeah, I'm that guy. Act like you don't know Babe," DeVonte jokingly responded

"We're on the road heading your way Babes, I'm riding solo in my car and the others are behind me riding with Stacey. I'll hit you on your cell when we are approximately ten minutes out okay" Erica said as she switched lanes with Stacey in pursuit of her.

"Okay no doubt, baby girl. I'll make sure everything will be set up upon your arrival," DeVonte said before they both exchanged good-byes and hung up as he placed the iPhone into its holder.

"You are one natural born BBQ chef dude. I gotta give you your props on that," Dennis said to Mike while making himself a Thug Passion (combination of Hennessy and Alize) at the Tiki bar.

"I do, what I do, when I do, On the fucking barbecue grill" Mike jokingly said in his imitation voice of the rapper DMX.

Stacey watched Erica switch in and out of lanes on the highway as she followed closely behind her.

"Damn, girlfriend pushing that beamer like she stole the bitch, don't she know that these New Jersey Troopers will pull that ass over with the quickness?" Doreen said while admiring Erica fancy driving.

"Well, she works in law enforcement. So if she gets pulled over, I guess she'll show them her credentials," Stacey replied.

"That won't stop them troopers from giving your ass a ticket. You're not law enforcement. Besides that, I hear New Jersey

Troppers don't really care for any other agency but there own.

"Girl since September 11th, it has been one big happy family in law enforcement," Stacey replied.

"Anyway, jumping off the driving subject. I hear Erica's man DeVonte has a nice relaxing indoor pool" Alexis said while sitting behind Doreen.

"Bitch, what the fuck you mean you heard. I'm the Bitch that told you" Stacey replied while laughing at the same time.

"I just can't wait to get there so I can relax my big ass in the Jacuzzi, drink and eat all night. I might even be in the mood to take a hard one up my bun hole tonight by one of DeVonte's big dick friends" Doreen said as she rubbed on her thick thighs.

There was a brief moment of silence in Stacey's vehicle for about five seconds before an explosion of laughter filled the car. Doreen was always known to be outspoken at work or when they did a night out on the town, but this time she was being a little extra. Stacy just smile as she continued to drive. She could picture Doreen being freaky enough to enjoy anal sex.

"Damn! You like it up the ass like that, huh? Girl! You must be on some Heather Hunter shit," Alexis said while bouncing up and down on her seat as if she was riding a stiff dick.

"I do have to admit it does feels good when a guy licks the rim of your asshole and slide his tongue in and out of it. But, letting them stick their big stiff dick up in your hole is a no go. That shit hurts so bad, it will make you scream," Stacey said as she expressed a little bit about her freaky side.

"Damn Stacy! You just as nasty as Doreen," Chantel said to Stacey while giggling her ass off. Doreen then turned around with a smile on her face

"Yall need to stop fronting! Everybody in this SUV got a fat ole booty. There's not a woman alive today with a big ass whom haven't had a man make an attempt to slide in their ass during sex, especially when you have a big one like mine okay" she said. "They love going near the asshole when you got a nice ass and always wanna rub they tip on it, until you shut them down if you feel it slipping in" She continued to say.

"Okay, next subject," Chantel said with a sneaky grin on her face. Stacey looked over at Doreen and shook her head.

"You are just too much and crazy as hell thick momma" Stacey said to her out spoken friend.

"Oh, yeah, I almost forgot! If any of you young ladies wanna get your grove on tonight, safe sex is on me," Doreen said while she checked her hair in sun visor mirror. "I got all flavors of condoms! I have Trojans, Magnum, Extra Magnum" Doreen continued as she pulled out some samples out of her pocket book.

Safe Sex, is no Sex! So, I guess I will be coming to see you on that, because I haven't had no dick up in me in a minute" Alexis said while pointing towards her watch.

DeVonte stood in the kitchen and took a little break as he completed some of the stuff he was doing.

Okay that takes care of the side dishes so now all I need to do is go freshen up a little before the ladies get here, DeVonte thought to himself.

"Hey Rick, I need you to take over the ship while I go upstairs and freshen up a little," DeVonte said as he headed towards the spiral staircase located in the kitchen leading to the second level.

"No doubt player I got you. Go pretty yourself up captain Rick on deck," Ricky replied as he saluted DeVonte as he went up the stairs.

DeVonte quickly entered his bathroom located in his master bedroom and took a shower. He then exited the shower and lotion up his body and got dress. His T-shirt, swimming trunks, sandals and sun visor cap were all made by Gucci and could be spotted in the magazines, making him look like a poster boy for the brand. He started to groom his wavy hair with his brush, until his cell phone began to ring. He could see it was Erica calling and decided to answer it.

"Hello, lady of my life! Are you almost here, yet?" DeVonte asked as he made his way back into the bathroom to look at himself in the mirror.

"Almost, Babes. We are about ten minutes away. Do you need me to stop, and pick up anything?" She asked as she got off of Interstate 80, while being followed by Stacey and her passengers.

"Nope, I already have everything we need. The grill is fired up and the music is pumping," DeVonte replied with the sounds of Jay Z playing over the stereo in the background.

"Oh Okay! I guess will head straight over then, I will see you when we touch down," Erica replied as they exchanged I love you and ended their phone call. DeVonte quickly ran downstairs and into his office and turned the music down. He then spoke into the remote after pressing the INTERCOM selection on its screen.

"Okay, my brothers it's on! Chef Mike let's get that grill popping player, the ladies will be touching down in about ten minutes. So, let's go people!" DeVonte said over the intercom.

Mike asked Dennis, if he could go retrieve the beef and chicken Shish-Kebab he put together at home from the picnic table.

"Okay operation barbecue is in full effect," Mike replied as he began to place steaks on one grill and chicken on the other. Dennis quickly returned with the request shush kebab and placed the beef and chicken in the order that Mike have done.

"Dennis! I know you gonna want to kick my ass, but could you bring out the rolls for the kebabs, it slipped my mind to ask you before," Mike asked as he was debating with himself if he should cook some burgers and sausage links.

"Do you need anything else chef, before I come back the fuck out here brotha?," Dennis said sarcastically while folding his arms with his head tilted to the side.

"Well, since you asked! Bring out some sausage links, burgers and those potato hamburger/hotdog rolls" Mike replied with a smile on his face while getting in a fighting stance.

Jason walked over to the Tiki bar and checked on the beverage stock.

"Hey Mike, you want me to hook you up with a drink to sip on while you do your thing on the grills of steel," Jason asked awaiting an answer. Mike was too focus on laying the meats on the hot grills that he didn't hear Jason offer at first. Jason then repeated himself and awaited Jason answer.

"I'll have a Coke with a smile please, if you don't mine my brother," Mike replied with a big smile on his face. Jason then walked behind the Tiki bar and removed a can of Coke from the Tiki bar refrigerator with his left hand. He then grabbed his crotch with his right hand and said,

"I got your Coke and here's your smile, right here little Mike," Jason jokingly said as he yanked his groin with a stupid smile on his face. Mike looked over at Jason and began to smile while shaking his head.

"Man, you must be proud of that little dick your grabbing. Me, personally, I wouldn't be smiling if I was packing a baby carrot like you. I'm just saying," Mike said jokingly.

"What?" Jason asked as if he was concerned.

"Jason, just treat these ladies with respect and we all have a great night and weekend," Mike continued as he pointed at Jason with the spatula in his hand. Jason then placed his right hand on his chest near his heart and his other hand in the air.

"Tonight, I will be a perfect gentleman, I will not disrespect DeVonte house nor will I embarrass myself, my homies by acting a fool tonight" He replied.

"Okay, It's a nice day today. We got all the homies on deck and some ladies in route to chill with us, food and drinks looking and smelling good, let's get it in fellas," Rick said as he held up a nice cold Corona.

"Oh, shit look at that pretty ass DeVonte come out this muthafucka all Gucci down for a got damn barbecue!" Ricky said while looking at DeVonte whited out in Gucci.

"A dark complexion brother like myself, should always wear light colored clothes to bring out the natural beauty in his dark skin. Especially, one with a body as chiseled as mine," DeVonte said as he reached the picnic area.

"Let me find out you fell into the man's trap by wearing all that Gucci shit as if it's gonna make you relevant to yourself my brother," Dennis said as he looked at DeVonte all decked out. DeVonte looked at Dennis as if he had to heads.

"Shut the fuck up Dennis! You know damn well, I don't need designer clothes and material shit to make me feel relevant on this planet! Plus, muthafucka, you were with me when I bought the shit. As a matter of fact, you even bought the same outfit but in a different color," DeVonte replied.

"Well, I'm Different! Because I bought that shit to be relevant in society," Dennis jokingly said. "And, Besides that! I forgot to pack the shit and bring it here. So, I'm hating on you right now, yah sexy muthafucka," Dennis continued as he blew a kiss in DeVonte direction.

"I always knew you was a half a bitch Dennis! My boy DeVonte can't even ride his own Dick without one of you hoes pushing him off and hopping on it," Jason yelled out with a smile on his face.

"Jason! Shut Yo half a dollar ass up! You just mad because nobody's talking about that Walmart shit you be wearing," Dennis replied as everyone started laughing.

"Excuse me Sweet Daddy DeVonte, but I think you forgot to

put on them Versace shades BIG AND PUFF use to rock in the videos," Ricky replied as he snapped a picture of DeVonte with his cell phone camera.

"See! That's what I'm talking about! Y'all niggas always Dick riding this man. His dick can't breathe" Jason blurted out before he started to laugh. Dennis and Jason continued to go back and forth with jokes that had the fellas laughing their heads off, while preparing things prior to the lady's arrival.

DeVonte was looking forward to relaxing in the pool with his lady. Especially after running into a problem earlier in the day, when he made a stop in New York City on his way home from Texas. The aroma of the barbecue pits began to fill the air, as well as the sounds of Ludacris song "Cadillac Grill" that flowed through the speakers of the surround sound system.

DeVonte cellphone started to vibrate in his pocket, He removed it from his pocket and looked at the caller ID. It was Erica

"Hello, babe what's up?" He answered. "Touch Down babes, we're here at the gate so buzz us in" Erica responded.

"Okay Babe, I'm gonna buzz you in" DeVonte said as they exchanged good-byes and he started heading into the house from the picnic area. On his way into the house, DeVonte notified the fellas that the women have arrived. He quickly entered the house and hit the buzzer button to open the front gate and watched Erica and her friends through the camera as the gate slide open.

"You may enter my Royal Queen," DeVonte said over the intercom located at the front gate. Erica followed by Stacey then drove down the stone paved driveway to an awaiting DeVonte who was standing next to his two vehicles parked out in front of the hours. Erica then parked alongside of DeVonte's vehicle and Stacey parked alongside of Erica's vehicle as well. DeVonte whom was standing watching the girls park, quickly walked over to Erica's car and opened her door as if he was a bell hop at a hotel resort. He then embraced Erica with a passionate kiss as she exited her vehicle and gave DeVonte an affectionate hug. The way they held each other was as if they haven't seen each other in years.

"You two need to go get a room or something," Stacey jokingly said after clearing her throat to get the two love birds attention, while she still remained in her car with the window down. The other girls looked on, and admired the site of the landscaping. DeVonte and Erica both blocked out the on-looker's presence for the moment, as if they weren't even present.

"Miss Stacey, glad to see you again." DeVonte said as he took a quick break from kissing on Erica. "I would ask how are you doing, but from the look of things, I see you doing very well," DeVonte continued while referring to Stacey's ride.

"Likewise, mister DeVonte, it's always a pleasure to see you too," Stacey replied.

"I'm loving that Q54 you push." DeVonte said just before going in for another kiss of Erica.

"Well thank you DeVonte, I only wish it compare to one of the hot rides in your display over there," Stacey replied as she walked over to admire DeVonte's vehicles closer. Erica then looked over at the other girls who were just standing there waiting to be introduced to their host for the weekend.

"Excuse my manners, Babes, these young ladies are my other friends. They all are nurses that work with Stacey at the hospital she works at," Erica said before introducing the other young ladies who were exiting Stacey's vehicle. "This is Doreen, Chantel and Alexis, you already know Stacey" Erica said while pointing to each one of her friends to identify them.

"Hello Ladies, my name is DeVonte. I am your host for the weekend. Please make yourselves at home and don't be shy because we are all family here," DeVonte said in his deep

Barry white tone voice as he started to remove bags from the trunk of Erica's beamer. The tone of DeVonte's voice sent a chill through the spines of his newly introduced guests. For some reasons unknown to a man, women are simulated by a deep masculine voice.

The female guests who were very impressed by their handsome host, returned their greetings as they began to retrieve their property from the rear of Stacey's vehicle.

"Do you ladies need help with your bags, I can have the fellas come out and help you ladies inside," DeVonte said showing general concern for his female guests.

"We're good, DeVonte. Thanks for asking anyway." Stacey replied.

"Something smells so good to my belly" Doreen said while inhaling the aroma of the barbecue that was in the air.

"The guys are inside and out back; you ladies can put your stuff down in the foyer and grab a bite to eat. Your property will be safe inside the house," DeVonte said while extending his hospitality.

"Oh, thank you and bless your soul DeVonte, because the ride here got me starving and your pleasant hospitality is right on time," Doreen said with a smile on her face, as she quickly rushed into the house and placed her bags down in the foyer. She quickly searched for the exit that led to the picnic area.

Stacey, Chantel and Alexis later entered the house after retrieving all their property from Stacey's vehicle. The ladies were very impressed by the interior of DeVonte's house, it was well furnished and decorated. It wasn't hard for them to recognize that DeVonte possess expensive taste as well as good manners and looks. They walked in only to see Doreen's bags sitting in the middle of the very elegant foyer, because she was nowhere in sight.

Doreen followed the strong aroma and walked down the long corridor towards the door leading to the deck elevated overseeing the picnic area, she observed Mike in an apron working the grill through the glass door. She exited the door and stood on the deck to get a better view. Mikes slanted eyes reminded Doreen of the model Tyson Beckford. The only difference, Mike was much darker than the buffed super model.

Erica done led them to the land of the Black Adonis's, Doreen thought to herself. After seeing DeVonte and now Mike, she knew for sure it would be some more eye candy to see this weekend.

That food smells so good. I love a man that knows how to prepare a meal. I wonder if his sexy ass could cook in the bed like he doing on that grill? Sometimes the fine ones that either have a small dick or they can't fuck. Doreen continued to ask and think to herself as she stared at the chef on the grill. Mike began to feel her presence and looked over towards the deck. He observed Doreen standing there looking at him through the smoke of the grill. He smiled and waved her over to him. Doreen stood still as if she didn't see him waving to her.

"Hello pretty lady, my name is Mike. I will be the chef working the grills of steel tonight," Mike said with a broad smile on his face, just before he started to remove some food off the grill and place it into a pan. Don't be shy, come on down here if you want something to nibble on," Mike continued as he continued to wave the sexy thick young lady over towards his direction.

After just standing there speechless, Doreen decided to head over toward Mike, while wanting to get a closer look at possible prey like a hungry tiger. Mike watched Doreen as she traveled down the deck towards him. He could see her beauty come closer and closer until she reached him.

"Pretty lady, I have a few appetizers already prepared

that you can nibble on," Mike said as he walked over to the picnic table and pointed at the aluminum pans. "We have Hot N Spicy beef sausage links, beef and turkey hamburgers, beef, chicken and shrimp kebabs. All are fresh off the grill a few seconds ago," Mike continued to say while looking into Doreen's slightly light brown eyes that glowed in the sun light. Doreen took a look at the great selection on the picnic table, then she looked at the grills. Mike tried not to stare too hard at the woman standing before so he tried to stay focused on the food for a minute.

"I would like to have the thickest, longest and juiciest link you have Mike the Chef" Doreen replied in a flirtatious tone of voice. Mike then looked into Doreen's eyes with a loss for words in regard to her comment.

Damn! If this Girl only knew, she's my type. Mike thought to himself as he played it off cool. Such a pretty face, nice thick ass with a small waist. Damn! She's blessed. Mike continued to think to himself as he secretly scanned her with his eyes.

"So, you like it long and thick huh? Well, before I give it to you, the way you like it. Can you at least tell me your name?" Mike said and asked. Doreen just stood there in a daze looking into Mike's eyes. She could see him crack a smile and figured she was on the road to breaking the ice with the stranger she wanted to get to know.

"My name? Oh! I'm sorry I didn't mean to be rude. My name is Doreen and I'm hungry" Doreen replied jokingly.

"Don't worry about it Doreen, around here we all family" Mike quickly responded. "I don't know about you being hungry, I could only see that your gorgeous," Mike continued as he complimented Doreen on her beauty. Doreen eyes lit up as she started to blush.

"Thank You for the compliment, your quite handsome yourself" she replied. "Since we're one big happy family here, should I be feeling the way I feel about you right now?" Doreen jokingly continued. Mike knew he had to respond quick to her flirtatious comment.

"If you don't believe in incest, we could be like kissing cousins if you like." Mike jokingly responded attempting to break the ice even harder. A blushing Doreen continued to smile as she walked over to the table and retrieved a hot dog potato bun and a paper plate. She then extended the plate with the open bun towards Mike whom gently placed a nice long thick link into it.

"Thank You." Doreen said as she seductively blew him a kiss and wrapped her lips onto the thick link before taking a large bite.

"The pleasure is all mine Doreen. If you need anything, and I do mean anything tonight come see me. I will be more than happy to give you what you want and what you need," Mike said while absorbing Doreen's beauty while she chewed on her thick link.

"Believe me Chef Mike, If I need anything long thick and juicy, you will be the first one I come looking for," Doreen said as she looked him up and down before slowly walking over to the picnic table area to sit down. She knew that Mike was watching her round bottom shake as she switched with every step she took. The aroma of the smoking grills began to lure the rest of the girls and guys to its source.

DeVonte and Erica still remained outside in front of the house embracing one another, while everybody started munching on the prepared appetizers in the picnic area. DeVonte figured it was the perfect time to devised his plan of getting Erica and her friend's out the house early Saturday.

"Babe, I want to do something nice for you and your friends tomorrow," DeVonte said as he looked into Erica's eyes. "I set you guys up, for a day at the spa in Wingate mall. You know the one you like, called TIA's?" DeVonte continued as Erica just smiled in regard to his gesture.

"Yes, that will be very nice. Thank you, I'm sure my friends will enjoy that," Erica said before giving DeVonte a

soft kiss on the lips and a hug to show her appreciation.

"I also arraigned for a limo service to pick you ladies up bright and early tomorrow. The limo will escort you to the mall and where ever else you want to go. Me and the fellas will be here chilling out, until you guys get back. I already mentioned to you that we are going to MAJOR SOUL'S tomorrow night. We have an 8 p.m. reservation, so you guys have to get back here, at least by 6 o'clock. Then we can all ride over there in the limo together," DeVonte gladly informed her.

The mention of MAJOR SOUL'S brought back fond memories for Erica. She started thinking of the many times, she has been there in New York, as well the one in New Jersey with DeVonte.

"I can't wait to go to MAJOR SOUL'S tomorrow," Erica said with a large smile on her face.

"I bet you can't. And you know on Saturday nights, they have R&B singers on deck doing their thing," DeVonte said to really sell his idea of the night's events to impress her friends.

"That sounds like a plan Babes. Who's going to be performing tomorrow night?" Erica asked as she started to get really excited about DeVonte's plans.

"I'm not sure, but I made sure we are set up for the usual V.I.P." DeVonte said.

Erica didn't know what to say or do.

"You never seem to amaze me, I really love and appreciate everything you do," she said just before pulling his face to hers for a kiss.

"I love you too, I just want your friends to have a good time and enjoy their time here," DeVonte said as he whispered in Erica's ear as he hugged her tightly.

"One of them bitches might want to steal my man from me" Erica jokingly said as she grabbed onto DeVonte ass cheek.

"If another woman could steal me away from you Babe, then I was never yours to begin with. I know what I want in my life and I know who I need in my life. And, I'm looking into that person's eyes right now," DeVonte said in a tone that warmed Erica's heart.

"That's exactly what I wanted to hear," Erica responded with a hug.

"Did you let your friends know, about my plan to take you guys out to MAJOR SOUL'S? So, they can be properly prepared for tomorrow night?" DeVonte asked.

"Yes, I mentioned it to Stacey. I don't know if she told the other girls," Erica replied.

MAJOR SOUL'S, also known as Major Soul's Club and Grill, is a well-known five-star night club, that is also known for their southern style cuisines as well as all types of other dishes. Many entertainers and athletes have been known to frequent their franchised locations. Along with the endorsements from celebrities, many articles about the establishment were printed in many magazines promoting the spot.

The owner, Kim Souls, a female native of New York City, always had the dream of owning her own restaurant since her days of working at an electrical company. Prior to working for the electrical company, she served as a Major in the United States Airforce. Kim started her hustle by selling plates of food and desserts to co-workers, whom steadily requested certain entrees, especially around the holiday seasons.

DeVonte met Kim many years ago prior to her becoming successful entrepreneur through a mutual friend who worked with her. DeVonte was advised by his friend, that Kim was one hell of a cook, and maybe he would like to do business with her. Upon their first meeting each other, she gave him a sample of one of her dishes which perked his interest.

The two met at a well-known bar and grill and she discussed her ideas with him over a few drinks. Not too long after their meeting, DeVonte and her developed a friendly bond and business relationship as he helped her connect with the right people as well as assisted in the funding of her first restaurant opened in New York City. She now has five-star franchise of four restaurants located in New York City, New Jersey, Atlanta and Charlotte.

"You want us to stay out the whole day? Then meet you guys back at the house, so we can head over together? Hmmm, what you guys up to? There better not be no strippers coming over when were gone." Erica jokingly said.

"Strippers?!" DeVonte shouted. "Oh, hell no. I love you and only you Babe, I just want to pamper you and your friends a little." DeVonte continued.

"You never cease to amaze me my love, that's why I love and appreciate you so much" Erica said just before pulling DeVonte's face to hers to kiss him again. Both DeVonte and Erica, wondered how their friends were getting along whom were all in the picnic area. Naturally the guys and girls didn't mix it up. The guys were sitting among themselves and so were the girls. Both groups were engaging in their own separate conversations.

DeVonte and Erica finally realized that they were so caught up in their romance that they were being rude to their guest whom awaited them. The happy couple then entered the house and could hear that everyone was out back. They headed out the door hand and hand to the deck and started walking down the steps towards the picnic area to join the rest.

It didn't take much for the couple to notice the separation between their friends. The ice needed to be broken, so everyone could enjoy the weekend. DeVonte attempted to get everyone's attention.

"Hello everybody! What's up with the segregation going on?" He asked. "I see the ladies sitting there and the guys over there. We all family people here people, lets mix and mingle!" DeVonte continued as he and Erica walked behind the Tiki bar together. No one practically paid him any attention and continued to engage in their conversations. DeVonte felt like a substitute teacher, attempting to get a class of student's attention. He knew how to gain their attention a different way. He pulled out his cellphone tapped the screen, the music went off. Like clockwork, everyone became silent and he had their attention.

"I just want everybody to loosen up a little. You know what I'm saying? Mix and mingle, is always the way to meet a new friend" DeVonte cheerfully said.

My man, is right! The weather is good, the food smelling good. Let's get this weekend started, I know it's hot out here and who's ready to take a dip in the pool," Erica asked to break some of the tension.

Everyone's hand went up as if they were in elementary school, trying to get the teachers attention.

"Okay boys and girls, get your swimming gear together and head to your locker room to change up" Erica said jokingly. Mike watched everyone disappear into DeVonte's house and quickly made their way back out to the pool house except for himself and DeVonte whom already had on his swim gear.

You guys go ahead and have fun, while I slave over a hot ass barbecue pit to feed Yall ungrateful asses Mike thought to himself as he continued to monitor the grill.

"Don't worry Mike! Let me know when you need a break and I got you" DeVonte said as he patted Mike on the shoulder and headed towards the pool house.

"DeVonte you know and I both know you not gonna get your gear all dirty and full of BBQ smoke my brother" Mike jokingly said as he looked DeVonte up and down while he walked away. DeVonte then stopped in his tracks and turned around and cracked a smile. He looked at his buddy while he took a quick sip of what was in his cup.

"Didn't I just say I had you on the grill or did I tell you I'm going to get one of the fellas to help you?" DeVonte responded.

"You, said you playboy," Mike said as he pointed his finger in DeVonte's direction.

"Man, what did I tell you about listen to muthafuckas that be drinking man," DeVonte jokingly responded.

"Man take your wanna be, Big Daddy Kane ass to the pool house. You must have traded in your cameo cut for them 360 waves you have flowing on your head" Mike jokingly said as he simulated brushing his hair into a wave pattern.

"Oh, you got jokes and could cook? You should have no problem in getting a little trim this weekend," DeVonte replied as he saluted Mike with his free hand and took another sip out of his cup with the other.

"Man, I want some of what you're having! Once I finish cooking up shop," Mike said replying to the cognac DeVonte was sipping on.

"This Privilege VSOP Cognac! Keeps your dick hard all night my brotha, fuck them blue pills that the weak dick muthafuckas be popping to impress they woman" DeVonte said as he began to feel some of the effect of the cognac with no chaser.

Mike looked at his longtime friend and placed his hand up as if to say stop. "PAUSE, on the dick talk homie. You my boy and all, But I ain't with that gay shit!" Mike jokingly said. DeVonte almost choked on his drink as he busted out laughing.

"You sound just like that fool Smokey from the movie Friday. Anyway! I'm off to the pool before you make me get cognac on my swim gear" DeVonte said as he about faced as if he was a solider and walked off.

"Yeah, get to stepping fool. Just make sure you don't jump in the pool with your cell phone in your pocket this time," Mike replied as he shook his head while smiling and continued to monitor the barbecue pits.

DeVonte phone began to ring as soon as Mike warned him about not jumping into the pool with it. He removed it from his pocket and seen a familiar number. He stopped for a moment and answered the call.

"My Man! What's up my friend?" DeVonte answered the phone

In a mellow voice.

"From the sounds of things in your background. Your What's up! My friend," DeVonte jokingly responded a male with a foreign distinctive voice on the other end of the phone whom could hear the music playing in the background.

"Yeah man, I got a glass full of Cognac in my hand, my lady and some friends are over partying and relaxing for the weekend with me" DeVonte responded.

"Excellent my friend. You should've had told me so I could've had a case of the finest champagne shipped to you express, for you and your guest" The distinctive voice responded.

"I would've told you. But, I thought you was overseas handling some business. So, I didn't want to bother you.

"You could never bother me my friend. Anyway, I'll give you a call when the weekend is over and your friends are gone. We have some very important business we need to discuss. With that being said, enjoy your weekend and have fun my friend," The male with the distinctive voice said.

"Thank You my friend. Enjoy your weekend as well. I'll talk to you later," DeVonte replied as the telephone conversation was ended on both ends of the phone.

R. Kelly and Jay Z's re-mix song "Fiesta" flooded the surround sound speakers filling DeVonte's whole environment with energy. Mikes gourmet touch seasoned the air with an out of this world aroma, that made the nearby neighbor's dog howl with hunger. Mike recited Jay Z lyrics as if he wrote them himself, while he worked the grills.

"Hey, what's up ladies. Would you two like to play a game of Taboo with me and my boy Jason over here?" Dennis asked as he held the board game in his hand.

"As long as you two don't try and cheat us. We're willing to play," Chantel responded with a smile on her face.

"I never played that before, what is that game based on?" Alexis asked as she looked at the cover of the box to see what it looked like.

"It's a guessing game almost similar to charades, but you're up against a timer" Dennis informed the two sisters.

"Like charades?" Chantel asked.

"Don't worry ladies, you'll catch on real fast once we get started," Jason responded as they all began to play.

CHAPTER 4

OLD SKOOL THUG

IT WAS THE CRACK ERA of the 1980's, a time when fast money ruled everything around it. Lives were ruthlessly taken as if they were meaningless due to greed and jealousy throughout the urban communities in America. Gun shots contentedly erupted among drug dealers on a daily basis, as they killed one another, as well as innocent bystanders during violent drug turf wars. The dealers mentally thought they owned the street corners and real estate where they sold their poison.

Young and old drug addicts, both male and female, were selling their bodies for money to support their habits. Most of these addicts, contacted and spread many sexual transmitted diseases like HIV. Some of the female addicts were at the point that they would perform oral and other sexual acts in front of their young children just to get high. Some of these same addicts even sold their children bodies to pedophile customers who took advantage of their addiction and need for money to get high.

It became a common occurrence during this time for newborn infants within the urban communities to be born addicted to crack cocaine and a high percentage were even infected with A.I.D.S virus. These poor infants were left in the hospital by their drug addicted mothers, who escaped all the responsibility of being a caring and nursing functional mother. Many of these children were fathered by the same drug dealer whom supplied their mother with the powerful drug after she exchanged sexual acts for the drugs.

Children who weren't born addicted to the drug were also affected. Some were torn away from their homes and placed in the foster care system, because their drug addicted parents were no longer functional to support them and deal with their addictions at the same time. The foster care system became overwhelmed with children who became lost in the system until they reached the age to be out on their own.

Drug addicts became the outcast of their families, once they began to steal money as well as other property located in their family home to support their addiction. It became a sad and common thing to see crack addicts also known as a Crack Heads pushing a shopping cart containing a television and other items, they just stole from their own family as well as many other victims in their community whom may have fallen victim to their addiction.

Elderly parents fell victim to their very own children, both physically and mentally as the addiction effectively destroyed the values their parents once taught them when they were younger. Grandparents were now raising their grandchildren as if they were their own, because their own children were on a mission to get high. An epidemic that spread like wildfire, destroying many families in its path in the urban communities as it soon spread to the suburbs.

Many male teenagers, traded in their souls to become ruthless drug pushers. They were willing to help spread the poisons of narcotics throughout their community to obtain money, power, and women. For the love of money, sells to pregnant woman, the elderly and even children went unquestioned or challenged. It was considered the life of the hustle by anyone involved in the life of getting fast money. While other young males chose the occupation of being a soldier for those who needed their services as enforcers to protect their illegal enterprise by any means necessary.

Back in the 1980's, a large percentage of teenage females in the urban communities, were very impressed by the flash of expensive materialistic things. Those teenage females who were so impressed by the fast life, usually traded in their bodies to receive gifts like mink coats, expensive bags, jewelry, and the latest fashion in clothes. Many of them became drug dealer's groupies and would only date and sleep with drug dealers. These young ladies wouldn't dare give a guy a second look if he wasn't out there hustling for that fast money. It became a fad to shop in the best stores like Bloomingdales, Lord & Taylors, Macy's among the people whom really had that type of money to shop there.

Purchasing and possessing expensive merchandise that only the middle class and rich could afford, made these young men and women feel relevant about themselves in society. They considered themselves ghetto fabulous, and if you weren't styling like them, you were a bum ass nigga.

Many of these young female groupies experienced things their young bodies weren't mature enough or ready to handle, as they used their bodies to get what they wanted from the young men they adored. The young males they admired ranged from the age of 16 to 30 years and so was getting that fast money hand over fist. Some of whom, were willing to spend it like there was no tomorrow. Young females ranging from the ages of 12-17 years old had no problem with sleeping with theses hustlers who lavished them with gifts. In return for their gifts, these young females engaged in multiple sexual acts like oral and anal sex. During the crack era, teenage pregnancy was on the rise and was getting way out of control.

Parents of a lot of these young women just stood by and watched their young teenage daughter enter their homes in the wee hours of the night and early morning with expensive merchandise that they did not or could possibly pay for. Someeven benefited from the situation, as the dealer also handed them over a few dollars for their household.

The dope dealers took advantage of their young female gold diggers who were willing to do anything to get a piece of their riches. A dealer would arrange to have sex with a young female he considered to be a gold digger, then pass her off to his buddies who waited they turn. Some even videotaped the sexual acts in order to degrade the female later in the community they live in. A high percentage of these young women bodies were destroyed in one way or another. Some of them were unable to conceive children due to multiple complications once they fully developed into a grown woman, after all the wear and tear their young bodies been through.

Their young vaginas looked like they had the lining ripped out of it as the lips hanged, making it look worn out and like it had a lot of mileage put on it.

In the hustle game of narcotics, some so-called soldiers remained loyal to their boss and some moved on to become bosses themselves. Many of the young men that were out there hustling, from the beginning of the crack cocaine era, lost their lives chasing the fast all mighty dollar. Many found themselves behind prison walls for many years and some became either addicted to narcotics or remained a menace to society like Nate Washington. There are some but very few who were wise enough to change their lifestyle and become legit members of society moved on, as there are many whom never snapped back to living a normal life, since they lost their innocence during their youth.

Harlem native Nate Washington, a 40-year-old ex-convict drove his large black Lincoln up and down the mean dark streets of Brooklyn. The Lincoln cruised down the street with the front windows rolled down and the Paid in Full album cassette by Eric B. And Rakim playing in the tape deck. The music from his car escaped through his window into the night air as well as the smoke from his Newport cigarette. He cruised around the neighborhood as if he was in a patrol car, so he can observe everything within his vision. Checking all the court yards and in between buildings for any activity that may benefit him. Nate on occasions would exit his vehicle and do a walk up in the midst of the project buildings to observe if anyone was hanging out on the stoop hustling.

Nate being only 5'6 tall and 135 pounds soaking wet had a non-intimidating look for a middle aged black male that walked with a limp, yet he was very notorious and considered a drug dealers nightmare in the streets of New York. He was a crack addict who carried two semi-automatic handguns, and was always on the hunt for drugs and dead presidents to support his habit by any means necessary.

Drug dealers had to stay on alert at all times, because if they were caught slipping by Nate, he would jack them for everything they had on them. Money, dope, jewelry, beepers and even Cazal glasses. Nate didn't give a fuck who he robbed and he let it be known. If he thought you were out there getting that fast money, he made it his business to get in your pockets. Most gave it up easy, and those whom didn't lost their lives.

It was an unusual cool fall night and sounds of gunshots ringed out like church bells into the night air. Nate continued to cruise around as he searched for drug dealers to rob. He knew that the weekends were a time when the dealers like to shop in the day time and party at night. Some dealers liked to gamble some of their hustle money and most showcased all the material things that their fast money helped them buy.

Jackpot! Look at these punk muthafuckas sleeping over there! Nate thought to himself as he observed a group of males hanging out on a handball court, enjoying a game of Celo right off the corner of Sutter and Stone Avenue. He slowly cruised by to get a better glimpse of his prey, while traveling down Stone Avenue towards Blake Avenue. Nate hungry eyes could see jewelry shining on them, fancy clothes on their backs and stacks of dollar bills on the ground, like a hungry tiger could spot a Buck in the jungle.

The group of drug dealers Nate had his eye on, were playing their game under a beam of light that came from a street light located outside of the fence. The handball court was located in a fenced space that consisted of a few basketball courts and concrete baseball field used by Public School 284 for lunch recess and recreation.

Large bottles of malt liquor and blunt cigars filled with marijuana was passed among the group who gambled. The smoke from the marijuana fogged up the entire hand-ball court and the smell scented up the whole park. Beeping of the dealer's pagers were going off on some of the hustler's hips from possible customers looking to buy some drugs or the females they were involved with.

Nate was happy that he found some jokers that would help him feed his addiction. He quickly made a right turn and traveled down Blake Avenue towards Rockaway Avenue. He looked at the time on his dash board.

11:15p.m., it's about that time for One-Time to change their tour (an old school term for the Police)" Nate thought to himself as he made another right turn onto Rockaway Avenue and traveled towards Sutter Avenue. The Housing and City police officers assigned to foot patrol in the area, could be seen heading back to their commands to go end of tour.

Nate was no stranger to the judicial system, and have been in and out many of Police precincts within the city as well as prisons upstate many times. He knew that the police started their midnight tours and conducted their rollcall at 11:00p.m., and it took them a least fifteen minutes for them to get out on the street to patrol the area. He also knew that the 4x12 tour where looking forward to getting off work on time at 11:30p.m. As they slowly headed back into the station house. Nate decided to circle the area in search of any lingering foot post, patrol cars, and unmarked vehicles.

As a teenager in 1965, Nate was an enforcer for a well-known heroin dealer. He was feared for his brutal tactics that lead to many painful deaths within the community. His favorite weapons of choice were two .38 Caliber Saturday Night Specials, and his gun play was fierce and highly respected among fellow thugs. Competitive heroin dealers and addict's delinquent with their payment, all knew if Nate came to pay you a visit, it was going to be nothing but gunfire.

The owners of the local funeral homes benefited and made lots of money from Nate's murder game, as they conducted many closed casket services for those who fell victim to his gun play. It was rumored that some of the funeral directors would tip Nate off if rivals wanted to retaliate against his boss or if there were any upcoming competition, just so Nate could deliver whomever they were in a box to them.

Nate enjoyed the lifestyle of driving a brand-new Cadillac, wearing expensive clothes, sporting expensive jewelry and having a pocket full of cash at the tender age of sixteen so he didn't mind eliminating the competition or those who came up short with the cash owed to his boss. The women in the neighborhood loved his bad boy image and clung onto him as their personal private protector. It's something about a dangerous man that makes some women sexually attracted to them.

Nate's terror to the neighborhood temporarily came to an end in the early 70's, when he got pinched for a homicide of a local cocaine dealer named Al Money from the Atlantic Towers Complex. Al Money decided he wanted to indulge in the sale of heroin instead of the cocaine that he usually pushed in the streets. The streets were talking and of course the hit was ordered by Nate's boss Huck, who didn't want anyone stepping into his hustle. Nate's murder game landed him in prison for a ten year stretch without parole for the hit on Al Money.

While being incarcerated in Napanoch, a correctional facility located in upstate New York for approximately 3 years. During Nate's incarceration, his boss Huck was gunned down by one of his own soldiers named Dirty. Dirty real name was Shamel Watts. He took over Nate's position as Huck's main enforcer as soon as Nate went to prison. The word on the street was, Dirty was tired of being the help and wanted to be the top dog. Huck was the only one standing in his way, so he decided to take Huck out.

It was unknown to Dirty, that Huck continued to take care of his favorite solider while he served time in prison, by keeping his commissary loaded with cash and made sure Nate wanted for nothing. The word on the street quickly made its way to Nate's facility, and he was not happy at all.

Dirty was quickly captured by the police the day after Hucks murder, as he attempted to board a Greyhound bus heading down to South Carolina at the Port Authority Terminal. The Police received a lead from a heroin addict named Eric that was currently on the hit list for owing Huck $500 in debt. Eric knew Dirty would come to collect or kill anyone that owed Huck, because he believed that any debt owed to Huck was now owed to him. Eric figured if he could get Dirty off the streets, he would get to live and get high another day.

Ironically Dirty died of multiple stab wounds to the face and body a day after he arrived at Napanoch. He was placed in the same prison facility that Nate was in. Dirty was sentenced there to serve a twenty-year prison bid issued by the courts.

That sentence was cut short, when Dirty's nude lifeless body was found laid out on a cold shower floor. He was last seen alive entering the showers along with other inmates and of course, no one saw or heard anything. It was rumored that Huck had a cousin who worked in the court system, this said cousin pulled some strings to get Dirty sent to Napanoch instead of the intended prison facility named Fishkill. Huck cousin knew that Nate would be there waiting on him.

The ten-year sentence quickly past and once again Nate was free to enter the society again and roam the streets. The 1980's have arrived, and Nate wanted to hustle his way back in the game, but could never gain the status he once had as a known enforcer. The game had changed, and cocaine was on top of the chain, even though heroin was still major, cocaine addict's kind of went unnoticed.

Nate searched for a position as an enforcer with the major drug kingpins, but after many failed attempts. He started selling foils of cocaine on 42nd Street aka THE FORTY DEUCE in mid-town Manhattan. The money rolled in fast, due to demand in the area from the Tourist from all over the world, New York City locals, Pimps, Whores and members of the Military that docked in the city.

Nate was making lots of cash as he hustled for long hours on THE FORTY DEUCE daily. The Deuce was a twenty-four-hour operation of non-stop hustling and was the right place to get paid in the city that never sleeps. Joey, Nate's new boss was very impressed with his new salesman energy and non-stop hustling. He was so impressed with Nate, that he bought Nate a brand-new Lincoln Town car. Joey was a dark complexion Italian whom was connected with the mob. He wore expensive jewelry and Sergio Tacchini track suits.

Nate bought two .45 caliber automatic handguns from one of Joey's connects for protection against possible robbers and competition that may want to step to him in the streets.

Like many drug dealers pushing dope before him, Nate decided to find out what all the hype was about the stuff he was selling on the street and took a hit of the famous white powder. It didn't take long before he became addicted himself to the white powder he was pushing, causing him to lose the trust of Joey, whom he once made a lot of money for at one time. Nate began to snort more than he sold, and came up short with Joey's money one too many times.

Joey took notice in Nate's transformation and had no choice but to fire him. He could no longer cover for him when the money came up short. Joey warned Nate that the higher ups wanted him dead, but he put his own neck on the line to save him. Joey liked Nate and hoped one day he would snap out his addiction, and work for him once again.

After fucking up the one hustle that got him some fast money in his hand, things became real ruff for Nate with his new addiction. Reality and addiction started to eat at Nate'sbrain. He decided to rob dope dealers, pimps, and whores whom worked THE FORTY DEUCE near the Port Authority Terminal where he used to sell his dope, to support his habit. After numerous robberies, Nate found himself getting shot at by retaliating dope dealers and pimps. This was bad for business on the Deuce. Joey was now under pressure to get rid of Nate. He sent a few of his boys to scoop up Nate.

After they beat Nate's ass in an abandoned warehouse for a few days. They dropped him off in Brooklyn and warned him to never return to the midtown Manhattan. They also informed him that a contract was placed on his life if he was spotted anywhere near the Forty Deuce, and that the reward would be paid to anyone who blew his brains out.

Nate realized he burnt his bridges in midtown and went to stay with his mom in Bedford-Stuyvesant. While in Bed-Stuy, he linked up with a few old friends he use to run the streets with. After years of hustling and living in motels in midtown, He was now back in the streets of Brooklyn. One day while hanging out on the corner, he ran into an old girlfriend named Kim. Nate and Kim started to get real close again, and he spent a lot of time at her apartment in Stuyvesant Projects.

One night, while having a few drinks and smoking some weed with Kim. She passed Nate a marijuana cigarette laced with crack cocaine to smoke. The high was like no other high he ever had before had from marijuana and asked her what the fuck she laced his joint with. She proudly told him she made him a bone. Nate not knowing what that was, she then explained she laced the weed with some crack cocaine to give the weed an extra kick.

Nate heard of crack cocaine, but had never tried it before until the day Kim gave it to him. He immediately fell in love with the high that it gave him. Nate had also heard that, crack was becoming one of the biggest money makers to ever had hit the streets. People were literally going crazy over this new drug and Nate was now one of those people.

It wasn't long before Nate graduated from smoking a bone to free basing it in a glass pipe. Nate tried to get a work relationship with the dealers he bought from, he figured if he brought them new customers; the would hook him up. After he gained the trust of the dealers, He then tried to get a job selling for them. Nate found out the hard way that nobody trusted a crackhead after repetitive rejections of landing a gig as dealers kicked. He decided to unite with the two things that have never let him down in getting money, his two Smith n Wesson's. It was time for him to start his mission of robbing drug dealers to support his habit.

CHAPTER 5

INFECTION WITHIN

In 1911, the New York City Police Department historically appointed its first black police officer Samuel J. Battle. During this time, the population of blacks in the city was approximately at 2 percent. Prior to Officer Battle's appointment, the City of Brooklyn had already hired a number of black officers to patrol the borough.

The New York City Police Department on the other hand, considered another black police officer by the name of Wiley G. Overton to be the first sworn in, back in 1891 by the City of Brooklyn. The City of Brooklyn may be the first to have hired black Police Officers, Samuel J. Battle was in fact, the first black person appointed to New York's combined 10,000-member force after the merge.

Since the historical hiring of the first minority whom later moved up the ranks to sergeant in 1926 and lieutenant in 1935. New York City Police Department have been infected with a strong racial bias, especially when it comes to accepting minority police officers into special units for many years. A bias that showed no exempt within the Narcotic Division Unit nor any other investigative unit the department had to offer.

This bias is highly visible when a minority police officer applies for a position in the Narcotic Division to become a narcotic investigator. Minority police officers could possess a very active arrest record, above average evaluations, awards as well as commendations in their career folder, making them qualified on paper. Yet, their quest to start a career path in investigations within the department would come up against a road block. That road block being a ranking Caucasian supervisor of the department assigned to interview all the applicants applying for special units.

In many cases, when minority police officers who have applied to join the Narcotic Division under the command of the Organized Crime Control Bureau also known as O.C.C.B., They are interviewed by a ranking Caucasian supervisor whom is assigned to interview all applicants. The Caucasian supervisor would say the following to the applying minority officer:

We have reviewed your application, as well as your career folder. Your arrest activity is quite impressive, as well as your evaluation and overall police performance. Your career points are above average, but it doesn't quite meet the criteria that we're looking for to qualify you into the unit as a narcotic investigator. We basically brought you in for this interview to offer you the position that we feel is more suitable for you, as a narcotic undercover. It's a foot in the door into the unit and after serving a total of 18 months as an active undercover, you'll be promoted to Detective 3rd grade. Once your promoted to Detective, this would set you on the career path to become a Detective investigator after a few more years of hard work.

The New York City Police Department will deny any sort of racial discrimination acts within the department when it comes to disciplinary actions enforced on its minorities officers, promoting of minorities supervisor the rank captain or above, As well as the positioning of qualified minorities into specialized units. The department cannot hide the fact that it exists or existed, especially prior to the 1996 merge of all three departments. Over the years, some things have changed for the better and the rest still remain the same.

In comparison of the departments treatment of its minorities on the force, the treatment of the Caucasian officers was quite different. An average Caucasian police officer would be assigned to a special unit like the Narcotic Division as a narcotic investigator based on an excellent to a fairly decent career folder. Some would either enter the narcotic unit solely because they had many years on the job.

And a lot of them got into the Unit based on a phone call made from a hook (political connect) on the job. Being related or associated with the higher ranks was a plus for career moves within the department.

While in other cases when it came to many minorities police Officers whom have received numerous merit medals and citations for excellent duties performed in the department, were told they would contribute better to the unit if they took the position of a Narcotic Undercover, because they had the look (appearance to be someone of the inner city and urban streets).

Now to explain the difference between the position of narcotic investigator and narcotic undercover and their functions:

THE NARCOTIC INVESTIGATOR:

Primary functions are to investigate narcotic complaints sent into the department whether received by the main narcotic division hot-line located in police headquarters or by a direct call to the individual narcotic borough command front operations desk.

The Investigator must conduct all available computer checks on the location as well as on all possible known sale subjects named in the complaint if available, these checks must be made before a narcotic undercover makes a Buy attempt.

Debrief prisoners and attempt to recruit confidential informants also known as C.I. Generate, obtain and execute search warrants when necessary.

Investigators, make the arrest and apprehensions of the persons committing the narcotic related offenses. Even though the narcotic unit is a plain clothes assignment the investigators are still required to have on the required equipment to engage with the public (armored vest, visible shield, handcuffs, radio and raid jacket when needed).

The narcotic investigators are usually depended on by the department to supply security detail at most major events (Labor Day Parade, New Year's Eve etc.) as well as many other units under the command of organized crime control bureau.

THE NARCOTIC UNDERCOVER:

Primary functions are to purchase narcotics or weapons and identify whom was the seller. Observe and transmit narcotic transaction.

Ghost their partner and report all the actions that are transpiring to the team supervisor as well as his team while the primary undercover is making a buy attempt.

Secure the safety of their partner by keeping a sharp eye on them and their surroundings.

Transmit any visible narcotic transaction to the team supervisor as well as members of the field team.

The narcotic undercover unlike the narcotic investigator are not required to carry required equipment (vest, radio, badge nor identification cards) and they are forbidden to wear a police department uniform at any time while assigned as a narcotic undercover.

The difference in the two roles caused many altercations between the narcotic investigators and the undercovers. The Caucasian supervisors would more than likely side with their fellow Caucasians investigators and down play any complaints that the minority officers made against them, and in many cases, would give the minority officer and more severe discipline.

Many Caucasian supervisors and investigators in the Unit believed that buying narcotics and illegal weapons were part of the minorities officers culture. Newly temporary minority transfers would be lined up in the corridor near the administrative office in certain borough units. Caucasian supervisors and investigators would visually exam them for scars, weight, height, body frame and whether the minority officer had the look of a junkie. They would put in their bid with the administrative supervisor for the minority officer as if it was a scene from a slave auction in the.

Many of the Caucasian personal in the unit also felt that the minority officers weren't intelligent enough to be in an investigative position within the unit and would boldly express their opinion to the minority officers. Numerous discrimination complaints within the narcotic units have been filed to the office of equal employment opportunity in regard to racially motivated comments that were mostly down played when they brought it to their immediate commanding officers attention.

The New York City Police Department has an Office of Equal Employment Opportunity unit office also known as O.E.E.O. located within the department's headquarters. The office consists of leaks and wasn't confidential as it should be. On numerous occasions OEEO personnel would notify the parties begin complained on, and told of the complaint against them. This resulted in retaliation and a hostile work environments toward the person whom made the complaint.

The terms "Giving a Heads Up" was and still remain the normal in the department today.

Minorities undercover officers whom were believed to not have a problem in purchasing narcotics in the selected narcotic prone locations by their predominately white investigator teammates and supervisor. And if that said undercover came up with negative results for their effort of making a buy. The investigators as well as the supervisor would take it personal by stating the undercover is shutting the team down (purposely not making a drug or weapons purchase and basically not doing their job).

The Narcotic Division is a unit that is under the command of the Organized Crime Control Bureau. The Division is very different from regular patrol, and its main purpose is to make arrest in drug prone locations, and close out numerous narcotic complaints in designated locations.

The main objective of joining the Narcotic Division was based on the high volume of overtime available. Police Officer to the rank of lieutenant, would benefited for their aggressive police work. Police Officers would join the unit to make rank of detective, a process that usually takes 18 months to accomplish. Once the police officer is promoted to the rank of detective, it's all about making cash overtime.

Supervisors with the rank of sergeant and lieutenant simply apply for the large amount of cash overtime availability. Supervisors with the rank of captain are usually dumped into the unit because they pissed someone at headquarters off, or got drafted by the unit while applying for a different special.

Narcotic borough commanding officers in the narcotic division basically ranked from deputy inspectors to one star chiefs. These guys get their asses handed to the at Comp stat meetings by the narcotics chief as well as the chief of department.

Deputy inspectors and above are usually promoted to the next rank after serving in the unit, especially if their command receives a unit citation.

In The New York City Police Department, supervisors of the rank of captain or above could not receive any cash overtime. Their salary is set and any overtime they concur must be used as compensation time.

The more people arrested during narcotic enforcement, the more overtime was afforded to the team. "Collars for Dollars," was the slogan and the main objective of enforcement. Well at least to those who could receive cash overtime. The Investigator detective/police Officer at one time along with the supervisor (lieutenant and sergeant) took approximately 95 percent of the overtime while the undercover was left with the scraps of the remaining 5 percent. An undercover officer would have to make two or more buys to generate a decent amount of overtime, in which was crazy due to the undercover generating 95 percent of the activity during the enforcement in most cases.

The minority undercover officers whom were promoted to the rank of detective, were forced to continue their undercover assignment beyond five years in their undercover assignment, while the department would assign newly assigned Caucasian officers to the unit as investigators. It wasn't until one year in the late 1990's, when a minority undercover detective assigned to the Bronx was fatally shot down in the line of duty, while performing a buy and bust operation. After this fatal incident, the experienced minority undercover detectives with five to six year's experience in the narcotics unit was allowed to be re-assign to narcotic investigator status. Many immediately transferred from their current command.

This was a typical technique of the New York City Police Department to wait until something tragic happens, to make adjustment and change. After this tragic incident, the investigators were challenged in their investigative skills by their Undercover teammate in regard to checking on certain drug prone locations. The narcotic unit was full of investigator detective/police officers whom were slackers (Lazy ass cops). They wouldn't have any useful material for the undercover to work with to obtain a successful buy attempt. As well as not investigate if there is any safety pre-cautions the Undercover should take prior to making the buy attempt at the location.

The following is a list of what an undercover detective/police officer needs to be informed of prior to making a buy attempt at designated residential and commercial locations:

» Type of narcotic sold at location

» Price of narcotic sold at location

» Narcotic sold business hours at location

» Any possible weapons at location

» Brand name (if any) of narcotic or street lingo for product

» Any pets at location

» Names of alleged narcotic dealer whether their government or street nick name or their Street

» Any previous arrest made at location, and if so, what where the charges and whom was arrested.

The above information is very vital and important towards the safety of the undercover and necessary to blend into the situation at hand. Knowledge is the key to all situations.

The undercover detective/police officer would request the needed information while out in the field, when a Kite Location is thrown into the mix during enforcement that wasn't discussed at the tactical meeting. The investigator would usually reply "Everything is unknown, or no further information is available". The Team Leader (Supervisor) would then instruct the Undercover to give it a quick attempt and make magic happen for a positive result. The undercovers were relied on to use their gift of gab to make something happen.

This practice in the New York City Police Department Narcotic Unit continued until another tragic incident took place approximately five years later. Two experienced minority undercover detectives were assassinated during an operation to purchase a weapon in early 2003. This tragic event shocked the city as well as the world. Once Again, the New York City Police Department decided to show a somewhat concern for its undercover detectives/officer's safety by granting the experience ones a re-assignment to detective investigator and transfer them to other investigative units within the department.

While out in the field, the undercover detectives/police Officers took on two different roles of Primary and Ghosting.

Primary undercover means the undercover who will be attempting to make a purchase, whether it was street level or a case buy.

Ghosting undercover means the undercover who will be observing the primary undercover actions while transmitting their every move. Transmit all activity to the team supervisor and other fellow team mates, as well as secure the safety of the primary undercover environment. Transmit the description and location of all possible subjects the primary may encounter out in the field. Basically, the ghosting undercover has a vital job to perform during any operation, he or she are the eyes and ears of the team.

CHAPTER 6

TRAINING DAY

A **New York City Narcotics Division lieutenant sat** at his desk preparing his team tactical plan for a buy and bust operation to be conducted for the four to twelve tours. A tactical plan usually consists of a list of names of at least one supervisor whether it's a lieutenant or sergeant, six detectives/police Officers assigned as investigators, two detectives/police Officers assigned as undercovers also known as UCs. A tactical plan must be prepared by a supervisor prior to conducting any type enforcement and faxed over to the division office located at police headquarters, whether it's for a buy and bust, case buy or a search warrant.

A buy and bust operation (also known as B&B) is basically street enforcement conducted by a narcotic team. The teams head out to targeted area where complaints of narcotic activity are reported to the Mayors Hotline, Precincts and community leaders. The detective/police Officer assigned as undercovers main function is to make a buy and make buy attempts at or in the vicinity of the locations listed on the tactical plan. The undercovers are to exchange pre-recorded buy money giving to them by the assigned arresting detective/police Officer prior to heading out the door for enforcement, with the dealers. Once a buy is made by the undercover out in the field, the rest of his field team members are notified to move in and apprehend persons involved in the transaction. Once a positive identification is made by the buying undercover, the person or persons involved in the transaction are then arrested.

Lieutenant Zaki reviewed his roll call and noticed his best undercover was out on vacation leave for a few weeks, and realized he needed to make an adjustment. Lieutenant Zaki supervised four teams in his module that covered one of the busiest precincts in South Jamaica Queens. There were three recent shootings in the confines of the 117th Precinct, one resulting in a double homicide.

The high-ranking officers at headquarters wanted full enforcement in the vicinity of the double homicide as they requested the issuance of summons (minor criminal violations, traffic violation and parking violations) and arrest. A strategic move commonly used by the New York City Police Department in an attempt to obtain information leading to an arrest in shooting and homicide cases.

The Chief of the Organized Crime Control Bureau Narcotic Division sent a memo to the Commanding Officer of Narcotic Bureau Queens, stating Queens Narcotics will be joining the enforcement initiative in the confines of the 117th Precinct, as per the Police Commissioner and Chief of Department.

This said memo quickly found its way onto the desk of a queens narcotics Lieutenant Zaki, whom had to prepare an enforcement tactical plans for the Sergeants and Detectives under his command.

Okay I have Sergeant Moreno as field supervising officer, Detective Dean as arresting officer, Detectives Rivera and Jones in the chase car, Detectives Boyd and Zapata in chase car 2, Detectives McRae and O'Keith in the prisoner van and

Detective Undercover number 98989! Looks like I'm short one undercover He thought to himself as he filled out the tactical plan.

The lieutenant knew his tactical plan was incomplete, due to the fact that an enforcement team cannot conduct an operation without two Undercover officers. His experienced undercover was out on vacation leave, and he doubted any other undercover could compare to his first-grade detective experience and skill in making narcotic buys at the drop of a dime. The lieutenant then got up from his desk and walked over to his door that was open.

"Eric! Step into my office for a minute and close the door behind you," the lieutenant yelled out as he poked his head out his office, that was located next to his team modules he was in command of.

Detective Eric Clayton, a well-seasoned undercover was sitting at his staring into his lap top. He looked over at the lieutenant whom called him. He then quickly got up and closed his laptop, before heading into the lieutenant's office as instructed.

"What's up lieu?" Eric said as he took a seat on the sofa located in the lieutenant's office. "Lieu" is a short abbreviation of lieutenant used by subordinates under that rank.

"Fucking South Jamaica section is getting crazy, and I need big things to happen, while you guys are out doing enforcement tonight. Since your partner is on vacation, I'm going to need you to step up your buying game and observation skills. I also need you to go find a partner to work with for tonight. Just do me a favor, find a worker and not one of them lazy bums UCs, we have sitting around here," Zaki said while placing the tactical plan down on his desk. Eric sat there staring at his lieutenant before responding.

"Come on lieu! You're the lieutenant and I'm just a detective. It's going to be hard for me to find a volunteer, to go out with me." Eric replied. Eric knew exactly what he was talking about, an undercover searching for a volunteer to be a partner was like searching for a needle in a hay stack in his command. Fellow undercover officers treated you as if you were a snitch, if you alerted a supervisor that someone was in the building chilling out and not assigned to go out in the field with any team for the day. Zaki just shook his head.

"Today is not a good day for dick measuring detective, I got a damn memo on my desk from headquarters today. The crime stats are up and the Chiefs are losing their fuckin minds over South Jamaica," Zaki explained. "We need some good enforcement numbers tonight and I'm counting on you and the rest of the team to get the job done." Zaki said as he looked Eric whom was sitting across from his desk.

"Lieu, Moreno could go out there and find another UC.

Why didn't you tell him to go look for one?" Eric asked as if the lieutenant owed him an answer. This muthafucka! Zaki thought to himself, before leaning back into his chair and folding his arms. After looking at Eric for a few seconds, he reached around his neck and pulled his shield out and let it dangle from the chain onto his chest, for Eric to see.

"You see this shield Eric?" Zaki asked. Eric acknowledged. "It's a lieutenant shield, meaning it out ranks a police officer's, detective's and sergeant's shield. I'm not gonna sit here and debate with you. But I will tell you this. I've been in narcotics for many years. It's always better if an undercover asks the assistance of another undercover. As we both know, UCs pretty much run the show.

Second, I'm asking you to do, not your sergeant. Do you want my request to turn into a direct order?" Zaki asked as he started to lean forward in his chair. Eric then shook his head to say no.

"Okay then, if you have any problems, just mention my name. I have a pretty good reputation with the UCs in this building. Everyone knows I'm no cheap sake when it comes to overtime and have no problem blowing the cap off it if necessary. When you find a volunteer let me know who he or she is so I can put them down on the tac plan," Zaki continued as he then placed his hands behind his head.

"Okay lieu, I'll give it a try. Hopefully somebody will step up to the plate." Eric said while getting up from the sofa and exiting the office.

"If you have no luck just let me know, then I will handle it from there," The lieutenant replied. Eric walked out the office and started to think to himself.

Why the fuck do I have to go out here looking for somebody to work with me tonight?! I ain't no fucking boss! He's a fucking boss and could order somebody to go out me without a problem Eric thought to himself soon as he exited the lieutenants office and down the corridor to another module.

Times have changed within the Narcotic Division since the early days and a new breed of undercovers had emerged over the years. A lot of the new and less experienced undercover police Officers were less aggressive in hitting the streets to do buy and bust enforcement. Some of them would rather hide out in their command all day bullshitting, watching movies, playing cards and playing on their laptop.

Many expected to skate thru the first 18 months to get promoted to third grade detective, then make second and first grade without putting in hard work or effort. Most of their activity was way less than the more experienced veterans whom were out there grinding hard prior to their arrival. The new breed was basically happy with a mere case buy and attempted to stretch it as far as they could.

A case buys is when the undercover detective/police Officer makes a purchase (narcotic/weapon) and the person whom sold it to them are not immediately apprehended. The person whom sold whatever to the undercover are known as a sale subject. The sale subject is further investigated to determine if he or she can lead the undercover to the bigger fish. In most cases, a case buy lead to a search warrant.

Damn! I knew I should've took off today and hung out with my partner this weekend! Eric thought to himself as he was referring to his partner Detective Major that also went by the name of MAJ.

Eric knew there was no way in hell he was going to get a day off too as he repeatedly approached and asked fellow UCs to go out with him to do enforcement. He received the cold shoulder as expected and ended up hanging out at the front desk. While standing near the FOD (Field Operation Desk) and engaging in a conversation with one of his ex-team members who retired on a line of duty injury, Eric observed Brandon walking down the corridor.

Brandon was an experienced undercover whom loved the deception of the buy and bust game along with the overtime he made from it. Brandon was the type of UC that would roll out on the set in a wheelchair or push a shopping cart full of recyclable cans and bottles just to make a buy on the streets. Brandon stayed focused on his goal of becoming one of the best undercover detectives the city ever had. While making lots of cash overtime and getting promoted to second and later on first grade detective.

In the New York City Police Department, there are two types of Detective and there are also three grades. The following is a brief definition of each:

DETECTIVE INVESTIGATOR: Conducts investigation and a usually promoted from detective squad, narcotic division, vice squad, internal affairs bureau among other investigative units.

DETECTIVE SPECIALIST: Newly appointed and promoted by the Commissioner of the Police Department to the rank from the rank of police Officer based on the police Officer's Commanding Officer of a Non-Investigative Unit recommendation.

THIRD GRADE DETECTIVE: Newly appointed and promoted by the Commissioner of the Police Department to the rank from the rank of police Officer based on the Police Officer's Commanding Officer of an Investigative Unit recommendation. Third Grade is investigative Status.

SECOND GRADE DETECTIVE: Promotion from third grade for extraordinarily work while having third grade status by the police commissioner based on the detective commanding officer of an investigative unit recommendation. Second grade detective receive a pay raise almost equivalent to the salary as a supervisory ranking Sergeant, there is no responsibility to supervise subordinates and no promotional exam required.

FIRST GRADE DETECTIVE: Promotion from second grade for extraordinarily work while having second grade detective status by the police commissioner based on the detective commanding officer of an investigative unit recommendation.

First grade detectives receive a pay raise equivalent to the salary as a supervisory ranking Lieutenant, there is no responsibility to supervise subordinates and no promotional exam is required.

The rank of first grade is the highest promotion that any detective could achieve, under that said rank.

"Brandon! What's up player?" Eric asked while embracing Brandon with a handshake and a brief hug, just before asking him the question of the day.

"Nothing much Eric, I'm just chilling out on my down day (Non-enforcement day), what are you up to today?" Brandon replied while looking at his cell phone. Yes! Eric thought to himself, once he heard Brandon was down for the day. His eyes lit up with hope that he didn't have to search no longer.

"B&B for me tonight. My lieutenant sent me out here looking for somebody to ghost me," Eric said as he watched Brandon stare at his phone and seem not interested. "Do you wanna roll with me out in the field and make this money?" Eric continued as he asked in the hope that he wouldn't be shut down again. Brandon still continued to stare at his cell phone as he shrugged his shoulders.

"Only if you can't find anybody else to go out with you dude! To tell the truth, I'm trying to get off work on time tonight," Brandon replied as he finally took his eyes off his phone. "Where's your partner at? Oh, let me guess. He's doing an operation with the D.E.A. or maybe major case?" Brandon asked as he looked back at his phone and started to send out a text message to some unknown receiver.

"Nope! He's on one of them long extended vacation he be taken every year. I'll be lucky to work with his first-grade ass in about three to four weeks," Eric replied as if he was exhausted from getting shut down by all his fellow undercover staff. Brandon started to laugh as he read a funny text message that appeared on his phone screen. He then looked up at Eric whom stood there looking all pitiful in the face.

Everyone assigned to Eric's command knew that MAJ was a living legend whom had a shit load of vacation days and comp time on the books to take off as long as he wanted. It wasn't a strange thing for him to be out for a month or two.

"Who's your lieutenant?" Brandon asked as he became curious to whom Eric boss was.

"Lieutenant Zaki! You know the big guy with the blond hair," Eric responded in hope that Brandon knew of his lieutenant.

"Zaki? That's my man! He's real cool, plus he's not stingy with the overtime," Brandon said as he began to smile and considered to work with Eric.

"Don't worry brother, I'm not going to leave you hanging! You can tell your lieutenant to put me down on the tac plan. My undercover number is 071. I'm gonna hit the gym real quick, so hit me when it's time to tac up," Brandon continued as he exchanged another handshake with Eric and walked down the corridor towards the locker room. Eric was relieved that the temporary stress was now off his neck of getting a partner for the night.

Brandon worked with Eric a few times in the past and didn't want to see one of Queens narcotics up and rising stars stuck with a lazy non-aggressive undercover ghosting him. Eric headed back down the corridor towards his module, with a sign of relief on his face for finding an active partner for enforcement. Before returning to his desk he knocked on the lieutenant's office door and remained outside of it until he was acknowledged.

"Come in!" The lieutenant yelled out as he sat at his desk going thru a couple of reports.

"Excuse me lieu! I found an undercover to ghost me while we're out there tonight. You can put Brandon down as the second Undercover on the tactical plan" Eric said as he poked his head into the office.

"What is his UC number?" The lieutenant asked as he picked up a pen to write it down on the tactical plan.

"His UC number is 071," Eric responded as he stood there watching the lieutenant take a sip of his big gulp cup containing ice water.

"I worked with that detective before, he's pretty good out there in the field. Good job Eric! We tac up at 1750 hours and the team is heading out the door 1800 hours sharp so be ready okay" The lieutenant said as he entered UC 071 onto the tactical plan.

"Okay lieu, I'll let Brandon know the time and the place we are meeting up." Eric replied as he returned to his desk and called Brandon to inform him of the times of the tac meeting and departure for enforcement.

Back when Eric first arrived at the narcotics unit in the borough of Queens, He was partnered up with Billy, a more experienced Undercover whom was recently promoted to detective. Billy seemed to be lacking the initiative to remain an active Undercover since he already received his detective shield and his reluctance to train Eric became evident.

For a month in a half, Billy would give Eric all types of bogus tips on how to make a buy and what to ask for in the streets. If one of the team investigators had a narcotic complaint also known as a kite on a local bodega in the confines of their module's command, Billy would tell Eric to place the money on the counter and ask the cashier for cheesecake or some other outrageous alleged code word to make a narcotic buy.

Eric was unaware of his partner attempts to keep him inactive, as he followed the instructions of his senior partner that always lead to negative results. The frustration of not making a buy began to take a toll on Eric after his first month in the unit.

New undercover police officers assigned to the narcotic unit were only temporary assigned for 90 days. The constant threat of being sent back to your prior command during that 90 days, inflicted pressure on the new undercover Officers to have very good activity or be embarrassed once your sent back to your old command as if you couldn't cut it in the detail.

When it came to the Organized Crime Control Bureau, once you were kicked out, your chances of getting into another detail within the department was very slim to none.

Billy, a male Hispanic whom was an approximately 6'3 tall 255lb and could pass for a Caucasian due to his very light complexion, was a standout in the South Jamaica section of Queens. The local dealers and residences quickly assumed he was a cop soon as he stepped his foot on the set. There was no Caucasians living in the area and a very low percentage of Hispanics living in that immediate area at the time. With that being said, Billy raised suspension with presence.

Eric's sergeant, as well as Billy both, knew if the big guy stepped out of the car and onto the set. The whole set would be blown and the dealers would shut down their street operation in a heartbeat. Billy knew he didn't fit in the area and became very apprehensive about not being out shined by the new jack undercover, whom blended very well into the community. Instead of being a mentor to his unexperienced partner and guide him in the right direction, Billy choose to misinform Eric on the street lingo and how to engage in a narcotic conversation with alleged dealers so it could lead to negative results.

Billy would look over at Eric when he returned to the vehicle after an unsuccessful buy attempt and say, "Don't worry kid you'll bust your cherry one day," with a sneaky conniving smirk on his face. Billy while ghosting Eric, would sometimes transmit a narcotics transaction observation over the radio to the team leader, once Eric returned to the car. This was his attempt to show his personal worth to the team and generate a little overtime for himself, since he was unable to make a buy attempt himself.

Eric's sergeant whom later transferred to another borough asked Eric to step into in his office one day and said the following:

You got too relax out their kid! I like you and I see your trying real hard to get the job done. You're all the team has as an undercover and I see you looking the part as well as you are giving it what you got for what your being taught. Just remember, you're here temporary on paper for 90 days and I don't wanna see you heading back to your old command and getting back in the bag (term for being in uniform). It's me and you kid! We walked into this building together.

These investigators on our team will be promoted automatically as long as they keep their ass clean. Some of them even have a few months to go before being promotion and that's if they don't already have their detective shield already. I know it's a harder for an undercover to do his job in this unit. You have to bring out a character in you that you have never lived before and separate it from the real you. I'm going to see if I can get you to go out in the field with this guy Anthony I've been hearing about, maybe after a few times so you can learn the ropes and take over the buying game in this building kid.

"Thanks, Sarge, I know I can learn a lot more from Anthony more than what Billy is showing me. For some reason, I don't think Billy is schooling me right!" Eric replied to his supervisor. Eric always wanted to work with Anthony. There wasn't a day he could remember since he was assigned in the Unit, that Anthony didn't make a buy.

Anthony, 6'1 tall 180 pounds dark complexion male black, was a Harlem native from the projects, whom arrived at the Narcotic Borough of Queens approximately eight months prior to Eric arrival. Anthony who was still an undercover police Officer at the time was a up and rising star in the unit. He looked like everything a cop didn't, and was willing to get down and dirty just to fit the part to complete his mission to purchase narcotics.

Eric remembered back when he was in undercover training, the instructors always stated that a new undercover officer should never attempt to make an inside buy attempt, but that day came sooner than Eric thought when he teamed up with Anthony.

Eric and Anthony along with the rest of the narcotic field team headed out the door of their command, and was in route to the south Jamaica Queens area for enforcement. The first set was in the vicinity of 205th and Hollis Avenue, a border line location for the 116th and 117th precinct. The field team arrived and quickly set up in position awaiting the supervisor instructions. The supervisor then conducted a brief roll call checking who were present in the vicinity already, and requested a Mic check from the Undercover Officers.

"Leader both of the UCs are going to step out on this set together, if you don't mind " The experience Undercover Anthony requested over the radio frequency.

"Both of you are going to step together? Why do you want to do that Anthony?" The supervisor replied.

"I want to give the new UC a more on hands feel of the game by watching me up close and personal. You know what I'm saying?" Anthony replied.

"Okay! That sounds good to me Anthony. I'm reading you guys loud and clear over the transmitter. You have the green light to step," The supervisor transmitted to let the undercovers know that their equipment was working properly and that they could get the ball rolling.

"Leader, Eric will have the transmitter device on him and I'll be wired up to my radio, to give you a play by play.

Both UCs are stepping out of the vehicle now leader." Anthony transmitted before both UCs exited their vehicle. The Undercovers headed down Hollis Avenue from Francise Lewis towards 205th Street. While they were walking Anthony started to engage in brief conversations with people walking along the street or hanging on the corners.

Eric was naïve to the game of buy and bust as he watched his experience partner work the area.

"Damn player! I guess we gotta hit the next set because you seem to know a lot of people over here. Did you use to live in Queens or something?" Eric asked as he just observed his partner give a hand shake and brief hug to a male who was passing by. The experience Undercover just looked at his unexperienced partner and cracked a smile.

"Hell No! I'm from Harlem World Baby! Land of the hustlers. Just stand by and Peep my game player. I don't know these muthafuckas from a hole in the wall, it's a mind game I'm running on them plus the set. You have to make them think they may know you from somewhere, but can't recall from where. You have to keep your face getting seen on the set socializing with the people in the neighborhood. You're always being watched at all times" Anthony said as he schooled the new jack undercover as he transmitted their location over the radio to the team leader.

Once the two undercovers reached the corner of 205th Street and Hollis Avenue, they observed a tall male black approximately 20 years old wearing all black clothing smoking a cigarette in front of the bodega. Anthony then turned towards his partner as if he was engaging in a conversation with him, but in reality, he was transmitting over the description and location of the male standing outside the bodega and notified the leader that his new jack partner Eric was going to make a buy attempt on him. Anthony then instructed Eric to approach the male and engage in a conversation about anything while he himself stepped into the bodega to purchase some beverages for cover.

"Hey! What's up player? Do you have a light on you?" Eric asked as he removed a single cigarette from a fresh pack he had in his jacket pocket. The young male without saying anything, just looked at Eric and reached into his pants pocket to retrieve a cigarette lighter. He then handed it to Eric.

"Good looking out playa!" Eric said as he took the lighter and lit his cigarette that he had dangling from his lip. "My lighter went on empty when I was at work earlier today" Eric continued after handing the young male back his lighter in an attempt to get the possible hustler into a conversation. The young male still didn't respond to Eric comment. He was more concerned with a beep he received on his pager and walked over to the pay phone that was located next to the bodegas entrance.

"Yo! I'm already on the AVE! How many you want? I got that for you! Come thru right now! Okay! How far are you away and what you are driving?" Eric overheard the young male saying as he attempted to ear hustle the conversation. Eric figured the young male was engaging in a narcotic conversation with whomever was on the other end of the phone and knew he had to get word to Anthony. Eric quickly walked into the bodega and notified his partner Anthony that a possible deal was about to go down with the young male he was trying to make a buy with.

"Okay, I'm going to set up outside in the cut and relate shit over to the leader, you just focused on trying to get a buy with home boy yourself" Anthony instructed his inexperienced partner as he handed him a forty-ounce bottle containing malt liquor wrapped in a paper bag. They both exited the bodega and observed that the male they were focusing on was off the phone and still hanging out.

"Son! I'm gonna go take a piss in the park," Anthony said to his partner loud enough for the hustler to hear, as he started to cross Hollis Avenue.

"Don't get locked up nigga! You know Police be out here giving tickets and locking niggas up for that shit out here every day!" Eric replied as he cracked open his bottle and took a quick sip before placing the cap back on.

Anthony pretended to wave Eric off and crossed Hollis Avenue and entered the darkly lit large school playground directly opposite of the bodega. He camouflaged himself into the darkness as he transmitted what was transpiring on the set and that an unknown vehicle should be arriving to make a purchased from the suspected hustler Eric was focusing on"

"Yo! Can I bum a cigarette off of you, homie?" The young male asked Eric whom was patiently waiting for the perfect opportunity to make a buy attempt. Eric already knew that the young male observed him with a full pack of smokes.

"Yeah! No doubt Player! I could bless you with one," Eric replied as he reached back into his pocket and removed the pack to retrieve a cigarette and handed it to the male.

"Thanks, my man, I gotta quit smoking. I never seen you around here before. Where you from?" The male asked trying to strike up a conversation with Eric as he lit his cigarette.

Eric was already previously warned while in training that Queens was one of the hardest boroughs to make a drug buy in. Basically because, everybody knew everybody in Queens especially on the south side.

"I'm from Queens Village playa, I'm just passing through to check on my baby momma on 198th Street," Eric replied as he looked down the block and suddenly placed his bottle on the ground while a marked police vehicle cruised down Hollis Avenue.

"You put that shit down at the perfect time, them motherfuckers would've jumped out on yo ass for that beer with the quickness" The young male said jokingly.

"I know, I shouldn't even be fucking around like this! I got my glass on me and shit," Eric replied as he patted his jacket pocket.

"Damn homie, I didn't take you for somebody that hit that glass at all! Yo ass definitely would been heading to the bookings for that shit, if them fools want some overtime," The young male said as a black Lincoln town car pulled up in front of the bodega and beeped the horn. The whole time Eric was in conversation with the male, Anthony was in the school park conducting a surveillance on his partner and possible sale subject. He also transmitted the description and direction of the vehicle that arrived on the scene.

"Excuse me for a minute homie! I gotta go make this paper real quick," The male said as he walked away from Eric and towards the vehicle. The male entered the vehicle just before Eric had a chance to make a buy attempt. Eric then walked over towards the vehicle a little, so he could get a better look at the male he was focusing on to make a buy with. He observed the male engaging in a conversation with another male whom was sitting in the driver's seat inside of the vehicle.

"Leader my possible subject is talking to a male black light complexion with a white baseball cap and white sweater seating in the driver's seat of a black Lincoln town car with a dent on the front passenger side," Eric transmitted while he hid his lips behind the brown paper bag containing the bottle of malt liquor he retrieved from the ground. He then observed the male he was talking to counting something in his hand and exchanged it with the driver for an undetermined amount of cash, just before his possible sale subject exited the car.

"My guy is out the vehicle leader and now the vehicle is about to drive off towards 204th street. Tell my ghost to let you know which way the car heads," Eric transmitted prior to taking another sip of his beer, just before his possible sale subject approached him.

Anthony was still in the darkness of the park ghosting the set and alerting the team of the Lincoln's location and movement.

"Damn, What the fuck is my boy doing in the park? How long does it take for a nigga to take a fucking piss? I wanna go cop some shit before I head to this bitch crib," Eric said out loud, in hope that the male standing next to him could hear him, so he could strike up a narcotic conversation. The male actually heard him and Eric's plan started to work.

"Yo! What you are you looking for?" The dealer asked as he looked Eric up and down.

"I'm looking to get some soft (a street term for powered cocaine) so I can make me a Fat Ruler (a street term for marijuana combined with cocaine cigarette) Eric replied.

"Soft?" The hustler asked. "Who you usually get it from around here?" The hustler suspiciously continued to ask, because Eric wasn't a familiar face to him in the neighborhood.

"My man, I already told you I'm from Queens Village. The last time I came through here, I copped from a nigga named Black," Eric replied without hesitation in hope that the name would ring a bell of some type, even though he was lying. Eric pretty much knew in every urban neighborhood in America, you could always find a dude nicknamed Black that was out there hustling.

"Oh, you're talking about short Black, with the gold fronts," The male questioned the undercover.

"Negative baby, I don't know what Black you are talking about playa, But the Black that hooked me up last time I was out here, was tall with a big ass scar on his face," Eric replied with confidence. The young hustler started to smile.

"Okay, I know that Black. I thought you was five-O (a street term for police) for a minute, so I had to feel you out, to see if you good. How much you looking to get?" The young hustler asked as he figured the undercover passed his little test.

"I need about three tins playa," Eric replied as he was getting eager to make his first buy. The young hustler seemed puzzled for a quick second.

"Hold up my nigga, if you smoke bones, why are you carrying that glass on you?" The hustler asked referring to the glass pipe the undercover claimed he had in his pocket, as he stared Eric in the eyes.

"I smoke rock too, but the shorty I be fucking with only smokes bones and don't know I be fucking rock. So, I just smoke rulers around her, you know what I'm saying?" Eric replied as if he memorized a script.

"I hear you playa. Take a walk with me to my crib, because I'm two short on what you looking for. I only have one tin on me," The hustler responded.

The Sergeant and the investigator heard what was transpiring over the hidden transmitter and notified Anthony whom was ghosting from across the street to head back to the bodega, so he can keep an eye on thee inexperienced undercover. As Anthony exited the park and got closer to where Eric was standing.

"Yo nigga! What the fuck ,was you doing in there? Shitting or pissing?" Eric jokingly asked, as soon as his ghost returned to the front of the bodega.

"You a real funny muthafucka Easy," Anthony replied while using Eric undercover aka name.

"Check this Tony, I'm about to slide off with my man and pick up a little package," Eric replied while also using Anthony's undercover aka name.

"Okay, hurry up man. I don't wanna hear Yo girl beefing I had you out here fucking with other bitches," Anthony said while looking at his watch.

"Yo playa you ready, I gotta get on the move or my girl ain't gonna want to give up no ass tonight," Eric said as he reached out and extended his hand to give the dealer a hand shake.

"I can dig that like a muthafucka my nigga. Take this walk with me real quick. I gotta go re-up on my shit," The dealer said as he guided both undercovers down Hollis Avenue towards 203rd Street.

The undercovers both walked with the deals down Hollis Avenue as they joked and laughed while engaging in a friendly conversation about the freaky shit a some of the crack addict woman would do just to get high. The young hustler pointed out a female whom was walking on the opposite side of the street and stated she was a major freak. She looked over and spotted him with the two undercovers and continued on her way as if she was in a hurry. Once they reached the corner of 203rd Street.

"Oh Shit! Here comes that nigga Chauncey who owe me twenty dollars. Let me go holla at this fool and I'll catch up with you two in a minute" Anthony said as he watched a male black walking from 202nd street towards 203rd. Eric thought to himself. What the fuck is he doing? He knows I'm new in this Undercover shit and I'm not supposed to attempt any buys inside yet, especially not alone he continued to think to himself.

"Pardon me playa! My name is Tony and this non-manner muthafucka you been kicking it with, name is Easy! What's your name player? And which house you gonna be in so I could catch up with you guys in a few once I get my money from this nigga" Anthony asked while pulling out a little pocket knife as if he was going to use it on the unsuspecting male who was approaching 203rd street if he don't get his money. Anthony knew he had to play the shit off the right way by pulling out his knife. He knew if someone owed you money in the streets you had to go at them hard.

The hustler was kind of hesitant at first to give the knife holding stranger his information, but decided to do so before he became a possible witness to a homicide from the look in the undercover eyes.

"My crib is the white and green house over there, come to the side door at the end of the drive way. By no means, should you knock on the front door. If anybody else answers the door, just ask for Dezo," The hustler instructed Anthony as he headed down the street towards his house with Eric.

Anthony quickly transmitted the description of the subject (hustler) who was now known to him as Dezo and gave a description of the house that Eric and Dezo were heading to, as the other male who Anthony identified as someone who owed him money reached the corner of 203rd street and Hollis Avenue. Anthony just merely asked him for a cigarette, in which the male gave him one.

The exchange to the unknown eye would've looked like the male handed him some dope or cash the way Anthony stuffed it in his pocket.

"Leader! The undercover just walked up the white and green house drive-way located on 203rd street, I will put over the address as soon as I get to the location" Anthony said as he quickly made it to the house. Eric and the hustler now known to him as Tony entered the home from the side door located in driveway of the green and white house.

Once inside, He notice a small flight of stairs leading to the basement that was dark and to his right there was four upward steps leading to a kitchen that was fairly lighted and had a strong aroma of Marijuana coming from it.

"You said you wanted three right?" Dezo asked as he whispered attempting not to be heard by whom ever was in the kitchen.

"Yeah Player! Three nice ones" Eric replied while scanning the entrance to the kitchen and the dark basement on guard for possible sneak attack. Tony then flicked on a light switch that lit up the basement.

"Give me a minute Fam, I'll be back up in a minute" Dezo said as he headed down stairs and out of the new undercover view. Suddenly there was a knock at the door, It was his partner Anthony. Anthony opened up the door.

"What's up Easy? You get served yet?" Anthony asked Eric as he was curious if the new undercover made his first buy.

"Nope! I'm just chilling out until my man comes back upstairs from the basement" Eric told his partner as he knew the whole conversation was transmitting over his hidden transmitter. A large shadow started to emerge toward the kitchen doorway.

"Yo! Who the fuck are you niggas?!, And what the fuck are you doing in my house?!" Shouted out a tall muscular male black whom was now standing at the kitchen door way smoking a long thick cigar stuffed with marijuana. He heard the unfamiliar voices near the door way and came over to investigate.

"Big Man, we just waiting on Dezo! He told us to wait here until he comes back upstairs," Eric replied while watching the hands of large muscular dude sporting the wife beater white T-shirt start to clinch. The tall male inhaled the marijuana smoke deep into his lungs, then blew the smoke into the two undercovers face.

"I don't give a fuck, what he told you! Y'all niggas need to get the fuck out!" The large male said as he stared both of the undercovers up and down.

"Okay! No problem Big Man! We out!" Anthony replied as both undercovers started to head out the door.

"Yo Murt! Ease up off my niggas! They good!" Dezo yelled up as his head appeared at the bottom of the staircase after over hearing the big guy yelling.

"Dezo! What the fuck I told you about bringing niggas up in the spot! I don't know these niggas, so they got to get the fuck out!" The tall male now known as Murt said as he angrily looked at Dezo. "These niggas smell like bacon! I just came home! And I ain't trying to go back to the pin again for nobody!" The hulking Murt said as he folded his arms and took an intimidating stance as he once again began to stare at the two undercovers.

"Nah, I serve them on the regular," Dezo said to justify himself to his brother on why he let the two strangers into the house. Murt wasn't impressed and continued to stare at the two undercovers.

"Dezo! We'll just wait outside player! We don't wanna cause any conflict with big man's house rules" Anthony said as both undercovers exited the side door and walked towards the end of the driveway near the street.

"Did you transmit the location and everything to the leader" Eric asked his experienced partner. Anthony quickly responded to the rookie undercover.

I did all of that player. The boss sent the arresting officer and another team member to draw up an emergency search warrant for this house as we speak. Just remember to get Dezo pager number after he hits you off" Anthony instructed Eric to do just before Dezo exited the side door and began to walk towards them. Dezo then walked over to Eric and simulated a hand shake while passing him three tin foils containing cocaine, Eric in return handed him the thirty dollars buy money.

"Yo! You niggas gotta pardon my brother, He just did a 5 year bid up north and is all paranoid cause he in there bagging up five pounds of weed" Dezo said as he placed the money Eric handed him into his rear pants pocket.

"Yo! Your brother is a big muthafucka! I don't blame him for being paranoid, we ain't trying to piss a big nigga like that off by standing in his crib, especially when he don't want us there!" Anthony replied as he gave Dezo a quick hand shake and a brief hug.

"Let me get your pager or home number so I can hit you up and avoid all the unnecessary" Eric asked while following his undercover training instructions.

"I never give out my number to the crib! But here's my pager number. Just input how many you want at the end of your number," Dezo said as he handed Eric a card containing his street name and his pager number.

"Will it be okay if I hit you up later player for another tin, if shit goes smooth with my girl?" Eric asked as he placed the card into his jacket pocket.

"Whatever you need my nigga, just hit me up. I'm about to get rid of these other tins, I just put together before I close up shop on 205th," Dezo replied as he showed the two undercovers his stash. The two undercover and the hustler began to head down the street towards Hollis Avenue away from Dezo House.

"Easy! I'm hungry my man. I'm gonna to go pick up a Hero sandwich from the deli on frannie lew. Do you want something while I'm there?" Anthony said referring to Francise Lewis

Boulevard, where he had the undercover vehicle parked.

"Yeah! Get me a turkey and cheese with lettuce and tomato on a hero. I'm gonna hurry over to ole girl house before I get shut out on the ass tonight" Eric replied as he started to head down Hollis Avenue towards 198th Street.

Anthony and Dezo headed in the other direction on Hollis Avenue, with Dezo returning back under the awning of the Bodega on the corner of 205th Street setting up shop again and Anthony returned to the undercover vehicle.

"Positive buy leader, Positive buy" Eric transmitted over the transmitter to notify the team that he made a buy.

Once in the vehicle, Anthony transmitted the results, and location of the subject whom sold his partner the narcotics.

"Leader I'm going to pick up the other UC and we're goonna set up on the sale subject to see how you want to handle this" Anthony transmitted over the radio transmitter as he quickly road down Hollis Avenue to pick up his partner.

"Player Player! I told you was gonna get done tonight! You finally bust your cherry and got your first buy!" Anthony said after he picked up Eric and traveled down a side street to set up in the vicinity of 205th Street and Hollis Avenue to watch Dezo.

"Thanks for coming out and helping me get on," Eric graciously said while smiling from ear to ear. Anthony smiled and gave Eric a thumbs up.

"Okay leader! Both UCs are in the vehicle and are set up with the sale subject in sight, You rolling in on him or what?" Anthony asked as he transmitted over the radio to the team supervisor.

"Good job guys! We're gonna sit on this guy for a while and watch him. I want you two guys to put over any observation of sales made by this guy Dezo. I need alldescriptions and directions of the buyers and where they're heading in after the hand to hand is done. We'll pick up all the buyer's then scoop Dezo up later," The supervisor instructed.

"10-4 leader! What's up with that emergency search warrant for the house?" Anthony curiously asked.

"The Search Warrant is in the works as we speak, I just want to get a few bodies in the van just in case shit don't work out the way we planned it" the supervisor responded.

"I hear that leader, loud and clear. Dezo showed us a nice stash he put together he plan on hustling off real quick," Anthony acknowledged back to his supervisor.

After placing six individuals under arrest based on the Undercovers observations, the supervisor then received word that the emergency search warrant was authorized and signed by the judge. He notified the team captain and lieutenant whom were now in route to supervise the warrant. Dezo was shortly picked up by members of the team prior to the search warrant being executed.

Dezo's brother Murt, was shot to death by members of the field team as he opened fire on them as they raided his home during the search warrant. Eric first buy resulted in a justified shooting, twelve arrests and the following property was recovered:

Two loaded Twelve Gauge Shot Guns

One fully loaded .357 Magnum hand gun

Four Ounces of Cocaine

Four Ounces of Marijuana

Eighteen Thousand Dollars Cash

One Police Scanner

All property was recovered and vouchered as evidence.

CHAPTER 7

CAUGHT SLIPPING

Once Nate reached the corner of Rockaway and Sutter Avenue, the traffic signal turned red. He then reached his arm back towards the rear passenger seat to retrieve his duffel bag and placed it in the front passenger's seat next to him, while the car idled at the light. Just before the light changed to green, he observed a well-dressed young male wearing two large Cuban link chains crossing in front of his vehicle and thought to himself.

I should take this nigga shit real quick Nate thought to himself until he recognized the male to be a local kid from the neighborhood named Denzel. Denzel once hooked Nate up with some free burgers at the fast food joint he worked at on Pitkin Avenue. Even though the jewelry would've been nice to pawn off for cash, Nate knew the kid earned it legal and wasn't out there hustling in the streets. He then decided to concentrate on his intended mission pin pointed at Sutter and Stone Avenue.

Nate traveled down Sutter Avenue towards Stone Avenue once the traffic signal turned green, and decided to park his vehicle on the opposite side of Stone Avenue near Van Dyke Projects. Once he was satisfied with his position, Nate quickly grabbed his duffel bag and exited the vehicle with the engine still running set to go. Nate zoned in on his prey as he limped across Stone Avenue, making his way to the entrance leading to the handball court located next to the B14 bus stop. Once he got inside the park, Nate swiftly moved at a quick pace.

The group's arrogance along with their misconceptions that they were untouchable, allowed Nate to approach them unnoticed. Nate suddenly tossed his duffel bag onto the rolling dice and stacks of money that laid on the ground, that drew everyone's attention automatically.

"Oh, Shit!" One of the cocky young males uttered as he notice that Nate was already on them like stink on shit in a blink of an eye.

"Yall niggas know what it is!" Nate yelled as he stood there with his two Smith n Wessons drawn on the small group, catching them all by surprise. "I want it all niggas! Cash! Jewels! And all that shit you niggas be slinging. As a matter of fact! Give up that weed Yall smoking too!" Nate forcefully said as he looked around to see if someone was coming. There was a quick moment of silence but Nate wasn't in the move for them to be dumb founded.

"Here!" One of Nate's victims said as he attempted to hand Nate over his gold chain.

"Put it in the bag muthafucka!" Nate quickly instructed his victim. The dealers were taking their time giving up what they had, causing Nate to grow impatient.

"Hurry the fuck up niggas! Before I start squeezing these cannons off," Nate continued to say as he nervously looked around into all his victim's eyes. Nate wanted to make this robbery as quick as possible. The quicker the robbery the less chance you could be recognized and identified by the victims, he had this theory logged in his head and lived by it.

Ain't this some shit! We suppose to be running these streets, Yet we let this fucking crackhead just run up on us like we bitch ass niggas! Thought one of the hustlers in the group as he removed two large gold rope chains from his neck and a bundle of cash from his pocket. Nate's bag was filling up nicely. Gold watches, chains with medallion pieces, bracelets, two three and four finger rings. Nate noticed his victims were starting to stare at him.

"Face the muthafuckin ground niggas! Yall niggas acting like you never heard about me! I'm that nigga in these streets they call Nate! And if you never heard of me! Nigga better ask about me," Nate said loud enough for them to hear him. "Keep reckless eyeballing me and the last thing you gonna see is these barrels flashing," Nate continued to say as he grew impatient of how slow his victims were moving.

Nate's victims, felt the tension in the air by the tone of Nate's voice. So, they picked up the pace on removing their property quickly and placed it in the duffel bag, Well all of them except for one who had a different plan in mind. Nate took notice of this particular victim, but went along with his plan to keep the others moving. Shakim, who was an ex-stickup kid himself turned drug dealer started to reach into his rear pants pocket, to retrieve his fully loaded nickel plated .25 Caliber semi-auto as Nate watched the others.

He figured if he could get the drop on the armed crack head, he would gain major street credit as someone not to fuck with in the hood. Becoming an urban legend as crazy as it may seem, meant the world to those who lived the life of crime. Being known as one of the biggest drug king pins, stickup men and murderers gained a lot the respect in the hood and built up street credit.

Nate's sensed Shakim was going to make a move on him, and with his keen eye and experienced street smarts zoned in on the glare coming from Shakim's shiny weapon before it was even fully pulled out. He quickly placed one of his handguns to Shakim's head, gaining his full attention.

"Too slow bitch!" Nate yelled out. "Anybody else got a burner on them?!" Nate violently asked. No one responded to Nate's question. "Okay since you niggas wanna play stupid, every body strip until your dick swinging! Before I start blasting! Except for this cowboy ass nigga over here whom think he about the murder game," Nate continued as his voice roared like thunder and he grew more furious of Shakim's attempt to pull out on him. All the hustlers except for Shakim stripped down butt naked and tossed their clothes all into one pile.

"Everybody get face down on the ground and put your hands on back of your neck. If I see a head come up! I'm blowing it the fuck off!" Nate instructed as he placed one of his handguns in his waste band and removed Shakim's weapon from his pocket, then placed it to its owner's head.

"What's your name cowboy?" Nate asked Shakim as he pressed the gun against his temple. "SHA-SHA-SHAKIM!" Shakim stuttered in response to Nate's question as he grew more nervous by the minute with a gun pressed against his skull.

Tears started to flow down Shakim's face. Nate could hear the thump of Shakim's heart beat, and could smell the fear coming from his body.

"Oh, don't cry now nigga!" Nate yelled into Shakim's with so much force that it caused Shakim's body jump with fear. "I bet you don't even know the rules to carrying a gun little nigga, so let me school you real quick." Nate said as he tapped the .25 Caliber against Shakim's head. "If you live by the gun, you die by the gun! So, man the fuck up and stop crying like a little bitch," He continued.

Thoughts of making a run for it crossed Shakim's mind, as his eyes scanned for an escape route, but the loaded gun he once possessed was now in the hands of a fearless junkie whom may end his life with one flinch. Brief thoughts of his life entered his mind. He realized the life he lived is the one he chose, and his possible death was his own destiny.

"I'm debating if I should pull this trigger. If I do, will it blow your brains out? Or is it empty?" Nate asked Shakim.

"I don't know?" Shakim answered.

"What the fuck do you mean that you don't know? You know what? I'll give you a few seconds to remember, before I pull the trigger," Nate responded. Hearing that, one of Shakim friends started to move as if he was gonna make a move to escape.

"Move again! And I'll put two holes in your head muthafucka!" Nate shouted.

Shakim knew he fucked up, and his life was at Nate's discretion. He thought about his past as a stick-up kid and all the lives he disrupted both physically and mentally throughout his life. Thoughts of his mother and all the pain he inflicted on her, with his choice of lifestyle.

"I wasn't gonna shoot you! I just wanted to back you off of us," Shakim said in an attempt to cop a bullshit plea, so his life would be spared.

"Get the fuck outer here with that dumb shit! Nigga, you gotta be a stupid muthafucka to pull out, when another nigga already got the drop on you! You ready to die nigga for this money?!" Nate asked, not really caring what Shakim's answer was. Shakim didn't answer. Nate been around for a long time and was no fool. He knew if he let Shakim live, that he and his boys would attempt to retaliate. He also knew if he didn't put the fear of god in them, he would always have to look over his shoulder.

Nate took a deep breath, then squeezed the trigger of Shakim's gun two times. Shakim was struck twice in the head just behind his ear at point blank range. Shakim lifeless body dropped like a sack of rocks. He was dead before he even hit the ground, and he landed face down on the ground. Nate boldly rolled Shakim onto his back then pointed the gun towards Shakim's face and fired until the gun was empty, giving him his signatured closed casket special.

The now terrorized group of hustlers covered their heads in fear that they would be next, as Nate gradually retrieved his duffel bag full of stolen goods.

"Snitch and I'll kill you!" Nate said as he removed the clip from Shakim's .25 Caliber and dropped the unloaded smoking weapon on his lifeless body.

Nate was wearing thin leather gloves, so he didn't give a shit about leaving any prints on Shakim's weapon for the police to trace. He quickly tossed the clip containing one bullet over the fence into the street and exited the location with his duffel bag while the scared hustlers remained on the ground. Once the close was clear, all but one of Shakim's nude buddies immediately scrambled to retrieve their clothes and quickly exited the handball court to safety. The one remaining friend, removed jewelry. After robbing his dead friend, He then anonymously alerted the police by calling 911 from the gas station across the street.

Nate quickly returned to his vehicle and sped off down Sutter Avenue towards the East New York Section of Brooklyn.

While making his getaway, he bypassed responding police cars with their sirens on racing towards the crime scene direction. Once Nate got deep into the jurisdiction of the 75th precinct, he pulled over on the corner of Sutter Avenue and Miller Street to change his license plates, just in case someone wrote down his plate as he pulled off in a hurry.

After he had changed his tags, Nate started to check the duffel bag containing stolen goods he just jacked from his young victims. *Damn that was a good hit* Nate thought to himself as he counted $3000 in cash. He had four large gold rope chains, five large gold rings and a couple of gold bracelets.

He no longer really cared for jewelry, he basically took it just to pawn it for cash. Sometimes he just exchanged it for a large quantity of crack with dealers willing to buy it Uptown and in Harlem. Nate only bought his crack from other boroughs especially Harlem, because he didn't want to slip up by running into someone he previously robbed in Brooklyn. He rarely bought in Queens, because dealers in Queens didn't like to sell to outsiders. The Bronx was where he spent most his money, because he thought the quality was better in Harlem and the Bronx.

Nate drove off until he found himself, what he believed to be a quiet spot to lay low until the heat cooled off.

CHAPTER 8

POSITIVE BUY

After completing his 90-day temporary assignment, Eric was then officially assigned to the unit. After completing his 18th month, Eric was promoted to detective and teamed up with an experienced undercover detective in the unit by the name of Denzel Major.

Detective Major, a highly decorated first grade detective that possessed the gift of gab and an active aggression to purchase narcotics and weapons throughout the tristate area. The first-grade Detective was spoken highly of by high ranking officers at headquarters and within the department. The word in the narcotic bureau division was, If MAJ didn't get a buy on his tour; then there was nothing out there to be bought.

Major whom went by the nickname of MAJ, ZEL at his work place was very charismatic and possessed many characteristics. He could easily play the role of a down and out crack addict to having the swagger of high profile dope dealer in the streets.

City wide in the narcotics unit, Major was classified a guarantee buy. The skill and charisma he possessed came with a price called envy. Many of his peers within his unit grew very jealous of his previous promotions. Major was aware of the jealousy, but continued to stay active and made loads of overtime. He took Eric under his wing once they became partners, and schooled him on how to make things happen in his career as an undercover.

Lieutenant Zaki stepped out of his office and walked to the center of his module.

"Tac-Up!" The lieutenant yelled out loud enough to get everyone's attention. Sergeant Moreno then stood up with the tactical plan in his hand.

"We are hitting the first set on the tac-plan in the vicinity of 134th to 137th Street on Guy Brewer Boulevard, in the confines of the 113th precinct. As you all may know or heard. There was a double homicide in front of David's Bodega across from Rochdale Village. So far there are no arrest or leads at this time" The Sergeant said loudly as Eric and Brandon both walked into the tac meeting after changing into their buy and bust clothes.

"Okay, Field Team! I need everybody to take a look at our two undercovers whom will be working in the field with us on the set tonight. Make sure you take a very close look at their faces and what they are wearing. I don't want no mistakes in the field in regard to our undercovers, is that understood?!" Said Sergeant Moreno. The field team acknowledged.

"Undercovers, please be safe out there and watch each other's back tonight. Be careful and keep your eyes and ears open to anything you see or hear on the set," The Lieutenant said to the two undercovers, as they acknowledged their lieutenant's order. Members of the field team started to prepare themselves to leave out into the field, by placing in the bullet proof vest and equipment.

"Are there any questions in regard to your assignments or the tac plan? If not, lets meet up in the vicinity of 134th Street and Guy Brewer Boulevard in thirty minutes," Sergeant Moreno yelled out as he reached into his desk and retrieved two sets of handcuffs.

The team headed out the door, as the lieutenant headed back into his office to handle some paper work. Some members of the team headed to the local Precinct to fuel up their vehicles that they were assigned to, and then continued towards the first set at 134th Street and Guy Brewer Boulevard.

"Team one, Team two, P-van and undercovers are you on the air?" Sergeant Moreno transmitted over the designated radio frequency, checking to see if the team was in place.

"We in the vicinity," Members of the team simultaneously responded. The sergeant then looked at his watch and placed his radio to his mouth to transmit.

"Undercovers! Are you guys ready to step to this set?" Moreno asked to see if his undercovers were ready to get the ball rolling. Eric acknowledged letting Moreno know that himself and his partner were ready.

"Okay, who's going to be the primary and who's going to be ghosting this set?" Sergeant Moreno asked as he transmitted over the point to point radio.

Primary Undercover means the Undercover who will be attempting to make a purchase, whether is street level or a case buy.

Ghosting Undercover means the Undercover who will be observing the Primary Undercover actions while transmitting their every move. Transmit all activity to the team supervisor and other fellow team mates, as well as secure the safety of the Primary Undercover environment. Transmit the description and location of all possible subjects the primary may encounter out in the field. Basically, The Ghosting Undercover has a vital job to perform during any operation, he or she are the eyes and ears of the team.

"UC 6969 is going to be the primary and Undercover 071 is going to be ghosting the primary," Eric who was listed on the tactical plan as UC 6969 said over the point to point radio transmitter.

"Okay undercovers, let's have a mic transmitter check (Device that transmits directly to a transmitter receiver that the supervisor possession his vehicle, that only said supervisor and whomever is in his vehicle can hear).

"Mic check one two one two. How are you reading that leader?" Eric stated as he transmitted over the Mic Transmitter.

"I'm reading you five by five (meaning audio transmission is coming over clear) responded Sergeant Moreno.

"Ten four (acknowledgement) leader UCs are ready to step out the vehicle.

Eric the primary undercover exited the vehicle first, and began to walk towards the set located at 134th Street and Guy Brewer Boulevard. He then turned around for a quick glance, to see if his ghost was out of the vehicle. Eric observed Brandon the ghosting undercover already out of the vehicle, and crossing the street walking, as he traveled at a normal pace parallel to him. Brandon began to transmit to the team leader (supervisor) the location of the primary undercover as well as the scenery of the set (targeted location) as soon as he came upon it.

"Leader the primary is on the corner of 134th Street and Guy Brewer Boulevard, there is also a few players (possible sale subjects) hanging out in front of the liquor store with the red and white awning. I will keep you posted if I see the primary engage in any type of conversation" Brandon transmitted over his point to point radio, he had connected to his ghost kit.

"Ten four ghost," Moreno acknowledged. "Field team the primary is set up on the corner of 134th and GRB. Ghost we have the primary loud and clear on the Mic," Moreno transmitted as the rest of the field team acknowledged.

Every time Eric steps foot on a set, he mentally goes back to his training with Anthony and Major. And every time he does, he comes up with positive results. Eric took a quick glimpse of the guys who were hanging out in front of the liquor store, then he entered David's Bodega that is located on Guy Brewer Boulevard between 134th Street and 137th Street. While inside the Bodega, he made his way towards the rear and removed a forty ounce of Old English Eight Hundred Malt Liquor Beer, and quickly made his way to the counter to purchase it for cover.

"Okay leader, the primary is inside of David's Bodega, it has a yellow and red awning and it is located on GRB between 134th and 137th Street" Brandon transmitted over his point to point radio while observing from across the street, while he stood at a bus stop.

"Okay TEN FOUR ghost I have the primary loud and clear, sounds like he is at the counter ready to make a purchase, field team the primary is inside David's Bodega, yellow and red bodega, possibly purchasing some food for cover, on GRB between 134th and 137th Street," Sergeant Moreno transmitted to the field team, while Detective Dean monitored the Mic transmitter closely.

Eric placed the forty-ounce bottle of malt liquor beer on the counter and asked the cashier also to give him a Dutch Master Cigar, he then purchased both items and exited the bodega.

"Leader the Primary has stepped out of the bodega, and is heading in the direction of the liquor store were a few players are hanging out in front; it's located on the strip of GRB Between 134th and 137th Street," Brandon transmitted while he closely ghosted his partner. "Ten Four ghost, field team the Primary is on the move and is heading towards the liquor store on GRB between 134th and 137th, standby for further" Sergeant Moreno transmitted to his field team. As Eric walked, he held the large bottle of beer concealed in brown paper bag in his left hand while having the exposed Dutch Master Cigar in his right hand.

Eric considered this to be a tactical measure he needed exercised, just in case the shit hits the fan, planning to use the bottle as a weapon by striking with the bottle as he reached for his weapon with the other hand. Eric also likes to use Dutch Master Cigars as a prop and made it available for a potential narcotic dealer to see. Eric decreased his walking pace then stood next to a pay phone that was posted next to the liquor store, and began to untwist the cap of the large bottle.

"Yo, you get that yet?" Asked one of the males whom was hanging outside of the liquor store, as he focused on the Dutch Master Cigar in Eric's hand. "Nah, not yet what's good?" Eric replied showing interest to the approaching male curiosity, and also to alert the team leader he's engaging in conversation so it would be monitored closely.

"Leader the Primary is engaged in a conversation with a Black Male, Light Complexion, approximately 6'2 tall, medium build and is wearing the following: Black Baseball Cap, Black Hooded Sweatshirt, Black Jeans, and Tan Boots. Both the Primary and the Possible Sale Subject are standing in front of Riddick's Liquor, it has a red and white awning and is located on the strip of GRB between 134th and 137th Street" Brandon transmitted over the point to point radio. "Okay Ten Four on that ghost, I'm picking the primary up loud and clear over the Mic transmitter, field team be advised the Primary is engaged in a conversation, the ghost has already transmitted the location and description, standby for further" Sergeant Moreno transmitted to the ghost and members of the field team, while Detective Dean carefully monitored the Mic Transmitter Receiver box.

"I got some fat tree sacks (plastic zips bags containing marijuana) son" the male said to the Primary Undercover as he removed one from his rear pants pocket to give the Primary a quick view of his product. "Damn, them shits are fat player, I was looking to get some HARD (crack cocaine) are you holding that too. "Nah son, I got you on the trees though but what you need on the hard?" Asked the curious potential sale subject. "Four Dimes of HARD, plus I'll take a couple of them sacks off your hands too" Eric replied.

The male then began to look around and over the Primary Undercover shoulder, until he spotted what or whom he was looking for. "Yo Mel, let me holla at you for a minute" the male yelled out as he waved over another male wearing a red baseball cap, who was standing in front of a barbershop located on the same strip.

"Okay leader and field team, the primary is still engaging in conversation with the male with the black baseball hat, but I'm now observing that same male calling over another male who is standing in front of a barbershop on the same strip, stand by for further," Brandon transmitted as he Ghosted the Primary from across the street.

"Ten four ghost, give us a quick description of the other guy and location," Moreno replied.

"Black male, dark complexion, approximately 5'6 to 5'7 tall slim build and wearing the following: Red hooded sweatshirt, red baseball cap, black jeans, red and black sneakers," Brandon transmitted over the point to point radio.

"Ghost, location of the guy and red hat," A unknown member of the field team transmitted with curiosity of the male in red location.

"The primary and both possible sale subjects are standing in front of the liquor store now, leader are you picking the primary up on the Mic?" Brandon stated and asked as he moved in a little closer to view the primary undercover surroundings.

"Ten four ghost, I have him loud and clear. Sounds like we are going to have at least one possible buy go down real soon, ghost keep your eyes peeled and field team be alert," Moreno transmitted over the point to point to his team.

"What's good my nigga?" The short male wearing the red baseball cap asked the male who called him over and the primary undercover.

"Yo, son right here need some hard. I'm blessing him with a few sacks of trees," The male wearing the black baseball cap said while referring to the Primary as the buyer.

"Yo! Do you know this nigga?" The male wearing the red baseball cap asked the male who called him over, as he looked the primary up and down in an intimidating manner.

"What?" Asked the male in the black baseball cap who was quite shocked of his buddy re-action.

"I'm just saying my nigga, shit it hot out here, niggas got murdered earlier today and poe poe is everywhere out this bitch hunting heads and locking niggas up," The male with the red baseball cap continued.

"I'm just trying to get me some get high playa before I go see this bitch up the block, if you don't wanna hit me off that's cool I'll keep it moving and find another player who ain't out here making scared money," Eric replied as if he didn't give a fuck about not making a buy at all, also he knew the phrase "MAKING SCARED MONEY" fucks with a hustler ego.

"Okay ghost, and field team. It seems like this other guy may be a little spooked about selling to the primary, but from the sounds of it, the primary may have a little more luck with the first guy. Ghost get a good eye on this for me," Moreno transmitted the members of his field team.

"Ten four leader, I'm on it," Brandon responded to the team leader. Brandon then crossed GRB and onto the strip between 134th and 137th Street.

"Let's move from over here son, we are standing too close to where them niggas that got blasted at," The male with the red baseball cap said as he pointed towards David's Grocery that was right next door to the liquor store. The male in the black baseball cap both acknowledged the male in the red baseball cap, and they all three walked over then stood in front of the barber shop a few doors away.

"My nigga, I don't make scared money. You know what I'm saying? You still want these sacks they twenties," The male in the black baseball cap asked while pulling out two zips containing marijuana.

"No doubt my nigga, but them shits you got are dimes!" Eric said as he took a good look at the product.

"Nigga, you bugging, these are some fat ass twenties sacks right here," The male in the black baseball cap responded attempting to stand by his product.

"Only way I'm gonna be spending forty cents on them shits, if I'm getting four of them, I work too hard for my paper nigga, I ain't poe poe,"

Eric responded in a manner to suggest we gonna do this or what. The male in the black baseball hat began to smile and reached out his hand to give the primary a hand shake while laughing.

"I'm just fucking with you my nigga, had to test you for a minute but it's all good," He continued. "

"Yeah baby, bless me," Eric said as he handed the male in the black baseball cap forty dollars as the male in return handed him two more bags, leaving him with the total of four bags.

"Okay ghost, and field team. Sounds like the primary just made a buy, ghost ten five (Repeat) the description of the sale subject the primary is with," Moreno transmitted over the point to point radio.

"Ten four leader, the primary hasn't left the set yet and is still standing with the male black wearing black hooded sweatshirt, black jeans and tan boot and also the male wearing the red baseball cap red hooded sweatshirt black jeans with red and black sneakers in front of the barbershop.

"Parton me earlier my nigga, shits hot out here and a nigga not trying to get locked down, with that being said how much you want?" The male with the red baseball cap asked the primary undercover.

"I feel you on that, I ain't trying to get bagged up either, I want four," Eric responded as he handed the male in the red baseball cap forty dollars of the buy money and in exchanged received four zips containing crack cocaine from the male in the red hat.

"Yo, take my number down so you can hit me up and it be no conflict, it's 917-555-5555 and ask for Mel," The male in the red baseball cap now known as Mel said as the primary undercover wrote his number down on the brown paper bag he concealed his large bottle of malt liquor in.

"Good looking out playa," Eric said as he shook hands withMel and began to walk away.

"Positive buy leader, two subjects, have my Ghost watch them as I step off the set Leader," Eric transmitted as he gave the buy sign (Signal to Ghost that a narcotic buy has been made) and continued to walk off the GRB set.

"Ghost speak to me! The primary transmitted a positive buy with the two sale subjects over the mic, field team get ready to move in," Moreno transmitted over the point to point radio.

"Leader, I got a positive buy sign. We got one male black wearing a black hooded sweatshirt, black jeans, black baseball cap and tan boots also a male black wearing a red baseball cap, red hooded sweatshirt, black jeans with red and black sneakers. Both sale subjects are standing in front of SHARP CUTZ barbershop located on GRB between 134th and 137th street. The barbershop has a purple and white awning leader.

"Move in leader, move in!" Brandon transmitted over the

point to point radio via hit ghost kit (Concealed wires that connect to point to point radio for transmitting by undercover detectives/police Officers) as he stood near the liquor store and made sure neither sale subject left the location without being seen.

"Field team move in!" Moreno transmitted and instructed his field team as he also responded to the set. The field team moved in swiftly and with force, and before the two sale subjects realized what was going on; they were already placed in handcuffs without incident.

Brandon the ghosting undercover quickly returned back to the vehicle and met up with Eric.

"Both the primary and ghost are back in the undercover vehicle, leader," Brandon transmitted as he sat in the passenger seat.

"Okay, good job undercovers. We need you guys to ride by the set and for a positive identification of the subjects (Required identification of apprehended sale subjects are to be made by primary undercover who made the purchase)" Moreno instructed his undercovers.

"Ten four leader, we are in route," Brandon replied as the two UCs headed back towards the set via the undercover vehicle, and observed both sale subjects in custody of the field team.

"It's a positive on both subjects, leader," Brandon related to the field team for Eric, so the sale subjects wouldn't recognize Eric's voice.

"Good job UCs, let's head over to the next set (Location for Operation on the Tactical Plan) Moreno transmitted to the undercovers as he observed the prisoner van field team members place the two handcuffed sale subjects in the vehicle without incident.

"Major is one hell of a trainer, ever since he took Eric under his wing and schooled him to the buy and bust game, it's been a rap!" Detective Dean excitedly said as he and the Moreno rode to the next set.

"I thought Anthony Rouhlac trained Eric?" Moreno replied as he scanned the streets in search of possible narcotic sale observation or possession violation (marijuana smoker).

"Nope, Rouhlac took him out showed him the ropes, but MAJ showed him the game and ever since then, he's been a buying machine," Dean responded as he continued to drive. "

Seems to be the beginning of a money-making night," Moreno cheerfully said as he rubbed both his hands together.

The Eric and Brandon luck continued the rest of the night, both made a total of four narcotic buys a piece, and ending the night with a total of twelve subjects apprehended.

"Okay field team it's wrap! (End of enforcement) Lets head into the 117th Precinct. UCs, good job, you guys can head back to the barn (Narcotic Unit Office)," Moreno transmitted to his field team while in route to the Precinct for arresting processing.

The members of the field team all acknowledge simultaneously and headed in towards their designated locations. Lieutenant Zaki sat in his office reviewing new kite folders that were recently placed in his box from the nitro office, until the telephone started to ring.

"Queens narcotics, lieutenant Zaki, how may help you?" The lieutenant answered.

"Hello lieu, this is Moreno. We grabbed subjects off that homicide location thanks to the UCs," Moreno informed his supervisor over his department issued cell phone.

"Great! What's the head count for the night?" The lieutenant asked as he wrote down the stats.

"We have a total of twelve bodies, including the two we got off the shooting location," Moreno responded.

"Good job sergeant, good job. Make sure every perp is debriefed by the squad, especially them two from the shooting location. Keep me posted.

"Ten four lieu," Moreno responded before ending the call.

CHAPTER 9

FLASH-BACK

DeV**onte decided to chill out with Erica** in the Jacuzzi to relax himself, while the others enjoyed the pool. The music playing in the pool house began to fade, as the effects of the numerous glasses of cognac he consumed began to take its toll on him. He started to think back to his years as a teenager, when he first started to make money. Growing up, He didn't have the designer clothes like others whom parents were fortunate to afford to pay for it.

Once he reached the age of fourteen, he became eligible to receive working papers and applied for summer youth employment. After getting that first taste of making his own money and not having to ask his parents for anything, he remained ambitious to find employment after school and on the weekends. He landed his first summer job right after graduating from Junior High School, and was assigned to the Bushwick section of Brooklyn New York. At the age of fourteen, DeVonte along with a former Junior High School classmate were the only two youths assigned to do custodian duties along with the regular porters.

At the age of fifteen, he worked summer youth at a Day Care center in the Bushwick section of Brooklyn. In the Mid to late Nineteen Eighties after turning sixteen years old, DeVonte started to work in the fast food industry. DeVonte was informed by his friend Rob, who was one of his schoolmates at his High School, that he just landed a job at the local Golden M Burger restaurant located on Pitkin Avenue in the Brownsville Section of Brooklyn. Rob suggested to DeVonte, that he should also apply for the job.

The sixteen-year-old DeVonte, knew he was now at the age he could forget about summer youth, and could make some money after school and on the weekends. DeVonte quickly applied for the job as soon as he got out of school that day. He was hired right there on the spot by a tall female black manager whom spoke with a Jamaican accent.

DeVonte's first assignment at the restaurant was to maintain the lobby (cleaning tables, dumping garbage, wiping tables and etc.) It was one of the worst assignment there. In the lobby, the worker must make sure the tables remained clean along with the seats, all the trays left in the lobby had to be collected and wiped clean, then issued back to the cashiers to issue with all the to stay orders. Spills, Vomit and all types of nasty shit was the usual to keep the lobby person busy working their ass off.

The garbage cans would fill up to the Max if they weren't monitored probably, and the managers would usually give you an ear full of shit for it, when they came out to check the conditions of the lobby area.

Being that it was the mid-eighties and the rise of the young drug dealers. DeVonte would see some of his former classmates from his elementary to present High school whom joined the drug dealing game, come to the fast food restaurant, while he worked in the lobby. Most of them, never made it to the nineties, due to the murder game that came along with their chosen profession.

During them times, many young men of the urban community fell game to the fast life, by slinging all types of narcotics and making a lot of money doing it. The fast flow of cash to an immature mind made many of these young hustlers very arrogant and they frowned upon does who earned a legal dollar. The young males who chose the legal life, were considered to being a square.

The fast food restaurant was located in a very known shopping area, and it was frequent by many shoppers from all over the borough of Brooklyn. Young drug dealers would do their shopping in the area, and hit known stores like Simons and Harry's located up the block on Belmont Avenue. They would later come into the fast food restaurant where DeVonte worked, with their girlfriends to grab something to eat.

Yellow gold teeth, large gold chains, two to four finger gold rings and latest designer clothes were worn like a uniform for a drug dealer who had little success in his line of work. Their female companions were usually very pretty with a sexy body. The ideal drug dealer's girlfriend, wore big gold earrings, carried designer hand bags that matched their boots or shoes they wore, as well as some gold name chains on their neck. A high percentage of these young ladies were gold diggers.

The Crack Era dawned the life in many gold diggers to rise to the surface. A guy could be the most handsome guy in the world b but if he wasn't hustling he was considered a cornball. Back then, if you weren't a drug dealer, hustler, ball player or a booster in the urban community, the gold diggers made sure they stood clear of you. Many of the young female gold diggers fell victim to physical abuse, sexual diseases and multiple visits to the abortion clinic destroying their young bodies at the hands of their dope dealing companion.

Many cases of HIV as well as many other sexual diseases was contracted from the drug dealers who slept with the drug abusing women as they exchanged sexual favors for drugs, and in many cases, this exchanged went unprotected. Mature drug addicted women giving birth to drug addicted children fathered by the young street hustler they sold their body to for crack or dope.

A lonely night hustling drugs led many drug dealers to make a sexual exchange for product, especially if the female addict had a fat ass. Female addicts would approach their drug supplier with money, ready to make a drug by and would be hit with a common proposal.

"Baby, you don't need to give me that money, hook me up with a quick blow job or some pussy, and I'll hook you up with some product," was a constant offer made to the female addicts who was out there feening hard.

Many women of the community, whether it was the average girl next door, a mother or grandmother whom came in the mist of this powerful drug, went from being functional within their family and their community. To sucking dick and getting fucked in urine odored staircases for crack cocaine.

DeVonte at his young age always kept a smooth swagger about himself even in his fast food uniform. He always tried to mimic the style of his favorite hip hop artist, and like Kane the ladies loved his smoothness. While working the lobby, if DeVonte noticed a dope hustler come in with a young lady he liked, he would work his way in her area as she waited on her male friend to return from the counter from purchasing food. Once he observed the hustler reach the counter and begin to place an order, he would politic the young lady and get her number at the drop of a hat.

Former class and school mates, as well as people from the neighborhood who became drug dealers, would offer him a job in the dope game stating:

"Son! Why you cleaning tables and flipping burgers for $3.35 An hour? I'm out here getting real money! I got pockets full of cash, I got the latest clothes, I got jewelry, I got two cars and I got a whole bunch of bad bitches. You want to get down with me and get this money or what? Or do you want to struggle for chump change?"

DeVonte wouldn't let the peer-pressure get to him and always rejected their offer. Some of those dealers respected his decision not to join them, while others would start a verbal confrontation.

"DeVonte was called a square or a cornball muthafucka so many times back then by the drug dealers he turned down to join them in the dope game, that he found it to be funny. Most of the guys whom called him that are now either serving many years in prison, dead or in the witness protection program for snitching. DeVonte got back on most of them by hooking up with their gold-digging girlfriends, when they went away out of state to hustle. Some of the young ladies even bought him designer clothes and nice gifts with their drug dealers boyfriends dope money is giving to them.

It was common for female boosters to hook up and become real friendly with most of the drug dealers back then. They would steal for their boyfriend or male buddy and save the guy a whole lot of money, in exchange the guy would lace her with fancy jewelry, designer bags and money. DeVonte always seem to catch the eye of a female booster that liked his swagger. On many occasion these females would hit Macys, Bloomingdales, Lord and Taylor and even A&S locations going unnoticed as they popped alarms and made off with expensive gear. DeVonte would be working in the lobby at the restaurant and they would stop by and hand him a shopping bag containing all types of Polo and Hilfiger gear.

DeVonte with his charismatic swagger even convinced the young ladies to go to the health clinic to check themselves out for sexual diseases, prior to him having sex with them.

The young ladies for some reason believed he was looking out for their best interest when he merely was looking out for his own. DeVonte was well knowledgeable of the hustler's sex for dope exchange, and didn't want to contract anything they may have passed onto their uninformed girlfriends.

The Manager at the fast food spot soon took notice of DeVonte's charisma with the female customers as well as the female co-workers, and he decided to re-assign DeVonte from duties in the lobby to working in the back near the grill: In which was a possible attempt to avoid possible future altercation with DeVonte's and the dope dealers that frequent the restaurant over their girlfriend.

"Welcome to the grill area! Pimp Daddy," said John as he started to load hamburger buns into the toaster in the work area. John was a very tall slim build guy with medium complexion male black whom spoke with a Caribbean accent and immigrated from the island of Trinidad, he also attended DeVonte's high school and played for the school basketball team, the school was located in the Flatbush section of Brooklyn next to Kings County Hospital.

"Excuse me pimping! But you need to ease up off them drug dealer's girlfriends, before you fuck around and get yourself shot up in here," Benny said as he stood next to John shaking his head. "Fuck, them punk ass niggas! If it wasn't for that drug money, half of them would still be that same ole piss smelling, nappy headed ass niggas they were before they started the drug game. Half of them didn't even know what pussy was, until they got some paper," DeVonte said as he looked at both John and Benny.

"Yo! I'm just trying to pull your coat to chill before you get fired or even worst shot. You should already know that the managers don't want any problems in here" Benny replied. Benny was a big tall strong guy. He played for his high school football team and had hopes of getting an athletic scholarship for college. Working at the restaurant kept him off the streets and away from temptation of fast money.

"Well, I'm just glad I'm back here to chill with the Big Dogs!

No more of that wiping dirty ass tables, moping vomit off the floor or dumping that stinky ass garbage out the trash cans shit for me. When do I get to these burgers and all that?" Devonte stated as he looked at his two co-workers with a smile on his face. John and Benny both looked at one each other for a quick minute and began to laugh.

"Your new jack-ass ain't cooking shit on this grill! You got the nuggets and the fish fillet station. Plus, you will be putting condiments on the buns and dressing the sandwich as we slide the patties on it," John said as he pointed out the area DeVonte would be working in. The smile on DeVonte face was now gone.

"John, you forgot to tell him the best thing about his new position," Benny said with a smirk on his face.

"And, what's that?" DeVonte asked.

"You have to wash all them dirty ass dishes piled up in the sink back there, and you have to filter all the oil fryers used to make the fries, fish, apple pies and nuggets before you go home," John quickly said to really erase DeVonte smile completely off his face.

DeVonte took a quick walk to the back to look at the sink full of dishes. He had an expression on his face when he returned to the grill area as if he wanted to quit. Wiping tables and the rest of the lobby duties didn't seem so bad all of a sudden. His strive for making more money, stopped him from turning down the alleged promotion. He realized the two experienced co-workers were just trying to school him on what he needed to know, if he decided to work in the grill area. John looked DeVonte up and down as he stood there in his uniform.

"Damn, the chicks you be talking to be hooking you up like crazy with all that Polo and Hilfiger gear," John said referring to the Polo Jacket and Flag Sweater DeVonte sported to work before changing into his uniform.

"That's why I keep them on my roster John; I take care of them and they take care of me," DeVonte responded with a smile on his face.

"I hear that! The chicks be keeping you clean like you they pimp or something. You must have the gift of gab or something, because you stay fresh," John responded as he complimented DeVonte on his wardrobe.

I don't get it. How the fuck does this skinny ass tooth pick, pull all these fine ass girls? And on top of that! What the fuck do he do to them to make them want to go out there and boost top notch gear for him? I must be doing something wrong Benny thought to himself as he began to shake his head and temporary hate for DeVonte's swagger.

"I wish I could get a chick to boost me some of them Gucci sneakers you were rocking the other day" Benny said as he snapped out his hate for a moment.

"Ain't nobody boosts them joints, I bought them with the money I've been saving. That extra overtime I make, from unloading the supply truck here comes in handy. I picked them Gucci's up from Bloomingdales last week for like three hundred and fifty bucks. It took me about three and a half paychecks to get them, "DeVonte quickly responded. Benny eyes opened up wide.

"Damn DeVonte! You paid three Hundred and fifty dollars! How much you be making on your check?" Benny asked as he wanted to know.

"Yo Ben! DeVonte be putting in mad overtime hours plus he scheduled for five days a week, unlike me and you. Don't be asking the next man about how much paper he makes! It makes you seem like a hater. You and I work around our athletic schedules at our schools. So, you should expect DeVonte to make more than us" John quickly said before DeVonte could reply.

"You're right, John your right! My bad DeVonte for my so nosey" Benny said as he took a sip of his courtesy cup containing orange soda, while not wanting to look like a hater.

After working at the fast food restaurant for a few months and getting to know John and Benny a little better, Deon decided to politic his co-worker by hooking them up with some gear, by asking his boosting female friends to pick up a few things in the fella's size. His female friends didn't mind at all when it came to DeVonte, and they also gained a free food connect with the fellas as well. DeVonte knew if he kept John and Benny happy they wouldn't snitch on him to the drug hustlers on how he be macking on their ladies, plus he got tired of looking at the two dressing like they shopped at the Bargain Center.

By June that summer, both John and Benny were high school graduates. John received an athletic scholarship to play basketball at a University in North Carolina, and Benny received an athletic scholarship to play football for a Miami University. They both increased their work hours at the fast food restaurant to earn extra bucks for college expenses, during the entire summer until it was time to head off to school mid-August.

Mr. Skate owner of the fast food restaurant DeVonte worked for, was a young black entrepreneur whom also owned another franchise in the state of New Jersey. The owner authorized a "GOING AWAY PARTY" at the request of his managers, for his two young hard working employees that were heading off to school in mid-August. The owner generously also threw in a $1500 bonus for the two, to use toward their college expenses.

It was a hot summer night on the first day of August, and Iron Mike Tyson was scheduled to fight in Las Vegas for the IBF (International Boxing Federation) title against Tony Tucker on Pay-Per-View. Mike Tyson, a Brownsville Brooklyn native, was working on his third title belt after winning the WBC (World

Boxing Council) and WBA (World Boxing Association) less than a year apart.

Tyson's ferocious and intimidating boxing style, took the boxing world by storm, and captivated the hearts of many living in New York, especially the Brownsville Brooklyn natives. Iron Mike would occasionally pass through his old neighborhood to visit some old friends and get a haircut from J-Rock, a local barber who claimed the title as "THE BARBER OF THE VILLE" as he perfected the high-top fade haircut.

Mike Tyson was the first heavyweight boxer to simultaneously hold all three titles, as well as the first individual to Unify all three titles since Leon Spinks in 1978. Beyond his personal and legal problems that followed during his career in the world of boxing, he set a great presentence in the urban communities all over the country, that anyone can rise from poverty with hard work and dedication.

On this hot August night, DeVonte took the day off work to attend a fight party hosted by an aunt of his friend Rick, so he was unable to make the "GOING AWAY PARTY" for John and Benny that was scheduled after closing time at the restaurant around midnight.

Rick's aunt resided in Rutland Plaza located in the Flatbush section of Brooklyn, that also went by the name of "THE NINETIES". Ricky's aunt always prepared a big feast for her fight parties, and only paid for fights when it was Tyson up deck, because she was a dedicated Mike Tyson fan. DeVonte and Rick were hoping to witness Tyson throw that vicious combo of "one shot to the body then an upper cut to the head" that usually sent his opponents crashing to the canvas.

DeVonte and Ricky walked to the Rockaway Avenue upper level train station in their neighborhood, and boarded the number three train. After two stops, they exited the train station at Sutter and Rutland Road and walked towards Rick's aunt building down Rutland Road

"Yo, I thought Michael Spinks was holding the IBF title." DeVonte said as he last recalled Spinks previously won the title a short time ago.

"They stripped the title from him, because he refused to fight Tony Tucker earlier this year" Rick said as he updated DeVonte on the current boxing events.

"Wow, they took his belt for that? Oh well, Tyson will beat Spinks ass next, if he decides he want to come for the title. He might change his mind after he see Iron Mike take the title from Tucker" DeVonte said having confidence that the Brownsville native was unbeatable.

"You think not? I just hope Tucker don't pull a Bone crusher Smith move, and hug Mike all night" Ricky replied referring to the fight Tyson had against Bone crusher Smith in Las Vegas when Tyson won the WBA title.

DeVonte and Rick arrived at Rick's aunt apartment, the aroma of fried chicken, fried fish, beef ribs and a whole lot of assorted soul food dishes minus pork, hit them in the face like a Mike Tyson punch. Mike Tyson's fight was scheduled as the main event, so everyone attending the fight party placed their bets on what round Tyson would finish Tucker. Everyone enjoyed themselves as they ate their delicious meal and engaged in friendly conversations during the opening fights.

The last fight of the three opening fights was over and it was now time for the main event. Every Tyson fan in the fight party, watched as their champion made his way to the ring. Tyson, the WBC and WBA Heavyweight Champ. Entered the ring first due to a coin toss. His record was thirty wins, with twenty-seven of them by knockout. Tyson entered the ring bare back with black trunks and black boxing shoes with no socks and red gloves. The signature jerking of the neck and small bald spot was observed once again by the world. Tyson paced the ring before he faced off with the six foot five-inch-tall Tucker and the center of the ring.

After a twelve round unanimous decision, Tyson earned his third title belt at the age of twenty-one years old. Even though Tyson didn't knock Tuckers block off, everyone was happy about Tyson's victory. Tony Tucker fought a good fight but was simply out matched by the young Tyson.

"Man, I thought Mike was gonna knock Tuckers Jeri curls out his head" DeVonte said as he and Rick left Rick's aunt apartment and exited her building.

"It was a good fight, and I'm glad Ike won" Rick replied as he looked at his watch once the mild night air hit them.

"Yo, lets hit your job for some grub" Rick suggested as his stomach began to rumble. DeVonte looked at his friend as if he was crazy. He could've sworn he saw Rick eat two large plates of food at the fight party, and just shook his head.

"Damn, you greedy muthafucka!" DeVonte responded as Rick started to smile. "If you really still hungry, we gotta hurry up to my job, before they pull down the gates and get rid of the leftover food," DeVonte said as they both began to pick up their step walking down East New York Avenue. Rick's greedy ass, decided to hail down a passing cab to get there faster. It only took a few minutes for them to arrive to DeVonte's job.

As they both exited the cab, DeVonte began to knock on the window to gain the attention of one of his co-worker whom was cleaning the lobby, once realizing the doors to the restaurant was locked. He could see that no customers were present and the place was closed for business, while the workers cleaned up their work areas. Teddy, one of the quietest guys at the fast food restaurant, took notice of DeVonte outside the window and dashed behind the counter towards the back of the restaurant. He quickly returned with the key and let DeVonte and Ricky in.

"Is the party still going on or what?" DeVonte asked Teddy as he looked around and noticed everyone looking a little stressed out.

"DeVonte, we just got robbed about a fucking hour ago!" Teddy replied as his hands was shaking while he wiped off a table.

"Robbed! Are you fucking serious?!" DeVonte shouted out loud gaining every one's attention.

"Yep, two muthafuckas came in here just before we closed. They were fronting like they were customers, until one pulled out a gun and put it to Brenda's face. He then threatens to shoot her, if she didn't do what he said," Teddy informed DeVonte as DeVonte remained in disbelief.

"Damn, that's fucking crazy! There's a fucking Police Station right up the block and they still had the nerve to rob this place," DeVonte responded while referring to the 12th Precinct located on East New York Avenue between Bristol Street and Thomas S.Boyland Avenue (formerly Hopkinson Avenue).

"Did anybody get hurt? Is everybody Okay?" DeVonte asked while showing concern for his co-workers.

"Brenda and Donald are shaking up, because they both had guns put to their head" said Teddy.

"Donald, why they pulled out on Donald?" DeVonte asked wondering what provoked that action by the thieves.

"One of the thieves ran to the back and put the gun to Donald's head and made him open up the safe" Teddy replied as he continued to clean the lobby as Donald appeared from the back of the restaurant to the front lobby behind the counter.

Donald was a husky dark complexion male black, that had a stuttered while under pressure. Donald was the youngest manager working at the restaurant. He was also the coolest.

As long as you did what you had to do, he would let you horse around until it was time to leave. On many occasions during closing hours, Donald would bring chicks in off the street and take them down to the basement storage area to have sex. He would have someone from the work crew, pack his female friends a bag of food, for them to take home after he finished with them.

"DeVonte! What What What you doing in here? We just just got robbed" Donald stuttered as sweat stood still on his dark forehead.

"I know, I just heard. Are you okay?" DeVonte asked as he noticed Donald was still stressed out.

"I feel like fucking quitting this job, but I got got got bills to pay you you know what I'm saying" Donald replied as He grabbed a broom and started to sweep the floors near the registers.

"I was heading home from catching the Tyson fight. I figured I'll drop in to see my boys off before they head off to school later this month, and I wanted to get some food." DeVonte explained to the young manager.

"The whole fucking 12th Precinct were here like forty five minutes ago, trying to get some free shit. I hooked them up all the time. You would think they would at least leave one cop car parked outside, but you know they don't give a fuck because this is a black neighborhood" Donald said referring to the precincts concern for the well-being of the restaurant workers after the robbery.

"The whole Precinct showed up to be nosey, but not one in sight as usual now huh?" DeVonte asked as he began to shake his head in disbelief.

"What did Mr. Skate have to say about you guys getting robbed?" DeVonte continued to ask.

"Mr. Skate is pissed off, and on his way here right now as we speak. So, don't take this the wrong way, but get you and your homie some food and say your good-byes to your boys now before Mr. Skate gets in here" Donald instructed DeVonte, knowing it wouldn't look right for DeVonte to be hanging out in the restaurant, while not being on the work schedule for the night.

DeVonte gave his congratulations and good lucks while he exchanged numbers with both John and Benny before existing the restaurant along with Rick and two full shopping bags containing fast food. Mr. Skate as well as many other business owners in the neighbor were insured, so he would be refunded for his lost in the robbery.

"Damn, I'm glad I didn't work tonight, everybody looking all stressed out and shit" DeVonte said as he and Rick walked towards their neighborhood down Pitkin Avenue.

"Of Course, they stressed out, with muthafuckas running up in there waving guns in their faces and all that" Rick responded while taking a quick peek into his shopping bag to see what type of goodies he have to munch on. "

"And the crazy shit is, the police are always in and out of the place. They either got to use the bathroom, cooling off from the summer heat or and staying warm from the cold weather outside," DeVonte said as he still tried to figure out the thief's chain of thought.

"Fool, God kept Yo ass out of there tonight. You don't know how to act under pressure" Rick said while remembering back to the time DeVonte knocked out a guy who tried to rob him at knife point. DeVonte broke the guy's jaw, after he continued to stomp him.

"You always bringing up old shit! That was a knife, these fools had guns" DeVonte quickly responded to let Ricky know he was no fool.

"Whatever man, you have a dark-side to you. And I'm not talking about your skin complexion" Rick jokingly said as he pulled a cheese burger to munch on as they continued to head home. DeVonte started to laugh, because Rick couldn't wait until he reached home to eat again.

The fall season quickly came, and John and Benny were off to their University. DeVonte and his friend Rob who put him on to the job, both took over as head grill crew members, and where joined by Teddy and a new guy named Sly. Rob and Sly both shared DeVonte's aggression in the hunt on making overtime at the restaurant, as they joined him when they came in before their shifts to unload the delivery trucks. The threesome, stocked the storage rooms as well as the freezer.

The extra hours put in weekly, had DeVonte, Rob and Sly average $150 to $200 a week after minor taxes withheld. It was a pretty good salary for teenagers to be making in the mid to late nineteen eighties. Teddy was now a senior at Art and Design High School in the City and worked only on the weekends. He focused more on going to college to pursue his dream of being a cartoon artist.

DeVonte and his partners in crime, would save their weekly salaries for a few months and go on mini shopping sprees at department stores like Macys, Bloomingdales and Lord and Taylors. On many occasions, they would run into friends or schoolmates at the department stores, whom where there boosting up a storm.

People who didn't really know the three hard working burger flippers, began to believe that they were dealing drugs or boosting clothes, because of the clothes they wore.

When in fact, they were working hard doing things the legal way. The customers waiting in line at the restaurant would observe the three as they came into work for their shift. They would be stared up and down in amazement.

"Damn, these burger flippers must be making money in here, to be rocking that fresh gear. Can I get an application to work here? Because I want to dress fly too like them dudes." Were the usual comments made by the customers as the trio walked behind the counter in their fresh gear.

Beyond DeVonte having a connection with drug dealer girlfriends and female boosters that adored and gave him gifts, when he first started working there. DeVonte had a connect with an old school mate that was down with a boosting crew called "Below Life" that were from Marcus Garvey Houses near Dumont Avenue in the Brownsville Section of Brooklyn.

Young Cee was a schoolmate of DeVonte since Elementary until High School. They remained friends throughout their entire school years together. While in high school, DeVonte bought a lot of merchandise from Young Cee and his crew of boosters. He later put Rob and Sly on to his hook up.

The Below Life Crew were out their getting theirs with all the latest gear magically appearing in their possession throughout the mid-eighties to late nineties. They were no joke when it came to popping alarms off shit they wanted. The young boosters appreciated the paper DeVonte and his work buddies were putting in their pockets in exchange for boosted merchandise, basically because it was their only means of income.

DeVonte at first had to use his gift of gab to convince the boosters to put him on, even though him and Young Cee were so cool. He first politic his longtime friend with the following question:

"What's the sense of having all that expensive gear on your back, if you don't have any money in your pocket?"

Young Cee was a smart kid and knew DeVonte was right, about him not having any money in his pocket. The two came up with a deal for Cee to boost certain things for him and he would pay him well for it. Cee and his crew went on later to boost for a number of people, especially for the local drug dealers.

DeVonte and Young Cee both attended G. W. Wingate High in the mid-eighties. While attending Wingate High, there was a few boosting crews and posse's that attended his school at the time. All the members of the boosting crews and posses mainly wore brands like Ralph Lauren Polo, Tommy Hilfiger, Benneton or whatever was on top back then.

Ralph Lauren Polo of course, was basically on top of the fly list, and had on lock in the urban hoods of New York City. If you had Ralph Lauren clothing with the Polo Flags, Ski Man on back of the Goose coat, the Polo Cookie symbol, Polo Teddy bear and Jean Jackets with the Ralph Lauren Flag emblem. You were someone that was labeled fly.

Working in a fast food restaurant as a teenager back then, didn't earn you any respect or street credit. Drug dealers and thugs, believed that anyone working in a restaurant was soft and a sucker. DeVonte liked his job and the money he made working there. He liked working in the grill area at the restaurant, because it had certain advantages and privileges. The advantage of not being easily seen by the public, compared to someone working the register or cleaning the lobby.

DeVonte's advantage was soon shorting one weekend, when he was observed near the cash register in uniform having conversation with a female co-worker, by Dexter a schoolmate of his. Dexter was a large framed, loud mouth West Indian guy from the island of Jamaica. Dexter was a member of a Caribbean gang called the RUDE BOY POSSE at DeVonte's High school. Dexter stood about 6'5" tall and possessed a very deep voice like the reggae recording artist Shaba Ranks. He was well known to intimidate people with his size, rugged voice and accent.

After spotting DeVonte in his work uniform at the fast food joint. Dexter decided to let it be known at the school, on how DeVonte made his money for some reason. Himself as well as many others, thought that fast food restaurant people were soft. So, the first day back at school after the weekend, he spotted DeVonte and a friend walking through the crowded corridor on the first floor. Dexter sat on a railing among his

Rude Boy Posse, that were all posted up in the corridor among the crowd of students.

Dexter started to stare at the passing DeVonte and placed a devilish grin on his face. The look in his eyes showed he didn't really care too much for DeVonte. It was later rumored that DeVonte allegedly stole a girlfriend away from him during his freshman year.

"Yo Dee!" The name DeVonte went by at the school, Dexter shouted. Me see Yo ras flipping burgers on Pitkin you know, at the bumbba clod restaurant," Dexter continued to yell out across the crowded corridor, causing everyone to stop and stare. Everyone in the corridor were kind of confused, because it was rumored DeVonte was a drug dealer or a booster, due to the expensive clothes he always wore every day.

"When you gonna hook me up mun, me thought you was flipping the beige rock or white powder, but you flip them blood clod burgers viciously" the hater continued to yell with laughter as DeVonte made his way towards him through the crowd of on lookers. The onlookers stopped their travels to their next class to be nosey and hungered for any type of action to go down.

As DeVonte smoothly made his way thru the crowd and approached Dexter who was still sitting on the rail.

"What the blood clod you looking at Yankee boy?" Dexter said as he raised his shirt to reveal the butt of a gun. The

Crowd of students started to back up a little, as DeVonte stopped in his tracks.

"Me knew you was a pussy! Yah better hook me up with a ras burger and fucking fries, when I come through to your job was last words Dexter could utter out before DeVonte slugged him with a crushing left hand to his face, causing Dexter to bang his head on glass window behind him. Dexter then fell off the rail in slow motion, as his posse looked at the action with amazement. DeVonte decided to go southpaw on the unsuspecting loud mouth, basically because he knew a right-handed punch would be more easily spotted traveling towards a face. A brief silence filled the corridor, as Dexter went down in slow motion like a falling giant.

"That's your hook up motherfucker! DeVonte said as he stood over Dexter who began to roll on the floor, while he held onto his eye grunting in pain.

"Dexter! Dexter! Yankee Boy, knocked Yo Ras the fuck out!" An onlooker loudly chanted as the crowd students erupted into laughter. One of the members of Dexter posse, started to reach into his waistband as if he was going to pull out on DeVonte, but was quickly stopped by Winston whom signaled him to stop.

Winston, the leader of the Rude Boy Posse at the school, looked on as one of his posse members got dropped like a sack of shit. He shook his head as Dexter laid on the ground in pain. Members of his posse awaited his signal to take DeVonte down, but only received the signal not to interfere. He basically knew that Dexter was wrong for starting shit, and wanted to give him the opportunity to walk the walk after he talked the talk. Dexter only proved to him that he was a fraud, and talk himself into an ass kicking.

Dexter! You played Yo self mun! Yah romp with the wrong Yankee, yah see. Give me yah pistol! You no longer a Rude Boy! Yah Gone, Pussy!" Winston said as he extended his hand for Dexter to hand over his gun. Dexter quickly handed Winston over his gun, got up and disappeared into the crowd. Winston then handed the gun over to another member of his posse, whom tucked the gun into his waist band.

"Much Respect to the Mun, everything is cool upon us you know?" Winston said as he extended his hand out towards DeVonte's to let him know he had no beef with the Rude Boy Posse. DeVonte acknowledged Winston as he notices the school safety guards making their way through the crowd of rowdy on lookers to locate the reason for all the commotion.

"Yo! No one better snitch upon this or they bumbba clod will get Ras dealt with!" Winston loudly warned the crowd, sending the message for everyone to keep their mouth shut.

DeVonte was then quickly pulled into a nearby stairwell as school safety officers approached the scene by his one of his classmates, giving him the opportunity to escape the scene unnoticed as he continued to his English classroom and taking his seat assigned to him without drawing unwanted attention from his teacher.

After the incident with Dexter, DeVonte gained major juice at his High School and was respected by all the posses and crews that thought they was running things. Winston put the word out if anyone tried to fuck with DeVonte, they were fucking with the Rude Boy Posse. DeVonte was suddenly transformed from a low key average guy that could dress, to a silent but deadly knockout artist, whom would put you on your ass if you fucked with him. Young ladies at the school became very attracted to the popular DeVonte, whom remained grounded and continued to hang with his real friends and ignored their unwanted attention.

"Are you going to sit in there all day rubbing your dick and daydreaming babes?" Erica asked as she snapped DeVonte out of his flashback while he laid back in the Jacuzzi.

"No babe, I was just relaxing letting my mind float back and forward in time" DeVonte replied as he looked up at his beautiful woman smiling. "Well float your gorgeous self out of that Jacuzzi, and join the rest of the party that's already getting their eat and groove on" Erica said as she placed her hands on her slim waist and returned a smile.

"Babe, I'm going to hit the shower first and be right out my love" DeVonte replied while he stood up and climbed out of the Jacuzzi gaining Erica's full attention towards his penis area, checking if it was still fully extended. Erica was happy with DeVonte's reply and exited the pool house, as she joined the others in the picnic area.

The sun was starting to set, and as soon as it did, the entire picnic area was lit up by the night lights DeVonte had installed that made it look like daylight.

CHAPTER 10

THE STREETS IS TALKING

Detective Dean cell phone started to ring, while he was filling out his arrest processing paperwork in the 117th Precinct. He checked his phone and noticed it was Slim, his confidential informant also known as CI in law enforcement, calling and he decided to answer it.

"What's up player?" Dean asked while answering his phone. He then stood up from the desk he was sitting at.

"Dean! What's up?" Slim quickly asked.

"Nothing much, what's up with you Slim?" Dean responded.

"I heard your people grabbed that fool that smoked them niggas in front of the store earlier today," He continued. Dean's eyes immediately popped open wide as he put a slight grin on his face and headed out the area in the precinct he was in. Dean began to think to himself that if this informant was telling the truth, his criminal sale of narcotics charge could also turn into a homicide apprehension.

Confidential Informants are really not to be trusted and would practically say anything to benefit in any way they could to survive. Most of them are part of the criminal element, and would give up their own mother for an extra dollar to get rid of the competition and mostly to reduce or avoid jail time. Many of the legendary street hustlers are either in jail or dead. There is also a number of them whom either quit the game entirely and those whom either in the past or are still in the present are still working for law enforcement on the down low.

Dean knew he would have to confirm that his informant wasn't blowing smoke up his ass and decided to quiz him with a few questions in the hope of receiving few good answers out of him before getting his hopes up high.

"Yeah right! We bagged up about twelve heads today, So I know the streets are talking. What make you think we got a killer out the bunch?" Dean asked as he threw Slim a line hoping he would bite.

"Yo Dean! Why you trying to play me like I'm thirsty or something? You know my info is always official and certified when it comes to the tales in the hood man!" Slim replied.

"Yeah, but you haven't informed me on nothing yet playboy. All you said was that we got the dude that smoked some cats today. You didn't hit me with a location, time or who got smoked! You know I need more than that Slim," Dean responded as he stepped outside of the precinct and into the parking lot.

"Dean! I could name the set you grabbed dude off of, but if you think I'm wasting your time. I'll just give the Crime Stoppers hotline a call and collect that reward. You want to let them take the credit after you drop home-boy off at the bookings later tonight?" Slim asked sarcastically.

"It's fine by me, if you think Crime Stoppers are going to pay you more money than I can get you for a non-high profile shooting of a couple of local jokers, "Dean replied.

"Did you forget, who put you on so you could afford to buy

that 750 BMW?" Dean continued as he asked Slim to help remind him who kept him on top of the game of getting money for important information.

"Damn Dean! Why you always got to bring up old shit" Slim jokingly replied. Slim knew that Dean was on point when he mentioned he kept him on top of the game. Dean practically helped him earn approximately $300,000 tax-free money from the City and Federal Government for pertinent information leading to numerous firearm and narcotic traffic take downs within one year. Slim practically was the best informant in the City and gave great information to law enforcement while he still continues to hustle on the streets 24/7. No one in Slim's community had any idea that he was the eyes and ears of the Police Department.

"Slim, I don't have the time to be out here playing games with you all night man! I got twelve bodies to process so let me know what's really good" Dean said while anxiously attempting to verify if Slim had any useful information.

"He's one of the dude's you guys bagged up on GRB (Guy Brewer Boulevard) near the liquor store earlier today" Slim replied.

"Which guy Slim! Which guy?" Dean repeatedly asked. "We locked up two guys over there," said Dean. Slim was becoming real hesitant on giving the shooter up so fast. He wanted to seal the deal on getting paid for his information.

"Come on Dean! Are you going to take care of me on this info? Shit been slow on the streets, and I need some paper you feel me?!" Slim asked while in hope he would be pulling in at least four grand for info on a double homicide.

"You have my word Slim; I will run it by the DA (District Attorney) and the Department like always! So, hit me off already with which guy already," Dean stated as he looked at his watch to check the time.

"The short muthafucka with the red on! His government name is Rahmel Jenkins, but we know him in the streets by the name of Mel. I think he might be a member of the Bloods or something, because he's always wearing red. But I can't confirm the gang shit, now and then he's flagging a red bandana out his rear pants pocket," Slim informed Dean as he cut to the chase.

"Rahmel, Rahme, Rahmel!" Dean mumbled to himself as he was trying to remember the names of the prisoners he arrested at the first set.

"Oh, Shit! Slim I'm going to hit you right back on your cell in a minute, I have to check on something real quick," Dean said as he quickly hung up with on Slim and ran back into the Precinct. Dean observed Detective Boyd standing by the photo copying machine making copies of the prisoner's property receipt forms.

"Hey Boyd, do we have a Rahmel Jenkins?" Dean asked. Detective Boyd then checked through some of the paperwork he was making copies of.

"Yeah, Why what's up?" Boyd asked. Dean looked over at the front desk and noticed the Desk Officer looking at him and Boyd have a conversation.

"Do me a favor, don't take any of our prisoners upstairs to the squad for debriefing yet, I just got a possible lead to today's homicide from my CI," Dean said as he whispered into Boyd's ear to avoid being heard by the Desk Officer at the front desk.

"You got it, I don't have the P-Van today, but I will give them guys a heads up to keep our prisoners in the holding cell after all the prints are done. I'll also let them know that you or the boss will keep them updated," Boyd responded as he completed his last copy and entered the holding cell area. Dean then walked off towards the area he was filling out paperwork, to inform his supervisor.

"Hey Boss, I have some good news. My CI Slim just called me on the phone. He told me that the streets were talking and that we got the shooter involved in that double homicide earlier today," Dean informed his supervisor whom happen to be pouring a small bag of Lays potatoes chips into his mouth.

"What!!" The sergeant mumbled, after nearly choking on the chips in his mouth.

"Slim just hit me up and said we got the shooter from the double homicide. I told him we would look out for him if the shit is legit," Dean repeated to his shocked supervisor.

"Ching, Ching, Muthafucka!" The happy sergeant shouted. A good day of enforcement leads an investigation that leads to cash overtime!" Sergeant continued to yell out as he pounded the desk with his large fist. Dean didn't want to draw too much attention, but his supervisor was starting to draw it. Dean put his hands up, to signal the sergeant to calm down.

"Chill out, before we get all hyped up. I have to call Slim back and really confirm this shit. Give me a few minutes to confirm so, we can get to work on this murder business," Dean said as he headed back out of the processing area. Sergeant Moreno wanted to congratulate Eric and his partner on a job well done. He reached into his pocket for his department cell phone, to place a call.

"Hello, Queens Narcotics Detective Porter, how may I help you?" Porter answered the telephone at the field operation desk.

"Dex what's up?, This is Sergeant Moreno," Moreno replied from the other end of the phone.

"What's up boss?" Porter replied as he picked up his pen and was prepared to take a message or notification.

"Nothing much Dex. I have two of my undercover's, Eric and Brandon heading back into the barn from the field. Have you seen them?" The sergeant asked as he awaited Dean's return.

"Hold on boss, let me check the movement log," Porter responded as he grabbed the rollcall to check if the two returned.

"Nope, they didn't sign back in yet boss," Porter stated as he closed the roll call folder.

"Okay, Do me a favor. Let them two guys know to give me a call as soon as they come in," the sergeant requested as he looked at his watch.

"Okay, no problem," Porter responded as they both ended their telephone conversation by hanging up.

Slim's cellular phone started to ring and vibrate on his glass coffee table, breaking Slim's concentration from his PlayStation game he was playing on the large screen television in his living room. Slim placed his black and mild cigar he was smoking into the ash tray then picked his phone up. He saw it was Dean and answered it

"What up?" Slim answered as he continued to play the game while placing the phone in between his ear and shoulder.

"Slim! Is that's you Slim?" The caller asked as he spoke with a whisper.

"Who else would it be answering my phone fool, yeah it's me!" Slim jokingly responded.

"Yo Slim! This is Dean. Are you alone? Do you have company?" Dean responded from the other end of the phone.

"Fool! I know who the fuck this is, you think you the only muthafucka out here with caller I.D.?" Slim stated as Dean could hear some laughter in the background after Slim's comments. Dean figured Slim had company in his apartment, because he seemed to be acting quite the comedian for the moment.

"Slim, what the fuck are you doing over there, man? Are you entertaining the troops again?" Dean asked as he wanted to cut to the chase.

"Yeah, I'm chilling with my niggas in the crib. As a matter of fact, I was just busting one of my boys ass in FIGHT NIGHT ROUND 4 on PlayStation," Slim said a he was pressing the buttons on the controller like a mad man. Dean was familiar with that PlayStation game, because he owned one himself.

"Nice game, which fighter you picked?" Dean asked.

"Mike Tyson of course! Give me two seconds because I'm about to knock George Foreman ass out!" Slim said as he continued to man-handle the controller and knocking the opponent out. Dean could hear the referee count out the fighter, then the people in the background laughing loudly.

"Told you I was gonna knock this nigga out!" Slim said to Dean as he passed the controller to one of his home boys whom was sitting on the recliner.

"Slim, I spoke to my boss about what you ran by me earlier, but I need some more information on this. Slim got up out his seat and started walking.

"Yo, I'll be right back! I got to go set up some quick paper," Slim said to his home boys as he headed out his apartment door.

"I guess you can't talk around your boys huh?" Dean asked as he overheard Slim conversation.

"Hell no, I'm not trying to let them fools in on my business and get labeled a Snitch. Why are you ear hustling my conversation, Dean?" Slim jokingly replied as he entered the stairwell of his building and headed downstairs towards the lobby.

"You know cops are nosey like a muthafucka, we ear hustle all day," Dean said as he started to laugh. Slim made his way to the lobby and exited his building. He wanted complete privacy so he walked to the parking lot and entered his car.

"Okay Dean, I'm downstairs in my car outside parked in the lot now, so listen up while I drop the jewels," Slim said as he closed his car door. He then started the engine, turned on the radio and prepared himself to tell the story.

"About a week ago, Mel got strongly armed robbed by them two mUtherfuckas that got smoked. I heard one of them fools tried to holler at Mel Shorty aka girlfriend, but she gave him no rhythm, while she waited on Mel outside his building. Dude got all upset because she ignored him, and started calling her all types of bitches and hoes, you know disrespecting her to the max. Dude knew shorty was Mel's girl, and I guess had that "What the fuck, that little nigga gonna do to me?" type of attitude. Mel's shorty got all upset and I guess told Mel, who arrived a few minutes later without his burner and stepped to them, dudes. I heard them niggas smashed Mel out. They stomped, punched and beat him none stop until his girl got on her cell to call the cops. Then they dug his pockets and took whatever money he had on him. He got lumped up pretty bad and his girl had to help him back upstairs to his apartment.

Now, here's the kicker, Dean! I heard them same two dudes got in a beef with Mel last night around 7 o'clock inside of David's Bodega at the front counter, in regard to them strong arming him and taking his paper. I guess he just happen to bump into them dudes on the humble and wasn't strapped with his burner once again. Anyway, after the beef in the store, the two fools decided they was gonna set up shop in front of the bodega like they owned the block. They wanted to send a message that they were taking over Mel's spot.

Once it got real late, say around 3 o'clock in the morning. Those two fools were still posted up, hustling in front of the bodega. All of a sudden, Mel just ran up on them fools dressed up in all black, and started blasting on them on some gangster shit. They said the little dude kept squeezing the trigger on them until his gun was on empty. Mel then ran across the street and cut through Rochdale Village so he reached his building.

"You have got to be shitting me, Slim!" Dean said as he was happy to get some information involving the double homicide that occurred earlier.

"Yeah Dean, go pull the surveillance tape from the bodega, so you can see the static at the counter they got into last night; then go pull the tape from Rochdale Village Security to check the movement coming out Mel's building early this morning," Slim instructed Dean as if he was schooling Dean on how to do his job.

"Slim, I can tell you have been watching your them cop investigation shows," Dean jokingly said as he finished writing the info giving to him down on his note pad.

"Yep, NYPD need to hire a real nigga like me to solve cases and shit," Slim said as he felt his information would put a few dollars in his pocket.

"In all my ten years on this job, I still can't figure out why these knuckle heads commit murder, then return to the scene as if nothing ever happened," Dean said, as he shook his head in disbelief of the same old pattern.

"It's the code of the streets. Your rep is all you got, and if a nigga violates, you better murder his ass. Then everybody would know, not to fuck with you," Slim explained as he started to look at his watch, noticing he spent too much time away from his apartment.

"Yo, Dean! I got to go playa. I got too many grimey ass muthafuckas hanging out in my crib, left unattended," Slim said as he was ready to hang up.

"More grimey than you?" Dean jokingly asked.

"Whatever officer asshole! Just make sure you take care of that money situation for me. As a matter of fact, hit me up when everything is a go, for it," Slim continued as he exited his car.

"Don't worry, I got you, Slim! Just make sure you listen out for your phone. And, be safe out there," Dean replied as they both hung up. Dean began to think to himself about how it was going to be a long night as well as a lot of overtime coming to him and his team. He knew that having a good informant like Slim, could enhance his career in law enforcement. Slim's loyalty to the streets came with a price tag, he would sell anyone out for a good price. Dean decided to call his wife to inform her, he wouldn't be coming home until possibly the next day evening due to extra overtime.

Working in the Narcotics Unit as well as other specialized units in the New York City Police Department, required many long hours from those members of the service whom choose to be assigned there. Many families were hit hard with separation and divorce due to less quality time spent by members in the Unit with their spouses and romantic partners. The more overtime you made, led to the less time you spent with your family. The term *Money Isn't Everything* is a true statement and exist on a day to day basis in law enforcement.

After hanging up with his wife, who wasn't so happy about not spending the morning with her husband. Dean then walked back into the precinct and gave his sergeant the full run down of what he was informed of by slim.

Moreno was pleased to hear the good information giving to his detective by the informant in regard to the double homicides. Moreno hoped of one day to be reassigned to the major case squad at his unit, in which his detectives would be handling the more high-profile cases. The current sergeant of the Major Case Squad is awaiting transfer to the Joint Terrorist Task Force, so many of the sergeants in the unit were trying to boost their evaluations up a notch to gain the soon to be available position; And thanks to all the good information Slim have been giving throughout the year, Moreno's name is at the top of the list.

CHAPTER 11

GOOD JOB

Eric and Brandon returned back to the barn, while the rest of the field team headed in to the precinct to conduct the arrest processing. He signed himself and Brandon back in the movement log, located at the field operation desk while Brandon returned the equipment to the equipment room.

"What's up TUC?" Detective Dexter Porter who was assigned to the field operation desk asked Eric as he monitored the surveillance camera monitors. The phrase "TUC" was a short-term name for Temporary Undercover that every newly assigned undercover Officer was labeled as they entered the unit. The veteran undercovers in the narcotics unit made it their business to call the new jacks and those with less experienced than themselves "TUC" to enforce their seniority in the game.

Porter was one of them detectives that grew up in the hard streets of Brooklyn in the 1970's and at the tender age of 18 he joined the United States Marines. Once he was honorably discharged two years later, he joined the New York City Police Department at the age of 20 years old. His recruiting investigator was so impressed with Porter's swagger and hard-core street appearance, that he made a phone call to a connect in headquarters to get Porter involved in a new pilot program that involved a joint taskforce between the police department and the federal government.

After six hard months of training in the police academy, Porter graduated with honors. Porter, along with a selected few of his classmates, never stepped their foot into a precinct to work. They were sent straight to special operations for undercover, narcotic and weapon trafficking training.

During his 25 years of undercover work, Porter had infiltrated hundreds of upcoming notorious narcotic drug organizations, made thousands of narcotic and weapon buys on a state and federal level, accumulated numerous combat medals from gun battles against stick up men posing as dealers. His impressive record pretty much spoke for itself, and the high-ranking officers at headquarters respected his work ethic.

Porter was quickly promoted to detective third grade after being on the job 18 months, while spending his whole time in the taskforce. He was then remarkably promoted to detective second grade a year later and reached the rank of detective first-grade within his fifth year on the job.

Lieutenants aren't too keen on supervising subordinates who earn just as much as they do. Porter's had major hooks (political connects) in the department, mostly all the rank of chiefs. If a supervisor under the rank of chief pissed Porter off, all it took was a mere phone call to one of his hooks and that supervisor would be administratively transferred or even demoted back to the rank of captain.

In the New York City Police Department, competitive promotional exams are taken to be promoted to sergeant, lieutenant and captain. Ranks beyond captain, are politically based on appointment by the department. Politics plays a major role in the promotion above captain. Officers ranked

Deputy Inspectors to the rank of Chief are at the mercy of the Mayor, Police Commissioner and Chief of Department to maintain that rank above captain. They are pressured to go with the flow of the Commissioner and Chief of Department or they may be at risk of demotion.

Everyone at the unit respected Porter, especially Eric whom thought of him as a legend. Eric knew Porter trained his partner Major to become one of the best undercovers in the city, and that all the skills Major taught him, originally came from Porter. Porter and Major had also known Major from way back when he was a quiet kid running around the hard streets of Brownsville, so when Porter found out Major joined the force and worked in the Housing Bureau; he made it his point to recruit him into the unit. It was ordered by a chief at headquarters, that Porter would be assigned to train Major once he entered the narcotics division.

After numerous years of good training, street level buys, high profile cases and some heroic actions made by Major on and off duty, he also reached the rank of detective first grade and gained a lot of respect at headquarters within a short length of time himself.

"Nothing much Dex! What's good with you?" Eric replied as he looked thru a file cabinet next to the desk for paperwork needed to process his buy.

"I'm good young man! Where's my main man at?" The veteran detective asked referring to Major as he leaned back in the reclining chair.

"He's on vacation for a week or two," Eric responded as he collected a few vouchers, narcotic substance testers and narcotic envelopes for himself and Brandon.

"Vacation! I just spoke to that sucker last week and he never mention to me he was going to be away. I have to give that chump a call later," Porter said as he handed Eric the property log book, that was located behind the desk so Eric could sign out the paperwork he was taking.

"Looks like you guys had a good night tonight," Porter continued as he noticed Eric collecting a lot of paperwork.

"Yep, Brandon and I did our thing out there tonight and made four buys a piece," Eric replied while feeling quite pleased with his activity for the night.

"Only four buys a piece? Man, that ain't shit! Me and Major use to have separate P-Vans (prisoner vans) and made sure we loaded them up with a least ten bodies a piece," Porter replied with a smirk on his face as he reminiscence of his past activity compared to Eric and Brandon's activity.

"Back then, we only got two hours overtime for each buy, so we had to grind hard to make our money," Porter continued.

That was back then, and this is now! Yah old bastard! Eric thought to himself after hearing the same old war stories from the experienced detective. Eric just looked at Porter and was ready to tell him to go fuck himself, but he knew better not to challenge the legendary veteran work record and status. Porter knew he pissed Eric off and cracked a smile.

"Where's your thick skin, kid?" Porter asked Eric, once he noticed he was starting to frown. "You got to have thick skin to survive in narcotics, Eric. Because, if you can't take criticism here in the office, you won't be able to handle the shit in the streets," Porter continued.

"Dex, I'm not even sweating, that shit you're talking about," Eric responded. Dex knew Eric was fronting, and knew he was growing more angry by the minute.

"Anyway! Times have changed since my days out in the field, so I'm going to salute you for a job well done my brother," Porter said as he leaned forward in his chair and extended his hand out to Eric for a handshake.

"Thanks, Dex, maybe one day I will make it to detective first grade after years of hard work," Eric replied after shaking Dex hand. Eric short spell of anger quickly disappeared once he received the compliment from Porter, in which meant a lot to him coming from the First Grader.

"Don't worry kid you'll get there one day, just keep your head in the game. If all fails, I'll give the commissioner a call." Porter said as he slammed his fist into the desk and began to laugh. Eric wasn't sure if Porter was joking or telling the truth about making the call to the commissioner, everyone knew Porter had connects, no one knew how far up the latter his connects went.

"I see your heading in the right direction, you're a hard worker unlike these other ass kissing, throat cutting muthafuckas getting promoted because they have political connects or blowing the higher ranks. I have seen a lot of do nothings at them promotion ceremonies making grade for just being a chief's secretary, making chief's coffee and being they hump buddies. I have no problem with making a call for a hard worker.

Keep your hustle on and make all the overtime you can. Money over fame is the name of the game. Fame ain't shit, and you are as good as your last buy. Fame don't pay bills or feed you. Money, is what you need to make the most of from this job, because the more you make, the more goes toward your pension. The bigger the pension, the more comfortable you will be when you retire," Porter stated to Eric while giving him a lesson on what's really important.

"I'm as good as my last buy, huh Dex? That's fucked up!" Eric said as he understood with the Veteran was hinting on.

"Exactly, remember that Janet Jackson song WHAT HAVE YOU DONE FOR ME LATELY? That's the Department! So, make that money," Porter replied. "

"From your mouth to my ears, I will be putting that in my mental Rolodex for sure," Eric said as he finished gathering up all the needed paperwork and started to head down the corridor towards his module. Porter suddenly realized he had forgotten to relate a message giving to him earlier, as he stood up and came around the desk.

"TUC! Your boss wants you to call him asap!" Porter yelled across the corridor as he caught Eric's attention before he turned the corner. Eric stopped in his tracks and turned around.

"Okay, thanks," Eric replied as he continued around the corner and towards his desk. Once he got to his desk, he made the call. Sergeant Moreno cell phone started to ring as he sat in the roll call room along with his team, whom were still conducting arrest processing. As he checked the caller I.D. He realized it was Eric that was calling and quickly answered.

"Hello" Moreno answered

"What's up Sarge?" Eric answered.

"Eric, You guys get back to the base yet?" Moreno asked as he looked at his watch.

"Yep, we just walked in, and I got the message from the desk to call you," Eric replied as he laid his paperwork on his desk. Sergeant Moreno then got up from his seat and exited the roll call room to head outside to the precinct's parking lot.

"Okay, good. Me and the rest of the field team gonna be at the 117 for a while, so make plans on staying later tonight and listen out for your phone," Moreno said while observing a patrol car pull into the parking lot.

"Later than usual? Why what's up?" Eric asked as he inserted a blank voucher into his word processor.

"Right now, it's very possible that you may have made a buy from the wanted shooter in that double homicide earlier today," Moreno informed the unaware detective. Eric heart started to beat fast.

"Stop playing Sarge," Eric responded as he thought the sergeant was pulling his leg.

"It's like you UCs like to say, I'm deadass!" Moreno replied.

"Which set? Which sale subject?" Eric curiously asked.

"The first set, on GRB. The guy with the red hat and hoody that sold you the crack," Moreno further replied.

"Oh shit!" Eric quickly responded. "No wonder dude was acting so nervous there," Eric said as he recalled his brief encounter with his sell subject.

"I'll have Dean give you a call with all the pedigree on all of the subjects. So just hang tight and soak up all of this overtime we are getting tonight," Moreno said as he was ready to head back into the precinct.

"No doubt Sarge, I'll see you guys when you come back in," Eric replied as he started to input information into the word processor.

"Eric!" Moreno shouted in the phone before Eric hung up.

"What's up Sarge?" Eric quickly answered.

"Good job detective, you're the man!" Moreno said as he checked his watch. Eric started to laugh.

"Thanks, Sarge, I'm the man today. But will you love me tomorrow? "Eric jokingly responded.

"You're a dick," Moreno said while laughing. "See you later" He continued as he hung up and ended their conversation.

Brandon suddenly entered into Eric's module area, as soon as Eric hung up from Moreno. He had already changed out of his buy and bust clothes and back into his regular causal street clothes. He walked over to Eric's desk looking for the paperwork Eric retrieved for him. Eric pointed over to his file cabinet once he realized what Brandon was looking for.

"Damn! Don't you think it's time you go change out them funky ass clothes?" Brandon asked. "I'll keep an eye on your product and paperwork until you get back," Brandon said as he observed Eric still dressed in his buy and bust clothes and sat at the desk directly across from him and turned on one of

Eric's teammate's word processor.

"Thanks Bee, I'll be right back" Eric responded as he quickly got up from his desk, placed the narcotics he purchased in his file cabinet and locked it. It wasn't that Eric didn't trust Brandon to watch the bought narcotics, he knew that it could end up missing at the drop of a hat if Brandon took his eyes off it for a second. The Narcotic Unit as well as many other specialized units possess many haters whom would do anything to fuck over someone who is shining.

"Hey E! Did the arresting officer call in the pedigree of the subjects yet? "Brandon asked as he loaded an evidence voucher into the word processor. Eric realized he didn't tell Brandon what was going on.

"Not yet, I just talked to Moreno before you walked in. He said for us to standby for pedigree and to prepare for a long night of overtime," Eric said just before heading out the module and to the locker room.

"Why? What happened?" Brandon asked.

"They think I brought from the shooter of that double homicide near Rochdale Village," Eric informed Brandon with a grin on his face.

"Yes! We about to get paid," Brandon responded as he rubbed his hands together.

"That's right playa! Paid very well tonight," Eric said as if he was about to make a million dollars in overtime. "I'm gonna leave my phone here, just in case Dean or Sarge call with the pedigree. Make sure you listen out for the phone, I'll be right back," Eric continued as he headed to the locker room to change his clothes.

"Okay, Okay already E! Go change them clothes dude. You're stinking up the place. It smells like funky feet and piss in this mutha," Brandon jokingly said as he waved Eric off. Eric threw up his middle finger and continued to head out his module.

CHAPTER 12

WEEKEND AT DEVONTE'S

THE SUN WAS STARTING TO SET, and as soon as it did, the entire picnic area as well as the entire backyard was lit up like a football field during Monday night football, by the night lights DeVonte had installed all over his landscaping. The music echoed through the air, and the stars above began to get brighter.

DeVonte quickly showered in the locker room, moisturized himself with body lotion and scented himself with his favorite cologne. He then changed into an all-white Gucci linen shorts set he had stored in his locker. He then exited the pool house with a fresh glass of cognac he prepared before he decided to head out into the picnic area.

"Yo Dee! I thought you fell asleep in the Jacuzzi my man." Rick said as he seen DeVonte approach the picnic area.

"Nah Rick, I just crashed a little to re-energize my brother," DeVonte said as he took a seat at the table next to Erica.

"Oh Babes, I'm loving that outfit you're wearing," Erica said as she leaned over and whispered into DeVonte ear.

"Thank you, Babe, and thank you for buying it for me my love," DeVonte replied just before giving Erica a soft kiss on the lips.

"Your welcome. You know, I love to see you in white" Erica said as she rubbed her hand up and down DeVonte's back. DeVonte began to tear into the large plate of food that Erica prepared for him, while he slept in the Jacuzzi.

"Mike! Thanks for blessing us with your skills on the grill, the food taste excellent as always," DeVonte said out loud as he demolished his plate within minutes and then washed it all down with a tall cold glass of lemonade ice tea.

"Thanks, Dee! I appreciate the compliment." Mike replied with a smile on his face as he stood up and took a quick bow.

"Man, sit your fake Chef Boyardee ass down or pass the damn hot sauce," Dennis jokingly said causing everyone to laugh out loud at the table. Mike quickly tossed the bottle of hot sauce across the table to Dennis. Hoping it would hit him upside the head. Dennis caught it without even looking in Mike's direction

"Whoa! Check out the reflex on that," Rick said as he observed the catch.

"My reflex sharp like a razor blade," Dennis replied as he untwisted the bottle cap and began to pour sauce on his barbecue chicken.

"Mike! You're a beast on the grill," Jason said, as he stood up and headed over to get a second serving of food.

"I second, that statement," Doreen yelled out without warning as she also jumped up to go get a second helping at the serving table close by the grill. Mike couldn't help but to look at Doreen as she walked over to get more food. Her thick goddess body physique and beautiful face made his blood flow in the right direction and demanded attention. DeVonte made his way towards the Tiki bar to make himself a fresh glass of cognac on the rocks with no chaser. He then hit the surround stereo system to mute and held his full glass up high for all to see.

"I will like to thank everyone for taking the time out to come hang with me and my lady this weekend. Having old and new friends surround you is a true blessing and I'm very thankful to have you all here. So for the remainder of the night and weekend, if you want a cocktail, beer, some wine, soda, a glass of water, snack or a bite to eat, don't ask me shit (He laughs). The Tiki Bar and Serving table is now self served, so get your eat, drink and groove on. DeVonte said as he watched everyone raise their glasses to join in his toast. DeVonte then scrolled down on the stereo remote control LCD screen that had a list of musical artists listed and clicked on R.Kelly's name.

"IT'S GONNA BE A PARTY YALL" blasted through the speakers as R.Kelly And Keith Murray song "House Party" filled the air and moved the small crowd.

"Anybody down to do a few shots," Rick asked as he made his way behind the bar and held up a large bottle of Patron in his hand.

"Pretty Ricky sit your ass down and stick to them sweet ass daiquiris you've been catching brain freeze from all night, that Patron right there will straighten out your

SCurls Nigga, you ain't built for that," Dennis said as he started to laugh. "Somebody done told you wrong my brother, Pretty Ricky could hang with the best of them and out do the rest of them" Rick replied to defined his liquor tolerance.

"Yo, Dee! Where's that bottle of Tequila with the fat ass worm in it? Since Pretty Ricky could hang, let's see him sip on straight fire," Dennis yelled over to DeVonte whom was hanging in the cut.

"Come on now, Rick! Last time you called yourself doing shots of Tequila, your ass woke up butt naked in the jacuzzi full of ice water the next morning," Jason said as he pointed towards the pool house while he along with all the guest laughing at the story. Rick then looked at Jason with a facial expression of embarrassment.

"Yall fools, didn't have to do a brotha like that. I almost froze my fucking balls off," Rick said as he started to smile from ear to ear.

"What did you expected us to do? You were screaming and whining like a bitch. I'm hot! I'm melting inside!, Help me lord! Help me! So, we figured we would cool you the fuck off by throwing your ass in a tub of ice water. That was the only thing that made you shut the fuck up!" Jason jokingly said as he reminiscence of the event. DeVonte started to laugh out loud, almost spilling his drink on his white linen as he rocked back and forth.

Stacey stood up from her chair, walked over to the Tiki Bar and sat down on a stool.

"I'll do a few shots with you Rick, if you like?" Stacy said as she dazed into Rick's hazel eyes.

"Rick before you do that, could you hook the rest of us ladies up with another one of those delicious daiquiri you've have been preparing all day" Erica shouted out as she held up her empty glass.

"Hey Issac!" Mike said jokingly (as he compared Rick to Isaac the bartender from the love boat)

"How about making some Thug Passions for me, Jason and Dennis, unless you're just serving the ladies tonight" Mike continued.

"Ladies first Jason" Rick replied to the request as he loaded up the blender with ice, to make the strawberry daiquiris. DeVonte whom was enjoying the atmosphere, the music from the surround sound and the glass of cognac he was still working on, leaned over towards Erica and whispered in her ear.

"Let's blow this scene for a little bit. I wanna shoot a little pool with my favorite girl," DeVonte softly whispered into Erica's ear, sending chills up her spine with his deep seductive voice tone. Erica started to smile and leaned her head back into DeVonte's chest as she wrapped his arms around her.

"Are you for real Babes because......." Erica responded before DeVonte cut her off.

"Babe I want you, right now. Walk with me" DeVonte quickly whispered cutting Erica's sentence short.

"Excuse me bartender," Erica said referring to Rick whom was preparing her drink. "Can you please put a rush on my drink, I'm gonna need it to go," She jokingly continued as she leaned back once again into DeVonte's chest and kissed him softly on the lips. Erica loves it when DeVonte gets in a freaky mood, it turns her on automatically. As she waited on her drink, she reached her hand under the table and grabbed onto DeVonte's already stiff cock. DeVonte then softly removed her hand and stood up from his chair and started walking towards the side door entrance into his home, while sipping on his glass of cognac and avoiding attention drawn to his hard penis. Erica watched DeVonte as he walked into the house, then she got up herself and walked towards the bar and impatiently waited for Rick to finish preparing her drink.

"Rick! What's up with my drink? My man is waiting on me," Erica said as she leaned her head onto Stacy's shoulder whom was sitting at the bar.

"One express daiquiri to go," Rick said as he completed his first drink and handed it to Erica.

"Thank you, you're the best," Erica said as she took a sip and quickly made her way to the house.

Once inside the house Erica walked down the corridor and into the darkened entertainment room. She called out DeVonte's name, then suddenly the hanging light above the pool table came on. DeVonte was laying on top of a black silk sheet across the pool table, with his feet dangling off the edge. He was shirtless exposing his chiseled chest as well as his ripped ABS. Erica then dimmed the light and removed all her clothing as she placed her hands on the large tent that stood up from his shorts. DeVonte was faded by the numerous glasses of cognac and had that numb feeling that let him know he was high.

Erica placed her drink down along side the edge of the pool table, and began to unfasten DeVonte's shorts gently.

Once she unfasten the top button, she began to kiss him gently along his abdominal area as she pulled down his zipper. The song "FORTUNATE" sung by the Brooklyn native Maxwell began to play over speakers as Erica reached into DeVonte's boxers and removed his long thick rod. She gave his fat mushroom tip a soft kiss, then reached over with her other hand and retrieved her drink. She took a long sip of it before placing it back down, then opened her mouth up wide and slid DeVonte's hard cock in and out of her mouth slowly while flickering her tongue on it. The cold tongue sent a chill thru DeVonte's body, causing him to get goose pimples as it made his body shiver.

The intense pleasure of Ericas soft warm mouth, caused DeVonte to moan. She used no hands in the act of her oral technique. DeVonte motioned to grab her by the hair, but Erica quickly pushed his hands away. One thing a man should know when it comes to having relations with a black woman, never mess with her hair, or it could end your whole night. The more Erica sucked on his hard rod, the thicker and harder it became. The hot wet saliva began to splatter on Erica's face as she began to motion her head up and down sliding DeVonte's cock further down her throat until her lips kissed his nuts.

Her clitoris stood erect as she gently massaged it with her finger, causing it to get soaking wet. It wasn't too long before her juices dripped down her inner thighs. DeVonte was turned on by her moans. The veins in his dick began to pop out from the mere thought of sliding into her hot pussy.

Erica couldn't wait any longer as she to climbed on top of the pool table. She hovered her wet pussy over his stiff dick and let her wet pussy drip onto it, as it slid down to his balls.

She straddled him and started humping on his stiff manhood, causing him to moan. Once her clit became too sensitive to touch, she took a deep breath and shoved him inside of her. Once he was inside of her, Erica rode DeVonte with force until the juice between her legs turned into milky cream.

Suddenly, an atomic climax erupted through out her ass beat his balls like a drum, as it smacked against them while she rode on top of him. DeVonte began to squeeze and suck on her breast as he stroked her from the bottom. The flickering of his wet tongue against her sweet brown nipples, aroused Erica more and more until she climaxed again, that her pussy began to squirt out hot love juices that leaked all over his nuts. The flickering of the nipples and rapid motion of his pipe sliding deeper and deeper into her body along his balls hitting up against her asshole, Erica body began to tremble uncontrollably as she gasps for air. Her eyes rolled up in her head. She began to dig her nails deeply into DeVonte's chiseled ripped chest, as she continued to grind her pelvic area against his.

"What the fuck! What the fuck you doing to me! Oh Shit! Ooooh Shit! Yeah, fuck me! Yeah, fuck me, baby! Ahhh Ahhhh Ahhhhhhhhh!," Erica roared as she started to cum and squirt all over DeVonte's pelvic area. Her sexual bodily fluids dripped down his waist and onto the silk sheets he laid on to protect the pool table. Erica body continued to tremble as she leaned over to kiss his chest as he squeezed her juicy ass.

"You think everything is alright in there with our girl, she has been MIA for a minute now," Alexis said as she whispered into Doreen's ear.

"What! Girl, she is doing way better than us right now, we out here talking among ourselves, while the men are over there talking sports and shit," Doreen responded as she continued to look in Mike's direction.

"Your right about that" Alexis said as she began to shake her head.

"Besides, she's probably in there fucking that big dick man of hers," Doreen continued as she simulated on how big she thought it was. Alexis nearly spit her drink out her mouth, because she wasn't prepared for Doreen's comment.

"Bitch, don't even act like you didn't see that long dick print in them linen shorts he had on. No disrespect to Erica, but I was about to yell snake out this muthafucka when he got up," Doreen said as she started to laugh. It was clear to her friends that the effect of her icy drink have taking over her.

"Girl, you are a hot mess. You know damn well you ain't suppose to be looking at Erica's man like that," Alexis said as she decided to have a sip of her drink without almost choking on it this time.

"Let me tell you girlfriend, I don't want her man. I plan on leaving a big wet mess on that one over there," Doreen said as she boldly pointed toward Mike whom was unaware of what was going on.

"Babe, I could still feel your pussy hole throbbing, it feels like a pair of lips sucking on my dick," DeVonte whispered to Erica as she laid her head on his chest and attempted to catch her breathe from the intense climax she just encountered that left her weak.

"Oh babes, your dick was in my belly," Erica joking said as she rubbed her stomach. "I'm so weak right now. I have no energy left. I can't even feel by legs; I'm ready to go to bed. My stomach hurts and I can't even feel my legs" Erica continued to babble. DeVonte started to laugh.

"For real? Did I do all that to you?" DeVonte jokingly asked as he held his lady in his arms.

"Yes! Your dick is excellent and I need some more," Erica said in a soft and weak whisper.

"No No No, you have to re-energize yourself. We have guest out there, whom might just pop up in this room at any minute looking for us. I'm gonna clean up real quick, so we could join the rest," DeVonte replied as he got up from the pool table, and lifted Erica up. Erica quickly wrapped her arms around his neck and her legs around his waist. He carried her across the room towards the bathroom located inside the entertainment room.

"Okay, put me down Babe. I need to go to the bathroom," Erica said as she kissed DeVonte on the neck, just before he placed her on her feet. Erica then walked into the bathroom and soaked two wash cloths with soap and water.

"Babe, I'm gonna need a cold cloth to kill this snake," DeVonte jokingly said as his manhood still stood at attention. "I hope you know your gonna have to feed this snake again later," DeVonte continued as he was referring to having more sex with her later. He walked back over to the pool table and laid back down, while awaiting Erica to wash him off. Erica returned and placed the cold soapy cloth on the tip of his manhood and slid it up and down with a gentle grip as she cleaned him off.

Once DeVonte was cleaned, Erica then cleaned herself with the warm cloth. They both got dressed then exited the entertainment room hand and hand with a smile on their faces.

Upon arriving back outside, DeVonte notice there was still separation of his male friends and Erica's friends.

"Hold Up! What's up with the segregation in here? Where's the love?" DeVonte shouted out. "I see the guys over here and the ladies over there! Where's the unity? Where's the love my people?" DeVonte continued to shout, as he and Erica made their way to the Tiki Bar. He reached for the remote to the surround sound that was sitting on top of the Tiki Bar counter and scrolled down the music selection LCD screen.

"My man Michael got something for you all to hear, so you can get them out your system and mix and mingle," DeVonte announced to his guest as he pressed play on the song BUTTERFLIES by the gloved one. As the beat of the song thumped Erica started to do her two step close and personal against DeVonte, who did his own two step of his own.

"Look at the cute couple dancing," Rick said referring to DeVonte and Erica, as he poured DeVonte a glass of cognac and passed it to him over Erica's shoulder while they danced.

Everyone stood around as they watched the two love birds do they thing on the dance floor.

"Yeah, look at them. Looking like a fake ass Martin and Gina," Stacey jokingly said causing everyone to burst out into laughter.

"Go Martin! Go Gina! Go Martin! Go Gina!" The onlookerschanted as DeVonte attempted to do the classic dance move Martin Lawrence did on his show, causing everyone to laugh before they all eventually joined in. Now the ice had finally been broken, and everyone was enjoying themselves.

As the night grew later, the whole party set turned from up tempo to chill out mode. The guys and girls started to pair up into couples, Of course Doreen got all close and personel with Mike. Stacey and Ricky set up post near the tiki bar and Dennis and Jason were entertaining the two sisters Alexis and

Chantel at the picnic table near the barbecue pits.

"Stacey! How have you been doing since I saw you?" Rick asked while he started to make Stacy another icy drink.

"I'm good Pretty Ricky and you?" She smoothly replied.

"Here you go, with that Pretty Ricky talk," Rick replied. Beyond me being pretty. I'm just living and enjoying life. Shit! I'm trying to look good and young as you. You know what I'm saying? Rick continued as he poured the icy drink out of the blender and into two glasses.

"Thank you Rick, or should I say, Slick Rick." Stacey replied. "Who's the lucky lady in your life? Stacey asked as she took a sip of her daiquiri while looking him in his eyes.

"I'm looking at her," Ricky quickly replied as he smiled and winked at Stacey, showing his perfect white teeth that nearly glowed in the dark.

"Wow, Is it my drink? Or are you just getting smoother and smoother by the minute?" Stacey asked as she started to smile. Rick always had a thing for Stacey from the first day they met, but last time he saw her she was seeing someone at the time.

"What up with you and the guy that came with you to the last event, the last time I saw you? Ricky asked curious to Stacey's relationship status.

"He's the past, and really wasn't nothing serious. We weren't even in a relationship," said Erica.

"What do you mean by that?" Rick asked.

"Well, we hung out and fucked on some occasions. Nothing major beyond that," Stacey explained.

"So, if yall was cool like that. What happened?" Rick asked as he grew more nosey.

"I started to see signs in him, that made me glad I made the choice not to be in a serious relationship with him.

"Signs? What type of signs?" Rick asked.

"Simple things, like him showing up to the club on girls night out," Stacey said as she took another sip of her drink.

"Damn, he was on it like that? But I thought you said you two weren't serious or nothing," Rick said as he became confused.

"We weren't at all! But dude use to ask me, what I was doing for the night? So, I would tell him about my plans on hanging out with the girls at a certain bar or club. Don't you know, that stupid muthafucka would be at the spot before I get there waiting on me to show up," Stacey said as she recalled the guys actions. Rick started to laugh, because he witness a few clowns doing the same thing at the clubs he has been to in the past.

"Hold up Rick, that's not even the half on why he got his walking papers. I moved upstate near Woodbury Commons, where I built a house for me and my kids. He was around when I was going through my building process and what not, and rode up there with me a few times when I went to check on things. I moved in last September and me and him of course blessed the house a few times. The last time we fucked was probably in October. After that, I really didn't have any time for him at all.

The commute back and forth, along with the other shit I had on my plate. What we had, turned into a mere phone call every now and then. By the next year, around May. He asked me could he use my mailing address for his car insurance and I told him no. A month later, I check my mail box and I noticed a letter from the Department of Motor Vehicles addressed to this muthafucka. It was a fucking drivers license with his name, photo with my address," Erica said as she became a little angry as she reminisce of the asshole she once dated.

"Damn! That nigga violated like that? Ricky asked.

"Hell yeah!" Stacey sarcastically replied.

"So, how did you handle that?" Rick asked as he grew nosey for the action taken.

"At first, I just called him and asked. Why would he do that? When I told him no. He just laughed and acted like it was no big deal. So, I gave him a few warnings to change the address, then I simply dropped the drivers license off at State Police station.

"How did he get to use your address? Didn't he need a bill or you to verify that he lived there?" Rick asked because he knew he had to have proof of address when he visited the Motor Vehicle and changed his residence.

"I have no idea of what that fool did, but what ever happens to him is his own fault," Stacey said as she shrugged her shoulders and took another sip of her drink.

"I hear you on that lady, you too fine to be dealing with a jerk like that," Rick said as he looked into Stacey's eyes.

"Well, you know at first he was cool and everything. Plus he was like a rebound from me just separating with my children father," Stacey said.

"Guess he came into your life when you were nice and vulnerable," Rick replied.

"I guess so. I let him know from jump street, I wasn't looking for a serious relationship at the time. And he claimed he was cool with that," Stacey said. "We kicked it for about ten months, and he made it pretty clear he was out there doing his own thing with other women. Yet, he would catch feelings if he sensed I was getting involved with another man. You know how you men are!" Stacey continued.

"Not all men get down like that," Rick responded as the two continued their conversation.

"Excuse me Mike are you still handling chef duty?" Doreen asked as she leaned over and whispered in Mike's ear.

"Only for you lady, what do you want me to bring you?" Mike responded.

"I was wondering if you can give me a long thick hot sausage, if you don't mind" Doreen said in a very seductive voice. Mike's eyes widen, as a result of Doreen's boldness that left him speechless for the moment.

"Don't get it twisted; I'm talking about the meat that's in the pan, not the one in your pants," Doreen jokingly said.

"I think I'll save that one for desert," Doreen continued as she started to laugh because it seemed like Mike was getting a little nervous. Mike started to smile.

"Are you always this bold?" He asked as he whispered back in Doreen's ear before standing up.

"Why? Do I scare you? Doreen responded as she licked around the rim of her glass.

"Nah, you need to be scared of me. I'm the last guy in this house you want to tease," Mike responded as he walked over to the table with the food and retrieved what Doreen wanted as well as food for himself.

"Oh, is that right?" Doreen said as she looked at Mike from the corner of her eye.

"Only time will tell, and my watch has been ticking since I first laid eyes on you," Mike said as he returned to where Doreen was sitting with both of their plates.

"Whatever father time, we will really see what time it is, when that time comes," Doreen said as she began to laugh out loud as she continued to work on her plate.

"Yes, we will," Mike responded with a devilish grin. "In the meantime, all jokes aside. Tell me a little about yourself. Are you seeing someone? Do you have kids? What do you do for a living?" Mike asked before biting into a cob of sweet buttered corn. Doreen took a sip of her drink, to wash down the food she was chewing.

"I'm very single; I have no children, I'm a registered nurse with goals to become a head nurse and I like men with big dicks," Doreen answered with a smile on her face.

"Nurse! The way you be talking smack, I would've never guessed that in a million years" Mike replied as if DeVonte didn't mention it earlier to the fellas. Doreen leaned back in her chair and started to laugh at Mike's comment

"I've been serving the people for about ten years now, and I love what I do," Doreen proudly responded to mike's comment as she gazed into his eyes.

"I don't doubt that at all. It's just that your so out spoken, that it's kind of hard to believe," Mike said to Doreen as he tried to cool off the conversation as he took another sip of his Thug Passion.

"What's so surprising about it?" Doreen responded as she stared him right in his eyes. "Are nurses supposed to be nerds and as quite as a church mouse? " Doreen asked.

"Well, most beautiful women like yourself are usually shy, laid back and conceited. But your different, your friendly, outgoing and may I say very bold," Mike said while giving Doreen his perception of how he views her character and tried to combine the thought of her being a nurse.

"I appreciate the compliment Mike, you're not a bad sight on the eye yourself, plus you're the type of eye candy I like," Doreen said as she began to blush while she gracefully returned the compliment of good looks to Mike.

"Eye candy! That's the first time I have ever been called that before. I appreciate the compliment, especially with it coming from such a beauty like yourself," Mike said as he looked into Doreen's light-colored eyes.

"I see you're as charming as you are handsome. I love it when a man looks me in the eye as he speaks to me," Doreen said as she took a brief look at Mike's bulging muscular chest.

"Who wouldn't want to look into those beautiful eyes?" Mike replied as he moved his face closer to hers as if he wanted a kiss. "I hope you have a sweet tooth, for this eye candy," Mike jokingly continued to say with a smile.

"Everything on me is sweet baby. My tooth, my tongue, my breast, my lips and everything in between and in the back of my hips," Doreen boldly said as she flexed her breast as if they were pecks. Damn Mike thought to himself, as he looked at her big breast jump up and down.

"I see, I can count on you to always say what's on your mind," Mike replied while he stared at Doreen's full set of lips that he imagined, was calling his name.

"Mike, we are both two grown adults, here right?" Doreen asked. Mike acknowledge yes, by shaking his head up and down.

"A woman knows from the first time when she meets a man, whether she would or would not fuck him. Most of the time if she selects that she would but doesn't, it's not because she just changed her mind. It's because the guy either said or did something stupid to fuck it all up. I want to hook up with you sometime during our short stay here, no strings attached. I am hoping you can handle all this woman, but if not, you can let me know now," Doreen said as she looked Mike up and down. Mike was at a loss for words at the moment.

"I really don't know if you're in a relationship with anyone and I really don't care. All I know is, I plan to get to know you better," Doreen said as she reached over to feel Mike's hand.

The softness of her hand sent a warm sensation to Mike's soul. Her glossy full lips shined from the reflection of the moonlight as it shined brightly among the stars down on the earth from above. Mike wanted to lean over and connect his lips with hers, but held his position to show his will power and remain respectful. They both just stared at one another for a brief moment as they faded out the music from their thoughts. Doreen snapped out of her trance.

"Since we both just had a moment of silence and I've already let you know some of my business. I might as well ask have a few similar questions of my own for you," Doreen said as she began to ask the following questions

"Do you have any kids? A baby mama drama? Are you single? And what do you do for a living?" Doreen asked.

"Please don't say your street pharmacist, "Doreen continued.

"I don't have any baby mama drama, because I don't have any kids. I'm single and date here and there, but nothing serious or committed. As for as what I do for a living. I work for the department of sanitation and co-owner of a security company called DIVINER INC. My company handles security and escorts for celebrities. We also supply security for night clubs in the city. I'm also on the waiting list for promotion to sanitation police in which I will be supervising sanitation workers. Mike informed Doreen while giving her a quick rundown of his occupation.

"That's very impressive. I'm happy to hear you're making positive moves for yourself, while doing it all legal," Doreen said as she sipped the last of her beverage in her glass.

"So, you said, you have no children, no woman in your life, a good job and you own your business?! Are you gay or living on the down low?" Doreen continued to ask as she wondered why was he still single.

"Gay! Oh, hell no! I have nothing against gay people, But I love women, from head to toe. I just get so caught up working hard and making that overtime with the city, and running DIVINER INC with my partner hustling to pull in more business, so much that I really haven't had time enough to get to know a woman long enough to select that special someone yet. Oh, it looks like someone could use a refill" Mike said to Doreen as he removed the empty glass from Doreen hand had to go get her a refill.

"I hear that, you focus on making that cheese and have no time for the rats" Doreen jokingly said as Mike stood up to walk over to the Tiki Bar.

"You got jokes pretty lady," Mike said as he laughed and walked over to the Tiki Bar where Rick was hanging out with Stacey.

"Excuse me my brother and sister, but could you hook me up with a refill for the lovely Doreen," Mike asked Rick as he observed a fresh blend in the blender.

"No problem Mike. Do you need a refill on that Thug Passion?" Rick asked as he filled up a fresh glass of daiquiri for Doreen.

"I will appreciate it, you're the best bartender Isaac," Mike said jokingly as he held Doreen's drink in his hand and awaited his fresh drink.

"Mike you're an excellent grill master, everything tasted delicious," Stacey said giving Mike his props on the grill.

"Thank You" Mike replied as Rick handed him his drink and he started to walk away back towards Doreen.

"That subject of us possibly hooking up could definitely happen between us whenever you're ready to make it happen lady, because I'm really feeling you and Yes I can handle all that woman plus more" Mike finally replied as he looked at her curvy body from head to toe as he handed her the fresh glass of strawberry daiquiri and leaned over placing a soft kiss on Doreen's cheek that she for some reason assumed would land on her lips.

How the hell, did he miss these juicy ass lips of mine, I must make him nervous or something Doreen thought to herself.

"A kiss on the lips would've been nice, but I'll take what I could get for now" Doreen jokingly said after receiving the kiss on the cheek.

"Well I like to take my time in whatever I do, it makes the enjoyment in what I'm doing better, longer and stronger." Mike said as he whispered in her ear just before placing his tongue on her earlobe.

Okay enough with the small talk, we have two nights to get it right, whatever happens, happens." Doreen said just before taking another sip of her drink.

"I'm feeling that, I'm feeling that like a muthafucka." Mike replied as he observed Doreen lick the rim of the glass before swallowing her drink.

"Looks like your boy Mike and my home girl are getting along very well over there" Stacey said as she observed Mike leaning towards Doreen and giving her a peck on the cheek as Doreen smiled as he did it. Rick then looked over Stacey shoulder to see what was going on between the two love birds sitting at the table.

"Yeah! They're connecting really well, but not like you and me," Rick jokingly said with a bright and wide smile on his face exposing his perfect white choppers.

"You may be fine as Rick Fox, but you're also a smooth talker like Slick Rick," Stacey said as she looked into Rick's eyes as she returned the smile.

"Oh, I'm Rick Fox, and Slick Rick combined Huh?" Rick asked jokingly as if he was never compared to the ball player/actor in regard to the resemblance.

Across at the other picnic table, the four-remaining guest engaged in all types of conversations leading to loud laughter. Dennis and Jason both figured they would take a crack at the two attractive sisters as they entertained them with conversation and jokes. Chantel and Alexis both found the guys they were sitting with to be very amusing. They also admired their buff physiques.

Dennis cell phone began to vibrate in his pocket. He pulled

it out of his pocket and noticed it was Brenda calling. Brenda was a young lady he was dating at the time who lived down the hall from his apartment in the condo complex he lived in. He sent her call directly to the voice mail and ignored her texts messages as he continued his conversation with the other three at the table. Brenda and he have only dated for about a month, but it didn't take long for things to get quite sour for Dennis taste buds.

Dennis started to become quite confused in regard to his new girlfriend's relationship status with her ex-boyfriend whom was also the father of her children. This confusion started when her ex popped up unannounced one day and spent the night at her apartment. On that same very night, she refused to answer any of Dennis calls as if she was on lock down and her explanations for not answering made him hip that she wasn't the type of woman he could have serious relationship with at all. She was still stuck in her past.

Why the fuck she keeps calling? Oh, her baby daddy must be with his other chick and don't have the time to cock block her life. That have to be the only reason why, she keeps blowing up my cell phone Dennis thought to himself as Brenda continued to call and text him.

I don't got no time for her bullshit today! When I fucking call her I get every excuse in the book Fuck It! She left me on stuck when I called her, Let's see how she deals with getting no answer He continued to think to himself.

"I have to go to the little girl's room. Chantel, come with me, because I know you gotta go too," Alexis stated as she stood up from the table, while exposing her belly ring.

Chantel then stood up from the table and started to stretch her curvy body. Both Chantel and Alexis were wearing apple bottom black leather leggings. The leggings style was low riders and looked like they were painted on. Their G-String panties were exposed, and the high platform sandals they wore made their asses poke out. The only difference was the two had on two different color G-Strings and sandals.

"Please excuse us fellas; we have to go freshen up a little. We will be right back," Alexis announced as both sisters collected their drinks from the table and headed to the rest room in the pool house. In this time and age, no one should leave their drinks unattended, due to people placing mickeys and all types of shit into one's drink to either take advantage of them or just to merely have them bug the fuck out.

"Okay, no problem ladies. There's a bathroom located in the game room if you don't feel like walking all the way back to the pool house," Dennis said while pointing towards the door leading to the game room. Both Chantel and Alexis stopped and made a U-turn.

"Thanks for the info, we will be right back," Chantel said as both sisters started to walk off towards the entrance leading to the game room, as if it was a runway. Their asses shook as if they were made of jello, all the men couldn't help but notice how sexy the two young ladies look.

Dennis and Jason watched the two sexy ladies until they disappeared into the house, then they looked at one another and shook their heads.

"Dennis, them broads just made my dick harder than Chinese math, when Chantel stood up and started stretching that plump round ass. She was flexing them ass muscle and everything playboy, did you peep that?" Jason said as he started to bang on the picnic table with his fist.

"Ray Charles could've seen that ass, but that belly ring Alexis was rocking caught my eye. They really must be trying to tease a muthafucka up in this piece. Damn! Did you see how they added a little extra shake to their asses as they walked away?" Dennis replied while he started grabbing his crotch area. Stacey looked over Rick shoulder to see what he was staring at. He made it more than obvious that his attention was no longer focused on Stacey.

"Is that what you like?" Stacey asked as she observed Rick looking at the two sisters walk away in the middle of their conversation.

"You're what I like lady. Why do you ask?" Ricky replied while he already knew the answer. "Because you stopped talking and turned your head in the middle of a sentence.

Plus, your eyes were popping out your head as my two buddies walked away. You know you was staring at their asses shaking and baking," Stacey said with a slight grin.

"Oh, you mean the two Cooley girls whom was just walking in slow motion into the house, Nah I was just wondering about something," Ricky said as he scratched his head full of waves.

"Wondering about what?" Stacey quickly asked.

"Just wondering how the fuck two sisters have the same identical asses," Rick jokingly said as he began to laugh out loud.

"Ha Ha Ha so you think that's funny huh pretty Ricky" Stacey said with a somewhat cold stare as her facial expression became serious.

Oh, shit fool, if you were going to get that pussy, you just fucked it up now saying that bullshit! Rick thought to himself.

"Pretty Ricky! I asked you a fucking question," Stacey continued as she seemed to grow angrier by the minute.

"I, I, I was just," was all Rick could utter out before Stacey burst into a loud laugh as she nearly fell off the stool.

"That's real cute how you were all stuttering and shit, like you under pressure and what not," Stacey said as she smiled. Rick was quite relieved that he didn't fuck up the possible pussy connect, and also that he wasn't dealing with a pyscho chick. "Damn, I thought you was going to bust me in my head with that glass or something lady, you had that look in your eye like that psycho chick in that Martin Lawrence flick a Thin Line

Between Love and Hate" Ricky said as he wiped his forehead.

"Nope, I was just fucking with you, If I was a man I would've been looking at them two also, you got to give credit where credit is due." Stacey said as she shrugged her shoulders.

"I didn't mean no disrespect you in any way, please excuse my rudeness if I offended you by my actions," Rick said as he apologized for dazing at the jello butt twins.

"No need to apologize, I already know my ass looks as good as both of theirs, so I'm really not sweating it," Stacey explained to Rick to let him know she was far from jealous. She then got up and twirled her body around to give him a sneak peek of her ass. Rick liked what he saw, and slapped her softly on the bottom.

"Look at them fools over there," Rick said as he pointed at Dennis and Jason. "I could see them drooling from over here," Rick continued.

"Oh my, they look they could tear my friends apart," Stacey responded. "Are they on steroids or something?" Stacey jokingly continued as she looked over in the fella's direction and commented on their muscular, stocky builds.

"They don't take steroids, that's all hard work in the gym. They both play football professionally, so they train to the max." Rick explained.

"Wow, look at their arms. Their bigger than my girlfriend's legs," Stacey said. Rick started to laugh.

"I might have to call 911 on them big boys. Before they put a hurting on my little friends," Stacey said as she started to laugh as the alcohol started to work on her brain.

"You like the big boys huh? Big, strong and athletic that could put a hurting on something huh?!" Rick jokingly asked while giving Stacey a dose of her own medicine. They both started looking in Dennis and Jason direction, as they attempted to ear hustle their conversation.

Alexis and Chantel returned from the rest room and joined Dennis and Jason once again. The evening grew later, and everyone started to connect very well even if some of the people present were envious of DeVonte and Erica's lifestyle and relationship.

CHAPTER 13

INVESTIGATING THE FACTS

Damn! It's going to be a long night. I better bust out my paperwork, so I can chill for the rest of the overtime Dean thought to himself soon as he hung up from slim. He was wise to the fact that having a reliable C.I. could be a career builder for an up rising star in the department and it could get him on the grid for promotions as well as assigned to wanted specialized detail assignments. He made it his business that Slim got paid for his service as promised, a one hand washes the other type of thing.

Dean looked at his watch, then walked back into the precinct. He immediately related all the information he received from Slim to Moreno. Moreno then contacted Lieutenant Zaki and filled him in on the information giving to him by Dean. Zaki seem to become happier than a pig in shit, by the sound of his voice. The lieutenant then stopped what he was doing, grabbed his radio off his desk and his gun belt and vest out of his locker. The lieutenant exited his office and made his way to the front desk to sign out. Once he signed out, he exited his command and jumped into his car, headed for the 117 precinct.

Working that night in the 117 squad was one sergeant and four detectives. They were working a four by twelve tour, and just swung back in for their first tour of the week. Many of the detectives assigned to the Detective Squad where formerly assigned to the Narcotics Unit at one time or another. Once reassigned to the Detective Squad for whatever reason, many of them forgot their roots and classified themselves as the top notched detectives and that the rest of the detectives in the department wasn't on their level. You could only guess that the polyester suits, numerous cups of coffee and loads of donuts, could affected their brains enough to make them believe such a thing.

"Dean, we got to go upstairs and fuck with the squad. We have to go see what they got on this double homicide," Moreno said as he stood up and placed a funny smirk on his face. The sergeant knew his team had one over the squad and wanted to rub it in their face.

"Sarge, you know them dicks going to act like they don't have shit, unless they're really desperate and have no type of leads in the case," Dean responded as he prepared himself to go upstairs.

"I know, but we still have to go up there and ask," Moreno said.

"Just make sure you bring all that shit you got on Jenkins upstairs with you," Moreno continued.

I already know that, asshole! Dean thought to himself as he gathered everything concerning the shooting suspect and placed it in a folder, before leaving the arrest process area.

Both exited the arrest process area and entered into the stairwell. The scent of French vanilla coffee tickled their nostrils as they walked up the stairs.

"It fucking smells like Dunkin Donuts in here; I can use a cup of that shit right now," Moreno jokingly said.

"You and me both," Dean responded as they reached the floor the squad was on and exited the stairwell. They walked down the short corridor and entered the door labeled 117 squad. Once in they noticed a coffee machine and a large box of donuts behind the desk counter on a table.

"NARCOTICS, IN THE HOUSE!" Shouted one of the detectives as soon as Dean and Moreno walked in.

"How many crackheads and weed smoker's you guys dragged in today?" The same detective sarcastically asked with a silly smirk on his face. Moreno scanned the room for the big mouth detective. He gave the guy a good stare down before asking.

"Where's your supervisor?" Moreno asked while pointing to his shield that was dangling on a beaded chain around his neck. The detective realized Moreno was a sergeant and chilled out with the remarks.

"He's in the supervisor's office," The detective responded as he pointed towards the back of the office, where the office was located.

"Hey sarge! There's a sergeant and a detective from narcotics here to see you," A different detective from the squad yelled out, to give the boss in the office a heads up.

"Okay, send them back here!" A raspy voice from the back yelled out. Dean and Moreno both headed to the back to the office and entered it. Sergeant Pelzer, the squad supervisor whom was sitting in the office, watched Moreno and Dean entered it. Moreno was a familiar face to the squad sergeant, so he got up and greeted his old buddy with a handshake and hug. The two sergeants were recruits together in the police academy and car pooled on many occasions.

"Moreno! Nice to see you, my friend. What bring you to my

neck of the woods?" Pelzer asked while he was happy to see an old friend from the past.

"Long time no see buddy. I'm doing great. I'm here, because we got a few bodies off the street tonight and the higher-ups wanted us to check in with you in regard to the double homicide. Beyond that, how's the squad treating you?" Moreno continued.

"Life is good, over here in the squad. I can't complain," Pelzer responded.

"That shit is a magilla," Pelzer responded as he went to take a seat at his desk and sipped his coffee.

"I bet it is," Moreno said as he and Dean sat down on the sofa in the office. "You guys have any leads? Any anything yet?" Dean continued to ask.

"So far, we don't have shit on it. The catching detective is still trying to gather information, but nothing is putting us in the right direction," Sergeant Pelzer said as he rocked back and front in his recliner desk chair.

"Sarge, who's the catching detective on this case?" Dean asked wanting to know if it was that dick head whom was talking that narcotics shit out front! Before Pelzer could answer, Detective Bland walked in.

"Speak of the devil; this is the catching detective right here. Detective Bland, I want you to meet Sergeant Moreno and Detective Dean from narcotics.

Detective Bland looked like Captain Ivan Drago from Rocky IV. He was tall, very muscular and intimidating. Bland walked over to Moreno and Dean, to shake their hands. He was carrying the pedigree sheets of both homicide victims in a folder. Moreno and Dean both stared at the hulking detective.

This guy must be juicing up Dean thought to himself as he shook Bland's hand.

"I was about to call you in here. These guys need to be updated on the homicide your handling as per the chief," Pelzer informed Bland.

This asshole knows damn well I don't have shit on this case yet. So, what the fuck does he expect me to tell these guys? Bland thought to himself as he stood there nearly speechless. Sergeant Pelzer just leaned back in his chair as he took another sip on his coffee mug.

"Not yet, I'm trying to work on a few leads, but I've been coming up short so far," Bland responded.

"Detective Bland, tonight is your lucky night. Me and my team have a gift for you today. And it's not a crackhead or weed smoker, like that asshole up front yelled out soon as we walked in," Sergeant Moreno continued.

"A gift for me? What?" Bland asked with the expression of confusion on his face as he stared at Moreno and Dean.

"Yep, a gift" Moreno responded. "We have your shooter downstairs," Moreno continued. Pelzer and Bland eyes both lit up like Christmas lights, in regard to the apprehension notification.

"Who? What? Where?" The shocked detective stuttered as he was caught off guard.

"We got him while doing B&B on GRB near the crime scene tonight. He sold crack to one of my UCs. He's downstairs in the cells and doesn't have a fucking clue that we are on to him yet," Moreno said to the tongue-tied detective whom was still in shock and disbelief.

"Here you go Sarge," Dean said as he handed Pelzer Jenkins paperwork. "This is our man right here." Dean continued. Pelzer became so excited that his hands started to tremble as he looked at the suspect photo.

"How do you guys know for sure, this guy is the shooter in the homicides? Did you recover any weapons off him? Or have any eye witnesses identifying him as the shooter?" Pelzer asked as he reviewed the suspect's rap sheet.

Dean pulled out his little note pad and started flipping the pages. Within the pad was information giving to him by Slim.

"No weapons were recovered from him nor do we have an eye witness, but what I have in my note-pad is just as good," Dean replied.

"Tonight, while processing my collars, I received a phone call from a very reliable C.I. that my teamed locked up the shooter involved in the double homicide. When I asked which guy was it? He named the guy in the photo your holding," Dean stated. "The informant also informed me that this guy acted alone in the shooting. Here's a brief rundown, of what I have so far from my informant," Detective Dean said as he began to read out loud the following:

Confidential Informant stated word on the streets, Rahmel Jenkins also known as Mel was the alleged only shooter involved in the double homicide that occurred on Guy Brewer Boulevard.

Confidential Informant also stated that the word on the streets, the two shooting victims known as Big D (Desean Wise) and Rock (Jaheim White) committed a strong-arm robbery against Jenkins approximately a week ago within Rochdale Village. Jenkins took quite a beating as well as had a large sum of cash removed from his possession by the two assailants whom are now both deceased.

Confidential Informant stated Jenkins was observed having a verbal altercation with Big D and Rock inside of David's Bodega near the front counter in regard to that robbery hours before the shooting. It was said that Jenkins left without incident basically because he had his little three-year-old son with him or he wasn't armed at the time.

Confidential Informant stated, Jenkins was observed

running through Rochdale Village to his building after the sound of shots being fired were heard, approximately three O'clock in the morning.

"That's all I have so far," Dean said after reading off his note. Pelzer and Bland seemed to be satisfied with what they heard.

"I owe you guys fucking lunch," Bland said once Dean finished reading the information he had. Pelzer passed Bland a copy of Jenkins photo and he just stared at it.

"We'll skip on the lunch, just make sure you put me and my team down for apprehension," Moreno said as he handed Bland a copy of his team tactical plan.

"No problem guys, I will make sure you get a copy of the compliant follow up report (also known as DD5) before the night is over.

"Maybe you should head over to David's Bodega and Rochdale Village security to get a hold on their surveillance tapes. According to the C.I., it will enhance your investigation in your case," Dean said to Bland as he and Moreno both got up from the sofa and exchanged handshakes with Pelzer and Bland.

"My guys will bring our perps(perpetrators) up here, that we grabbed tonight for your detectives to debrief. Jenkins will be up, for debriefing and interrogation." Moreno said to Pelzer, as he and Dean was about to exit Pelzer's office.

"Okay, I'll let my detectives know to get ready to debrief." Pelzer responded.

"Should I go get a warrant for the tapes?" Bland asked Pelzer, before heading out his office.

"You shouldn't need one, if they are both cooperative with giving you access. If they give you a hard time, let me know. I will have one drawn up and signed by a judge quicker than a rabbit gets fucked," Pelzer said as he cracked a smile.

"The chief of security over in Rochdale Village is a retired lieutenant, so I know he wouldn't have a problem in hooking you up with no problem. The workers at the bodega are a little shady. The shady fucks, let the players hangout inside and out in front of the store. One of my C.I.s said they sometimes even hold their drug stash from time to time" Dean said to advise Bland of what he may come up against, while trying to get access to the bodega's surveillance tape.

"Here's my cell, if the muthafuckas at the bodega give you a hard time. Call me. I will send a C.I. in there to buy a crack pipe or some other type of drug paraphernalia and hit them with an emergency search warrant. That will pressure them assholes into cooperating," Moreno said as he wrote down both his and Dean's cell numbers onto a sheet in his note pad, then ripped the page out and handed it to Bland.

"Thanks, Sarge, I really appreciate you guys help with this case. Hopefully one day I could return the favor and be as helpful as you guys are to me," Bland said as he expressed how grateful he was for the help in his case in which he had no leads until the Narcotics Unit showed up.

"No problem for a former narco ranger," Dean replied as he just realized he remembered seeing Detective Bland a few years ago at a narcotics tactical training in Rodman's Neck out in the Bronx. Bland was formerly assigned to Manhattan North narcotics located in Harlem as an investigator for approximately six years before putting in for the squad.

Moreno and Dean headed out of Pelzer's office and walked down the short corridor pass the desks of the detectives whom worked in the Squad. Bland caught up to the two before they exited out the Squad Office.

"I need to speak to your C.I. soon as I get back from picking up the surveillance tapes, If that's okay with you Dean?" Bland yelled out to get the attention of the narcotics detective while the other detectives in the squad, ear hustled on the conversation.

"Of course, just let us know when your back and I'll make the connect," Dean responded as he and Moreno stopped in their tracks, before exiting the squad room.

"Okay thanks" Bland replied as he headed back into Pelzer's office. Dean and Moreno then exited the squad room and headed back down towards their team.

"Bland, tell the other guys out there to drop whatever they're doing, and get in here," Pelzer instructed his detective as he strolled through his cellular phone book for numbers. Bland followed Pelzer's instructions and related the message to the other members of the squad. Detectives Sweeney Carey and Williams walked into the office to see what was going on.

"Sweeney! Carey! I need you two to debrief a shit load of collars, that narcotics brought in tonight. Williams! I need you to head out with Bland and help him out," Pelzer instructed his detectives. Sweeney, Carey, and Williams stood there looking at each other, because they didn't have an idea what was going on. Pelzer then looked at Bland and gestured with his hand, for him to show the other detectives the photo of Jenkins. Bland then passed the photo to Carey, whom looked at it briefly before passing it to the others.

"Who's this guy supposed to be sarge?" Carey asked after he passed the photo off to Sweeney.

"That guy right there?! Oh, he's our special guest Jahmel Jenkins. He sold to an undercover near the double homicide scene tonight, during a buy and bust operation. Bland will be debriefing him personally, when he returns from a quick run out in the field.

"What he do? Sell a micro pebble of crack?" Sweeney asked sarcastically, once he took a glance at the photo. Pelzer paused for a moment and looked at Sweeney as if he was an asshole.

"Sweeney! Until you out rank as a lieutenant, which will take you two exams to do. Shut the fuck up!" Pelzer yelled at his detective. "As I was saying, narcotics got a call from one of their C.I.s who's pointing the finger at Jenkins as the lone shooter in the double homicide," Pelzer continued.

"Nice!" Williams said as he patted Bland on the back. You see Sweeney! Your dumb ass was fucking with narco soon as they walked in, and they had valuable information along with the body to go with it," Williams said while as he started to laugh. Sweeney shrugged his shoulders.

"That shit isn't confirmed yet, and if it is. It's about time they did something right," Sweeney responded while sticking to his guns for being an arrogant asshole.

"Just be lucky your ass wasn't the catching detective in this case, because them narco guys think you're a real asshole and I bet they wouldn't have told you shit," Carey said to Sweeney just before sipping his coffee. Sweeney put his hands up in the air as if he didn't give a shit.

"I would've eventually solved the case myself, like I been doing," Sweeney said as he stuck out his chest with pride. Pelzer looked Carey and Sweeney as if they were idiots.

"Okay guys, forget all that bullshit for now," Pelzer said while interrupting the two-detective's conversation.

"It's time, for all you guys to earn your keep. So, get to work," Pelzer instructed his detectives. Sweeney, Carey and Williams headed out of Pelzer's office. "Sweeney, Carey! Check with narco to see if Jenkins was collared with somebody else. If so, give him a good briefing. Maybe the joker will finger Jenkins also.

"You got it Sarge," Sweeney replied knowing he will generate a lot of overtime off this case as he and Carey headed towards their desk.

Bland retained the paperwork giving to him by Dean from his Pelzer's office, as he walked out of it and back towards his desk; After removing a set of keys for a department vehicle and signing it out on the log book behind the sergeants desk. He then walked into the squad locker room to get his bullet proof vest, two pairs of handcuffs and small canister of mace.

He then returned to his desk and placed his equipment on it, before walking over to a file cabinet containing the portable digital cameras and assorted paperwork. He signed out one digital camera and returned to his desk, he put the camera on it. He then began to place his vest on.

Bland observed Detectives McRae and O'Keith from the narcotics team enter the squad room with the first prisoner to be debriefed. He knew it was time for him to get the ball bouncing, so he got all his stuff he needed together and headed out the squad and made his way towards the front desk to sign out of the precinct movement log.

The holding cells of the 117 precinct, were located next to the finger printing machine. The cells were packed with prisoner arrested by patrol and other units working within the confines of the 117th precinct. So, the narco unit made use of the other holding cells located in the back to separate their twelve prisoners from the rest. The holding cells in the back looked like a real prison cell, except for there was no beds and possibly a little smaller.

The funk of stale urine coming from the silver toilets in some of the cells, hit you in the face as soon as the main gate was open. The cell area in the back were the most secure cells in the building and was secured by a surveillance camera that was monitored by the desk officer (sergeant/lieutenant) who had to make periodic checks of the area and make a command log entry stating their finding of the conditions.

"Yo, officer! When are you guys going to take us to the bookings, man? Do you think we going to see the judge tonight," One prisoner yelled out from his cell to the detective he observed sitting on a chair with his arms folded.

"I don't know about you seeing the judge tonight, but soon as everybody done speaking to the detectives upstairs, I'm taking you players next door to get some grub," Detective Boyd said as he looked at his watch and hoped the members of the prisoner van hurried up with their escorts to the squad room.

"Fuck grub! I want to get to the bookings to see the judge," yelled out another prisoner from his cell.

"Yo, whoever said that shit must never got bagged before, or you a nukka who just like eating a thick ass cheese sandwich" yelled out another prisoner whom more than likely have been thru the system before.

Detective Boyd was a cool ass Irish cop, whom once was an undercover assigned to Staten Island and Manhattan South Narcotics Units. He went by the name of Red Top in the streets of Staten Island and the Lower East Side of Manhattan. He had long burning fire colored red hair with a long red beard to match. When he wore shades, he looked like a member of the musical group ZZ Top.

Boyd served three years as a New York City Correction Officer prior to joining the Police Department. As an undercover, he used his knowledge of the jail system to his advantage in the streets. He was up on the latest street lingo and used jail terms very frequent as he interacted with the people in the streets. After numerous incidents and a on duty shooting, in which two males made a robbery attempt on him and in return sent them to an early grave, he decided to flip over to an investigative detective assignment.

He always told the people he arrested or apprehended depending on his assignment for the day, that it was all part of the game and hustle. He had to break it down half the time to fools who thought they would never get caught, and blamed everyone but themselves for getting caught doing their illegal activities. The mental state of a lot of the street hustlers was that they supposed to be untouchable and should never get caught, as if whatever they were doing was all legal. Hooking up the prisoners with food to keep them mellow as long as they were cool and respectful, was no big thing to him.

His years and experience in the unit taught him that a full belly leads to a calm mind. Frustration, stress and anger builds in the mind of someone whom just been arrested and could possibly spend a lot of time in prison depending upon on whatever their circumstance may be. The fresh feeling of losing your freedom whether for short or long term could be mind boggling to one's mind, so just imagine going through this transition on an empty belly.

"I'm hitting Popeye's Chicken to grab a few buckets and some sodas, so if you got something against eating chicken, then you shit out of luck," Boyd yelled out in the cell area to alert all of his team prisoners, what their dinner was going to be.

"Yo! Why you got to get us chicken? Huh? Because we black huh?" One of the prisoners yelled out from his cell.

"First of all, asshole! I don't have to get anybody shit! I'm just trying to hook yall up with something hot and quick to eat, before you hit the bookings. Chicken and biscuits isn't a racial statement, it's food. White people eat chicken too muthafucka! So, if you don't want it. Just say you don't, or shut the fuck up" Boyd said jokingly as other prisoners started to laugh loudly.

"You a cool ass white boy, detective. Whatever you hook us up with will be appreciated," A prisoner yelled out.

"Hell yeah! The uniform cops be treating nukkas like shit, but you narco cats are cool as fuck and get the process moving quick," A different prisoner yelled out, as he knew the difference from the narco arrest processing from regular patrol.

"Shit is never personal; it's always business" Boyd stated as he got up and began to check on all the prisoners in their cells.

"Hey, Patrick! Bring another one out the cell, we have one returning," Yelled out McRae whom along with O'Keith were the two detectives assigned to the prisoner van was escorting the prisoners back and forth to the squad room. The stood outside the entrance to the cell room with a prisoner rear cuffed. All law enforcement officers no matter what rank, are not allowed to enter holding cells, debriefing rooms or any other area designated for prisoners.

"Okay! Give me a minute Chuck (Detective McRae)," Boyd replied as he removed the large cell key from his rear pants pocket. He then grabbed a set of cuffs that was laying on the desk next to the chair he was sitting in. He then walked over to one of the cells and instructed one of the two prisoners in the cell to walk towards the rear of the cell and face the wall away from him, as he instructed the other to back up towards him. He then instructed the prisoner who backed up to place his palms together and next to the open slot of the cell to be rear cuffed. Once the prisoner is cuffed, he then opened the cell and instructed the cuffed prisoner to step out the cell and stand to the side as he then closed the cell that slam locks upon impact. He then walked the prisoner over to the awaiting Detectives as the exchanged prisoners, then he walked the returning prisoner back to his cell and locked him in.

"Detective! Can I make a phone call?" Asked Curtis Johnson whom was the prisoner sharing the cell with the returning prisoner.

"Nope! You should've done all that before or after you got finger printed. Boyd answered as he reached into his pocket and checked his cell phone for missed calls and text messages.

"I asked the Detective that printed me, but he told me to wait until after everybody else is printed.

"And did you ask after that?" Boyd asked loud enough for the prisoner to hear him.

"I haven't seen him since he brought me back here after being printed" The prisoner replied as he attempted to plead his case.

"Okay check this player, he'll be back down here soon to take you up to the Squad room. So, ask him when he comes back," Boyd said as he sat down and leaned back in the chair. The prisoner realized that the young detective wasn't budging on his decision not to let him make a phone call, so he just remained silent until he was taken upstairs to the squad room.

Upstairs in the squad room, both Carey and Sweeney simultaneously interviewed and debriefed eleven out of twelve prisoners that the narcotics unit brought in. They both took their time with their interviews while stalling enough to give Detective Bland time enough to review and recover the video surveillance tapes from both David's Bodega and Rochdale Village Security.

"Hey, Sarge! All the guys narco brought up here to be debriefed are all done, except for Jenkins. The other eleven have been sent back downstairs to the holding cell and we have all their names logged in the log book as being debriefed," Carey said as he poked his head in Pelzer office.

"Did you guys find out from narco, who got picked up with Jenkins?" Pelzer asked.

"Yeah, we found out," Carey responded. "But the kid doesn't seem to know anything," Carey continued.

"Of course not," Pelzer said with a smirk on his face.

"He is not going to snitch on his boy," He continued.

"And you know it! Nobody knows nothing about nothing," Carey replied as he remained standing there waiting on further instructions.

"Okay, well I guess it's time for me to start making some notification then," Pelzer said.

"What you want us to do now Sarge?" Carey asked.

"Bring that knucklehead upstairs and let his ass marinate in the debriefing room until Bland gets back. And make sure you toss that muthafucka good; We don't need any surprises," Pelzer instructed Carey prior to him calling the 117th precinct commanding officer and Chief of Detective office at headquarters.

I know what to do! Asshole! Carey thought to himself, as he looked at his watch.

"No problem Sarge," Carey replied without saying what he was really thinking.

"I also want you guys to monitor this dude at all times, and watch what you say around him. I don't want him to have any slight ideas that we are on to him," Pelzer said as he picked up the phone and began to dial the 117th precinct commanding officer contact number. Carey left his supervisors office and headed out front to hook up with Sweeney.

The two detectives headed downstairs toward the holding cells to go get Rahmel as instructed by their supervisor. As they got closer to the holding cells; they came across McRae and O'Keith whom were standing next to the photocopying machine.

"Hey, what's up guys?" McRae asked as he saw the two squad detectives approaching.

"Nothing much my friend. Our boss sent us down here to get Jenkins. He wants the guy to sweat it out in the squad holding cell," Sweeney said as he dangled a pair of cuffs in his hand.

"We'll bring him up the way we brought the others up. We don't want this guy catching on, by getting a special escort upstairs with you guys," O'Keith wisely said. Carey and Sweeney looked at each other.

"That makes good enough sense to me," Sweeney replied as both he and Carey headed back upstairs to the squad room.

"Hey, Pat! Bring out Jenkins," McRae yelled out to Boyd whom still was temporarily assigned to the holding cells while they escorted prisoners to and from the squad room to the holding cells.

"About time! We back here starving like a muthafucka!" Boyd yelled back as he got up to get Jenkins out of his cell.

"Detective! Can you save a brother a chicken leg and biscuit if you get back with the food before I get back downstairs?" Jahmel asked Boyd as his stomach started to rumble from hunger.

"Don't worry playa; I'll make sure you get something to eat," Boyd replied as he rears cuffed Jenkins and escorted him to the two awaiting detectives. Once Boyd handed Jenkins off, he spotted his partner for the day, enjoying a cigarette near the precinct back door.

"Chuck! Can you go over there and tell Tommy to come to the holding cells? So, I could go make a food run," Boyd said referring to Detective Thomas O'Connor who was hanging outside of the holding cell area.

"He's standing out in the parking lot having a smoke, but we will let him know to come back here to relieve you," Chuck answered as he held onto Jenkins's arm as he escorted him.

"You know what? I'll wait until you guys return. It only takes a minute to walk him to the squad, plus you two are assigned to the prisoners today, not me." Boyd said as it finally dawned on him that McRae and O'Keith were trying to get over on their duties.

CHAPTER 14

SLEEP WALKING

It was the early 1990's, a time when New York City crime and murders was on the rise. The streets were filled with predators looking to feed on the weak while corruption within the New York City Police Department was at an all-time high. A change was needed. A day when the sheep was no longer hunted, as the wolf now became the prey.

"Fuck you, Denzel! And here! You can take this piece of shit with you on your way out, muthafucka!" Calise yelled out in the hallway of her apartment building as she unhooked the large gold chain from around her neck and tossed it down the staircase, where Denzel was standing. The thick gold Crucifix medallion came off the link and landed on Denzel's foot.

Calise, was Denzel's girlfriend when he was 17 years old. The two met at the fast food restaurant they both worked, when they were 16 years old, and started out as good friends. After ending his relationship with his previous girlfriend, Denzel decided to ask Calise to go out with him on Easter Sunday for a date. The two decided to head to 42nd Street aka Forty Deuce.

The two soon after, became a couple. And their relationship lasted for many years. Denzel after just two years in the relationship with Calise found out that she had a lot of issues, that lead to a lot of grief for him.

Denzel bent down to picked up the gold medallion as well as the gold chain from the stairwell, and stood there looking up at Calise. He placed the medallion back on the chain, without saying another word. He didn't want to continue the verbal altercation with her, so he simply placed the link around his neck and headed downstairs to the lobby of her apartment building. Once he made it to the lobby, he looked at his watch and placed his ear phones on his ears before he exited the building. He stood on the stoop for a minute to search through his jacket pockets for his favorite cassette tape.

It was now 2:20 in the morning as the lyrics of his favorite rap artist flowed through Denzel's headphones he walked off the stoop and headed down Pacific Street towards Hopkinson Avenue on his way home. He then placed his Walkman cassette player into his inside jacket pocket, and left his jacket open exposing his jewelry. Denzel took a short cut, as he made a left on Bergen Street and cut through the dark playground rear of the Junior High School IS 55. He continued to walk over to Rockaway Avenue, where he walked straight down the hill towards home.

"I'm gotta leave this fucking girl alone! She's always starting some dumb shit for nothing and had the nerve to throw this fucking chain I bought her down the stairs at me with her ungrateful ass," Denzel mumbled to himself as he listened to his walk-man. As he crossed Pitkin Avenue, he was approached by a male black that was about six inches shorter than him, that just appeared out of nowhere.

The male started walking along side of him and was saying something, But Denzel was unable to hear him due to the loud music playing in his ear. Denzel then stopped in his tracks and removed one ear piece of his headphones from one of his ears so he could hear what the male was saying.

"What's up homie? I wasn't trying to run up on you like that. I just wanted to know, if you had the time," The short dark complexion male whom spoke with a lisp said as he scratched the top of his head. Denzel then looked at his watch and responded.

"It's 2:30," as he proceeded on with his walk home. The male continued to walk along side of him, as if he was headed in the same direction.

"Damn! It's 2:30 already? Good looking out," The male responded. "You from around here? What's your name homie?" The male continued to ask as while walking along side of Denzel closely and acting in a strange manner.

"What's my name!?" Denzel responded sarcastically as a warning signal went off inside of his head telling him to turn around. Denzel followed his mind and turned around, He observed two very large muscular males, who looked as if they just came home from prison creeping up behind him.

The short male whom originally approached Denzel then grabbed at his neck, causing Denzel's attention to be drawn back to him and away from the two other thugs behind him. Denzel whom was unaware at the time, that the short male just snatched both of his chains from around his neck, thought the male just took a swing at him. Denzel retaliated by throwing a left hook that landed on the male's jaw. The male was sent crashing to the ground from the uninspected blow. Denzel then positioned himself into a battle stance. He was now face to face with the two larger thugs, as their smaller partner in crime laid on the ground. The first thing that came to Denzel's mind was that Calise set him up for a beat down by her male friends.

Denzel was determined to fuck up at least one of his attackers, while being jumped. He got into a fighting stance and awaited their next move. For a split second, he glanced down at the guy, he knocked out. He noticed one of his Medallion was laying on the ground, while the temporarily unconscious thug held onto both of Denzel's chains. Denzel quickly checked his neck and realized, he wasn't being jumped in retaliation for the argument with Calise, he was being robbed.

Now realizing what was going down, Denzel then lunged forward in an attempt to stomp the shit out of the unconscious thug and retrieve his chains. One of the other thugs grabbed Denzel from behind in the nick of time preventing him from stomping his size 12 forty below timberland boots, that he was wearing into the skull of their unconscious partner in crime.

Forty-Belows, were a favorite type of Timberland boot in style back in the early 1990's, within the inner cities. The boot possessed a rugged appearance and style. This particular boot was used as a weapon in many assaults in the urban community. They were the perfect boots to have on, if you wanted to stomp the breaks off of somebody's ass and possibly cause their death. The short thief finally awakened as he shook off the blow to the jaw and quickly jumped up from the ground and took off running. He fled down Rockaway Avenue and cut a right turn on Pitkin Avenue.

Denzel was pissed, he didn't give the unconscious punk a taste of his boot and get his chains back. He attempted to give chase but was blocked by the two other thugs whom wouldn't let him get pass them. The two muscled up accomplices acted as if they were two offensive linemen protecting the quarterback from getting sacked. Denzel realizing, he couldn't get through the two punks, began to take his frustrations out on the two remaining thugs. He started to shove both of them and got into a fighting stance as if he was ready to mix it up with them.

One of the thugs cracked a smile and began to back up

slowly in the same direction as his partner in crime that took off with the chains, before he took off running.

"Why you running like a little bitch? I bet you was one of them jail house faggots, that got fucked in the showers!" Denzel shouted at the fleeing thug as his voice echoed across the empty street. The fleeing thug, placed his middle finger up as he cut the corner on Pitkin Avenue and was out of Denzel's site.

Denzel was now standing face to face with the last remaining thug. He sized the thug up, and decided to grab him by the collar with one hand and was ready to strike him with the other hand. The thug simply pulled out a dark 9 mm handgun and pressed it up against Denzel's stomach.

"Don't do it money!" said the armed thug. "You fucking put one finger on me and I'll body you muthafucka!" The thug continued as he looked Denzel straight in the eyes while his finger was on the trigger. Denzel quickly unclenched his fist and loosened up his grip of the thug collar, once he felt the gun poking him in the gut. He then stepped back and quickly reached into his jacket. The armed thug thinking Denzel had a gun, jumped back and fired two shots, just missing Denzel.

The thug realized the two shots he fired missed their mark and just stared at Denzel as if he saw a ghost. Denzel with a demented look in his eyes, stood there as if he wasn't faded by the sound of the gunfire. He began to walk toward the thug as if he was possessed by something unnatural.

"Nigga! You better back the fuck up!" The Thug yelled out as he himself, began to slowly back up while still pointing his gun at Denzel. Denzel ignored the armed thug request and continued to walk closer and closer with his fist balled up ready to fight. He stared deeply into the thug eyes whom just tried to end his life over two gold chains. He could see signs of fear beginning to form in the eyes of the armed thug, and wanted to take the thug weapon away from him and kill him with his own shit. The armed thug attempted to make small talk, for some reason or another.

"Yo! Ain't you one of them Big Daddy Kane dancers or something?" The thug asked, thinking he recognized Denzel's face from somewhere. Denzel whole persona, made him appear to be a dancer or entertainer of the up and rising hip hop world of entertainment. Sometimes people would approach him and ask him who did he dance for. He sported a sharply cut high flat-top fade haircut with three parts and three strips on his eyebrow. He wore the latest designer clothing, that the rappers and dancers wore in their music videos and on stage at the concerts. Denzel just shook his head.

"Nigga, I ain't no dancer! I'm just a nigga you robbed and shot at tonight!" Denzel sarcastically replied as he noticeably started to stare at the weapon aimed at his body as he got closer. Thoughts of a television show based on disarming gunman, came into Denzel's mind. He felt if he could get close enough to it, he could grab it by the top slide so it wouldn't fire. And disarm the gunman easily.

"Oh, you must be getting money out here. I like taking drug dealers shit!" The gun man said as he started to laugh just before turning around and fleeing the scene in the same direction as his partners in crime. Denzel started to take off running behind him, but stopped dead in his tracks. He realized it would be crazy to run behind a man with a gun. Especially when he didn't have a gun of his own. All he could do is yell out his frustrations in the air.

"You should've killed me, muthafucka! I'm going to get all you niggas, watch! Closed caskets! I'm gonna come to all of yall funerals, and piss in yall caskets," Denzel yelled out loudly as he threatens the fleeing gun man, who ran down Rockaway Avenue and turned the corner on Pitkin towards Thatford Avenue.

"Suck a dick! You bitch ass nigga! And, thanks for the chains chump!" The fleeing thug yelled out as his voice echoed through air. Denzel started to let his rage get the best of him. He picks up a large empty beer bottle off the ground and broke the bottom off of it to transform it into a weapon. He then slowly jogged over to Belmont Avenue and made a quick left turn on Thatford avenue. Howard and Langston Hughes were two of the local projects in the area and Denzel figured these thugs had to live somewhere near the scene of the crime.

For a quick moment, his anger starts to grow and get the best of him. He grabbed a bottle from the ground and broke the base off it. He thought about running around the corner, in an attempt to catch up with the thugs so he could confront them. An old phrase *Never Bring a Knife to a Gunfight* popped into his head as reality set into his brain. He dropped the bottle to the ground and stood still for a moment to think.

Fool! Why would you even cross your mind to think you was going to run up on them with a fucking broken bottle? You already know one of them got a gun, because he bust two shots at Yo ass. A broken bottle means nothing to a nigga with a gun in his hand. Damn! I wish I had a fucking gun He thought to himself as he stood there on the darken street, as he let the robbery marinate into his mind.

I have no gun, no nothing to get these niggas with. There's only one thing left to do, to get these punk muthafuckas Denzel continued to think to himself as he began to walk fast down Rockaway Avenue towards the corner of Sutter Avenue. Frustrated and angered, he approached a telephone booth located at the corner, lift up the receiver and started dialing.

"911, where's your emergency?" Answered a female 911 operator, after Denzel placed an emergency call on the pay phone.

"Brooklyn, on the corner of Rockaway and Sutter Avenue." Denzel replied with his bottom lip trembling from anger.

"Okay, what is the emergency sir?" The operator asked as

Denzel could hear her typing on a keyboard.

"I just got robbed and shot at by three punks! They took my jewelry and then one of them shot at me two times," Denzel explained to the 911 operator as he started to stutter into the phone as his emotions began to get the best of him.

"Okay Sir, are you hurt? Do you need any medical attention?" The 911 operator asked. Denzel responded no.

"Okay, sir where did this happen?" Where there any weapons involved?" The 911 Operator asked.

"Rockaway Avenue between Pitkin and Belmont! Yes, there were weapons! Didn't I just tell you they tried to shoot me! I'm okay, I haven't been shot" Denzel said as he started to speak loudly into the phone.

"Okay, sir calm down! Do you know which direction the person or persons headed in and could you, please give a description if you can?" The operator asked.

"It was three male blacks wearing dark clothing. One of them is very short with a dark complexion and the other two are very muscular like they just came out of jail. They ran up Rockaway Avenue and made a right towards Thatford on Pitkin Avenue" Denzel stated as he looked around to see if one of the thugs was in his area.

"Okay sir, we will have a unit respond to you as soon as possible. Where are you now sir?" The operator asked as she typed in the information into her system.

"I'm standing at the pay phone next to the 24-hour store on the corner of Sutter and Rockaway Avenue.

"Okay Sir a unit will be there soon to assist you, please remain where you are until they arrive," The operator said just before she hung up.

The Violation of being robbed in his own neighborhood started to overtake Denzel's mind as he waited for the Police to arrive. It felt like a big dark cloud was over his head that squeezed at his brain. He wondered if the thugs spotted him walking with his jacket open exposing his jewelry, while they rode around in a vehicle looking for victims to rob. It was strange to him how he didn't observe anyone on the street, until the little chain snatcher approached him.

While he stood on the corner trying to analyze how he got caught slipping, he spotted a Blue and White marked police patrol car stop at the traffic light on the corner of Sutter Avenue and Rockaway. Denzel then stepped into the street and began waving his arms as he attempted to get the attention of the officers.

The officer driving the police vehicle, simply waved back to Denzel and continued to cruise down Sutter Avenue towards Osborne Street in which the patrol car then stopped at another red signal traffic light. Denzel started to yell out to the patrol car to no avail. He only gained the attention of the people whom were hanging out in the street in the early wee hours of the morning.

"Who you ready to snitch on, nigga?" A dirty crack addict asked as he stood near the store trying to bum some change to support his habit, while stinking up the block. Denzel looked over at the filthy drug addict in disgust.

"Mind your fucking business! You fucking, nosey ass crackhead!" Denzel yelled out loud enough for the crack addict to hear. "Instead of minding nigga's business! You need to go figure out who dick you gotta suck, so you could go get some crack to smoke!" Denzel continued to yell out as he started to run out in the street towards Osbourne to catch up with the Patrol car.

"Run snitch! Run! I may be a crackhead! But You a snitch, nigga!" The drug addict shouted back at Denzel, as he laughed loudly and smiled exposing all his rotten teeth. The crack addict started to draw attention to himself by people passing by and those whom were hanging out in the wee hours of the morning. Denzel didn't like to be called a snitch nor the attention the drug addict was drawing towards him and decided to give him a warning.

"Call me a fucking snitch again! You half dead muthafucka! And I'll come over there and kicked whatever life you have left out of your smoked-out ass!" Denzel shouted out with enough force that made the crack addict shut his raggedy mouth.

Denzel then zeroed in on the patrol car as he attempted to ignore the crack addict who was taunting him. He continued to run as he got closer and closer to the patrol car before they had a chance to pull off. As the patrol car was about to drive off once the traffic light changed, Denzel caught up to it and began to bang on the rear passenger window on the driver's side.

He basically scared the shit out of both officers who threw their guns out their holsters.

"What the fuck!" The startled officer driving the car said as he nearly jumped out his seat while he grabbed for his weapon. He then rolled down the window to see what the hell was going on.

"I'm the one you guys are looking for! I'm the one that got robbed and called 911!" Denzel said while trying to catch his breath after he chased down the car.

"Dude! You almost got your fucking head blown off for scarring the shit out of us! Especially in this fucking battle zone" The Officer sitting on the passenger side said as he pointed his weapon towards Denzel's head with his hands shaking.

Denzel wisely put his hands up slowly and looked at both of the Officers. He realized that he just scarred the shit out of them. He also realized he could've got blasted by the two scared to death Officers that patrolled the ruff neighborhood and knew it was best for him not to make any more sudden moves.

"Sorry Officers, I didn't mean to run up on you like that, But I just got robbed and one of the guys pulled out gun and shot at me. I called 911, and they said that the police were on their way" Denzel said as he watched the two Officer get more relaxed as they both holstered their weapons.

"Okay buddy, just relax, where did you get robbed at? And around what time?" The officer sitting in the driver seat asked.

"On Rockaway Avenue between Pitkin and Belmont around about five or ten minutes ago" Denzel responded. Both officers then looked at each other for a few seconds strangely.

"We going to call for that unit your looking for to come over here," The officer in the passenger seat said just before placing his radio to his mouth.

"Get on the other side of the car, so you don't get ran over by someone in the street" The Officer sitting in the driver seat instructed Denzel. Denzel then walked around the Police vehicle following the Officer's instructions to avoid the on-coming traffic that traveled up and down Sutter Avenue.

"Twelve Charlie Central," The officer on the Passenger transmitted over his radio.

"GO ahead Twelve Charlie," The dispatcher responded in regard to the officer's transmission.

"We have a pickup of a past robbery at gunpoint over here on the corner of Osbourne and Sutter Avenue. The victim stated he called it in central" The officer transmitted over his radio.

"Ten Four," The dispatcher acknowledged as she could be heard typing in the location on a keyword in search of the call in.

"Twelve Charlie," The dispatcher transmitted over the radio in response to the officer's transmission.

"Twelve Charlie," The officer in the passenger seat acknowledged.

"I'm not seeing any past robberies at gun point called in at that location. The only past robbery I have occurred on Rockaway Avenue between Pitkin and Belmont. The complainant on that call also complained that one of the perp shot at him during the robbery. Responding units stated they could not locate the complainant. It may be one in the same. Please keep central advised," The dispatcher responded.

"Well, central marked it down as a pick up then! We have a complainant here stating he was robbed at gunpoint.

"Housing Conditions Central," a deep male voice transmitted over the radio.

"Housing Conditions," The dispatcher acknowledged the deep male voice transmission.

"Show us responding over to Osbourne and Sutter to meet up with Twelve Charlie, so we could handle that robbery complaint central," The Deep Male voice stated over the radio.

"TEN FOUR Housing Conditions! I have you responding. Housing Condition, please keep central advised," The dispatcher responded and requested.

"TEN FOUR Central, Show us in route in route" Housing Conditions responded while heading to the location.

"We have another car coming over to take your complaint buddy! It's out of our jurisdiction, but we will help the other unit look for these guys, okay?" The driver of the patrol car said as he looked at his watch. The driver started to put one and one together that the complainant before them was the one whom placed the call-in regard to the past robbery within their jurisdiction, but he was more concerned with going to lunch than anything else.

"Hey buddy! Where did they rob you at? And what did they take?" The officer seating in the passenger seat asked.

"They got me on Rockaway Avenue between Pitkin and Belmont Avenue" Denzel responded as he leaned over to see the officer face.

"Did you just say Rockaway Avenue between Pitkin and Belmont?" The officer in the driver's seat asked. Before Denzel could answer, a gray unmarked Plymouth Grand Fury quickly pulled up beside the Patrol car. Inside the Plymouth Grand Fury were three very large male Caucasian officers in uniform.

An officer whom had a very thick blonde mustache sitting in the passenger seat of the Grand-Fury rolled down his window and dumped the ashes from his large cigar he was smoking. He stared at Denzel with his bright blue eyes and reddish face and asked the officers in the marked patrol car.

"Is this guy the perp or the victim?" As he continued to stare at Denzel and watch him closely.

"Yep! This is the complainant," The officer sitting in the driver's seat of the patrol car responded. The officers from th twelfth precinct then filled the housing officers on the little information Denzel had told them. The twelfth precinct officers then requested that the housing officers keep them updated on the description of the perps so they could assist on the canvass.

"Okay kid! These guys are going to take it from here" The Officer driving the mark patrol car said just before he drove off leaving Denzel with the Housing Conditions Officers. The Officer in the Passenger seat of the unmarked car then exited the vehicle and walked over to where Denzel was standing on the curb. He was very tall and had a solid build.

"Housing Conditions Central, "The officer transmitted over his portable radio as he looked at Denzel.

"Go ahead housing conditions," The dispatcher quickly responded.

"Show us out canvassing the area with the victim of a past

robbery, victim states, he was also shot at by the suspects, I will update you with further information in regard to the descriptions and directions of flight of the perpretrators in a minute," The officer transmitted.

"Do me a favor buddy, put your hands on your head," The tall Officer instructed Denzel.

"But officer I'm a victim, not the criminal, I get robbed and shot at and you want to search me?" Denzel said as he couldn't understand why the Officer was giving him instructions.

"Calm down young man! I got to check you for weapons before you get in my car, it's all about safety" The tall officer explained to Denzel letting him know it wasn't personal. Denzel then complied and let the Officer search him. The tall officer signaled to his partners that Denzel was clean and okay to get in the car.

"Okay get in my man, we're going to find these muthafuckas for you," The officer who was driving the unmarked police vehicle said. The Officer was a real wide body, who had sky blue eyes and blond hair. Denzel quickly jumped in the car and sat behind the Officer who was sitting in the front passenger seat.

"So, my man, where did this robbery take place?" The Officer seating in the rear of the Officer driving asked.

"It happened on Rockaway Avenue Between Pitkin and Belmont" Denzel said as he watched the Officer write down the information on a pad.

The officer driving the unmarked vehicle then pulled off and headed towards the location. The officer in the front passenger seat took a long pull of his cigar and blew the smoke out his window.

"Did you tell them other officers the same location?" The Officer in the front passenger seat asked.

"Yeah, I told them, and they said some other cops were

coming to help me," Denzel informed the Officers as they rode to the location where he was robbed.

"All that shit talking, about Housing Cops never available! But them lazy fucks from the Seven Three always shit canning jobs!" The officer driving said as he referred to the first responding officers on the scene.

The officer seating next to Denzel started to collect the description of the assailants as well as all his personal information, so he could complete the police complaint report (Name, Address etc.) As well information pertaining to the stolen property. The officer in the passenger seat then turned around.

"Give us a quick description of these three punks that robbed you kid," The officer sitting up front anxiously asked as he looked at Denzel.

"I'm getting that now from him now, you fucking jerkoff!" The officer in the back seat sitting next to Denzel said.

"You back there taking notes and wasting time, I'm looking to fuck somebody up and make this armed robbery collar tonight before them muthafuckas disappear!" The officer in the front seat said as he raised the radio towards his mouth. Denzel then repeated the description to the requesting officer in the front passenger seat.

Once Denzel completed the description, the officer driving then turned the vehicle back around, while his partner transmitted the description over the radio. The Central dispatcher, repeated the description of the three males and asked all units in the area to be on the lookout for the trio.

The officer driving the vehicle overheard Denzel give his address to the officer in the back whom was taking the report and started to say.

"You got to be fucking kidding me! These mutts are out here robbing people from their own neighborhood now?!" As he started to shake his head while driving. Denzel looked over at the Officer sitting next to him whose uniform patch read "New York City Housing Authority Police Department." Now back in the days during this time, all three Police Agency were separate and had different patches on their uniforms as well as patrol cars and scooters.

"You guys are housing cops? I didn't know that Housing Cops could lock people up," Denzel said unaware of the duties of a housing police officer.

"Didn't you hear me just talking about them City pricks shit canning your robbery just a few minutes ago?!" The officer driving shouted. "Can't lock people up?! Who's been feeding you this bullshit kid?" The driver continued as he drove the unmarked vehicle to the scene of the robbery.

"The regular cops, in the blue and white cars," Denzel said to the officers sitting in the unmarked vehicle surprise.

"Well, I got stopped and patted down the other day by some cops in a blue and white car. While being searched by them, I asked did they work out of the Police Room on Stone Avenue in back of one of the project building. The officers responded that they were on the real job, and that housing police were security guards and not the real police like themselves," Denzel said to explain his remark while he looked out the window scanning the streets with his eyes looking for the thugs that robbed him.

"Real police huh! Those lazy fucks who was in that blue and white marked patrol car you were talking to when we got over here, didn't even want to help you while knowing you got robbed in their jurisdiction" The Officer in the front passenger seat said in an angry tone of voice. Denzel didn't realize it was a long-lasting feud between the Housing and Transit Police Departments against the City Cops.

"Oh no wonder when I tried to flag them down, the driver looked me in the face and kept it moving. I had to chase the car down until they stopped at the traffic light" Denzel informed the Trio who started to laugh.

"Don't worry kid; Us Security Guards are going to find these punks that robbed you," The Officer Driving said as he cruised up and down the vicinity of where Denzel got robbed.

"Beep Beep Beep 10-10 shots fired! Corner of East New York and Stone Avenue! No further information giving at this time and no call-back," A transmission blasted over the Officers radio from the dispatcher. The officer driving accelerated the gas, as the officer in the front passenger seat quickly grabbed the metallic cherry red light from the middle console of the vehicle and placed it on the round sheet of metal on the dashboard while acknowledging the transmission and placed the red light on the hood of the car.

"What's going on?" Denzel asked the officers as the car sped towards Howard Projects and he observed the officers preparing themselves for some type of combat. It was like the sound of the Police siren transformed them into something else.

"We're heading to a shooting in Howard Projects, Maybe the guys that robbed you are involved," The officer sitting next to Denzel said. Denzel looked at the Officer like he was crazy.

CHAPTER 15

A NEED TO LAY LOW

NATE **sat in his car looking into his nap sack**. It was filled with vials of crack cocaine, jewelry, and cash. It was a nice hit for him, minus the body he caught.

Young Blood, had that shit coming to him! What the fuck, was that nigga thinking? I know he didn't think, I was gonna let that shit fly. You not gonna try to pull out on Nate, and live Nate thought as he questioned himself as he reached into his glove compartment, and pulled out his crack pipe. He then sorted through his nap sack and pulled out a crack vial and placed a crack rock into the pipe and lite it up with his lighter. As the fumes from the narcotic substance traveled through the pipe right into his lung then into his mind. Nate mentally started to thrift away.

He leaned his seat back to relax and enjoy the hit. He closed his eyes and was slowly falling asleep, until he was quickly awakened by the sound of gun fire. Nate jumped up and became very paranoid. He had already pulled out one of his guns and looked around in search of shooters shooting at him. He then realized the gunfire was coming from up the block and put his weapon down into his lap.

"Damn! These muthafuckas just fucked up my high," Nate mumbled as he started his vehicle and drove off in search of another spot to lay low. He knew the sound of gun fire would bring unwanted police attention to the area and anyone hanging it, whether if they spotted you walking on or merely sitting in a vehicle, it was a chance you would be questioned and frisked by the police.

Nate was no fool, and he knew shit was going to be hot for him in Brownsville, especially after he gun downed Shakim in front of his crew. Retaliation was the code of the streets and no one was above the code.

I got to get the fuck out of Brooklyn Nate thought to himself as he observed a patrol car slowly driving up the block and bypassing him. Nate continued to travel away from the sound of the gun shots and decided to pull over to a telephone booth not too far from the 175th Precinct. He exited his vehicle and left the engine running. He approached the telephone booth that was stationed right next to the 24/7 local bodega window under a lit awning. He inserted a dime and started dialing.

"What's Up, Cuzzo? It's me! Nate!" Nate said as he spoke into the phone after he heard a voice say hello.

"Nate! Why the hell, are you calling me this early in the morning?" Eugene said in a harsh tone as if he was in the middle of something important.

"Damn Cuz! I just called to see what's up with you and the family," Nate replied as he looked around for police and Shakim's homeboys.

"To see what's up? Dez nutts, nigga! I'm in here beating up some pussy, like you should be doing! Anyway, spare me the rah-rah shit and tell me what you want," Eugene said while knowing something must really be important for Nate to call him so early. Nate knew he might as well come clean with his situation already.

"Yo, Cuz! I just got caught up in some ole bullshit with some young niggas out here in Brooklyn, and I need to lay low for a few days. Can I come through?" Nate confessed and asked, letting his cousin know he was in some type of trouble and needed help.

"Damn! Your old ass always getting in some shit!" Eugene said in a sarcastic tone. "You know your always welcome to crash here for a little bit cuz, as long as you leave that Brooklyn state of mind bullshit in Brooklyn. I don't need no static on my home front," Eugene continued as he looked over at the young lady who was lying next to him.

"Good looking out cousin! But what about the shorty you in there smashing? Will she be cool with me laying low at your crib?" Nate responded after getting the okay from his cousin to crash at his apartment.

"Nigga this my crib! I'm about to wake this bitch up for round three, then I'm going to send her ass home in a cab," Eugene said as he thought the young female was sound asleep.

"Okay Cuzzo, I don't want to cause any problems in your love life," Nate said as he looked at his watch.

"Okay, hurry up then and make sure you get here before it's time for me to go to work Nate" Eugene said as he started to rub on the female next to him round ass.

"Soon as I get off the phone, I'm heading back home to Harlem USA," Nate said jokingly referring to the borough he once lived in and Eugene currently still lives in as they both hung up.

Eugene and Nate were first cousins. Their mothers were identical twin sisters and the daughters of a well-known preacher in East Harlem area. Even though they were the daughters of a preacher, both of the twins had a thing for street thugs. It was as if it was a common thing for daughters of preachers to do at the time.

Nate's mom, fell for Nate's dad whom was a stick-up kid in Harlem. He did everything from strong arm to armed robbery, and was in and out of jail on a regular basis. When Nate was two years old, his dad was killed during an armored car robbery by police. It was said, He almost made it home with the $250,000 he took, before the police caught up with him and gunned him down in front of his apartment building.

Mysteriously, only $100,000 of the $250,000 was reported recovered by the police. Nate whom was only two years old at the time of the shooting, never got to know his dad and soon moved to Brooklyn with his mom after his father's death.

Eugene's father name was James Currie. James, son of a heart surgeon and nurse at Harlem Hospital had a fortunate up bringing in Harlem. He once studied at New York University, but gave up his education to become a well-known dope dealer and pimp in Harlem. James had a good run with his career in crime until he was murdered inside his brownstone that was also set on fire. It was rumored that the Italians paid him a little visit for not giving them a share of the income he made, and for refusing their so-called protection.

Prior to James's death, he purchased himself a life insurance policy, but he never took the time to purchase a home insurance and neglected to pay his home property tax, so the home just went up in smoke, and his son wasn't able to benefit or inherit the property.

Eugene and his mom remained in East Harlem after James death, and moved to a New York City Housing Authority Project called Wagner Houses that overlooked the Franklin D. Roosevelt Highway, when she exhausted half of the money from James's life insurance policy.

Nate took on the job of looking out for his younger cousin by hooking him up with the latest gear and keeping his pockets full of cash, when he was on top enforcing for his now deceased heroin kingpin. When Eugene got older, he landed a job with the New York City Housing Authority as a plaster on the lower east side of Manhattan. He later recruited young teenagers whom lived in the projects where he worked to sling crack cocaine for him, along with some of his co-workers whom worked in housing maintenance. Back in the Mid 1980's until today, employees of New York City Housing Authority assigned to the projects, were deeply involved in the narcotic business.

During this time in the Mid 1980's, there was four young major players in Harlem that stood out, who were getting a lot of paper on the streets of Harlem. These guys were high rollers and were known to drive fancy cars. All the money hungry gold diggers were riding their dicks hard. These chicks did everything from sucking dick to fucking just to get an outfit, designer hand bag or a ride in a hot car.

The four major players were the connect to go see if you wanted some quality product for a good price, if you were dope dealing. Everybody involved in the dope game in Harlem was eating, as the money rolled in. Eugene had a connect with these guys, and was a loyal customer. He would purchase cocaine from them, cook it up into crack cocaine, then bag it up for sale by

Eugene workers would store their stash in the mail boxes and slop sinks located in the lobbies of the project building they were working out of. Some even hid it in a small container with a sliding slot that had a magnet attached to it, in which they would attach it to an overhead hallway light knowing many Police Officers never think to look up.

Eugene was wise enough not to set up shop in Harlem. The word was out about a violent crew of thugs that were out there in the streets of Harlem, who were terrorizing and extorting local dealers from the area as well as the Bronx that was making a lot of money. This crew had a reputation of making those who crossed their path disappear and were for hire for the right price.

Eugene also didn't want to cross his suppliers, who had a large fan base in the neighborhood. The four young major players that supplied him were making millions of dollars in Harlem. They sponsored and funded many events like block parties, cookouts, basketball tournaments, and funerals (of their fallen soldiers), so everybody showed them mad love in the community.

If word got out and it would've, that someone was stepping on their toes, it would be more than likely shit was about to go down. One of the three players, whom you could've spotted zipping down the street popping wheelies of his motorcycle was a real live wire. He was a male Hispanic that could pass for a male black due to his hair texture and his complexion. This guy didn't take well to those who crossed the trio, and had no problem laying down a murder game to build his reputation.

Instead of buying flashy jewelry, clothing and a whole fleet of expensive cars, drawing that unwanted attention to himself. Eugene took advantaging of the opportunity giving by the city of New York to purchase a few brown-stone townhouses in Harlem for practically nothing with the promise to renovate. He also purchased vacant properties for cheap in Charlotte North Carolina, Atlanta Georgia as well as in many other Southern States with his illegal income that he mixed with his legal money. Eugene some-how knew that real estate and property held much more value than the basic material things that others sold their poisons for. He didn't care for the flash, probably because the flash and fame was the thing that got his father killed, and he didn't want to follow in his footsteps.

Eugene began to hug his girlfriend who was laying right next to him. He pressed his naked body very close to her from behind as her round bottom quickly aroused him. Her naked body embraced his hug as she backed her ass closer to his harden cocked that twitched at her very movement. He began to lick the back of her neck along her hair line, in search of her sexual arousal spot to make her pussy drip wet. She Began to breathe heavier and heavier, because his tongue was sending chills through her body as it began to jerk on and off.

Eugene then reached over to his night stand and retrieved a condom as his cock stood up at full attention. He quickly slid the condom on as he squeezed her breasts with the other hand. The sexual encounter lasted for about thirty minutes, because Eugene was in a rush due to his cousin coming over.

"Okay now since you gave me a rush job! Are you going to drop me off home or do you want me to stay?" Monique the young lady laying with Eugene asked.

"Mo! I'm going to send you in a cab. If I drive you, it's a good chance I would miss my cousin when he gets here," Eugene replied while looking at his alarm clock on top of his dresser. Monique looked at Eugene as if she wanted to slap the shit out of him.

"Oh, since your cousin is coming I got too get sent home in a cab like a fucking side bitch huh?" She asked as her facial expression grew angry.

"Baby, I will make it up to you I promise. I just don't want this fool to try his stupid Brooklyn shit up here in Harlem okay" Eugene said as he watched the frustrated female get up and start to get dressed as he admired her shapely body.

"Do you really think I rather have my cousin here than you?" Eugene continued to ask as he began to fill bad that she was leaving.

"No, I understand that you have a family emergency, I just thought I was going to break day with you that's all," Monique said as she struggled to put on her Gucci Boots after placing her Gucci hat on along with her other clothing.

"Next Weekend, me and you are going shopping to any store

of your choice my treat," Eugene said hoping it would change Monique mood. Monique's eyes lit up from Eugene offer to go shopping next week.

"Oh, that would be very nice of you," She said as she placed her Gucci handbag on her shoulder and began to smile from ear to ear. Monique was far from a gold digger head looking to fuck and suck her way into a man's pocket. She was an Assistant District Attorney in Queens Supreme Courts and owned a duplex condo in the Chelsea Area in Manhattan. Monique father held the rank of a one-star chief in the New York City Police Department and her mother was a judge in Bronx Criminal Court.

"Gene (A nick name she called Eugene) when your cousin gets here, make sure your black ass let him know I'm more than some bitch, and not to make this shit a habit or we all going to have a problem," Monique said in a very sarcastic tone as she sent a message to Eugene who looked at her speechless for the moment while she held her hands on her hips. "And yes, I heard what the fuck you said," She continued as she began to fold her arms.

"Damn baby! You were ear hustling on me?" Eugene responded as Monique put up her middle finger.

"You know I was just fronting like I had it like that," Eugene said while copping a plea. "I really didn't mean nothing by it, I will straighten all that shit out with him when he gets here Mo okay!" Eugene continued as he extended his arms out in search of a warm embrace from his lady.

"Hug these nuts nigga!" Monique replied. Call me a damn cab, so I can get the fuck out of here," Monique continued as she was already set to leave his apartment. Eugene knew that Monique was a fly girl that had it going on. She had a great career and comes from a well-established family. He also knew if it wasn't for his down low drug money flow that kept him on top, He probably would look like a gold digger himself, if you compared the salaries they made, the car they drove and where they each lived. Monique could see that Eugene apology was sincere and began to smile as she walked over to embrace him.

"Next time you pick me up to bring me to your house, you better be taken me home! Okay!" Monique said as she looked Eugene in the eyes.

"Mo! (A kick name Eugene called Monique) You know I got you baby! And I promise this it won't happen again," Eugene said as he reached sled his hand down from the waist to squeeze her ass.

"Get your hands off my ass! I'm serious! Don't try to treat me like one of these bum ass bitches out in the streets, Eugene! You know I would drive my car over here but you got too many jealous muthafuckas on your block, that would fuck with my car," Monique continued. She was referring to her brand new red BMW, that she keeps parked in her indoor garage located at the condo complex she lived in on West 25th Street and 8th Avenue.

"I said I got you! Right?" Eugene yelled. Causing Monique to give him a look like, Who the fuck you yelling at?

"Now, I know you are bugging. Don't make me have to wake up your whole fucking building," Monique shouted.

"Oh, here you go! Chill out love, chill out" Eugene said as he gestured for Monique to keep her voice down and gave her a tighter hug. "Speaking of BMWs, I've been thinking about getting one myself. I've been putting in all that overtime at work, and saving up," Eugene continued as he released his tight hug, and released his grip on her ass. He then walked over to the telephone to call a cab. Monique smiled at Eugene with an expression as if he couldn't afford it, as she was unaware that he had enough cash stashed in his safety deposit box to buy at least six new beamers.

"For real baby! Make sure you get one with a phone in it like mine," Monique replied sarcastically.

"I'm dead ass serious Mo, I'm going to get me a beamer for real," Eugene repeated as he dialed the cab service.

"Whatever Babe, just let me know when you serious about making that move, and I will hook you up with a good friend of my family over at the dealership," Monique said in regard to having a connection at the BMW dealership. She was already on her second BMW, she got the new one when the first one turned four years old. Eugene could feel her doubt.

"I know you probably thinking to yourself, that I should be trying to get out the projects first before buying an expensive car. But I figured, I would buy the car first and move in with you later," Eugene jokingly said after he placed a pick-up request call with the cab service.

"Live with me huh? So, your family members could come pop up anytime they want early in the morning after getting into who knows what type of trouble, Oh Hell No!" Monique replied while laughing out loud as Eugene cracked a smile.

"Wow! I see you got jokes baby; You should be on a stage somewhere doing stand-up," Eugene sarcastically replied to her comment as he walked over to his apartment window that faces the street.

"Your cab should be here in a few minutes" Eugene continued as he looked at his watch.

"Okay, hurry up and get dressed so you can walk me down to the cab Gene" Monique requested as she watched Eugene walk back into the bedroom to get dressed.

Eugene lived in a New York City Housing Authority affiliated building, where the tenants had to pay electric bills and the buildings didn't possess any elevators. His apartment was located on the fifth floor and his window was located in the front and side of the building. The building possessed an intercom and a secured door to avoid all trespassers. Eugene got dressed and they both walked down the stairwell to the first floor and then they exited the building.

While standing on the stoop outside in front the building, a car pulled up and beeped its horn two times. It was the cab service Eugene called, so they both walked down the small set of steps off the stoop and towards the vehicle. Eugene then handed her three hundred dollars in twenty dollar bills, just before giving her a goodbye kiss. She then entered the cab as Eugene held the door. Once she was settled, Eugene closed the door and watched it roll away. He then headed back into his building and back to his apartment.

Eugene telephone started to ring, and he could hear it just before he re-entered his apartment.

"Damn, who the fuck is it now?" He thought to himself as he entered his apartment. He then walked over to the telephone and picked it up.

"HELLO" He answered.

"What up cousin? I just touched down in Harlem. I'm going to make a quick stop near the ROOFTOP before I come through to your crib," Nate said as he spoke from the other end of the telephone.

The ROOFTOP was a roller skating rink with an after-hours spot upstairs. It was a well-known spot in Harlem back in the mid 80's early 90's, where all the hustlers hung out and showcased themselves as being major players that was getting money. It was only open on Wednesday, Friday, and Saturday.

If you weren't hip to the latest in hot cars, jewelry, clothes or every seeing some of the finest women alive, this was the perfect place to get a glimpse of everything you been missing.

"Nate! What the fuck you mean you making a quick stop

before you come through? I just had my girl break out and all that for your crazy ass. Don't be coming up to Harlem starting that robbing niggas shit! Because I got to live here and I don't need no problems with any of these niggas out here. They have a team of niggas out here that got dirty cops rolling with them," Eugene said as he hoped Nate wasn't planning to pull his robbery game in his neighborhood.

"It's nothing like that cousin; I just want to hustle off some of these jewels I picked up in Brooklyn, unless you want to buy it?" Nate replied in regard to getting rid of the jewelry he jacked from his victims in Brownsville.

"You know I don't fuck with that flashy shit, so do what you got to do. Just get to my crib, before it's time for me to go to work," Eugene replied as he started to yawn.

"I just figure I ask you first. I'll be there soon as I finish meeting up with one of my boys," Nate said as they both hung up.

Nate drove down to West 132nd Street just off of 7th Avenue, after he didn't see his boys hanging out near the ROOFTOP. He was hoping to run into Money, before he turned in for the night. Nate met Money in prison and schooled him how to survive in there. Money thought of Nate of being a true old school thug. He heard of Nate's past as a true soldier to the game. So, every now and then, Nate would pass through Harlem and sell Money workers jewels, because the product Money was connected with was some real quality shit. Money respected Nate but would never put him on to work for him, basically, because he knew that Nate was using and also that he would probably bump heads with Polo.

Polo, who was a hot-blooded Cuban was well known all over Harlem. He was, and his demand for attention was off the charts. If he wasn't seen riding down the road in a foreign expensive car, he was tearing down the block on motorcycles popping willies as his groupies cheered him on as they watched. Polo would be on the set flossing with the type of clothes and jewelry that the upcoming rappers of the nineteen eighties would soon mimic as a sign of success. He would even pose in photos with weapons drawn while being surrounded by friends and fellow hustlers, showing no fear of law enforcement.

Polo and Nate also met in prison when Polo was serving a short bid for a minor narcotics charge. While in prison Polo once witness Nate strangle an inmate nick named APOLLO to death with a barbell in the weight room. On that day, Polo was in the gym getting his work out on while Apollo was in their bench pressing some heavy weights. Suddenly, out of nowhere Nate rushed Apollo as he went to press the barbell against his chest. Nate pushed the barbell downwards toward Apollo's neck and applied extra pressure by putting his knee on it.

Rumors had it that Apollo raped a new inmate, whom was related to a family friend of Nate's. Apollo was a big muscular guy that had a thing for committing rapes against the smaller inmates. He terrorized the weak on his tier and used his muscular body to intimidate selected inmates to submit to his sexual advances. Physical threats were made if an inmate didn't easy comply and some acts of violence would take place. If an inmate Apollo targeted didn't comply, he would DEAD ARM them. DEAD ARM is a street term for throwing a vicious blow with your arm putting all your body weight behind it. His victims would then be knocked unconscious, then thrown over his shoulder and taken to a secluded area, to engage in a little sexual activity.

Nate had a dislike for the so-called prison thugs that went around raping other male inmates and used this act to terrorize the prisons. During his numerous bids with the prison walls, His definition of dominating another male was to beat them down and put the fear of god in them, not to rape them. Nate was old fashioned and believed that a man should be a man and woman should always remain a woman. Any man with thoughts and urges to have any type of sexual encounter with another man for whatever reason, was simply a homosexual.

Incarceration was a mere excuse for many whom committed rape within the prison walls, as only being part of their prison lifestyle. Some claimed it to be a way of life in the prison and a symbol of strength and dominance within the prison walls. Polo respected Nate crazy murder game inside and outside of the prison walls. He would occasionally fuck with Nate in regard to how Nate fell off by getting hooked to the drugs on the street.

They argued on many occasions in the prison yard like father and son, but backed each other up when shit hit the fan. Polo let it be known to all the soldiers and hustlers under his rank in Harlem, not to cheat nor disrespect Nate when he steps on the set to cop some rock. And if word got to him that someone did, they would be personally dealt with by him.

As Nate parked his car on the corner after circling the block a few times; he then heard the sound of loud music blasting, and then observed a tinted out black BMW with chrome wheels pull up alongside off his vehicle. Nate sneakily reached over to get a grip of one of his weapons. He slowly turned his head, only to see Polo looking over at him with a smile on his face.

"What up Old Skool?!" Polo yelled out as he turned down the volume of his car stereo.

"Polo, my man! What's up young blood?!" Nate answered as he was happy to see him.

"Chilling nigga! I just dropped off one of bitches, I just finished fucking. I would let your old ass see the tape, but you might fuck around and catch a heart attack," Polo jokingly said as he started to laugh.

"Nigga you still taping yourself beating up some pussy

huh?!" Nate asked as he shook his head.

"Hell, yeah nigga! You know how I do Old Skool! These hoes out here be loving me," Polo said as he checked his watch while flashing his gold presidential Rolex.

"You better chill with that taping shit! You going to fuck around and catch a charge for fucking one of them fast ass young girls out here. God forbid, one of them girls catch feelings, and you shit on them. All they got to do is walk in the precinct and say you took that young pussy and taped the shit. The cops will draw up a warrant on your ass crib so fast, and your ass will be facing a statutory rape case," Nate explained to his young friend. Polo just looked at Nate as if he was crazy.

"So, you came all the way to Harlem, just to tell me that shit Old Skool?" Polo sarcastically asked.

"Hell, no Young Blood, I got some nice jewels for you to check out, to go with that Presidential you are rocking," Nate said while finding that the perfect opportunity to get rid of some of his stolen stash.

"Word, let me pull over and see what you are holding," Polo said as he pulled his car over in front of Nate's vehicle. Polo got out his car and walked over to Nate's. He could see Nate's hand on his gun.

"Fuck you got your hand on your burner for?" Polo asked as he climbed in into the front passenger seat.

"What the fuck you expect when you just rolled up on me like that Young Blood? I was ready for battle," Nate replied as he placed his .45 Caliber semi-auto in between his legs.

"My nigga Old Skool always set on go, and still thugging it like a muthafucka," Polo said while giving Nate a hand shake. "I just copped this nickel-plated baby yesterday" Polo continued as he lifts up his shirt to expose the .357 Magnum he had tucked in his waist line. He was basically letting Nate know he also stayed packing.

"What is the fascination you young muthafuckas got with these nickel-plated guns man? That nickel-plated shit will get you killed, it's too shiny, and niggas could see that shit coming," Nate said as he reached into his rear passenger seat and retrieved his duffle bag. Polo didn't give a fuck what Nate was talking about as he shrugged his shoulders. Nate then passed the bag over to Polo who examined its contents.

"Damn nigga! How you get all this shit?" Polo asked.

"What you think?" Nate sarcastically replied.

"I know you didn't jack none of my peoples up here in Harlem, right? "Polo asked Nate as he looked over at Nate.

"Nah man, I caught all that shit in Brooklyn." Nate replied as he took a quick glance in his side view mirror, looking for police. Polo fumbled through the jewelry in the bag, in search of something that he liked.

"Nate, you know this shit right here is basic Chinatown shit, way below my money level. I'm rocking Rolex's and foreign cars. We are getting money up here in Harlem! The Brooklyn niggas ain't getting it like we are getting it out here you heard!" Polo said as he continued to sort through the stuff. Nate started to get a little disappointed, because he wanted to get the shit off his hands. Polo stopped searching through the bag and looked at Nate.

"Old Skool, since you my man and all, I'll cop this shit off your hands. I probably will give it to some of these little niggas out here, when they go to the store for me or something. How much you want for it?" Polo asked. Nate started to smile. His time wasn't wasted.

"Hit me off with what you think it's worth in product," Nate replied.

"Product? Damn nigga! You still getting high?" Polo asked as if he didn't know. "You want hard aka crack cocaine or soft aka powdered cocaine?" Polo continued asked as he checked his pager.

"Let me get half and half," Nate answered. "Well I don't have shit on me right now, but I'm going to give you my pager to hit me up tomorrow for your package," Polo said as he opened of Nate's glove compartment and took out a piece of paper towel. He wrote down his pager number, as well as Money's and Smooth's. He handed the paper towel to Nate.

"Hit me on my pager for that package around twelve noon today. It looks like you got enough crack in this bag to hold you down until then. Let me get a bag or something for this shit I'm taking, "Polo said, because he was ready to take the stolen jewelry and leave. Nate handed Polo a plastic bag, and Polo took the bag and placed the jewelry inside of it. He then handed Nate back the duffle bag that still contained an undetermined amount of cash and vials crack cocaine.

"Old Skool! You know I only fuck with you, because your originally from Harlem, right? Because if you weren't, we wouldn't be doing any type of business," Polo said.

"Why not?" Nate asked.

"Most Brooklyn niggas be on that grimey shit! Robbing and setting niggas up all day, even down to the bitches from there," Polo said as Nate looked at him, like why you are telling me that. "Nah! Don't get me wrong Old Skool, I got a few homies down there I'm cool with. I just don't do business with them. Shit! I'm surprised they didn't kill your ass yet, as much as you be doing them dirty," Polo continued as he started to exit the car after giving Nate a hand shake.

"You can't kill the Boogie Man nigga!" Nate jokingly said as he watched Polo exit his car. Polo walked around to Nate's driver's side door, and motioned for him to lower his window.

"Next week, we are doing it up with a block party for all my peoples on the East Side, come through and check us out." Polo said as he checked his watch again.

"Sounds like a plan to me," Nate responded.

"Yall Harlem niggas be doing it big, you know I got love for my home team," Nate said as he watched Polo exit his car and re-entered his own. "I'll try and pass through for that Block Party Young Blood, I know how Yall Nukka do," Nate continued as he knew Polo and the other three players hosted nothing but the best for they people. Nate then started his vehicle and pulled out from behind Polo car that was still sitting there.

"Go home already! You know you need to be washing that dirty Puerto Rican Panamanian Cuban Spanish Dick! These hoes will have your little webo pissing fire," Nate hollered out the window with a smile on his face just before he drove off.

"Fuck you! Yah old bastard! You need to be worried about them dirty crackheads bitches you be fucking," Polo yelled back while laughing as he pulled out the parking spot and sped down the street with music blasting in the opposite direction that Nate was heading in.

Nate started driving towards Eugene's apartment building, once he got there he noticed there was no parking available on Eugene's block. He then drove around the block about three times until a postal worker came out of the building next to Eugene's building to head to work. As the postal worker entered his car, Nate then drove up and parallel parked near the postal worker so no one else could steal the parking space, in which was right in front of Eugene's building. The Postal Worker then drove off, and Nate took the parking space, and gathered his things before he exited the vehicle. He then walked onto the stoop and pressed the intercom.

"Who is it?" Nate asked over the intercom.

"It's Santa Claus Muthafucka! Open the door," Nate answered while having a little fun with fucking with Eugene.

"Santa Claus?!" Eugene replied. "You better get the fuck out of the hood Santa, before Yo fat ass get killed," Nate replied.

Nate started laughing at Eugene's reply.

"What up cousin? It's me, Nate," Nate said as he started to yawn as he grew a little tired.

"Whatever fool, it took you long enough to get here," Eugene replied as he buzzed Nate into the building.

Damn, Now I got to climb five flights of stairs, to get to this nigga crib. Why the fuck would somebody move to an apartment in the Projects, and the damn building don't got a fucking elevator! And you gotta pay a light bill on top of that Nate thought to himself as he started climbing up the steps. As Nate reaches the fifth floor, he observes Eugene standing next at the top of the fifth-floor staircase with his arms folded.

"Nigga! Is that you breathing, like Dark Vader?" Eugene asked as he started to laugh at his older cousins whom was breathing very hard from his trip up five flights of stairs.

"Whatever! Mr. Funny Man. Your ass going to get old too one day, if you're lucky," Nate said as he finally reached the top flight and bent over trying to catch his breathe.

"Old! You just are out of shape muthafuka," Eugene said while laughing as he placed his hand on Nate's shoulder. They both then greeted each other with a hug just before entering Eugene's apartment.

"Did you take care of your business out here already?" Eugene asked as he closed his apartment door behind him.

"Yeah, that's what took me so long. I ended up running into one of my boys and I have to check him later in regard to that," Nate replied as he walked down the apartment corridor and into the living room.

"Oh okay, just make yourself comfortable I guess. I'm going to jump in the shower and get ready for work," Eugene yelled out as he entered the bathroom and started the shower water running.

"Thanks, cousin, I figure I'll just chill out on this sofa right here for a little bit," Nate said as he removed his shoes from his feet and grabbed a throw pillow to lay his head on.

Eugene proceeded to take his shower and once he was done

he got ready for work. He returned to the living to find Nate fast asleep on the sofa with one of his guns tucked in his pants and the other on Eugene's coffee table. He shook his head at the sight of the guns, and placed a spare set of apartment keys next to the gun on the on table. He then walked back into his bedroom and called Monique to see if she made it home safely. Monique answered and told Eugene she called him when she got in, but she got no answer. Eugene explained he probably was in the shower at that time of the missed call.

"Baby! My cousin got here a few minutes ago, and that fool is already knocked out sleep on the sofa," Eugene informed Monique whom really didn't care. "I'm still a little tired my damn self, but I got to go make this paper to pay the bills," Eugene continued as he checked his watch to see how much time he has left before he heads out.

"Well, you better be going to work since you rushed me the fuck out your house, for your cousin," Monique said in a joking manner. Eugene could hear the animosity in her voice.

"I thought we squashed that already baby. I already promised you, it was the first, and the last time it's going to happen," Eugene replied as he was set to leave, as he grabbed his car keys and headed out the door.

CHAPTER 16

WHEN BLACK ICE EMERGES

"**Oh Shit! Officer! Let me get out first**. I don't want to get shot!" Denzel said with in a panic tone of voice.

"Don't worry you're in safe hands with us," The officer in the front passenger seat said.

These crazy muthafuckas are really taking me with them to where niggas are shooting at! First, I get fucking robbed, then shot at! Now, I'm going to get shot while riding in back of a police car, looking like a snitch Denzel thought to himself as they traveled to the corner of East New York and Stone Avenue at a fast speed. Once they arrived at the corner, the sound of three more shots echoed through the air as Denzel ducked down in the back seat.

"I know these muthafuckas ain't shooting at us!" Said the Officer who was driving the unmarked vehicle. The officers told Denzel to stay down, but he was too curious to see what was going on.

As he peeked out the window, he saw all types of police vehicles rolling up on the scene, as the officers he rode with jumped out and started run towards the corner with their weapons out. Police Officers were jumping out of all types of vehicles. He observed marked vehicles, unmarked vehicles, cargo vans, Sports Utility Vehicles and mini vans that people would've never guessed had cops in them pull up. Before you knew it, the whole Howard Projects was flooded with the Police Department. The bright lights from their vehicles lit up the night like Christmas lights.

The officers quickly returned back to vehicle as Denzel waited for them slumped down in his seat. They all got in the vehicle and the officer driving pulled off away from the shooting location.

"Well if them punks that robbed you came over here to Howard Projects, more than likely they won't be coming back outside no time soon now," The Officer seating next to Denzel said as he started to write something on his pad.

"Why do you say that officer?" Denzel asked as he looked out the window to see if he could spot the crooks walking around.

"Punks like that aren't too stupid. They know that the place is flooded with cops right now, and they will get grabbed and searched just for being outside at this time in the morning in a heartbeat," The officer driving said as he slowly drove down East New York Avenue towards Rockaway Avenue.

"We're going to ride by a few pawn shops to see if we can find these guys, If they're still out here. Some thieves like to hurry up and get the evidence off their hands for that quick cash," The officer sitting in the front passenger seat said just before instructing the driver to do a U turn to head towards a pawn shop on Stone Avenue. The unmarked police vehicle then drove back down East New York Avenue towards Stone. Once they reached Stone Avenue, the driver made a right and traveled slowly in the direction of Belmont Avenue.

Denzel scanned Stone Avenue like a hawk until he noticed three males walking. Two of the males where big guys and the shorter male was slim and dark complexion. His eyes widen as he thought he had spotted the punks that caught him sleeping on the streets. Denzel tapped the Officer sitting next to him.

"That looks like..." was all Denzel got to say as he pointed in the three-male's direction, before the Officer driving the Police vehicle immediately spinned the car towards the three males and cut them off as he drove up on the sidewalk. Before Denzel knew it, all three Officers had exited the vehicle and slammed all three males up against the wall, something that he had experienced many times before in the past.

The officer who was sitting in the front passenger seat pulled the short male he was holding off the wall after conducting a weapon search of him and walked him towards the unmarked police vehicle. Denzel was shocked that the officer brought the male over to the car to see his face, he then slumped down in his seat, because didn't want to look like a punk ass snitch.

"Look at these, and tell me if any of them belong to you," The officer said as he lifted the male left arm up while he was holding on tight to the back of the short male's neck. The short male had about seven gold chains wrapped around his wrist as if they were bracelets. Denzel examined all the jewelry on the short male's wrist as the male looked him in the face, but couldn't spot his jewelry. The male slightly resembled the male who struck up the conversation with him before snatching his chain, But Denzel wasn't sure so he shook his head to inform the Officer that he wasn't the guy.

Are you sure?! Are you sure?! The officer whom was in disbelief and became a little angered repeatedly asked Denzel.

Denzel continued to shake his head to say no to him once again that wasn't the guy nor was that his jewelry.

"I told you, I didn't do shit! You fucking dirty ass cop! The short male started to yell soon as he saw Denzel shaking his head no. The Officer then slightly banged the short male head against the window, basically because the guy was mouthing off and then he walked him back over to the wall to get the guy's information.

"Yo, snitch! I see your face," One of the other guys that was stopped said.

"And what does that supposed to mean muthafucka?!" The very large officer whom was riding in the passenger seat said as he walked the loud mouth over to the car and banged his head onto of the hood.

"Yo, what the fuck?! The male yelled out as he felt his forehead throbbing in pain.

"Don't ever threaten nobody in front of me punk, you fucking punk," The officer said as he held the guy by the back of his collar. Denzel thought to himself that these three cops was some old school beat your ass type of muthafuckas whom didn't give a fuck about the rules. The officers then let all three of the males go on their way, after completing their search and gathering their information.

The other two officers then returned to the vehicle and all three got in, then the driver pulled off and continued to head towards the Pawn Shop near Stone and Sutter Avenue. The officer then parked the unmarked vehicle in the gas station directly opposite of the pawn shop. After watching the traffic in and out of the location with negative sightings of the perpetrator, the officers decided it was time to head over to the pawn shop located on Rockaway Avenue and Livonia.

"We're going to chill out here for a few minutes and watch this spot, but if it comes up negative within the next ten minutes, we're going to drop you off home," The officer driving the unmarked police vehicle said as he parked the vehicle next to 265 Livonia Avenue to car lengths back from the corner of Rockaway Avenue. This location had a good view facing the Pawn Shop.

"You sure that wasn't the punks that robbed you? Trust me

you don't have to be scared kid. We got your back and don't have no problem with bringing them in," The officer sitting in the back seat with him.

"I know for a fact that those punks are dirty and up to no good. There's no doubt in my mind that all them chains don't belong to him. But if you say that it's not them, then it's not them" The officer in the front passenger seat said as he pulled out a set of binoculars to look at the front entrance of the pawn shop.

"I'm just hoping you weren't so scared of them punks so much that you wouldn't identify them. And on top of that possibly allowing us to let them walk away free because of your fear" The officer in the driver's seat said while looking into the rear-view mirror looking at Denzel.

"I wasn't scared at all! They just didn't look like the guys, plus none of those chains were mine," Denzel answered as he watches people walk in and out of the pawn shop. Denzel knew that the Officers would've locked up anybody he pointed a finger to just for an arrest. He was also smart enough to know that without his identification of the assailants they had nothing.

As time started to pass by quickly, Denzel sat there in back of the unmarked Police vehicle and started to build an uncontrollable level of hate that burnt his heart as well as his soul. After many years of being picked on and tested for having heart and not being a punk in the neighborhood by the local thugs. This new violation added to his hardship elevated him to a new high of hidden rage. It was like he stepped into the darkness and there was no glimpse of light to guide him back, and for some strange reason he didn't want it to.

He could no longer hide his anger as it showed in his facial expression and his eyes began to water up.

"This pawn, stays open 24/7 unlike the others around here, so if them punks wanna cash in tonight, this is the spot to do it at," The Officer driving the vehicle said.

Denzel listened very carefully as the officers spoke. While staking out the palm shops he realized patience could become a virtue if needed to find someone. And a little voice within him suggested that he devise a plan to find the thieves himself.

"Officer! It's getting real late and I have to be a work in a few hours. Can you drop me off on the corner of Livonia and Stone Avenue?" Denzel asked as he realized it was becoming hopeless in finding the three thugs that robbed him.

"I thought you said you lived near Blake and Rockawawy Avenue," The officer driving said as he started up the vehicle and began to pull out.

"I do officer! I just can't be seen getting out of a Police Car to close to my neighborhood. The drug dealers around my way would think I'm snitching on them and I don't need them types of problem in my life," Denzel said as he slumped down in his seat not to be seen.

"Okay, no problem," the officer driving said as he pulled off and did a U-turn on Livonia and towards Stone and let Denzel out. Across the street stood a group of males engaging in a dice game. The officer in the driver's seat watched them closely as the officer in the rear seat exited the vehicle, so Denzel can slide over and exit the car. The officer then got back in once Denzel was out.

"Thanks a lot officers for trying to help me find them punks. I really do appreciate it." Denzel said as the unmarked patrol car parked on the corner.

"Sorry, we couldn't find them punks for you kid. If we come across anything; you'll be contacted to come down to the precinct for a lineup," said the Officer seating in the front passenger seat.

The officer sitting in the rear of the unmarked car noticed the strange look in Denzel's eyes. The young victim eyes told its story, and it sent a chill through the officer's body. The observing officer had over ten years of experience and was up for promotion to detective in a month. Within his years on the force, the officer has come across many stone cold killers and a few vigilante's.

The vigilantes were feed up with the bullshit in their neighborhood and decided it was better if they took matters into their own hands. Each one of these vigilantes possessed the same look in their eyes that Denzel now possessed. The officer in the rear passenger seat then made the following statement to Denzel just before the young crime victim exited the Police vehicle.

We have all your information, so don't come back out here seeking revenge. Let us handle it. You seem to be a good kid, and I don't want you out here getting hurt or in trouble. If three punks fitting the description, you gave us turn up dead today, tomorrow or next week. Guess who's gonna be our number one suspect? We will be looking for your ass for questioning.

And as a matter of fact, don't even let us catch you out here looking for these guys, because we will know you're out here hunting.

"I don't look for trouble officer; I'm taking my ass in the house officer. I don't need any more excitement in my life right now," Denzel said as stood there talking to the officers.

"Yeah kid, just go in and get some rest," The officer in the Driver seat said as he looked at Denzel as he started to walk away. Denzel then crosses the street and bypassed the males shooting dice. He observed the large stack of bills laying on the ground as the rolling dice hit against the Day Care Center's wall. The men gambling ignored him as they only focused on the dice and money. Denzel began to cut through the projects toward his apartment building.

"That kid got that look in his eyes," said the officer seating in the rear passenger seat as he watched Denzel disappear into the projects.

"And, what look is that?" Asked the officer seating in the front passenger seat.

"Vengeance! As I looked into his eyes, I could see fire burning. It was like looking at flames burning beneath black ice. I can tell you both this. We haven't seen the last of this kid," The officer in the rear passenger seat responded. The two officers sitting in the front seat looked at one another then back at the officer in the back seat.

"Who gives a shit, if he kills them niggas that robbed him anyway? He'll be doing the neighborhood a favor taking them out, if you ask me," The officer in the front passenger seat said.

"Okay, tell us how you really feel," The officer in the back seat replied as he started to laugh.

"I'm serious! These fucking savages always running around here robbing and killing one another, so if one of the good ones take them out. What's the problem?" The officer in the front passenger seat continued.

"I know, I wouldn't lose no sleep over it," The officer in the driver's seat said,"

"Exactly! These savages be killing each-other every day. We just here to pick up the pieces, like sanitation collects the trash," Said the officer in the driver seat.

"But forget all that bullshit, because right now, I see enough money on the ground over there to pay off a few of my bills and your bills too. How about we go over there and tax them assholes for that dice game?" Said the officer in the passenger seat, referring to the group of males shooting dice. He wanted to make a few extra dollars before he gets promoted. The officer in the rear seat was feeling a little hesitant about taxing the illegal street gamblers. He didn't want to ruin his upcoming promotion for street taxing.

Denzel headed home as he cut through the six-story building in Brownsville Houses to get to his building. The closer he got to home the angrier he became. Suddenly! Shots rang out from a distance behind him, that was soon followed by the sounds of police sirens. Denzel wondered if it was the cops whom just dropped him off, but he had other things running through his mind, so he continued home. The feeling of being vulnerable in his own neighborhood, did not sit too well with him at this point in his life. All the past test heart and bravery since he moved to the neighborhood, started to reach it's boiling point.

As he approached his building, he noticed someone hanging out in front of it on the stoop near the entrance door. The person was wearing all black clothing with a large hooded sweatshirt covering they head hiding his or her face. The first thing that entered Denzel mind was that it was one of the guys who robbed him, that possibly spotted him snitching to the cops and wanted to shut him up. He then thought to himself that the thieves shouldn't even know where he lived. Was a stick-up kid looking for an early morning victim to feed on.

Aah Shit! Here goes another stick up kid, out here looking to rob somebody Denzel thought to himself. While referring to someone he spotted standing on the stoop of his apartment building. Already angered and mentally drained from his earlier experience, he could only imagine what could happen to him next, if the person standing is actually a stick-up man looking for a victim.

"Yo, what up Kane?" The male all dressed up in black asked as he removed his hood from his head revealing his face. It was Belly from upstairs. Kane was a nickname that Belly called Denzel, basically because Denzel kept his hair styled similar to the rapper Big Daddy Kane, who was known for the sharp flattop Cameo haircut.

"I just got robbed! That's what's up!" Denzel said with a pissed off look on his face. "I thought you were another thief ready to rob me again," Denzel continued.

"Maybe if you didn't live in the building, I probably would've robbed your ass for them chains you be rocking" Belly said as he cracked a smile. Denzel knew Belly was well known in the neighborhood to be out on the prowl jacking fools in the hood for they shit on the late-night tip, and spent the rest of his time being a lady's man. Even with his chubby physique, Belly was a nice-looking male who had the gift of gab and swagger that threw many pretty chicks in the hood to his bedroom. Belly whom never worked a day in his life always seem to have pretty young ladies and even ones whom already had boyfriends on his roster. These young women would financially take care of him and lavish him with clothes.

"Chains! What chains?! The muthafuckas already took them shits!" Denzel responded. Belly thought Denzel was joking, when he said he got robbed.

"Say word! I thought you were just joking about that. I was wondering why you was walking so fast as if you were paranoid about something. What happen?" Belly asked.

"I was coming from my girl house, and three niggas rushed me, took my shit and shot at me" Denzel reported as his eyes started to get glassy.

"Where? Up the Hill?" Belly asked.

"Nah! On Rockaway, between Pitkin and Belmont! I think they might be from Howard Projects," Denzel replied while shaking his head.

"Howard or L.H. (Langston Hughes) to be exact! How you get caught out there like that nigga?" Belly replied.

"One of them, a short nigga. Ran up on me, asking me what time it was and all that dumb shit. Then next thing I know, I was surrounded by three of them. I thought I had beef, because me and my girl got into it earlier. So, when dude went to grab my chains; I thought he was just swinging on me. So, I knocked that muthafucka out. I forgot all about them chains hanging on my neck, my jacket wasn't zipped up when I walked home.

That nigga snatched both my chains, before he hit the ground. Then I grabbed one of his boy up and that nigga pulled out a burner on me. I guess I was so mad that I tried to act like I had a burner on me and the muthafucka shot at me," Denzel said to give his friend brief details.

"Oh shit! They got you for that fat link you had? The Cuban shits? Damn!" Belly said as his eyes widen as if he wishes he would've caught the lick (aka robbery) himself, because he liked that chain Denzel had.

"Belly, they got me for two of them. I bought her one just like mine, but she gave it back today. I had both hers and mine on," Denzel said letting Belly know he got caught for two links.

"Damn, Kane! Them niggas caught you slipping hard," Belly said as he shook his head. Belly seemed to get a little angry that niggas in the hood jacked one of his friends and worst of all tried to shoot him. Denzel watched Belly as he started to pace back and forth.

"Damn, you look like you are getting more upset than me, and I'm the muthafucka that just got robbed and almost killed." Denzel said as he stood there and watched Belly pace like he was preparing to set shit off. Belly was one of those type of wanna be stick up kids in every hood, that was involved in all types dirty shit, yet couldn't respond well when, shit came close to home base. He knew Denzel since he was eight years old, and considered him to be like, a little brother as well as he did the other younger guys in their building.

"So, what did you do when that nigga shot at you?" Belly asked just out of curiosity.

"Nothing, I didn't even flinch," Denzel said as he thought back at the moments the shots went off.

"You didn't flinch? Get the fuck out of here!" Belly said as he didn't expect that answer to come out Denzel Mouth.

"Yep, the shit went down so fast. I didn't have a chance

to react to it, plus I was mad," Denzel said while recalling his action.

"Do you remember what these muthafuckas look like, Kane?" Belly asked.

"Yeah" Denzel responded.

"You know, I know a lot of these stick up kids out here. I bet you, I can tell you who did it." Belly said as he looked Denzel in the eyes.

"The short nigga that ran up on me, was real dark skinned with a big gap in his teeth. The other two niggas was brown skinned with short waved up haircuts and were built like they just did a bid in jail." Denzel stated as he simulated how big they were in size.

"Okay, that short nigga you are talking about. Did he talk with a Lips's?" Belly asked while thinking he may have an idea whom the short stick up kid was.

"Yeah! He talked funny, like he was holding a mouth full of spit." Denzel replied as he recalled on the way the little thief spoke. Belly knew exactly whom the short thief was, where he lived and where him and his crew usually hangout at, when they not out doing their dirty work. In the past belly did a few stick ups with the short thief and his crew, but later disconnected himself from the crew after they got in a big beef over money. Belly vowed to blast any member of that stick-up crew on sight, if they crossed his path.

"That's that nigga Unique that got you Kane! He's from Howard Projects," Belly said as he narrowed it all down in his mind.

"Unique? You sure that's his name?" Denzel asked because he wasn't familiar with the thief street name.

"Yeah Unique! I use to run around the hood with him and his crew back in the days, until they tried to jerk me on some paper. You have to had seen him before Kane. He one of them muthafuckas, that always use to be out there snatching chains, earring, and pocketbooks from people on Pitkin and

Belmont Avenue." Belly said while briefing Denzel on the guy that snatched his chain.

"All I know about Unique is, I knocked his ass out and dude jumped back up and ran," Denzel said while he performed a re-enactment of how he swung on the thief and put him down.

"Yo! Don't get gassed up off that. You better be lucky he didn't shoot you for that shit. That short muthafucka, real hot headed and is known to be strapped. He probably didn't have his burner on him if he ran, plus you would've never have caught him if you gave chase. He's, one of those little fast ass niggas, that could've been on a professional track team or something," Belly explained to Denzel.

"I was about to stomp that nigga out, until his fucking boy pulled out his burner on me and that's when that little muthafucka jumped up and took off running with my shit," Denzel informed Belly as his eyes began to water up as he grew angry.

"Kane, like I said. You better be lucky Unique wasn't strapped," Belly said while ignoring Denzel patting himself on the back for knocking Unique out. "Which one of them niggas pulled out on you? What kind of burner was it?" Belly asked as he started to pace again.

"One of them big niggas! He pulled out a black gun that looked like a 9mm or something, when I went to grab him. I let go of him and went in my pocket like I had shit in it. Boom Boom, that nigga started shooting at me," Denzel explained.

Belly looked at Denzel, and could see that look in his eye, the look that he wanted revenge. He rarely seen Denzel pissed off, but when he did he knew it was going to be all hell breaking loose.

"Are you looking to get at these muthafuckas or what?" Belly asked to see what state of mind his friend was in.

"Hell Yeah! I'm tired of these punk ass niggas out here fucking with me Belly, I'm tired of this shit! Niggas taking my silence for weakness!" Denzel started to say loudly.

"Calm the fuck down Kane, and go in the lobby," Belly instructed Denzel whom listened without hesitation and entered the building.

"I'm going to let you hold a burner if you serious about handling your business, but you going to need to change up them clothes you got on," Belly said as soon as they entered the lobby.

"Change my clothes? For what? So, the cops won't recognize me?" Denzel asked.

"No Dummy! So, them niggas that robbed your ass won't! Cops?! What cops? Why are you talking about cops recognizing you, nigga?" Belly wanted to know.

"I called them after I got robbed! I was just in their car riding with them around the neighborhood, looking for them niggas that jacked me for my shit. Belly just looked at Denzel like he was stupid and shook his head.

"What the fuck you called the cops for nigga? They ain't gonna handle that shit for you," Belly said as he frowned at Denzel.

"What else was I supposed to do? I wasn't strapped and I was hoping they could find them quick and get my shit back." Denzel replied as he shrugged his shoulders.

"Kane! You were out there riding around the hood looking like a snitch! You just lost some cool points in the hood, if niggas peeped you riding in a cop car," Belly said as he started contemplating if he should help Denzel out.

"Fuck the niggas, out in the hood! I panicked! I didn't know what else to do," Denzel explained.

Belly then looked at Denzel again and realized Denzel wasn't really keen to the rules of the streets, so he decided to give him a pass. Belly reached into his pocket and pulled out a key. He unlocked the padlock that secured the slop sink door located in the lobby and opened it. He quickly stepped inside then back out with small towel. He then unwrapped the towel revealing a shiny .44 Caliber revolver.

Denzel eyes widen as Belly handed the weapon to him. Denzel just looked down into his hands with amazement, because he never held a weapon in his entire life. The gun was shiny and had Black duck taped wrapped around the handle.

"Is this shit loaded?" Denzel asked as he stuttered a little at the sight of the weapon laying on the towel in his trembling hands.

"Hell yeah, that shit is loaded. Be careful how you handle it Kane, that shit ain't no water gun," Belly said as he looked at Denzel hold the gun with a serious expression on his face.

"You got extra ammo?" Denzel asked

"Nope, you don't need it," Belly responded

"Well, how many shots those this shit got then?" Denzel asked due to him being unfamiliar with guns.

"Nigga, this a .44 Caliber. This shit right here, holds seven hot ones. The power on this bitch, will put a big hole in an elephant's ass." Belly said as he started to smirk.

"Only seven shots? You sure that's enough for me to handle these niggas with?" Denzel asked. Belly looked at his friend as if he was an idiot.

"Kane, I'm not letting you hold this shit just so you can go out there and scare muthafuckas or get in a shootout with them! Nigga, it only takes one bullet to kill a muthafucka! Okay?" Belly stated as Denzel shook his head up and down to acknowledge yes. "If you could, get up close on them niggas and make sure they don't even see it coming. Just ease up on them niggas really quick, and start dumping them bullets into them until you got seven bullets in that bitch you holding! Don't waste them. Steal their life, like they stole your shit!"

Belly instructed Denzel in an influential manner. Denzel listened closely, as Belly schooled him. He then looked at the gun, as if he was confused.

"I never shot a gun off in my life, suppose I miss?" Denzel asked hoping for some type of guidance.

"Just line this shit up, aim and pull the trigger. Don't stop blasting them muthafuckas until their laid out!" Belly said as he took the gun out of Denzel's hand and simulated what to do just before handing the weapon back to him.

"How long can I hold on to this for? I know you going to need your burner back soon," Denzel asked while wanting to know how long he could hold on to the gun. Belly just looked at Denzel and lifted up his sweatshirt exposing the handle of a .45 caliber semi-auto handgun he had tucked in his waist line.

"Hold on to that, until you find them niggas! But you need to go look for them while they face are still fresh in your mind. You don't want to fuck around and forget their faces," Belly said as he pulled his sweat shirt back over his weapon to conceal it. "And make sure you put that shit up so your mom doesn't find it," Belly continued. Denzel felt he was schooled enough on how to handle the gun, but needed more information about Unique.

"Where does Unique rest his head at? "Denzel asked because he wanted to know where he could easily find one of the thieves.

"You know that little park with the Basketball Courts on Stone Avenue, just before you hit East New York Avenue in Howard Projects?" Belly asked Denzel.

"You talking about Howard Park? The one across the street from that public school?" Denzel asked trying to picture in his mind what playground Belly was talking about.

"Yeah, that park. Cut through that park, and you will see a building numbered 300 Stone Avenue. You can't miss it because it has Day Care center playground across from it. That nigga Unique lives in that building on the fifth floor. I think the apartment number is 5W, I'm not sure though." Belly informed his friend.

Denzel knew exactly what building Belly was speaking of, because he had relatives that use to live in Howard Projects, in that exact same building. Denzel and his cousin Hype, back in the days use to play basketball from dust to dawn on the basketball courts in that park.

"My cousin use to live in 300, but I don't rememberUnique. He must have moved in there, after my cousin moved to Red-hook. Anyway, I can't fuck around over there right now." Denzel said as Belly looked at him with a puzzled face.

"Why not? You scared you might know him or you just scared?" Belly asked as he was curious to why Denzel didn't want to head to Howard Projects.

"Fuck if I know him or not! That didn't stop that nigga and his boys, from robbing my black ass. I'm just hesitant because, niggas were over there shooting earlier and the cops got the whole project on lock." Denzel explained as he looked at his watch.

"Word? How you know all that?" Belly asked.

"Them crazy ass housing cops, drove me over there, when they were shooting! Shit was crazy over there," Denzel responded while shaking his head.

"Maybe somebody blasted on Unique and his boys that robbed you. Them niggas made a lot of enemies in the streets. They be robbing drug dealers and all that" Belly suggested.

"I doubt anybody got hit and I hope nobody killed them niggas. I want to be the one, who get them niggas!" Denzel said as Belly realized that his friend has been pushed too far and wants blood on his own hands.

"Fuck the police Kane, you need to get out there right now

and start hunting them niggas. Because if you don't, you gonna forget what them niggas look like. You got to get them when their faces are still fresh in your mind" Belly said as he opened up the elevator door. Denzel then stepped into the elevator as Belly reached over to give him a hand shake as he held the door.

"Kane, I'm just letting you know. If you catch bodies on that gun, you bought it. And if you get caught by police, don't even mention my name or where you got the gun from." Belly advised Denzel in a tone that seemed like a warning not to snitch.

"I already know that," Denzel replied as he observed Belly not entering the elevator. "You not going up?" Denzel asked.

"Nah Kane! I'm waiting on this shorty to come thru to drop me off some new kicks she bought me and to give me some pussy" Belly said as he started simulating how he was gonna hit the pussy from the back.

Denzel started to laugh as he watches Belly act like a fool. Belly was quite the hood comedian that would make you laugh, even when he was snapping on you.

"Nigga! You only gonna be in it pussy for a minute before you bust off," Denzel said while laughing at Belly.

"Kane! You just started getting Yo dick wet, I be knocking the lining out these bitches pussy! You can go ask your sister! That's why she bow legged now." Belly jokingly said as he closed the elevator door in Denzel face.

"Fuck You! You fat bastard!!!" Denzel yelled out as his voice echoed in the elevator, while he traveled up to his floor.

Once the elevator reached his floor, Denzel exited it and made sure the weapon was well concealed in his waist band and out of view of his mother whom may be awake. He stood in the hallway for a few minutes, thinking of what he should do.

I think I better go handle this shit now. All that changing

clothes shit is gonna take too long. And suppose my mom is up, there's no way she gonna allow me to head back outside. Denzel thought to himself as he contemplated on what move to make.

"Fuck it! I'm out," Denzel said as he headed down the staircase to the lobby. Belly was no longer hanging out on the stoop, so Denzel proceeded out the building and turned the corner towards the street. As he got closer to Blake Avenue, a Gypsy cab pulled up to drop off its passenger. As the passenger paid the drive, Denzel picked up his pace and grabbed the rear passenger door, soon as the passenger exited. He got in and closed the door.

"Where to my friend?" Asked the middle age Hispanic driver, who turned around to look at Denzel.

"Glenmore and Stone," Denzel responded, just before the driver pulled off. Denzel remained silent, until they reached the corner of Glenmore and Stone Avenue.

"Right here is good" Denzel alerted the driver as he pulled over. After paying the driver and exiting the car, Denzel crossed the street and began to cut through the park towards 300. He looked around to see if Unique and his boys were hanging out in there, but no one was outside. The front of 300 Stone was empty, so Denzel decided to check the lobby and back entrance with negative results. He walked over to the elevator, and pressed the button. After a few seconds, the elevator arrived and Denzel got on it and pressed the 5th floor button. While riding up, he removed the weapon he was carrying from his waist band and placed it behind his back. The elevator stopped, and the door opened. He stuck his head out to see if anyone was hanging out in the hallway, just before he exited it.

The strong stench of burning marijuana filled the 5th floor hallway. A common thing in New York City Housing Authority at any time during the day. Denzel slowly walked through the hallway, while checking apartment numbers, until he approached apartment 5W. He placed his ear to the door, in an attempt to listen in on what was going on inside. The faint sound of a radio playing, could be heard from his side of the door. Denzel lifted up the door knocker, and was about to knock when. He heard someone coughing on the stairwell.

He placed the knocker down slowly and made his way to the stairwell door. The smell of the marijuana, escaped the cracks of the stairwell door and into the hallway. Denzel carefully peeked into the glass window of the door leading to the stairwell. He could see Unique leaning on the wall smoking a blunt, while his partners in crime sat on the staircase leading to the up-level floor. He placed his gun alongside his leg, while placing the other hand on the door knob. He thought of Belly's instruction on how to approach them, as his heart began to beat fast. He then made up his mind, on who was going to get it first.

Denzel quickly open the door and rushed towards Unique, who was too high to react for a weapon and placed the gun close to his face and fired. He then opened fire on the other two thugs sitting on staircase, until his gun clicked from being empty. Denzel wanted his property back and wasted no time in trying to find it. He squatted down to check Unique's pocket for his jewelry, while Unique's splattered brains dripped down the wall. After finding it in Unique's jacket pocket, he concealed his smoking hot weapon in his waistband and fled down the staircase and out the building.

Everything seemed to be moving in slow motion for Denzel, once he exited the building. He was temporarily traumatized of his actions. The loud gunfire from the .44 Caliber deafened his ears to the point, he couldn't hear himself think. His hands began to tremble as he attempted to walk calmly down the street. The faint sound of police siren and the vision of flashing lights were getting closer, causing his heart to beat faster. Denzel watched as patrol cars raced passed him, as they headed to 300 Stone.

I did it! Denzel thought to himself as he clinched to his two chains inside of his jacket pocket, while walking home from the crime scene. Denzel looked up into the still darkened sky. He stared at the full moon, because there were no stars.

Forgive me Lord, For I have sinned. And have mercy on

My Soul, when I do it again Denzel thought to himself, just before the Housing Crime Officers whom previously drove him around earlier looking for the thieves, flashed their police spotlight on him.

Oh Shit! Denzel gasped.

CHAPTER 17

I DON'T SPEAK PIG

Rahmel "Mel" Jenkins sat cuffed to a desk in the precinct squads debriefing room, under the surveillance of Detective Carey. The room had corked paneling that decorated the walls except for the 3x4 foot two-way window that faced the desk, making it nearly sound proof. Conversations could be heard over the intercom and a visual could be seen through the other side of the glass unknown to whomever was being interviewed, or from the monitor located in the next room. Mel pretty much knew the drill, when it came to the debriefing room, because he's had a few prior arrests in the past.

He thought to himself, that it was just a normal procedure he had to go through before heading down to Central Booking on a bullshit narcotics sale. Rahmel was a little different from the other local drug dealers. He was into saving his money for a rainy day, and put away enough to the side to pay for bail and top lawyers, just in case he got pinched for anything that might land him in jail.

Scared Money, Don't Make Money was a slogan Mel lived by, so he hustled hard to the max to get it all. His customers were loyal, and helped increased his clientele. A dealer like Mel, with good product, made large amounts of money. Unlike most dealers in his neighborhood, Mel didn't like to attract attention and had a job. He worked maintenance at Rochdale Village during the day, and hustled his product after work hours on the Boulevard. He kept his cash stash in different spots, and trusted only one person to pick it up when needed, that person was his mother.

The heat in the squad debriefing room began to steam, causing Mel to sweat heavily. He was still wearing that thick red hooded sweatshirt, that was now beginning drenched in sweat. As he began to daze into the two-way window that only showed his reflection, he also stared at the reflection of the clock located on the wall behind him.

Carey watched Mel on the monitor and noticed the suspect was starting to get uncomfortable, and liked what he was seeing. Room temperature, was used as an investigative tactic to make suspects brought in for questioning very uncomfortable. Heat and Cold could expedite a confession and other situations, in which a suspect could no longer stand begin uncomfortable and rather get things over with faster than they would if they were comfortable.

The 117th squad sergeant cell phone began to ring as it nearly scared the shit out of him, while he gazed into his laptop. "Hello," he answered.

"Hello, boss, this is Bland! It's a positive on the surveillance tape over here at The Rochdale Security Office" Bland informed his boss on his results so far.

"That's Great! So, are you heading back in yet?" The sergeant asked wondering if the ball was going to start rolling soon.

"Yeah boss, I just have to make that trip to David's Bodega on the way back to check something out real quick" Detective Bland said as he entered his unmarked vehicle that was parked outside of the Rochdale Security Office.

"Okay hurry up detective, let's try to get this show on the road, I want this guy booked as soon as possible." The sergeant said as he looked up at the clock on the wall.

"No problem boss, I should be there in 15 to 20 minutes and by the way boss can you have Carey or Sweeney run a sheet on the two victims?" Bland asked as he started to drive off.

"Don't worry about that, I'll handle that myself so just get back in here ASAP, The Chief of Detectives gonna want an update soon," Pelzer said trying to put his rush on the catching Detective.

"Ten Four boss," Bland replied before their conversation came to an end. Once Bland arrived in front of David's Bodega, He quickly entered it and asked the employee to view the original surveillance tape in search to find the answer to the question that has been ringing in his head since he last viewed it. He wondered why the two victims whom allegedly robbed the shooter would remain unarmed, if they knew Mel had a reputation of being strapped. He reviewed the tape and went even further back on it to check something out.

"Jack Pot," Bland shouted out as he banged the desk located in a rear office located in David's Bodega where he viewed the surveillance tape. He quickly walked out the office and over to a refrigerator that held the cold soft drinks. Over the refrigerator where stacks of baby diapers, along with feminine napkins.

Bland then reached his hand up on top of the shelf and under a pack of diapers and recovered a nickel plated .357 Magnum that was fully loaded. The video surveillance tape revealed to him prior to him recovering the weapon, that DeSean "BIG D" Wise placed the weapon there moments after having the verbal altercation with Mel. The Detective believes BIG D placed it there for safe keeping avoiding a gun possession arrest and from being frisked, just in case Mel decided to snitch on him to the Police.

The Squad Sergeant was back at the squad room pulling the rap sheets of both victims DeSean "BIG D" Wise nicked named for his height and Jaheim "ROCK" White for his solid build as it was supplied to him by night watch who conducted many checks and they sent it over via fax machine upon the Squad Sergeant's request.

Jaheim White arrest history goes way back to when he was 16 years old, when he got pinched for his first strong arm robbery. He was age 22 and stood at 6'o feet tall and was a solid muscle 235 pounds. He could be found working out in the neighborhood parks doing pushups, pull-ups, dips or whatever type of hard body workout he may have learned in the past while in prison and continued to train as a free man. He knew in his line of criminal activity, that he had to stay fit to execute his robberies with force and sometimes by intimating his victims with his presence. He made a decision to hustle from marijuana to crack cocaine once he realized the hustlers were getting money faster and easier than he was out there taking it.

DeSean's arrest history was nothing like Jaheim's. He only had two misdemeanor charges, one for sell and the other for possession. He was a local dealer that frequent the corner of Guy Brewer Boulevard and Baisley Avenue not too far from the 117th Precinct. He grew up in Baisley Houses as a kid, and was known to be seen on the Basketball court in all types of weather. DeSean Wise also known as BIG D, a name he gained because of his height was a prime example of wasted talent. He stood at 6'7 235 lbs. and was a High School All American Basket Ball Player at one of the local schools in his area. He received a full scholarship at West Virginia University, and was a starter during his freshman year.

During the summer break, DeSean returned to his neighborhood and got caught up in the life of the hood. The fast money, women and material things influenced him to hang with the hustlers who was getting that type of money.

They put him on to the game of the streets, and he made school a secondary priority. He decided he would participate in the local Basketball tournaments in the neighborhood, drawing a lot of attention from the female basketball groupies as he was now surrounded by so called friends.

Everyone wanted a piece of the fame of the person they thought was a possible NBA prospect, and every female in search of a Pro Ball Player wanted to be under his arm when he made it. Once the fall semester was in session, DeSean returned back to his University in full style. He was driving a BMW, flashing large amounts of cash as well as wearing very expensive clothing on campus. It was speculated that he was getting kickbacks from sponsors of the school to play basketball in their program, and that would've jeopardize the team season with the NCAA.

After an investigation was conducted it was concluded that DeSean was selling Cocaine and Marijuana to students at the campus. It didn't take long before he was expelled and lost his full scholarship.

By that January, DeSean was back in his home town before he could complete his sophomore year. Word had already traveled out to the scouts and representatives of the NBA about his involvement with narcotics and wanted no part of him in their organization. DeSean chance of getting selected in the NBA lottery was at zero percent. By this time, DeSean had already impregnated three different females whom were a little older than him, and had contracted a STD from one of his groupies.

All the big-time hustlers that befriended and supported him who thought he was heading to the NBA, distance themselves from him once word got out that he fucked up his chances to go to the Big Leagues. They basically took the bad news like he fucked up their chances to rub elbows with the NBA players. Many of these hustlers invested a lot of money in him just so he could stay focus on school and build his skills on the court and away from trouble. They were in hope that they could live their dreams by him getting drafted. But instead his greed for attention for flash and the spot light led him to do extra shit that ruined all his opportunity.

People back home in his neighborhood wondered what kind of deal did he worked out with the University and State of West Virginia to exempt him from getting locked up for the amount of shit he was slinging at school.

He became very depressed after losing his scholarship at the University and his chances of going to the NBA, as he began to abuse alcohol on a regular basis to drown his sorrows. A former team mate of his advised him to try to get in the NBA D(Development)League. The NBA D-league is like the National Basketball Association's official Minor League. It started in the fall of 2001. By the summer of 2005, it is known as NBDL (National Basketball Development League).

DeSean former team mate advice went unheard as his new-found addiction to alcohol left him unable to focus, train and to play to his potential as he once did. DeSean basically went from competing with the top athletes in the nation, to hanging with the local thugs in the neighborhood selling whatever he could to earn some quick money. DeSean became what most urban youths whom couldn't leave the old neighborhood alone *A HOOD HOOP LEGION DEFLATED, WHO COULD'VE MADE IT.*

Bland returned to the precinct with both surveillance tapes and the recovered weapon in hand. Once inside he walked over to the roll call room and announced his return to Moreno and Dean. Once he got their attention, he asked them both to come upstairs to the squad room. He wanted to talk to them, before he began to debrief the alleged shooter.

Bland then signed himself back into the Command Log at the front desk, then headed up the staircase towards the squad room.

"Yo Detective! What's the deal? Why the fuck Ya'll got me boiling, in this hot ass room?! Detective! I know you can hear me from behind that mirror! Rahmel yelled out as he stared directly into the mirror.

"We'll have you out that room in a few minutes Mr. Jenkins," Carey said over the intercom speaker, that was located up high up on the wall in the debriefing room.

"What! A few minutes? I've been in here for about a fucking hour now! Yall be on that bullshit, turning up the heat, when you know damn well I got on a thick ass hoody!" Rahmel continued to rant and rave.

"Like I said before Mr. Jenkins, give us a few minutes and we will get you back downstairs," Carey repeated in a professional manner. Rahmel started to figure something was up. He wondered why he had to wait so long while others been up and down the stairs quickly.

Bland made it up to the second floor where he walked over to the designated unloading area, located next to the squad room to carefully unload the loaded .357 Magnum he recovered from the bodega. Once he unloaded the weapon, he placed all the ammo in his pocket. He then walked into the squad room and bypassed his desk as he headed to the supervisor office.

"I got a gift for your boss" Bland said as he placed the recovered weapon on the sergeant's desk. Pelzer looked at the big piece of steel on his desk, stopped what he was doing and looked up at Bland.

"Detective! I hope you have a good reason for putting that firearm on my desk, and I know that shit better not be fucking loaded!" Pelzer said with a low tolerance expression on his face.

"It belongs to one of the shooting victims," Bland said while looking down at Pelzer.

"Shooting victim?! Which one? Who informed you that the victim had a weapon detective?" Pelzer asked with a stun look on his face.

"It's all on the surveillance tape boss, it's all on tape," Bland said while taping his finger on one of the surveillance tapes he was holding in his hand.

Moreno, Dean along with Zaki then entered the squad room and walked into Pelzer's office. Bland explained the evidence he recovered to the members of the narcotics unit as well as his supervisor, just before placing the surveillance tape recovered from David's Bodega into the VCR located in the Supervisor's office. Everyone gathered around the 25-inch television as Bland fast forward to a clip when DeSean Wise was placing the weapon on top of the refrigerator for safe keeping in the rear of the store minutes after the verbal altercation with Rahmel. He then rewinds the tape to let everyone see the verbal altercation take place next to the counter in front of the store.

"Damn! Was that cannon loaded?" Dean asked referring to the recovered .357 Magnum.

"It sure was, with armor piercing bullets," Bland said as he pulled out one of the rounds from his pocket.

"I heard this guy DeSean was a good basketball player at one time. He went from being a NBA hopeful to a street level hustler carrying a big ass gun with cop killing bullets? Shit is getting real out in the streets," Dean said while shaking his head as he stared at the weapon.

"Shit been real! Be lucky you guys are carrying 9mm now, back in my day, we went up against high powered shit with just a six-shooter and a backup five-shooter," Zaki said thinking back to when he first came on the job and the officers where short on fire power as they were only authorized to carry a

6 inch .38 Caliber and their 4-5 inch off duty .38 Caliber they used as back up.

Bland then removed the surveillance tape, and placed in the other tape from Rochdale Village. The tape showed Rahmel heading out the front lobby door wearing a black hooded sweat shirt as he then placed the hood on his head once he exited the building. The surveillance tape then showed Rahmel quickly returning to the building as he removed his hood from his head, he then took a quick look up towards the surveillance camera and continued to jog towards the direction of the elevator.

"He might as well pose for the camera, because his ass is cold busted," Dean said as he started to smile after seeing Rahmel face clear as day in the video. "I guess he figured no one would point the figure to him and live by the code of STOP SNITCHING! But that code did nothing for his ass he's going down for this one," Dean continued to laugh.

"Well I've seen enough, I'm going to head back to the base," Zaki said as he extended his hand out to shake Bland and Pelzer's hand.

"Good job Detective on that gun recovery, thank God that weapon didn't fall into another knuckle head hands," the lieutenant said as he stood next to the door before leaving the office.

"Thanks, Lieutenant," Bland said as he ejected the tape from the video player and tucked it under his arm. Moreno and Dean prepared to leave the Squad Supervisor Office also, right after their lieutenant headed out.

"Thanks, for apprehending this guy and for supplying us with a major lead from your informant. I've already notified my Inspector as well as the Chief of Detectives in regard to the good work you guys put in, and I will make sure that Detective Bland insert you guys on the paperwork for the apprehension," Pelzer said as he stood up from his desk and exchanged handshakes with the three narcotic team personnel.

"No problem sergeant, I'm going to have my sergeant instruct members of my team to transport the rest of our perps to central booking, and the remainder of the team will be heading back to the narcotic base to complete the arrest processing. They will be available on standby if you need them, just give us a call with an update when you can," Zaki said as he exited the Squad Sergeant Office and walked down the corridor. Bland went to shake hands with Dean and Moreno who was still standing in the office.

"I owe you guys big time and once again thanks for the lead," Bland said as he exchanged handshakes with the narcotic sergeant and detective.

"No problem Bland! But you should really be thanking our undercover for making the buy, at the shooting location. And of course, my informant. My informant is the one, who put this guy on a silver platter for us to crack this case. He's looking to get paid for his services, I'll make sure that you get forward the bill," Dean said with a silly smirk on his face causing Bland to crack a smile.

"Detective Bland, I will have one of the guys bring up a copy of our tac plan so you could put our whole team on the paperwork for the apprehension," Moreno said.

"No problem boss, they could place it on my desk, if I'm still debriefing Jenkins," Bland said as he looked at his watch.

Moreno and Dean then exited the Squad office and walked over to the debriefing room surveillance monitor to take a look at Rahmel.

"I wonder, if this dude knows he's fucked?" Moreno asked Dean.

"Well, if he doesn't know now, he will soon enough," Dean responded as he shook his head and both him and Moreno made their way out of the squad room to join the rest of their team.

"Okay, Detective! I say it's time you get this show on the roll, so get your game face on, because it's about that time for you to get in there," Pelzer said to Bland as he handed him copies of the victim's information he received from night watch. Bland then reviewed the paperwork he was just handed by Pelzer.

"Boss, I got this stuff already, when I first caught the case," Bland said as he matched it with the paperwork he already had in his folder. Pelzer shrugged his shoulders.

"Take it anyway, Detective! Read this guy his Miranda Rights, debrief and book him ASAP!"

"Boss shouldn't I wait for the D.A. to get here before debriefing this guy?" Bland asked.

"Not necessarily detective, once they got word, they should've gotten their asses over here already. Plus, you have to get this started, the clock is ticking," Pelzer instructed his detective while pointing to his watch. The sergeant watched on as Bland took his time to exited his office, then glanced again at his watch. He knew his Inspector and someone from the Chief of Detectives office would be calling soon, to be updated on the case.

Bland, prior to exiting Pelzer's office, inserted all the needed paperwork into his folder, and gathered all his evidence, before exiting the supervisor's office. He walked over to his desk and placed all his paperwork and evidence on it, and he then quickly exited the squad room to go to the vending machine out in the hallway.

He returned with two cans of soda that he purchased and walked over to the debriefing room surveillance monitor. He noticed Rahmel had taken his hooded sweat shirt off and was looking quite uncomfortable from the heated room. He then walked back over to his desk, sat down and began to write out a list of questions to ask Rahmel on a large pad. He knew the right times and dates to question Rahmel on, coinciding it with the video surveillance tapes he recovered.

After writing down his questions, he placed the surveillance video tapes, His duty weapon and the recovered .357 Revolver in his file cabinet and locked it. He didn't want anybody fooling around with the evidence before he got a chance to voucher it, and he needed to safe-guard his weapon.

In the New York City Police Department, it's against regulations for anyone to be armed in the debriefing room, as well as areas like the prisoner holding cells for safety reasons. This regulation, came to life due to past incidents.

After, squaring himself away. Bland then walked back into the supervisor's office, to inform Pelzer he was ready to debrief the prisoner. Pelzer acknowledged him with a nod as he rose from his desk to exit his office. Pelzer then made his way over to the location where the surveillance monitor was located and sat down along with the two other detectives, who were already sitting there. Carey reached over to turn up the volume as he observed Bland enter the debriefing room.

"Damn, it's hot as hell in here," Bland said after entering the room. He placed his paperwork and the two cans of soda on the desk, just before walking over to the large fan located in the corner to turn it on. Rahmel sat there with sweat dripping down his face as he looked at the tall hulking Detective.

"I'm Detective Bland. I will be interviewing you before you head off to central bookings Mr. Jenkins," Bland said as he extended his hand to shake Rahmel's hand to break the ice. Rahmel just stared at the Bland without a response and left him hanging. Bland wasn't too surprised Rahmel wouldn't return the jester to shake his hand, so he just sat down in the seat across from him.

"I'm going to ask you a few questions, and you can respond Yes or No if you choose to, do you understand me?" Bland asked as he opened up his folder. Rahmel just nodded his head to acknowledge he understood.

"You want one of these sodas? Since it's so hot in here, I figure it should cool you off a little," Bland said as he cracked open one of them and took a sip.

"Yeah, I want one detective. Could you take this cuff off this hand first? You know, so I can open it," Rahmel said with a smirk on his face. Bland looked over at Rahmel like he wanted to smack the shit out of him. He hated a smart ass, especially one half his size.

"You already have a free hand to open it, plus I wouldn't want to endanger your safety Mister Jenkins by removing the handcuff," Bland responded as he stared into Rahmel eyes.

Rahmel noticed Bland face, started to get a little red after his sly comment about the cuffs and started to focus on the cold drink he was offered.

"Okay, detective. Since you're too scared to remove my cuff, I'll open it up myself. Can you slide it over to me?" Rahmel asked. Bland then slid the can of soda over to Rahmel who opened up it quickly without hesitation, while Bland waited for the prisoner to open it and take a swallow before he began with his questioning. The cold refreshment sent a nice chill through Rahmel's body, that stopped his insides from burning.

"Like I said before Mister Jenkins, I will be asking you a few questions," Bland said just before Rahmel yelled out

"Whatever, Detective! I know the fucking drill already, okay!" Rahmel yelled out before the detective could finish saying what he had to say. "Let's do this shit already, so I can get fuck outta here and down to the bookings and post bail," Rahmel continued in a cocky tone of voice. Bland just bit his tongue as he looked over at Rahmel and then down at his folder.

"I see you were picked up by narcotics for a direct sale, so I won't bother to ask you anything about that. But I will ask you the following questions and you can answer them any way you choose," Bland said just before beginning his questioning. He then asked the following questions and received the following answers from Rahmel:

Do you have any knowledge of any illegal weapon possessions?

Rahmel: Nope

Do you have any knowledge of any robberies?

Rahmel: Nope

Do you have any knowledge of any Burglaries?

Rahmel: Nope

Do you have any knowledge of any type of Prostitutions?

Rahmel: If I did, I would've been with a hoe fucking and getting my dick sucked, instead of riding in back of a Narco van, all fucking night.

Do you have any knowledge of any assaults?

Rahmel: Detective, you might as well write No straight down the line, because I don't know shit! And I if I did, I still wouldn't tell you shit. I'm no snitch. I don't fuck with the Police, period! So, do yourself a favor, and stop wasting both our time.

Okay, Mister Jenkins! Do you have any knowledge of any shootings or Homicides?

Rahmel: No

Are you sure Mister Jenkins? You saying you don't have any knowledge of any shootings or Homicides?

Rahmel: Last time I checked, No means No in English and Spanish Detective.

"Well Mister Jenkins I was hoping that you could help me out with some information, because I figured we could work something out if you had any information," Detective Bland said as he watched the body motion of Rahmel.

"I just told you I don't know shit, and I don't talk, snitch, nothing with the Police," Rahmel replied as he started to get agitated. Bland looked at Rahmel and started to write on his note pad. He knew the prisoner was starting to get uncomfortable.

"Could yall please, send in another detective, who don't have a damn hearing problem! Because this dude right here doesn't speak English! I don't talk to the PIGS! I don't eat pork and I damn sure don't speak PIG language," Rahmel continued to rant very loudly at the top of his lungs.

"Mister Jenkins, please lower your voice," Bland requested very calmly.

"Nah! Send me the fuck downstairs, before I miss my ride to the bookings! I wanna see the fucking judge today," Rahmel said as he continued to yell. He then picked his can of soda and tossed it across the room striking the two-way mirror, doing little damage to it.

Bland stood up and did a signal with his hands, for the onlookers watching the monitor to turn it off as well as the video recording. As the hulking Detective face suddenly became red. He swiftly walked towards Rahmel, and towered over him. Rahmel looked up at the red faced detective.

"What the fuck you swelling up for detective? I don't give a fuck, if you look like Ivan Drago from Rocky IV. I'm not Apollo Creed, weights don't hit back. I'll fuck you up in here," Rahmel said just before he got his head slammed into the cold steel desk by Bland who had enough of his shit for the day. Bland then walked over towards the tossed can of soda laying on the floor and picked it up, before all of the soda spilled out.

He then walked back over towards Rahmel whom was dazed from the slamming of the face to the desk and then poured whatever soda that was left on top of Rahmel's head.

Rahmel felt his forehead throbbing and felt like it was bleeding inside from the contact with the table. The cold soda kept him from passing out as it dripped down his face soaking up his T-shirt. Bland then grabbed Rahmel by the back of the neck and whispered a few words in his ear.

"Listen hear you piece of shit! I'm your fucking ride to the bookings now! We could make it an easy ride or a hard ride, it's up to you," Bland said as he squeezed the back of Rahmel's neck tighter. Rahmel squinted in pain as the large paws of the Detective nearly cut off his blood circulation.

"Yo! Get the fuck off me! I hope Yall got this shit on camera on the other side of that mirror, keep that camera rolling! I'm suing all you muthafuckas!" Rahmel yelled as if that was going to help him.

Bland started to laugh as he continued to squeeze Rahmel neck tighter and tighter.

"The camera is off, yah dumb fuck, so go ahead and scream like the bitch made little muthafucka that you are if you want," Bland said as he released the grip. Once the detective let go of his grip, Rahmel couldn't help himself not to say anything.

"Man, if I wasn't fucking cuffed, I would!" was the last words Rahmel could get out his mouth, just before catching a back-hand slap from Bland whom cut his words short. After striking Rahmel, Bland then kneeled forward and looked in the eye. Rahmel mouth hung open, as if the taste was slapped out of it.

"Would what? Huh?" Bland asked, as he was prepared to back-slap after the smart mouth prisoner. Bland didn't take threats very well and it didn't take much for him to change someone's mind who even thought of doing him some harm.

Tears began to form in his eyes as Rahmel felt like he just got hit across the face with a sludge hammer. The blow sent a sensation that felt like all the blood in his body just rushed to his face at one time. Throbbing was more severe since it wasn't too long ago that his head was slammed into the steel table.

"We can go at it all night Mister Jenkins if you want! Just be warned, if you throw anything, spit or doing anything to piss me the fuck off. It's going to be a rough and long night for you. Do you understand or over stand me? You little bitch?" Bland asked as he walked back towards his seat.

"And don't fucking think, I have a problem with taken off them cuffs just for you to attempt to kick my ass, it's been a while since I kicked the cowboy shit out of a punk's ass! Do you understand what I'm saying?" Bland continued.

Rahmel acknowledged yes by nodding his head, as he kind of learned his lesson that Bland was no cop to fuck with. The warm room quickly dried the soda that was on Rahmel's face and T-shirt, so Detective Bland signaled for the monitor and the video of the debriefing to begin again. Rahmel looked over at the Detective with a slight sign of pain and shock all over his face. He never experiences the hands-on action of a Detective in the debriefing room before, and realized he ran into the wrong one today. Bland began to continue his questioning and hoped he could complete it without fucking Rahmel up so bad, that it might cause him to lose his job.

Okay Mister Jenkins, did you hear anything about a shooting that happen earlier today?

Rahmel: No, I haven't heard anything about nothing today

Mister Jenkins, you were overheard saying that the Block was hot because muthafuckas got murdered by the officer you made a direct sale to.

Rahmel: Oh! You're talking about that shit! Yeah, I heard two niggas got murked, but I don't know who did it and I won't tell you if I did know.

I see your memory is coming back now! That's good. Now when you say murked, do you mean murdered?

Rahmel: Yeah murked means murdered! It's not about memory, I got my own shit to worry about, not what's going on in the hood, you feel me?

Yeah, I feel you. Do you know the two guys that got killed?

Rahmel: Nah! Word on the streets was that two fools got murked, I don't know who they were or nothing.

So, you saying you don't know who the two victims Mister Jenkins?

Rahmel: No, detective I don't.

Bland then reached into his folder and pulled out both of the victim's pedigree photos and showed it to Rahmel.

Rahmel heart dropped as he looked at the photos of the two victims that he killed. He then realized that the police probably was on to him, but he chooses to stand his ground and play it off as if he knew nothing. He wanted to know what the police already knew, and how did they choose him out of all the others arrested as the shooter.

"The two guys right there seem to believe you know a little something about something Mister Jenkins or should I say MEL," Detective Bland said as he observed Rahmel staring hard at the victim's photos. Rahmel then placed the photos back on the table and slid them towards the Detective.

"I don't know what you are getting at detective," Rahmel said as he looked up at the clock.

"Do you or do you not know ROCK and BIG D?" Bland asked as he held both pictures up so Rahmel could view them again.

"NO DETECTIVE! I NEVER SEEN THEM NIGGAS BEFORE!" Rahmel yelled out as he jumped up from his seat knocking his chair backward, forgetting he could catch a beat down for raising up on the detective.

"I suggest you sit the fuck down, Mister Jenkins!, Please pick up that fucking chair up and remain seated during this interview," Detective Bland said knowing that the video was rolling. Rahmel then kneeled down and picked up his chair and sat down. He didn't want to go through the shit again with the Detective for acting a fool, because he knew he would have no wins.

A knock on the debriefing door, caused the detective to walk over to it and answer. When he opened it, Pelzer was standing there? He instructed Bland to read Rahmel his rights, before asking him any other questions. Pelzer wanted to speed shit up, because time was running out. Bland then returned to his seat and looked at Rahmel.

"We gonna be here all night if you keep up with the bullshit, I'm fucking hungry and tired, What about you?" Bland stated and asked.

"Detective, I don't have any answers for you, because I don't know shit, I don't fuck with cops. So, you just wasting your and my time," Rahmel said as he leaned back in his chair.

Bland took a deep breath and looked at his watch. He was hoping that Rahmel would just make it easy for himself and confess to what he had done. He also knew that it was time for him to read Rahmel his Miranda Rights, so he wouldn't fuck up the case once it goes to court.

"Okay, Mister Rahmel Jenkins, since you want to play it this way. I'm placing you under arrest for.

"What the fuck you mean you placing me under arrest? For what?!" Rahmel yelled out cutting Bland words short.

"I'm already under arrest by Narco, so what the fuck are you talking about, you're placing me under arrest?" Rahmel continued. Rahmel felt the room get even hotter as he knew the cops must have some type of lead on him. Carey then stepped into the room, just in case shit starts to get out of hand with Rahmel provoking Detective Bland enough to get his ass kicked.

"Rahmel Jenkins, I'm placing you under arrest for the murder of DeSean Wise and Jahiem White," Bland said as he stood up. Rahmel just sat their speechless as Bland started to read him his Miranda Rights.

You have the right to remain silent

Anything you say can and will be held against you in the court of law

If you can't afford a lawyer one will be provided to you before any questioning if you wish.

Do you understand?

Yes- Rahmel replied without emotion

If you decide to answer questions now without an attorney present you will still have the right to stop answering at any time until you talk to an attorney.

Do you understand?

Yes- Rahmel replied

Knowing and understanding your rights as I have explained them to you, are you willing to answer my question without an attorney present?

I'm willing! To speak to my lawyer! You Fucking Pig!!!! Rahmel responded, as he leaned back in his chair.

CHAPTER 18

THE ENTERTAINMENT ROOM

After a brief conversation, Stacey and Rick began to wonder off from the Tiki Bar with their drinks in hand. They decided to take a walking tour of the well-lit two acres of land Deon owned as the moon was full and the stars were bright. The two walked off as Stacey held onto Rick's arm as he escorted her away, as they left unnoticed to the small group of four whom was sitting at the picnic table and loud talking.

"You're not going to turn into a Were Wolf, like Michael Jackson did in that music video Thriller, right? Because I'm no Ola Ray, I will beat your ass!" Stacey jokingly said with a bright smile on her face as they walked across the thick green golf course like lawn.

"Maybe I will, maybe I won't," Rick answered as he looked up at the full moon, that shined so bright. He started to howl like a wolf, as they continued to walk.

"The four of us, should shoot a nice game of pool. You know, boys against the girls," Jason suggested to Dennis, Chantel and Alexis.

"Sounds like a plan to me, I just need a refill on my drink before we head inside," Alexis said as she stood up from the picnic table.

"There's a bar in the entertainment room; you can refill it in there," Dennis suggested as he notice the girl's glasses were on almost empty.

"Not unless you can make a bomb ass strawberry daiquiri like Rick," Alexis responded. Chantel then stood up and stretched her body.

"She's right, Rick daiquiri was good. We'll just meet you guys in there, after Rick, takes care of us at the bar," Chantel said as she sucked the last of her drink through her straw. Alexis looked towards the bar to see if Rick was still hanging out at the bar. Rick was nowhere to be found. Dennis also looked towards the bar and also notice Rick wasn't there.

"Looks like Rick and Stacey stepped off for a minute, but don't worry ladies, I can make a pretty good daiquiri my damn self," Dennis stated as he extended his big forearms to escort the two ladies over to the unoccupied Tiki Bar. "I might as well hook up your daiquiris right here for you. All the stuff I need to make them is already set up right here. Dennis continued as he started to go to work on the drinks for the two ladies.

"DeVonte! Erica! Do you two love birds want anything from the bar?" Jason yelled over to the happy couple. "Dennis is holding it down, until Rick gets back," Jason continued before getting an answer.

"We're good!" DeVonte and Erica answered at the same time as then began to laugh at themselves for doing so.

"Damn! You two get me sick. Yall over there answering in acappella," Alexis said as she started to laugh herself.

Jason enviously started to stare at the two love birds sitting in the cut. *This muthafucka DeVonte got it all. Nice house, nice cars, an expensive wardrobe, stacks of cash and above that to top it all off, he has the finest bitch in the house Jason* thought to himself.

"Jason! What you want?" Dennis asked as he snapped Jason out of his envious trance of DeVonte's lifestyle, while pouring himself a nice glass of coconut Vodka and pineapple juice.

"Pour me some of that Henney," Jason answered as he turned his attention away from DeVonte and Erica and cracked a smile.

"You want it on the rocks or with a chaser?" Dennis asked before pouring the cognac into the glass.

"Nope, straight. I don't want anything to dilute the effects of the cognac," Jason jokingly said as the girls started to giggle.

"Okay, one glass of straight to the vein cognac, coming right up." Dennis replied as he tilted the bottle of Hennessy Privilege into the cocktail glass. He damn near filled it up to the rim.

After making the drinks, Dennis and Jason escorted the two sisters into the house. The fresh smell of Fabreeze deodorizer scented up the entertainment room as the four entered it. Jason went to hit the light switch and placed his drink down on the bar counter, just before walking over to the pool table. Dennis then pulled four bar stools closer to the pool table while Jason racked up the pool balls and handed out pool sticks to everyone. The four played a few sets of pool and enjoyed the music playing on the surround sound.

Dennis cell phone began to ring, as he leaned over to shoot during his turn. He simply took a look at the caller I.D. and hit the ignore button, sending the call straight to voice mail. After taking his shot, the phone immediately began to ring again and again, as he continued to ignore it over and over again. Jason began to shake his head, as the repetitive ringing of Dennis phone began to annoy him as well as the two ladies that joined them in the game room.

"Come on player, answer that fucking phone already.

Before I snatch that shit off your hip and stomp the shit out of it!" Jason threatened. Dennis cringed every time his phone ranged and placed it on vibrate.

"It's that chic I've been telling you guys about earlier. She usually doesn't speak to me this late on the regular, so she must be checking up on me or something," Dennis explained after he took the phone off the belt case and held it in his hand.

"You damn right she is checking up on you, it's like two in the morning. You need to answer, the way she keeps calling you. It might be an emergency or something," Jason sarcastically said as he started to shake his head at Dennis. Dennis began to grow frustrated, every time the phone would vibrate.

"You see, this is that bullshit right here. When I call her when she's hanging out, I never get an answer. As a matter of fact, she never picks up the fucking phone call to give me a call to say if she made it home safely or nothing. Now that I'm out chilling having a good time; she wants to be the queen of communication!" Dennis said as he sent another incoming call to voice mail to stop the vibration.

"Dennis! GO handle that shit outside, so we could finish up this game. You fucking up the atmosphere in here right now with all that drama," Jason continued as he placed his pool stick onto the pool table. Dennis then looked at Jason and the two young ladies.

"Sorry ladies for the interruptions, I will be right back," Dennis said as he excused himself from the game room and placed his drink down on the bar table, before he headed out into DeVonte's very large corridor. Once he was outside of the game room, Dennis decided to answer his phone.

"Hello," a female voice said before Dennis could say hello when he answered.

"Hey, what's up?" Dennis responded.

"How's everything going at your friend house?" The female voice asked.

"It's going good; everybody seems to be enjoying themselves and I'm chilling of course," Dennis said as he started to pace back and forward.

"Sounds like y'all getting it in over there," The female said as she could hear the two sisters laughing in the background as well as the music playing.

"Yep, it's a nice get together among friends. Food, drinks, music and good people. All the perfect elements to have a good time," Dennis responded as he took a sip of his drink.

"I wish I was there to party with you, baby," The female said as she whispered into the phone.

"Well, we both know that's was not going to happening at all. Now, don't we?" Dennis sarcastically asked.

"What do you mean by that?" The female voice asked.

"You never extend an invitation for me to join you to any of your friends or family functions. So why would I ask you to join me to one?" Dennis continued to sarcastically ask to remind her of many occasions when she left him behind to do her own thing.

"What are you talking about?" The female asked as if she was confused. Dennis figured she would play stupid.

"As a matter of fact, forget all of that. You don't even pick up the phone to call or answer when you're out on the town or having a good time with family or friends. So, I'm about to get off the phone with you, and finish enjoying myself for the evening like you do," Dennis said just before hanging up. Dennis then turned his phone completely off and walked back into the entertainment room to join the others.

"Will there be any more distractions from you know who my brotha?" Jason asked as he approached Dennis soon as he returned inside. He could see the disgust on his friend face and that he wasn't happy. Dennis simply shook his head as to say no and picked his drink up and swallowed it down until his glass was empty.

"Dude, I don't know what's going on with you, but forget all that shit. I think Chantel is really feeling you. Don't blow it with her with all that girlfriend drama. I doubt that chick you are stressing over is finer than Chantel, so snap out of it," Jason said as he could see Chantel watching Dennis over his shoulder. Dennis thought about it, and decided to erase the stress and enjoy the rest of his night.

"Wow! That had to be one heck of a phone call, for you to kill that drink like it was a glass of water," Chantel jokingly said as she started to smile. Dennis couldn't help but smile after Chantel's comment. It also confirmed him of what Jason just told him, on how she was possibly feeling him.

"We're here to relax handsome, so pour yourself another glass and let's get this game going again. It's us ladies turn to shoot." Chantel flirtatiously said as she took a sip of her glass.

Every time Alexis and Chantel were up to shoot, they would purposely put on a little show for the fellas, by seductively bending over and making exotic body movements.

Dennis and Jason both enjoyed the little sexual exhibition the girls were putting on so much, that they would fuck up their shots, just so it would be the ladies turn again. Chantel whom was starting to fill the full effect of the coconut rum that was put into her daiquiri, started to dance closely on Dennis who was sitting on a stool, while the song Shake Your Money Maker" by Ludacris played over the speakers.

Dennis immediately caught a hard on from the mere touch of Chantel's body. He could feel his dick travel down his leg towards her soft ass cheeks, as she pressed against him.

Alexis joyfully watched her sister and decided to join into the fun. She made her way to Jason and started dancing the same way against him. Jason excuse himself for a second and quickly deemed the lights and returned back to Alexis to dance. The dances became more intense as R. Kelly's song Slow Wind shuffled into play and through the speakers, as the two ladies began to wind to the rhythm of the beat.

"What the fuck is going on up in here?!" Rick shouted as he and Stacey entered the entertainment room. "Yall decided to have a private party in here without inviting the rest of the us?" Rick continued as he undimmed the lights. The two couples in the room were so caught up in their dance, that they just ignored Rick rants and continued what they were doing. Rick and Stacey then look at one another with a smile.

"Fuck it!" Rick said as he shrugged his shoulder and re-dimmed the lights. He then grabbed Stacey by the hand and lead her over to the others and joined in on the fun. The pace on the dance floor picked up, when the stereo play-list shuffled to the song Change the Game by Jay Z. The instrumental bass boomed as everyone began to bounce as instructed by the rapper in the song. Rick, Mike and the other girls weren't in the room.

"I'll be right back lady," Rick said to Stacy while interrupting their dance. "I'm gonna let DeVonte and them know that, there's a party going down in here!" Rick continued while shouting, as he tried to talk over the music.

"I was just thinking the same thing," Stacey responded.

"It's like a club in here; they need to hurry and get in her asap," Stacey jokingly said as she continued to shake her hips and sip her drink.

Rick danced his way over to the bar and went behind it to get something. He removed a Mini Disco 24 LED White Flashing Strobe Light from a shelf under the counter and placed it on the bar counter. He adjusted it to flash quickly and everyone got excited as he transformed the room into a disco. Rick then exited the game room and headed out to notify DeVonte, Erica, Mike, and Doreen to come to the entertainment room. He spotted Mike who was still in the picnic area packing up food, soon as he got in the area.

"Yo Mike! Yall need to come to the entertainment room. It's going down in there, we are having a blast," Rick yelled out to inform him, while Doreen danced to the music playing, while sipping her drink.

"Okay! I'll be in soon as I finish up out here." Mike responded.

"You need help with that?" Rick asked.

"Nah, I'm good. I'll catch up with you in a minute," Mike said as he continued to clean up.

"We'll let DeVonte and them know where we at, I'll see you in a few," Rick responded as he turned around and headed back inside the house.

"Fool, I can hear you! I'm right here," DeVonte yelled over to Rick who didn't see him in the cut. Rick looked over in the area, DeVonte voice was coming from.

"Sorry my brotha, but it hard to see your sexy chocolate ass sitting in total darkness," Rick jokingly said while smiling. "Let's go then." Rick continued.

"We'll be there in a minute, after we help Mike clean up." DeVonte responded. Rick put up the peace sign with his two fingers and headed back into the house.

"Nah DeVonte, yall could bounce. I got this under control," Mike informed his buddy.

"Yeah, you and Erica could go in. I will help him get everything together out here." Doreen said as she continued to dance a little.

"I appreciate the thought, but technically you're my guest and I should be cleaning up. I refuse to take advantage of your generosity, so me and my babe gonna help you," DeVonte responded as he and Erica started to help Mike load pans with left-over food.

"Wow, I noticed that everybody was gradually disappearing

from over here," Doreen said as she sealed up a large aluminum pan containing food.

"Yeah, once I noticed it. I thought Dennis and Jason made their way down to the theatre to catch a flick," Mike said while stacking a few pans with food in it.

"Hold up! You have a movie theater in your house DeVonte?" Doreen asked as if she was very impressed by the thought of it.

"Yeah, just a little sumethin sumethin to keep me off the long lines," DeVonte modestly responded, not trying to toot his own horn. Doreen started to zone out. She's never been to a home, where someone actually had their very own movie theater in it. She unknowingly started to stare at DeVonte.

Erica's my girl and all, but this bitch better watch her back. DeVonte is one fine nigga, and he could definitely get it from me. This big house, those nice cars and his expensive taste in clothes, put him at the top of the food chain. I'm not sure if he likes a big bitch like me, but I would be all over him if giving the chance Doreen thought to herself as she stared at the man of Erica's dreams.

"Girl, what's up with you and Mike? I notice yall two getting sort of close," Erica asked while whispering in Doreen's ear and snapping Doreen out her trance of DeVonte.

"Mike? Oh, I'm feeling him girl. He's not as fine as your DeVonte, but he will do just fine," Doreen answered as she and Erica started to walk towards the entrance to the kitchen. Erica took key to Doreen's words but said nothing.

From what Erica heard from Stacey, Doreen is that type of horny bitch that wouldn't hesitate to fuck the next woman's man. She peeped how Doreen looked at DeVonte, but chose not to speak on it. Keep your friends close and your enemies even closer phrase popped in the back of her head as she looked at Doreen.

"Well, DeVonte is one of a kind Doreen. I'm really glad he's in my life and so blessed that we met." Erica said as she placed some of the food in the very large refrigerator in the kitchen.

"Girl, you sure he's not married?" Doreen asked Erica.

"Married? Who Mike?" Erica responded.

"Not Mike, DeVonte," Doreen quickly responded.

"Hell no!" Erica quickly responded as she started to frown in disgust. Why the fuck would you ask me a dumb question like that?" Erica asked as if Doreen questioned her integrity as a woman. "I never dealt with a married man in my life and never plan to." Erica continued. Doreen realized she struck a nerve and didn't want to shorten her stay by pissing Erica off.

"No disrespect girl. I'm just saying. It seems like all the good ones are always taking or married. So, I was just wondering if he was. I didn't mean anything by it," Doreen continued as she explained her question. Just before the two of them headed back outside to get more food to bring in.

"Well, DeVonte been married before when he was younger, but he has been divorced for a minute now. He also has a son and a daughter," Erica informed Doreen.

"Married? And have two kids?" Doreen asked as if she cared and wasn't just being nosey. "Well, I hope he's already divorced, and isn't trying to play my girl. Did you asked to see the divorce papers?" Doreen continued as she wanted to get more into the happy couple's business.

"I didn't have to ask. He showed me when we first started dating. Like I said before, I don't do married men at all, I don't even play that separation shit," Erica said to let Doreen know; she didn't play that game. Doreen started to smile as she just picked Erica's brain for a little information.

"Well I do, and I fuck them very well. These lucky hoes get these good men and stop fucking like they should, after they get that wedding band on the finger. So, I have no problem with helping them brothas out in their time of need to be pleased," Doreen said while grinding her hips as if she was getting some sex and laughing.

"You are so damn nasty! Keep fucking with them married men, and your going to whined up in hell," Erica replied as she started to laugh out loud while they headed back to the picnic area. Doreen shrugged her shoulders.

"Hell? I'm not gonna be the only one at the eternal barbecue, especially for fucking a married man. It's gonna be a whole club of bitches in the fire, waiting on their turn with the devil," Doreen jokingly said. Erica just shook her head and started to laugh, as Doreen grabbed her hand and bowed her head.

"I just need you pray for me," Doreen gestured as Erica entertained her, by bowing her head also.

"I sure will, because you're a hot mess in need of prayer," Erica yelled out as Doreen then grabbed her in a bear hug and kissed her on the cheek. They observed DeVonte and Mike shooting the breeze.

DeVonte and Mike had everything prepared to go inside the house by the time the two ladies returned. They both where sitting on the stools at the Tiki Bar, while they engaged in a conversation among themselves. The diamonds on DeVonte's Rolex shined as the full moon light shined down on it, catching Mike's eye. Looking at his friend's watch, made Mike bring himself to ask DeVonte to let him in on how to get one.

"Why you didn't tell me you were heading out there to pick up them bricks? I know you could've used the help and company," Mike asked awaiting DeVonte's response.

"Nigga, I called you. But you must have been so caught up some pussy, that you couldn't function right by answering or returning my call," DeVonte said jokingly as Mike began to think back to the day he had a missed call from DeVonte.

"It's hard to think with your mind when you're getting brain, and boy was she tutoring me like a genius," Mike answered with a smile on his face as he remembered what was going down when DeVonte called him.

"See, you are thinking with the wrong head baby boy. There's always going to be time for play, you just got to learn to put business first," DeVonte said as he looked over at the ladies whom were heading back into the house, with a few trays of food.

"You right, I shouldn't have left you hanging on that man," Mike said as he extended his hand to DeVonte's for a handshake.

"Don't worry baby, I got something lined up, we both could do to make a little money. I'll let you know when it's a go, soon as this weekend is over. I have a few things set up before I return to work, so try and have yourself available," DeVonte said as he knew his boy wanted to get put on to his side job. Mike started to smile.

"Good looking out my brotha. I appreciate you thinking of me like that. You know I want to get one of them watches you wearing, in the worst way." Mike said as he pointed to DeVonte's watch. DeVonte looked at his watch then took the Rolex off his wrist and handed it to Mike.

"Try this on for size and let me know how it feels to you," DeVonte said as he handed Mike the watch. Mike took the watch and placed it on his wrist. He stared at it in amazement.

"That shit looking good on you Homie, that's you all the way" DeVonte said giving his friend a compliment on how the bling bling looked on his wrist.

"Man, I am feeling this shit for real," Mike said all excited to have diamonds on his wrist.

"Don't worry, as long as you think with the right head, you'll have a few of those joints in due time," DeVonte said.

"But in the meantime, give me back my damn watch nigga!"

DeVonte jokingly said as he extended his hand to retrieve his Rolex back.

"Let's help these women out so we can go inside with the rest of the crew." Mike said as he got up from the stool.

"Okay, let's go," DeVonte responded as he also got up from the stool. Mike looked at DeVonte and wondered if he was ready to tie the knot.

"Are you sure you're ready to make that move tomorrow playboy?" Mike asked referring to what DeVonte had planned for the next day. DeVonte nodded yes.

"Yeah, my brother, it's time I make it official. She's a true treasure and I really think she's the one for me," DeVonte replied in a low tone so the women couldn't hear his and Mike's conversation. Mike then walked behind the bar and pulled out a shopping cart. For some reason, he would always leave it folded up behind the bar, knowing that at the end of the barbecue he could shorten his trips to the kitchen, as he loaded the cart with pans of food.

"We could stack the rest of the pans in this" Mike said referring to the shopping cart. "See I knew you could put that brain to use," DeVonte said as he placed three pans into the cart.

"Whatever fool!" Mike quickly said as he also stacked pans into the cart. The two finished up packing the remainder of the food and brought everything into the kitchen. Erica and Doreen then placed the food in the refrigerator.

"You ladies ready yet?" DeVonte asked as he leaned against the centered island. "Yes Babes, let's go see what the kids are up to" Erica jokingly said while laughing. The four of them then walked down the long corridor and couldn't help but hear the sound of laughter as they approached the entertainment room. The site of everyone dancing and smiling only made the four wants to join in. So, as they entered the room, they smoothly made their way to the dance floor.

"Oh shit! We got VIP in this muthafucka now!" Yelled out Dennis whom was feeling real nice off his alcohol buzz and noticed the four enter the room.

"Shut your ass up! And finish doing the CHICKEN NOODLE SOUP dance Big DEE" Mike said as he danced with Doreen.

"Nah player, I'm gonna do that two step you over there doing" Dennis said while laughing and pointing at Mike choice of dance to every song. Mike started to laugh as well as everybody else.

"Like Fifty said, I'M IN THE CLUB DOING THE SAME OLE TWO STEPS" Mike said as he added a little energy to his dance.

"You're a mess," Doreen said as she admired the way, Mike was loosening up on the dance floor.

"Just watch sexy lady, I don't want you to lose a toe, since I know how to cut a rug," Mike said as he got closer to Doreen.

"Rug? What rug? You need to be cutting them sharp as toe nails um hmm," Jason said as everybody burst into laughter.

The remainder of that late night into early morning, while DeVonte and Erica made their way up to his bedroom, everyone continued to party, until they drifted away one by one to go get some rest.

CHAPTER 19

CALL FOR HELP

In early fall of 1999, The New York City Police Department was on high alert for a sexual predator who has been terrorizing the female residences within the Linden Housing projects, for approximately three months. Linden Houses consist of 19 apartment buildings that are from 8 to 14 stories tall. Linden Projects is located in the East New York Section of Brooklyn and within the confines of the 15th Precinct.

All of the known attacks were reported to be committed at gun point. The predator was becoming more and more violent during each attack, as he chose a more brutal approach each time. The fear within the community was at all-time high, and speculations of the attacks becoming deadly raised many concerns. There have been nine attacks reported so far, with no leads for the police to make an arrest.

Victims, ranging from the age of 12 to 64, have all giving similar descriptions of their attacker. A police sketch as well as a reward of $15,000 had been posted, for information leading to the arrest and conviction of this menace to society. The police department increased its patrol in targeted areas, in an attempt to present a high police presence in the community.

It was approximately 2:00 o'clock on a chilly Sunday morning, when Denzel arrived at Linden Projects along with his daughter and his mother in-law. Denzel, a newly promoted detective was dropping his family off home, as they just returned from another family member birthday party that took place in the Bed Stuy section of Brooklyn. Denzel picked them up from the party on his way home from work. He was very aware of the sexual assaults, and made it his point to make sure his family made it home safely.

As the three entered the apartment, Denzel quickly made his way to the bathroom. He had to go bad, and knew he wouldn't make it home fast enough, without pissing on himself. After using the rest room, he exited the bathroom and was ready to head home.

"Denzel! What are you rushing home for?" His mother in law asked. "You know you should just stay here until day light, instead of going home this late," His mother in-law continued as she looked at the clock.

"Late? I'm the Police! I should be good in the streets of New York," Denzel jokingly replied as he patted his waist line, where his weapon was.

"A bullet doesn't care if you're a police officer or not! Anybody could get it these days. These young boys over here be shooting like crazy everyday around here," His mother in-law said as she walked over to the window and lifted up the shade.

"Grandma's right daddy, they be shooting around here all night. I don't want anything to happen to you, I wish you would stay the night with us," His daughter said as she gave him a look a father couldn't refuse from his little girl. Denzel thought about it and decided to grant his daughter and her grandmother's wish, by remaining at the apartment for the rest of the early hours of the morning. He was basically tired from putting in a lot of overtime hours prior to picking them up.

Denzel's mother-in-law went and got him a blanket and pillow from out of her linen closet, so he could set up the sofa to sleep on. After making up the sofa, Denzel then turned on the television and began to watch one of his favorite television shows. He removed the sneakers he was wearing and laid down on the sofa.

"Daddy, you just love watching that show for some reason," His daughter said as she walked in the living room to give Denzel a hug and good night kiss. After saying good night, his daughter then walked down the corridor towards her room to go to sleep.

Denzel made himself comfortable on the sofa and quickly fell asleep, before seeing the ending of the flick he was watching. As he slept, he was awakened by a noise that he believed to be a scream.

What the fuck was that? He thought to himself as he sat up on the sofa, trying to focus his hearing on the sound. He heard the noise again and quickly placed his detective shield around his neck, while tucking his weapon in his waist band of his pants. He put on his shoes and made his way to the front door. He opened the door and stuck his head out, to see what was going on. He could hear a muffled scream that started to fade away. Denzel then closed the front door and knocked on his mother in-law's bedroom door.

"What!" The mother-in-law yelled out, as she was awakening from her sleep by the knock on the door.

"Call 911! I think I hear somebody screaming in the hallway for help," Denzel yelled enough for her to hear through the bedroom door.

"Oh My God" She responded as she jumped up out her bed and reached for her cordless phone.

"Make sure you tell the 911 operator, that a black off-duty officer needs assistance and to get here as soon as possible.

Tell them I have on a white T-shirt and black jeans," Denzel yelled out to Mary as he prepared to exit the apartment.

"Be careful out there Denzel! Don't be no hero!" His mother-in-law yelled out just before talking to the 911 operator whom answered her call.

"I'll be okay as long as you let them know what I'm wearing, so they don't shoot me," Denzel said as he headed out the door.

During Denzel's time spent in the New York City Housing Authority Police Department, he was trained to listen and focus on sounds. Once inside of the hallway he opened the door to one of the stairwells and stuck his head in to listen. Sounds travel throughout the stairwell from the lobby all the way to the roof, giving whomever listening an idea on where the noise is coming from. As he listened closely, he heard a muffled scream coming from the higher floors and took off running up the staircase swiftly towards the noise.

With his adrenaline pumping and his heart racing from the swift scaling of the staircase, Denzel was finally approaching the top floor where the muffled scream grew louder. He removed his weapon from his waist band and slowly walked up the last flight of stairs leading to the roof landing.

"Please don't do this! Please don't do this!" A female voice screamed as she pleaded with her assailant. The violent predator banged her head on the cold cement floor of the roof landing.

"Shut the fuck up bitch! You better open them fucking legs and give me that pussy! Before I blow your fucking head off!" Denzel could hear a male voice say in a very violent tone of voice. Denzel eased up closer to get a peek at what was going on. Before he could look.

"Bitch! If you don't open them fucking legs, I'm going to fuck you up the ass first!" The male yell as he struggled to get his victim's legs open. He then struck her in the head, in an attempt to knock her unconscious. Denzel then took a quick peek around the corner and observed a very large male on top of a female's back trying to pull her thick tights down with one hand as he struck her repeatedly in back of her head with the other hand containing a handgun.

The female squeezed her thighs together tight to avoid the predator penetration as best she could, while he continued to strike her in the hope that she would loosen up. Denzel then lowered his body as until he laid across the staircase. He used the wall as cover as he took aim at the predator. Tactical thought entered his mind as he continued to take aim.

I'm sending this muthafucka to hell! Not jail! Denzel thought as his finger itched on the trigger. He had no intentions of letting the predator surrender nor survive from what he was about to unleash on him. The court system has failed the society it is supposed to protect many times, by giving predators second chances to commit the same crime again.

"Yo Muthafucka!" Denzel yelled out while scaring the shit out of the unsuspecting predator, as he took cover and aim.

The startled predator quickly jumped up, turned around and fired a single shot striking the concrete wall. He seemed amazed to see no one standing there in his path. Temporarily confused, the predator slowly glanced downward and spotted Denzel. The flash coming from the barrel of Denzel's gun, was the last thing the predator saw in his final seconds on earth. A bullet traveled between his eyes, rocked his head backwards and sent him slowly crashing down. Denzel then fired two more times, striking him in the chest area, before he hit the ground. Denzel then yelled out.

"Police Don't Move!" Soon as the large predator hit the floor and laid there unconscious. The .22 caliber semi-auto handgun the male possessed laid close to his body, until Denzel quickly kicked it away from the predators reach. Denzel was trained never to assume anything when it comes to weapon involvement. Denzel knew if he yelled out the police warning, it would've given the predator more time to figure out if he was going to give up or shoot his way out.

History has shown that in many cases of off-duty Police Officer who were involved in off-duty incidents have announced themselves as being Police Officers, resulting in them receiving serious injuries, or death.

The female victim started to scream uncontrollably due to the action she just witnessed. She covered her ears in an attempt to stop the ringing sounds in it. The sound of the gunshots continued to echo through her head, over and over again.

"Are you okay?" Denzel Yelled out to gain the young woman's attention. The female victim then looked over her shoulder to observe her savior, who was standing there with his police detective shield dangling around his neck and gun smoking in his hand. Denzel extended his hand over to her for her to grab onto, so he can guide her closer to him as he kept an eye on the lifeless predator. Tears streamed down her cheeks as she crawled on all fours towards Denzel, while bypassing the bleeding predator whose body remained motionless. She then recognized Denzel's face as someone she has seen many times before in her apartment building. Once she bypassed the predator, she grabbed onto Denzel's hand and he helped her up to her feet.

Denzel then placed his weapon inside his rear waist band so it would be visible to the arriving officers responding to the roof landing. The victim bled from the back of the head, and began to shake uncontrollably. In an attempt to console her, Denzel started to hold her in his arms and told her that everything will be okay.

"Oh my God! Oh my God! You saved my life! You saved my life!" The victim shouted as her bottom lip trembled. "Thank you Jesus! Thank you for sending me an angel!" She continued as she looked up towards the ceiling. Denzel could feel the warm blood traveling down her back, and removed his T-shirt from off his back and applied pressure to her womb.

The sound of police sirens grew closer and within seconds the apartment building was flooded with the famous New York Finest. Before Denzel and the victim knew it, uninformed officers quickly stormed the roof landing from the staircase with weapons drawn. The blood of the lifeless predator started to flow heavily and traveled towards the staircase, where it began to leak down the stairwell.

"Police! Don't Fucking Move!" Yelled out a uniformed officer whom was the first to respond to the roof landing and noticed Denzel weapon, tucked in his waist line behind him.

Right away Denzel knew if he made any sudden moves it could be fatal for him, so he remained still as the female victim continued to hug him tightly around the waist. It was way too much excitement for her to handle as she was unable to calm herself down.

As the history of New York City Police Department would reflect. On numerous occasions in the past, minority police officers especially African American were quickly gunned down by responding Officers either while on duty in plain clothes or off duty. The officers gunning them down were non-African American nor possibly any other race than Caucasian. The Police Department in response to such a tragic incident would label it friendly fire. When in fact, there is nothing friendly about being shot or even killed by a fellow member of the service.

As of today, there is no recorded incident within the New York City Police Department of an African American or Caucasian police officer tragically gunning down any Caucasian undercover, plain clothed or off-duty police officer, ever. If there is any record of such an incident occurring, the incident was hardly publicized and the percentage compared to minorities officers gunned down in friendly fire.

"I'm on the Job! Don't shoot!" Denzel yelled out, with his back to the responding officers and without making any sudden moves. The female victim looked over his shoulder.

"He's a cop! He saved me! Don't shoot him! He saved my life!" The female started to scream at the responding officers as she became hysterical and hugged Denzel's waist tightly. One of the many officers on the roof landing, radioed into dispatch that they were present at the scene and requested EMS. The officer also transmitted that they were holding a possible suspect act gunpoint.

More responding officers attempted to enter the roof landing, but it was far too crowded with officers already. All the officers on the roof landing focused on Denzel, the female victim and the lifeless predator that was lying face down on the cold roof landing floor.

"Okay, buddy! If you're on the job. You should already know the procedure," The officer behind Denzel whom he later found out to be a sergeant yelled out as he focused on Denzel's exposed weapon in his waistband, just under the victim's arm.

"Excuse me, Ma'am! I'm gonna need you to release your grip from around his waist, step away from him and make your way over towards me," The sergeant shouted as he instructed the shaking victim to move away from Denzel. The victim then clinched Denzel waist tighter as if it was her turn to protect him.

"Miss, go with them. I'll be okay. Just do whatever the officer ask you to do, and everything is going to be okay," Denzel assured the victim as she began to loosen up her grip from around his waist.

"Officer! She may need some help walking. She was hit in the head numerous times by that punk," Denzel informed the responding Officers as he stood there.

"Okay ma'am, I need you to try your best to walk over to me, and away from him. I will meet you half way, if you need me to," The officer said as he extended his hand out to the woman as he kept aim of Denzel with the other hand. The female then took a grip of the officer's hand and was guided by him to the officers behind him. The victim was escorted by officers down the staircase to the 8th-floor hallway. It was now time to identify Denzel.

"Okay buddy, do yourself a favor and don't move until we verify who you are," The sergeant shouted as he started to move in closer to Denzel, while his fellow officers covered him.

"I have my shield around my neck, and my Identification card in my rear left pants pocket" Denzel yelled out as he sensed the officer approaching him while he remained still.

The sergeant got closer to Denzel then ordered him to slowly place his hand behind his neck, and interlock his fingers. Once Denzel complied, the officer quickly removed the weapon from Denzel rear waist-band and handed it to an officer who stood behind him. Denzel was then quickly handcuffed and frisked for safety reasons. The sergeant removed Denzel's wallet containing his department-issued identification and quickly examined its credentials.

"Sorry about that detective, we had to confirm who you are," The sergeant said as he removed the handcuffs from Denzel wrists and patted him on the shoulders.

"I understand," Denzel replied as he was happy enough not to be shot by his fellow members of the service, and be added to the list of those whom historically have been.

"Are you okay detective?" A Lieutenant on the scene asked Denzel, as he stared at the predator he removed from this earth.

"I'm okay boss, I'm okay," Denzel replied as he started rubbing his eyes from being tired from a long night of work and the heroic act he just committed.

"Detective, I know you said you're okay. But I want you to let EMS take a quick look at you, just to make sure," The concerned lieutenant said as he instructed one of his officers to escort Denzel to see EMS, who was awaiting him on the floor below, stationed in the hallway.

Denzel took one last look at the lifeless rapist, before heading down the roof landing staircase. *Tell the devil I sent yah, you nasty muthafucka! May you rest in shit*! Denzel thought to himself on his way down the steps. Once they reached the bottom landing, the escorting officer opened the stairwell door leading to the six-floor hallway that was very noisy. The hallway was filled with cops and civilians whom lived on that floor. A few police chiefs were on the scene, talking on their mobile phones to report updates on the shooting.

Word traveled fast in the neighborhood about the shooting, as well as in the police department. The media was quickly notified of the events, and they set up outside of the apartment building the shooting occurred in at the blink of an eye. The Police Commissioner and Mayor raced lights and sirens, to the scene to make their media statements with the press. Finally, it was a positive incident involving the New York City Police Department that has been getting a lot of negative publicity for the last few years.

The female victim who was now being treated by EMS in the sixth-floor hallway. Once she noticed Denzel step into the hallway she began to burst into tears and ran over to Denzel while everyone looked on.

"That's him! That's the man that saved me!" The victim yelled soon as she spotted Denzel in the hallway. She then jumped up from the chair EMS had her sitting in and raced towards Denzel direction. Denzel seeing her dashing his way, and open up his arms awaiting the hug. The victim started to cry hysterically as she held Denzel tight.

"That monster beat me like I was nothing! He tried to kill

you, but you still saved me!" The victim said to Denzel, nearly bringing tears to his eyes. The emotions from the female victim brought tears to many eyes that witness her outburst, even a chief at the scene had to fight back his tears. The victim was then escorted away from Denzel by two female officers whom comforted her and walked her back over to EMS.

Someone in the crowded hallway began to applaud, next thing you know the crowd erupted into cheers. A few of the residence on that floor recognized Denzel as a familiar face.

"Thank you, Jesus! Thanking you for sending one of your angels to save this young woman!" Yelled out an older woman holding a bible in her hand.

"Isn't that what's her name son?" A different older female resident in the crowd asked, while getting a reply of yes from another.

"Damn! That niggas a cop? I've been seeing him come in and out this building for years and had no clue," said a young male whom usually sold marijuana from the lobby of the building.

"Man, you never know who's five-o these days, they look and dress like a regular nigga," said another marijuana dealer whom frequent the building.

"Detective! What's your name and what command are you from?" Asked a captain who was covering the duty for the 75th precinct and police service area. "I need to make a notification to your command and commanding officer," The captain continued.

"My name is Denzel Major, and I'm an undercover assigned to Queens Narcotics," Denzel responded while EMS ran a few simple field tests on him.

"Thanks, detective, I will notify your command of the events that occurred and good job," The short and chubby Duty captain said before walking away to give an awaiting chief the rundown of what he knew.

Chief Whitaker, a female three-star, focused her attention on Denzel and questioned his mental state of mind as the captain gave her the run down. She recognized Denzel to be a fellow undercover of hers, from her former command at Queens Narcotics; where she was once an undercover detective herself prior to her rise in the ranks of the Police Department. Denzel was also the cousin of one of her very close friend and ex-partner of hers from her patrol days in the confines of the 12th Precinct.

"Captain make sure that detective goes to the hospital to be treated for trauma and I want a mental evaluation conducted on him. He's a personal friend of mine! And I want to make sure he's okay," Chief Whitaker instructed the duty captain in charge of the scene.

"I will get on it, right away Chief," The duty captain replied as he quickly walked away and delegated the instruction to a lieutenant at the scene.

After a brief check-up by EMS in the crowded hallway, the female victim was escorted by EMS on a wheel chair and two female officers into the elevator as they prepared to leave the scene. Once elevator made it to the lobby, the female victim couldn't help but notice the large presence of Police Officers, On lookers and Media Camera Crews. The two female officers along with some other officers surrounded the victim like a human shield. The EMS tech placed a blanket over the victim's head to shield her from photos and Television cameras and she was escorted to the awaiting ambulance that would take her directly to Kings County Hospital for further treatment.

The duty captain then instructed officers to clear the hallways of all civilians, so a crime scene investigation could be established and undisturbed. The officers followed his orders by asking all the occupants in the hallway to either enter their apartment or exit the building. Once the hallway was cleared of all civilians; Major began to get handshakes and pats on the shoulders by his fellow members of the service. The congratulations came from the rank of police officer to three star chiefs whom where all on the scene, and very proud that the young detective did not get hurt while risking his life.

The Internal Affairs Bureau (IAB) where notified of Denzel's act of heroism as part of procedure and are required to ask a few questions to assure it was a good shooting with no foul play by the now popular Detective. It's a standard procedure for IAB to respond to all shooting incidents involving an Officer whether on duty or off, all notifications and responses by this unit receives a log number that is recorded into the incident file.

The body of the deceased predator whom terrorized the neighborhood of East New York Brooklyn remained face down where he took his last breath on the roof landing floor. The

Flashes from the Night Watch Detective's cameras lite up the dimly lit roof landing as they snapped photos of the deceased to submit with their paper work. It didn't take too long before the deceased predator was identified as Curtis Holland from the Ocean hill Brownsville part of Brooklyn. The hulking predator served many years in prison for charges of Robbery, Assault and of course Rape. This 6'5 300lb menace like many others before him slipped through the cracks of the judicial system and continued to walk the streets of New York City.

The State of New York as well as other City, furnish these menace to society with recreation (Gyms, Body Building Equipment), Education (GED and College) and three hot meals a day, while they're incarcerated. All these things funded by the honest tax payers of the City and State. This same State and City system whom would refuse a child that attends public school free meals basing it on the parent's income, but would supply an inmate with the best fruits and vegetables that money could buy.

Many violent fatal incidents occur in New York City as well as others within the United States, involving Parolees whom continue their life of crime while out on Parolee. The increase of Homicides, Assaults, Rapes, and Robberies by these repeat offenders has risen over the years and is still on the rise.

New York City as well as New York State, has awarded many incarcerated inmates Lawsuit Settlement for improper treatment towards the inmate while being imprisoned. If an inmate falls victim to another inmate's attack, slips and falls in the jail or feel he or she has been treated in an unfair manner, they usually file suit. Most of these inmates whom has a history of violence and have violated many innocent people rights and safety during their time of freedom, learned how to work the system and cash in on it.

The attacks on correction officers have gone up, and the officers attacked cannot file suit against the job nor the inmate. If an inmate is assaulted by an officer during a use of force, the officer is usually held accountable and disciplined by the department, as well as sued by the inmate.

Instead of the City and State, fighting the allegations in Civil Court, they usually settle and payout the inmate an undetermined amount of United States Currency (Cash). The City and State should grant the settlement won by the inmate to all the victims of all the Murders, Assault and Rape victims instead of the criminals who has inflicted pain in so many lives.

The Department of Human Resources also aid these menace to society by granting them Welfare, Health Care, Food Stamps and some even collect Social Security Insurance(SSI) checks, all on the tax payers dime. Many of these inmates and free criminally minded predators never worked a day in their life, but yet benefit from the hard work of others who earn a decent living. The easiest way for them to collect an SSI check is to act mentally disturbed while in prison. An inmate mental status is documented during his incarceration by a

Doctor supplied and employed by the City or State. Upon the inmate's release, he or she is giving a referral to follow up and continue treatment.

The elevator door opened and out walked a very slim tall male white along with a very short female black. They were both wearing their shields on the outside of their blazers and carried their transmission radios in their hands. The male approached an officer that stood near the elevator and engaged in a brief conversation with him, just before the two were directed to Major's direction. As the two started to head down the corridor, Major took notice of them heading in his direction and figured they could only be from one place and came for only one purpose.

"Excuse me, Detective Major, I'm Lieutenant Iaccino and this is Sergeant Williams, and we're from Internal Affairs." The tall male said as he stood over Major whom was getting looked over by an EMS tech.

"Hello Lieutenant, Sergeant" Major replied as he looked up while he was having his blood pressure checked. The female Sergeant then extended her hand to shake Majors, who extended his free arm in return.

"How are you Detective?" She asked showing concern based on the dazed look in Majors eyes.

"I'm okay I guess, I'm still alive, and I'm blessed to be that" Major said as he touched the female Sergeants hand as they shook hands. The look in Majors eyes sent a tingle through the Sergeant's body, that warmed her heart. Major then extended his hand out to the Lieutenant after shaking the Sergeants hand. The Lieutenant then shook Major's hand, and then removed a memo pad from inside of his blazer pocket.

"Detective, me and the sergeant know you just experienced a hell of a lot today but you already know we need to ask you a few questions in regard to what have taken place," The Lieutenant quickly said getting to the point. Before Major could even respond, he heard a familiar voice shout out across the corridor

"My detective has 48 hours to give a summary of what occurred, and will not answer nor be asked anything by your unit until then. He's being treated right now by the EMT right now as you can see, and he will be transported to the hospital for trauma," Captain Jently, Major's module captain from Queens Narcotics shouted, as he approached Major and the two supervisors from the Internal Affairs Bureau with a BIG GULP 7 ELEVEN CUP filled with Coca-Cola. Captain Jently was accompanied by two Detectives whom a worked on the Midnight Team at his command.

"Excuse us Captain, but we just need to ask the detective a few of the record questions involving today's incident." The Lieutenant dared to say, thinking his position in the Internal Affairs Bureau could hold a candle to the rank of captain.

"Maybe you don't see my fucking shield, nor do you see these two fucking bars on my shoulder Lieutenant," The captain said referring to his rank over the lieutenant.

"I just told you, LIEUTENANT! My Detective has 48 fucking hours to make a statement and he will be heading to the hospital! Do I make myself perfectly clear LIEUTENANT?!" He continued as he started to get louder and turn red in the face. The Lieutenant just looked and stared at the red face Captain and nodded his head.

"His firearm has already been confiscated by patrol and sent to the Lab, so you two can head back into that little rat hole command of yours Lieutenant," The hyper Captain continued to attack.

The Lieutenant and Sergeant didn't dare to challenge or question what the Captain order for them to return to their command. The Lieutenant just took a quick glance at the Captains name tag before both him and the Sergeant decided to walk away towards the elevator. The Lieutenant started to write in his memo pad once the two reached the elevator, and entered it once it arrived on the floor.

"Can you believe these rat bastards! Half of them muthafuckas were zeros while out on patrol, but now they rather go hard and lock up cops than pursue perpetrators. I was assigned to that fucking Bureau once I made Lieutenant, and I see so much shit going on in there you wouldn't fucking believe it" The Captain continued to rant and rave as other Officers listened in closely.

Chief Whitaker, whom was still present at the scene then walked over and tapped Captain Jently on the shoulder and asked him to take a walk with her down to the other end of the corridor. As the two walked away, Major as well as the other two Detectives from his command looked on. They thought for sure the Captain was gonna get scrutinized for yelling at the two members of the service from the Internal Affairs Bureau, but once the two reached the end of the corridor, they engaged in a brief conversation that ended in a handshake. Captain Jently quickly headed back towards Major.

"Okay my hero Detective, are you ready to head to the hospital now?" The extra jolly Captain said as he took a sip on the very large cup of what was believed to be soda. Major thought to himself "This dude probably has rum or Jack Daniels mixed with that Coca Cola or this dude was just bipolar" as he looked up at the Captain.

"Captain Jay I'm okay. Could you please have someone send a message to my family that I'm okay, and that I'm heading over to the hospital?" Major asked not knowing if his family was already notified.

"Detective! Man, you got the Mayor, Commissioner and every News Media van downstairs right now. I'm pretty sure your family got word that you're a Hero by now" The Captain said as he cracked a smile at Major.

"Don't worry Detective; your family have already been notified and the Chief of the Housing Bureau has already set up a fixed post to safe guard your Mother in Laws apartment for 24 hours until the emergency transfer is granted," Chief Whitaker said as she heard Major make a request for a notification. Denzel looked at the Chief and smiled. Even though she was a friend of the family and an ex-partner at work he remained professional.

"Thanks a lot, Chief, I really appreciate it Ma'am," Major said as he stood up and was prepared to leave with the EMS Techs.

"No Detective! I would like to thank you as well as the rest of the city of New York for your dedication bravery and service to us all," The Chief said as she extended her hand out to shake Major's hand. Major then shook the Chief's hand and headed down the corridor towards the elevator along with the two Detectives from his command, his Captain and two uniformed officers assigned to escort him to the hospital along with the EMS Techs and they all entered the elevator once it arrived.

Once the elevator reached the first floor, one of Major's co-worker placed a Police raid jacket over his head to conceal his identity; then everyone exited the elevator and headed into the lobby. The bright lights from the video camera crews blinded them as they exited the building, while a press conference with the Mayor and Police Commissioner was in process right in front of the entrance.

A roar of cheers erupted from the crowd of on-lookers as the hero off-duty detective exited the building. The applause and cheers sent chills up his spine as his eyes began to tear up from the love expressed to him by the on-lookers and fellow co-worker. The Mayor and Commissioner proudly looked on as their hero detective, escorted by other officers made their way through the crowd to the awaiting ambulance. Once Denzel was inside of the ambulance; it was escorted by many marked police vehicle with lights and sirens straight to Kings County Hospital.

Denzel's eyes started to tear up during the ride to the hospital, the mere appreciation from the crowd overwhelmed him. They appreciate my thirst for dirty blood. He thought to himself with the cheers he received from the crowd whom named him a hero, but deep within his heart lived a stone-cold killer that didn't give a fuck about a low life motherfucker that wasn't worth shit to the world. He figured he served the citizens of New York City and satisfied his own fetish to eliminate the menace to society that deserved it. He repeatedly visualized the large predator hitting the deck in slow motion as he caught some hot ones from his handgun. The vision quickly disappeared out his mind as soon the ambulance came to a stop, as he arrived at the Emergency Room entrance and prepared himself to exit it.

"Don't forget to put that jacket on your head before you get out; there might be some media out there filming and taking photos" said one of the EMT Techs warning Denzel to protect his identity. After putting the raid jacket over his head once again, Denzel stepped out of the Ambulance and couldn't help but observe the army of blue uniform officers that stood outside the Emergency room entrance whom started to cheer him once he exited the ambulance and was escorted into the Emergency Room.

While waiting in Triage Denzel was approached by Captain Jently.

"Hey Detective, I have some great news for you" The Captain said as he looked down at Denzel who was sitting on a stool awaiting the triage nurse.

"Good News Cap?" Denzel asked not having a clue to what the Captain was talking about as he looked up.

"Yes detective! That three-star chief at the scene said you're going to get grade, a combat cross and possibly a medal of honor for your heroic act," Captain Jently informed the Detective.

Oh shit! I just took out a piece of shit, and the department wants to reward me for It, with a promotion and citations. Nice! Denzel thought to himself as he held in his smile.

"Get your good suit ready detective, this a high-profile case. That promotion should be right around the corner, soon as the smoke. Congratulations on a job well done," Jently said as he extended his hand out to Denzel to congratulate him.

"Thanks, cap," Denzel replied with a smile. In back of his mind he was wondering, why the Captain was so happy for him? Denzel was only an undercover, and that position was treated as the lowest of the low at his command. Jently had a history of sending new undercovers back to their former command in a heartbeat, if he thought they didn't meet his standards of making narcotic buys. Even though Denzel was one of his top undercovers under his command, Jently would still call him into his office, if he thought Denzel's buy numbers where getting low.

"Don't let him fool you, player! That muthafucka only happy because he thinks he might get promoted to Deputy Inspector (D.I.) off your shit! Don't think for one second that he even gives a fuck about you," Rock, a detective from Denzel's command who rode with Jently to the scene informed him. "Jently was on the phone talking about it on the way to the hospital," Rock continued.

"What the fuck?! You think I'm stupid Rock? I know what time it is with him, but right now I need him to do whatever he got to do to expedite my promotion," Denzel replied to his co-worker comment. "That chief he was talking to, me and her go way back even before I got on the job," Denzel continued.

"Wow, that's cool. You know rumor has it that Jently, has a red flag in his folder and will never get promoted to deputy inspector, right?" Rock asked.

"Yeah," Denzel replied.

"So, he thinks he's going to shine at headquarters, because of you," Rock stated just before the nurse in Triage called Denzel in to exam him.

Denzel was then examined by both medical and psychological doctors who treated him for signs of physical and mental trauma. He was released and escorted home by detectives from his unit and was left alone to gain some rest to prepare himself to talk to his union representatives later that day.

The Media was all over the story as the news traveled nationwide with television footage that took over the air waves.

The deceased predator mug shot photos was posted all over television and on the front page of every newspaper.

The new paper articles contained his long criminal record rap sheet on the following page. The rap sheet was an embarrassment to the judicial system, since they once again allowed another career criminal to roam the streets to terrorize the citizens of the city.

The mayor and police commissioner continuously took to the podium at many press conferences during that week, as if they were the ones whom made the city proud. The mayor wanted to boost things up to enhance his upcoming re-election run, and spread the word that New York City is one of the safest cities in the country under his watch. He gave much praise to the police commissioner for his great tactics and strategies on how to decrease crime. The Pressure was on them both to promote the young Detective's whom heroic act, shined a positive light on the Police Department as well as the City.

While in the shower, Denzel could hear his cell phone ringing. He just finished doing an intense workout of pushups and pull-ups to burn off some stress and was in need of a hot shower. He picked up his phone to check all missed calls once he exited the shower and dried himself off and applied lotion and cologne. He noticed he missed a call from the F.O.D. and thought to himself "What the Fuck Now!" As he placed the phone down on his bed as he got dressed. He figured it must be a Departmental Investigative Interview also known a GO-15 Notification called in to the F.O.D. by the Internal Affairs Bureau in regard to the shooting.

The Phone ringed again, and he picked it up from the bed only to see that his girlfriend Nicole was calling him as he looked at the caller I.D. Screen. Nicole was a very pretty Carmel complexion black woman that possessed deep dimples and smile that could brighten up any room. Denzel was immediately attracted to her when he first laid eyes on her, basically because her body was a show stopper and her face was like baby dolls. He didn't hesitate to engage in a conversation with her, when she first moved into his neighborhood. He came to realize that she was very ambitious in succeeding to provide for her two children and worked very hard to get what she wanted. After five months after meeting, Denzel and Nicole started dating and have continued for about ten months. They have traveled to the Caribbean together and even went to Disney World along with all of their children as a family united vacation.

"Hello, baby," Nicole said as Denzel answered the phone just before the call got sent to voicemail.

"Hello love. How are you today?" Denzel replied as he laid back on his bed from his sitting position.

"I'm good, just checking on my man to see how you're doing," Nicole said in her sexy voice.

"I just got out the shower a few minutes ago," Denzel replied as he turned on his television with the remote that was also on his bed.

"Oh, okay baby, give me a call when your finish getting yourself together," Nicole quickly responded thinking Denzel was still undressed.

"I'm dressed already, but I will call you back, I have to return a call to my job. They called me earlier," Denzel said to Nicole letting her know he had to handle some job-related business real quick, before he could have a decent conversation with her.

"Okay, handle your business and hit me later," Nicole said as both she and Denzel said their good-byes and ended their phone conversation.

Denzel decided to check all his voice messages.

"Yo Denzel! Call the FOD asap man!" A male voice Denzel recognized to be his Detective Porter said.

"Oh, hell no! I'm calling your fucking Cell Phone!" Denzel said out loud, thinking Porter was setting him up for a job-related notification. He then dialed Porter's cell phone number, wanting to speak to him directly to find out what was going on.

"What up player?" Porter answered, knowing it was Denzel on the other end of it.

"Yo chill out man! Don't be yelling out my name. Where the fuck are you?" Denzel responded.

"I'm sitting on the fucking thrown, taking a shit!" Porter quickly said as he continued to read an article in the magazine he was holding.

"You one nasty muthafucka, to be answering the phone while you taking a shit man. Hit me on the cell after you whip your stink ass," Denzel said while shaking his head on how gross Porter was. "What the fuck you call me for anyway? Denzel continued.

"I left a message for you to call the FOD, not me fool." Porter responded as he started to laugh.

"Like I said! Call me when you're off your thrown, and don't let nobody know you heard from me," Denzel requested of his friend.

"Whatever you say, hero! I'll call you back in a few," Porter responded just before he hung up his phone.

Denzel then laid back on his bed and started to flip the television channels. He stopped and looked at a media press conference with the commissioner and the Mayor up at the podium in regard to his shooting.

"So, Mr. Mayor, will the identity of the heroic detective be revealed and will he receive the reward money posted for the capture of the deceased predator?" Asked one of the members of the press, as he yelled out from the back of the press room.

"No, is the answer to your first question of the detective's identity being revealed. Before this incident, the detective in question has generated many cases, and the release of his identity will jeopardize his as well as many other undercover detectives/police officer's lives. Also, members of the police department, do not receive cash rewards. They are sworn in to protect and serve the citizens of the New York City. The detective will be promoted to second grade and will receive a citation and accommodation for his heroic act of bravery in the near future. I personally would like to give him the key to the city," The mayor stated as Denzel listened closely until his cell phone started to ring.

"Hero! I'm all done handling mine. What do you want from my life?" Porter asked as soon as Denzel answered his phone on the second ring.

"Why did you leave me a message, to call the FOD earlier?" Denzel curiously asked.

"Your notification for promotion to second grade came down from the police commissioner's(PC)office, plus I hear you up for The Medal of Honor and get a Combat Cross," Porter stated.

"What?" Denzel asked while being surprised that the mention of him being up to receive the highest citation in the police department along with a promotion to second grade detective.

"Damn! Did they test you for trauma, because you acting as if you can't hear me fool," Porter jokingly responded.

"Stop bullshitting me, Porter! I can't believe the department going to do all that for a black man," Denzel asked as he thought Porter was adding spice to shit.

"Man, that shooting was high profile. One of that punk's victims is related to a well-known congressman up in Washington and I guess he among others pushed the issue. You're the department's golden child right now. Enjoy the moment." Porter explained to a confused Denzel.

"I guess you're right," Denzel said as he laughed while still hoping to himself that Porter wasn't jerking him off.

"Well, if you think I don't got nothing else to do but call your ass up and lie to you. Why don't you just call the fucking FOD and get notified the normal way? Bitch!" Porter said just before hanging up. Denzel looked at his phone and smiled.

Did his punk ass just call me a bitch and hang up? That old school, half dead muthafucka! Denzel jokingly thought to himself. He decided to call the FOD just to get it over with, he wanted to really find out if Porter was fucking with his mind or not.

Porter was known at Denzel's Office as a practical joker, who would set you up for the kill just for a few laughs. So, the thought of him calling and receiving a IAB Interview Notification from the FOD never slipped his mind.

"Queens Narcotics! Detective Watson, how may I help you?" Answered Detective Watson whom was assigned to the FOD during that tour.

"What's Up Watson? This your boy Major," Denzel said as he turned down his television and grabbed a pen and a piece of paper.

"Oh, Shit! It's Detective Muthafuckin Major! A real life super hero!" Watson jokingly said as he recognized Denzel's voice.

"Hero? You and I both know that ain't nothing but a sandwich, player. Just call me a dark angel like or Shaft," Denzel responded before he started to laugh.

"I hear that my brother, you definitely earned your wings for that good deed," Watson said as he opened up the telephone message log, already knowing the reason Denzel was calling.

"I missed that call from the FOD earlier, and got the message to call back. Hit me with the good or bad news." Denzel said as he prepared himself for the notification.

Detective Watson then read off the following telephone message log notification to Denzel.

At 0700 hours on Friday, Detective Denzel Major shield 6969 is to report to the Chief of the Organized Crime Control Bureau office at headquarters in business attire for promotion to second-grade detective. At 0800 hours on Friday Detective Denzel Major is also to report to the auditorium located on the first floor of headquarters, to attend the award ceremony to receive citations for his act of bravery.

Due to Detective Major position as an undercover detective, all members of the press and public are not permitted nor allowed in the auditorium during his time of presentation. He will be allowed to bring four members of his immediate family to attend, as they will be allowed to take photos with the mayor, commissioner, chief of the department, chief of OOCB and chief of detectives after the ceremony.

Detective Major will be the recipient of The Medal of Honor as well as Combat Cross for his act of Bravery.

Denzel started to smile as he listened to the notification being read. A weird indescribable warmth traveled through Denzel's body. The idea of getting promoted to second grade detective just four months after his initial first promotion to detective was a positive sign to him that he was heading towards a lovely career in the New York City Police Department.

The once happy go lucky Brooklyn native, later transformed to a vindictive vigilante who roamed the violent streets of Brooklyn to hunt down those undesirable that crossed his path, was on his way to being a decorated detective in the police department. The hidden dark side of him, made him a rising star, in the eyes of the police department. But to him, it was self-rewarding just to eliminate those of whom he thought deserved to die. And on the day, he was promoted and received citations, all he could think of was, who he had to take out to make first grade.

CHAPTER 20

MAJOR ENGAGEMENT

The early morning sun was shining bright over DeVonte's estate, as the sun's rays entered his bedroom window warming his forehead. The activities just a few hours before, along with numerous sexual encounters between the happy couple, left him exhausted and plagued with fatigue. DeVonte and Erica basically slept for a few hours, unlike their guest who practically broke day and stayed up until the sunrise. The combination of good food, drinks, and dancing made the night a good one for all.

Oh shit! It's 7 o'clock DeVonte thought to himself once he awakened and looked over at his alarm clock sitting on his dresser. He smoothly and unsuccessfully attempted to ease out of his bed to avoid waking Erica, who had her head laying on his chest while her one of her legs wrapped around his waist.

He kissed her on her forehead and whispered Babe slide over so I can go to the bathroom. Erica, still half sleep, kissed him on the chest and rolled her body over onto her side, facing the opposite direction of the bed.

Once Erica released her body of DeVonte, he quickly got up the bed and picked up his cellphone from the night stand while on his way to the bathroom. He closed the door behind him as he entered it and immediately turned on the shower to muffle the conversation he was about to engage in over the phone. After engaging in a ten-minute conversation, he then placed his cell phone down near the sink and entered the shower. DeVonte exited the bathroom after taking his shower and looked at Erica as she laid there.

"Babe! Are you up yet?" DeVonte asked. Erica did not answer as she laid still on her belly. After receiving no response from his sexy companion, he then climbed on top of the bed placing his face under her see through gown, and placed his head on top of her lower back just above her perfectly round bottom. He then slid his tongue down the crack of her ass cheeks and licking around the rim of her anus until her pussy began to moisten. The sound of faint moans began to escape her lips as he slowly stroked his wet tongue on her.

Erica's eyes slowly opened as they rolled up into her head from the sensation of DeVonte's tongue. She gradually raised her ass north, while her head went south onto the bed, once she started feeling the sensation. After a few licks of his wet tongue, she then lifted her body upward on to her knees in a doggie style position. The erotic sensation had her hoping that the pleasure of his tongue would soon change into the pleasure of his stiff hard penis. DeVonte rose his head up once he felt her sexual cream escaping her pussy and he started to laugh.

"I knew that would wake you up Babe!" He said as he raised his body up from the position he was in.

"Oh no, don't stop! Finish what you were doing Babe! Can't you see how wet you got me?" Erica said in the heat of passion. DeVonte just watched her as his manhood became harder and harder.

"Why are you stopping?" Erica asked as her body burned up inside with passion causing her to gyrate her body in a highly sexual matter. She turned her head around only to find DeVonte just staring at her. The way he was looking at her turned her on even more as the creamy lather between her legs began to slowly drip onto the bed.

DeVonte continued to look down at Erica as the towel he had wrapped around his waist became a large tent. The scent of her heavenly essence flowed through the room, arousing him to his hardest peak. His half moist chiseled chest, Abs and pelvis area aroused Erica even more as she looked at his manhood grow longer and thicker. He knew if he granted her wish, he would fall behind in his plans. DeVonte couldn't resist the temptation to feel that soft round ass of hers, so he climbed back onto the bed and pressed his hard cock against her ass cheeks.

Erica began to grind her body up against the hard-long cock that was concealed by his towel, and reached her arm around to try to remove it in an attempt to stop it from blocking out the flesh of his mushroom tip. DeVonte anticipating her action grabbed her by the wrist and kissed her hand, as he leaned over to kiss her on the back of her neck while he continued to hump her ass. After a few strong thrusts, DeVonte slowed himself down as his manhood pulsated.

"My body wants you, my body needs you to be inside of me! My body is burning inside for you, your lady needs to be fucked!" Erica moaned more and more aggressive as DeVonte slid one of his hands between her legs and massaged her clit that stuck out at attention.

DeVonte knew once he had a hold on the clit it wouldn't be too long before she was ready to cum. Erica clinched her legs tightly attempting to hold it inside, but in reality, she was ready to spread them while her pussy started leaking as her juices wanted to escape. The temptation was over baring as

DeVonte placed his towel covered just below her ass cheeks and began to hump her from behind as he continued to massage her clit and kiss the back of her neck. The sensation of the towel covered rock hard cock unleashed a stream of warm sexual fluids from her over heated pussy.

"Oh shit! It's slipping into my ass Babes!!" Erica shouted while letting DeVonte know he is falling deep into the rim of her ass hole. DeVonte quickly re-adjusted his hard cock, by placing it near her soaking wet pussy as he continued to massage it with his hand.

"Move that fucking towel! I want to feel that thick mushroom tip and thick dick slide into me!" Erica shouted, as she turned her face around towards DeVonte, who began to suck hard on her neck.

"No Babe! The way I feel right now! If I move this towel, it's gonna be all cream and baby squirting in your body," DeVonte said as he felt Erica ass cheeks griping his Dick tightly. Erica then shifted her body onto her bell and raised it up and leaned her head backwards with her mouth wide open and her eyes rolled up in her head. Her body started to tremble uncontrollably until she climaxed like a wild woman. DeVonte knew she was busting a nutt but continued to flicker the clit and suck on the back of her neck.

"Aah! I'm cumming again! I'm cumming again!" She moaned out loud making DeVonte dick harder.

"You cumming? You cumming for me Babe?!" DeVonte asked already knowing the answer, especially seeing how creamy she got his dick.

"You know I did!" Erica replied as she tried to catch her breath after her sensational climax.

"Okay, now relax for a minute! We both got a lot of shit to do today, so please don't get me started again," DeVonte said as he softly grabbed onto her wrist that she used to stroke him with. Erica continued her sexual attack, by licking on his chest and sucking his nipples. DeVonte wrapped her arms around his neck and lifted her up by her waist as she wrapped her legs around his hips.

"Oh, I see you really want me to get all up in that bee hive for that warm honey Babe," DeVonte said as he slid her body up against his stiff making her pussy over flow with wetness, but at the same time he avoided the penetration once he felt it about to enter her warm body. Erica stuffed her sweet tongue into DeVonte's mouth and reached down with her hand in an attempt to fill herself with him.

"You better get off me Babe, before I cancel the Spa, and relax you myself," DeVonte jokingly said as he swiftly tossed Erica across the room and onto the bed. Erica thought about the limo ride to the Spa.

"I would love for you to relax me right now, but mama didn't raise no fool. It's not every day, a girl gets a ride to a Spa via limo," She said as she started to giggle.

"I know, that's right. But you better get up and get yourself ready, because the limo will be her at 9 o'clock on the dot. Erica then looked over at the clock to see what time it was. She knew it would take a little time for her and her friends to get ready for their lady's day out.

"I'll run the shower for you, or do you want a hot relaxing bath Babe?" DeVonte asked as he stood near the bathroom entrance looking at the woman he's so in love with.

"A shower, is good enough for me, my love; It slipped my mind to tell them yesterday, so let me call them and let them know to be ready by nine," Erica replied as she reached over to get her cellular phone.

The guests were all up by this time and were enjoying the leftover food from the night before, as if the party never stopped. No one dared to hit the bar as of yet, but they demolished the food as they put the microwave and toaster oven to work. Doreen was already on her second plate of food like she didn't eat the night before, as she stayed close to Mike whom was eating just as much as her.

Stacey, who had a slight hangover from the way too many strawberry daiquiris, sat at the island in the kitchen nibbling on a small portion of fruit salad, while she read missed texts and listened to her missed voice messages. Dennis and Jason both made themselves a platter of food and stepped out onto the patio to enjoy their meal in the sun light.

Stacey started to dial out on her phone after returning text messages to whomever text earlier. Erica crossed her mind and she figured she should give her a call.

"Hello, Miss Thang! Where are You?" She asked knowing her friend probably was lying next to DeVonte.

"I'm in the presidential suite, nosey! What are you ladies doing right now?" Erica asked.

"Everybody's up except for you love birds. We're downstairs in the kitchen and patio eating. I have a hangover so I'm taking it easy," Stacey informed her friend.

"Well, DeVonte is treating us ladies to some spa time today, and a limo will be picking us up to go there," Erica said with excitement in her voice for. Stacey eyes lit up like Christmas lights, from the thought of a relaxing day after a good night of partying.

"Girl, it's way too early in the morning for jokes, okay! My head feels like somebody beat me in the head. So, stop playing with my emotions," She said as she curved her lip in disbelief of the free treat to the Spa.

"Playing! Girl nine o'clock you better be ready! This is not a test, I repeat this is not a test!" Erica jokingly said as DeVonte exited the bathroom and let her know her shower was running.

"Are you really serious? Because I'm in no condition to be

played with right now, I've been up all night," Stacey said as she still continued to doubt her friend word.

"I'm dead serious! We can do a little shopping at the mall and relax at the spa. Plus, later on tonight, we're all going out to MAJOR SOULS," Erica said as she watched DeVonte get dressed.

"Damn, Bitch! You must've sucked the shit out of his balls, last night," Stacey jokingly said loudly as she got a little excited herself.

"Well, he told me about it yesterday. I just forgot to tell you guys. And, on top of that, I always aim to please my man. But girl, between me and you girl, I think he has something up his fine ass sleeve though," Erica said while wondering what the big treat was all about.

"Well, you keep wondering, while I tell the girls to get ready. Make sure you tell DeVonte I said thank you," Stacey said as she glanced her phone to check for the time.

"I will let him know the best way, I know how! You just make sure you let the girls know now! We have to be ready by nine o'clock for the limo," Erica said to remind her friend while she was still staring DeVonte up and down.

"I'm going to handle that, soon as we get off the phone, and don't forget to thank him for me! Just don't thank him too much, we don't need to be late for our ride," Stacey said as she got up off her ass and started to walk towards Doreen whom was still eating.

"Okay, I won't over do it! I'm about to jump in the shower right now. I will see you in a few" Erica replied as she took off her gown as DeVonte took notice of her sexy body.

"Yeah okay! We will be ready. Just make sure you don't trip and fall on that dick and fuck up the class trip," Stacey joked just before they disconnected their conversation.

Erica began to laugh as she hung up her cell in regard to

Stacey's last comment. She got up off the bed and her nipples were at full attention as she slowly walked towards DeVonte. DeVonte stared at her as she approached him like he was hypnotized by her beauty. She stood up very close to him and wrapped her arms around his slim waist, while pressing her nude body up against him. DeVonte pulled her closer and kissed her softly on the forehead as he ran his fingers through her hair. Erica then lifted up her head as a kiss met her lips, causing her to reveal her deep dimples as she began to smile.

"My love! Did I just feel a track?" DeVonte said before cracking a smile, showing his bright white teeth. Erica started to laugh as she attempted to pull away from Deon as he held on tightly.

"You are such a jerk!! Get off of me!!" Erica yelled out while laughing as she attempted to escape DeVonte's hug.

"I was only joking Babe! Just a little jokey joke with my beautiful Queen," DeVonte said as he lifted her up and attempted to kiss her again on the lips as she resisted. Erica pretended that she didn't want to be kissed, knowing damn well she loved how she was held tightly and up in the air.

"Babes stop, why you gotta keep making me Horney, when you know I have to get myself ready?" Erica yelled out as she giggled as DeVonte tried to put his tongue in her mouth as he licked her closed lips.

"Okay, my love! Your right! Because your morning breathe is giving me a headache right now!" DeVonte jokingly said while laughing as he placed her down on the floor. Erica was no longer smiling and had an expression on her face that could kill.

"Oh, you're full of jokes today huh?! I'm gonna remember all that smack you talking tonight, when you want some ass" Erica said as she headed into the bathroom and watched DeVonte looking at her ass. DeVonte quickly ran behind her and kissed her on the ass cheek.

"Please Babe! Babe Please! I'll kiss your ass for all that good loving," He jokingly said as he got down on his knees and held his hands together as if he was praying.

"Whatever!" Erica said as she stepped into the shower and began to wash her body. DeVonte watched her as the creamy soap began to lather on her curvy body.

"My Love! I'm heading downstairs to see what's up with our guests okay," DeVonte yelled out hoping Erica could hear him over the sound of the water running as he started to head out the bathroom and back into the bedroom. The sound of the warm water hitting her body faded DeVonte out, preventing Erica to respond to him. DeVonte picked up his cell phone and headed out his bedroom and down the corridor towards his office.

Stacey popped two aspirins and washed it down with a bottle of water. She looked at her friends whom where all enjoying a bite to eat and wanted to break the good news to them. Doreen of course was eating like she was building strength to fight a war.

"Girl! Make that your last plate and hurry up so you can get ready," Stacey said as she walked over to Doreen.

"Hurry up for what?" Doreen asked as she sipped on a cold glass of ice tea to wash down her second serving of food.

"Erica just called me and said we are getting treated to the spa today" Stacey said as she jokingly placed her hands on her hip.

"Bitch, stop playing with me! Erica ain't just tell you no shit like that," Doreen said as she sucked her teeth and looked Stacey up and down.

"You better slow down with all that BITCH calling! Don't let this bitch, have to fuck you up in here. As a matter of fact, I'm Miss Bitch to you! And if you don't want to be the only Bitch left in this house today not pampered with all these men. I suggest you go get your big ass ready," Stacey replied as she rolled her eyes, smiled and looked at Doreen as if she was stupid.

"Whatever you say, Miss Bitch! What made you decide to walk over here and playing games with me? Talking about we are getting treated to the spa. I got to hear that come out of Erica's mouth, before this big ole ass start moving," Doreen said while still not believing Stacey.

"Okay forget it then! I guess you will believe me when you see the rest of us rolling off in the stretch limo at nine O'clock," Stacey said as she began to walk towards Alexis and Chantel. Doreen watched Alexis, and Chantel get excited after Stacey whispered a few words in their ear, while she finished off the last of her iced tea. Stacey then walked back over to Doreen, who was still sitting in the same spot, while Chantel and Alexis hurried their way into the house to prepare themselves.

"You must really think I'm playing with you, Doreen! This dude is the real deal and willing to treat us all to some woman time and you still sitting there like it's a game and shit. Finish feeding your face, handle your business and make sure you dress your best because we're hitting MAJOR SOUL'S tonight right after," Stacy said just before she started to head into the house.

"You must be dead ass serious, huh?" Doreen asked as she started to realize that Stacey wasn't playing around with her. We going all the way to NYC to eat at Major Souls?" Doreen continued.

"Hell No! I'm not playing with you, Doreen! And, no we're not going to the MAJOR SOULS in New York City. There is one close by in Jersey," Stacey answered as she continued into the house.

So, I guess I better get off my ass and go get ready then, this dude DeVonte is the truth for real if this bitch ain't fucking with me Doreen thought to herself as she finished her plate, cleaned up behind herself and headed in the house.

DeVonte bypassed Doreen on his way towards his boys whom were still hanging out in the kitchen and said hello to her as their eyes met. She gave him a seductive stare as she said good afternoon and followed it with a warm smile. Her thick curvy body nearly brushed against him as they passed one another, and DeVonte avoided the contact. To him it seemed that Doreen did it intentionally, but he knew better not to give her flirting any attention.

"Dang Miss Lady! You trying to knock me down on my ass or what?" DeVonte jokingly asked Doreen.

"Sorry about that DeVonte. I always seem to lose my balance when I smell a seductive cologne. My body just gets drawn to it, it's beyond my control," Doreen said as she stopped and turned around to look at DeVonte.

"Oh okay, I thought you wanted to fight or something. You look like you might know a little bit about ultimate fighting the way you tried to hip check a brotha," DeVonte jokingly said as he got into a fighting stance and placed his hands up.

"I'm not into that ultimate fighting stuff, but I do like to wrestle strong men! And when I do! I always end up on top controlling the battle" Doreen said as she started to laugh while walking away.

"I'm scared of you lady! I am truly scared of you!" DeVonte said while shaking his head and watching the flirtish Doreen ass shaking like a big bowl of Jell-O while she walked away until she disappeared from his site.

"That's a whole lot of woman right there Dee" Rick said as he spotted DeVonte looking back at Doreen, when he finally made his way into the kitchen.

"Man! That big ole bootie ain't nothing but, a big cloud that could never block my sunshine. Erica outshines everything and everyone" DeVonte said as he looked over at Mike whom was out on the patio eating.

"I feel you on that my brother! Especially when you're about to propose to your Queen by the end of the night. But, like most Kings say, "Your eyes are only for the Queen doesn't mean you have to keep your eyes shut to the rest of the kingdom" Rick said.

"Rick! How many years have you known me?" DeVonte asked Rick. "We have known each other, way before we both started getting pussy. I'm a changed man! I'm not playing games no more! Games are just way too stressful. Even if I was still the old me! I would never disrespect my lady by eyeballing her home girls no matter how good they may look," DeVonte continued as he checked his watch to see what time it was.

Mike walked into the kitchen and looked over at DeVonte and Rick as they stood near the large island.

"Damn! Did I just interrupt you two ladies from kissing or something?" Mike said as he observed the two staring at him as he walked in the room. "

"Nah Playboy! We were just talking about your girl Doreen," Rick said as he put a grin on his face.

"Doreen look like she's kind of sweet on you Mike. You think you could handle all that bro?" DeVonte jokingly asked.

"First of all! That's not my girl! And, second of all, you two fools got me a little nervous right now! I walk in and you two are asking me what my Dick can handle! Yall niggas suspect," Mike said as he shook his head. DeVonte and Rick started to laugh loudly at Mike's facial expression.

"You know we far from suspect! We just fucking with you with your sensitive, ass," Rick said as Dennis and Jason entered the kitchen from the patio.

"Glad you two came in to join us," DeVonte said referring to Jason and Dennis. Now since I got all my boys together in one room while the ladies are upstairs getting themselves ready to head out for a little lady time," DeVonte said as all his buddies gathered around the island as if it was a conference table. He reached into his rear pants pocket and pulled out a list of things to do and wanted to delegate it to his friends whom where there to help him.

Rick, did you call my girl over at MAJOR SOULS to make sure everything is going according to plan the way me and her discussed it a few days ago for tonight?" DeVonte asked.

"Yep," Rick quickly responded.

"And did you let her know, my decorator Nicole will be there around noon to hook up our V.I.P. section, and to leave five dozen of them long-stem roses in the VIP area for Nicole to hook up for the evening?" DeVonte asked Rick.

"Yep, and I made sure she still had our catered breakfast scheduled for your delivery here, for tomorrow morning," Rick responded.

"Good, Nicole should be here around eight to set the scene, while we're at Major Souls," DeVonte said as he gave Rick a hand shake of approval.

Mike, did you call up the limo service to make sure that the limo will be on time today? And the florist to get an exact time of arrival on all the locations, I arraigned to have roses delivered to?" DeVonte asked Mike.

"Yeah man, rose petals for the staircase and master suite will arrive on time. The long stem roses for the VIP area and your girl Kim should be delivered by now. I called over to the limo service not too long ago, and they stated that the limo should arrive at the scheduled time," Mike answered.

"Thanks," DeVonte said as he looked at his watch.

"Dennis and Jason! I need you two big intimidating brothers to ride with me to Jersey to pick up some currency one of my contracts owes me. I got a funny vibe last time I pass through there. You two muscle heads would make jokers think twice about scheming and looking at me sideways," DeVonte said as he requested the two big guys backup.

"Man! You already know we got your back." Dennis said as both he and Jason began to flex their biceps.

"Since we all on the same page, I'm gonna check on my lady real quick," DeVonte said as he excused himself from his buddies and headed out the kitchen and down the corridor towards the foyer next to the staircase. He bypassed Erica's girlfriends who greeted him with a hello and smile as they headed back towards the kitchen.

The love of his life wasn't among them, so he proceeded up the stairs and down the corridor. Once he opened the French doors leading to his bedroom, he could smell the sweet fragrance of Flower bomb floating in the air. He followed the scent towards his master bathroom, as he entered he observed Erica leaning her body forward towards the mirror over the sink, placing a lovely purple lip stick on her soft lips.

The white with purple screen print terry cloth sweat suit, fit her well-curved body like a glove. The purple embroidered Rhine stones imprinted on her white panties read "BEYOND SEXY" were visible to the eye, as it described her to a perfect tee. Her shell toe Adidas tennis sneakers coordinated with her outfit as well as the purple Rhine-stone custom jewelry hooped earrings.

DeVonte walked up behind Erica and wrapped his arms around her thin waist, as he kissed her on the neck. She then leaned her head back to receive one on the cheek as she still looked into the mirror. DeVonte then placed a nice soft kiss on it, and whispered something in her ear just before he let her go to walk out of the bathroom. Erica proceeded to place her lipstick on as if she was a makeup artist, she wanted to place it on her full lips perfectly.

DeVonte then headed down his second-floor corridor towards his office, entered it and closed the door behind him.

He walked around his large desk and pulled forward the large painting that hung on the wall behind his chair revealing a keypad safe, that was embedded into the wall. He inserted a four-digit code, pulled the safe open and removed a thick envelope. He checked its content and quickly closed the safe. He then pushed the painting that concealed it back in its rightful place. He glanced at the surveillance monitor that was mounted on the wall under his 80' inch screen television and noticed a white van with blue letters marked exterminator parked outside across from his front gate. DeVonte had noticed the van before in the past but, thought nothing of it. Since it was the weekend, it caught his attention today.

"What the fuck do we have here? I wonder if it's potential burglars or the Feds? Any which way, I know how to make them move and set up somewhere else," DeVonte said to himself as he picked up his cordless phone on his desk. He then called 911 and let the operator know that there was a suspicious vehicle parked outside his home and it has been sitting there for days. After giving the 911 operator the location and description of the van, DeVonte exited his office and headed back to his bedroom.

Erica was still working on herself in the mirror, when DeVonte walked back in the room. He took position behind her again and pulled her close to his body as they looked into the mirror together.

"Damn! We look so good together Babe! What do you think?" DeVonte asked the love of his life. Erica smiled and without a word nodded yes.

"Babe here's a little something for you and the girls to work on while you're out and about at the mall. Hopefully this can cover a little shopping, brunch while you're at the spa." DeVonte continued as he placed the envelope he took out of the safe into her jacket pocket.

"Thank You, Babes! Your one in a million," Erica said as she smiled and blew a kiss to DeVonte's mirror reflection.

"Only for you my love! Only for you," DeVonte replied as he smiled and looked into her eyes. Erica started to blush as DeVonte's kind words warmed her heart.

"So, Babes, how do I look?" Erica asked as she struck a quick pose in the mirror with her hands on her hips looking extra sexy.

"You are simply Beyond Sexy! Like the back of what you're VS say," DeVonte said as he started to laugh. Erica just stared at DeVonte without saying a word as she started to blush. She then turned her back towards the mirror and looked over her shoulder to examine her sexy bottom.

"I didn't know that my ass could be read through these pants Babes. You think I need to change them?" Erica said as if she was surprised and didn't want it to seem if she was trying to draw attention to her bottom.

"Whatever, I don't mind you getting a little attention just as long as that's where it stops. There's nothing wrong with giving the world a little eye candy to look at" DeVonte said as he looked at his watch.

"You have nothing to worry about my love; I'm all yours if you want me to be," Erica said just before her cell phone began to ring. Erica asked DeVonte to retrieve her cell phone from his bedroom, while she remained looking in the mirror.

"Erica! Where you at girl? It's almost 9 o'clock and your MIA," Stacey immediately said as soon as Erica answered her phone. Oh, Shit Erica thought to herself as she quickly adjusted her hair to the way she wanted it. Here she was, after warning everybody else to be ready, running late this time.

"Is everyone else ready?" Erica asked as she picked up her pace.

"Yeah, girl! Everybody is downstairs in the kitchen with the guys just waiting on you to come down" Stacey said as Erica could hear the others in the background talking.

"Babes, I'm running late, and my girls are waiting for me downstairs. I guess I will see you later, just before dinner.

I'll have dessert ready for you, when we get back home to show you my appreciation," Erica said as she winked her eye at DeVonte and gave him a hug.

"Okay Babe, I'm gonna hold you to that dessert tonight and then some. I'll grab your bag and walk you downstairs and await the arrival of the limo" DeVonte said after placing a soft kiss to Erica's lips. He then walked over to the foot of his bed and picked up her Gucci duffel bag that contained her outfit for the evening and escorted his lady downstairs.

Erica then walked into the kitchen and greeted the fellas and told her girlfriends that she was ready to go. The fellas couldn't help but notice how good Erica looked in her sweat-suit, especially when she and her friends walked away towards the front door. The words on her VS panties were visible to see.

All the ladies walked outside of the house and stood in front awaiting the limo. DeVonte walked into the entertainment room to hit the switch to open the gate to his estate. He then walked outside and awaited the limo arrival with the ladies. At 9 o'clock on the dot, DeVonte along with the ladies observed a shiny white long stretch Range Rover HSE limousine pulling up in front of the house.

The door opened up like a small jet plane, and everyone could see the flashing decorative lights and hear the smooth sounds of Mary J Blige playing on the stereo. Out stepped an older black male chauffeur who looked very similar to Billy Dee Williams in his prime with a blue Boss suit and hot pink shirt. He walked over to the small group and introduced himself as Robert and that he will be their escort for the day.

The aroma of his cologne caught the smell of everyone

standing there. Erica and her friends were very impressed with the limousine and looked forward to riding in style to wherever they wanted to go. DeVonte extended his hand out to Robert for a handshake and introduced himself. The diamond rings on the chauffeur hand sparkled from the sun light nearly blinding everyone.

"Please take care of my lady and her friends Robert," DeVonte said as he hugged and kissed Erica on the cheek.

"If there is any problem please feel free to call me at this number," DeVonte said as Robert acknowledged him and input DeVonte's number into his cell phone. Robert then escorted all the ladies into the limo as if they were royalty. He gently held each of their hands as they stepped onto the little step stool, he placed on the ground for them to enter the elevated limo.

After all the ladies were in, he then pressed a button and stepped away as the passenger door closed.

Damn, this old school player looks like he was a pimp or a big-time hustler in his younger days DeVonte thought to himself.

"Are there anymore further instructions you need to fill me in on before I pull off sir," Robert asked.

"Robert, you don't have to call me sir. I see that you got that sweet Eve rosé gold Date-Just Rolex on your wrist, along with rings filled with rocks my brother. It doesn't take a rocket scientist to see this is just a hobby for you driving a limo," DeVonte said as both him and Robert began to smile.

"I guess game, recognize game young blood. My brother owns this limo service, so sometimes I take on the light gigs to get out of the house and away from the wife. I like to earn a little extra paper, so I can add to my watch collection. Looks like you're doing very well for yourself DeVonte," Robert said as he looked at the vehicles DeVonte had parked out front.

"Yeah, I'm out here trying to get what life has to offer. But, me and you could talk later, I don't want to hold the ladies up from having their time at the mall and SPA, while I prepared for tonight," DeVonte said as he looked at his watch exposing his Rolex for Robert to see.

"That was my first real piece of jewelry, I treated myself to back when I was a young player," Robert said referring to DeVonte Presidential Rolex that sparkled with diamonds. DeVonte wanted to chew the rag with Robert hoping he could make a new connect and associate, but knew he was only wasting time and needed to get the ball rolling.

"Robert, please try your best to get them ladies back in time, so we can reach MAJOR SOULS by eight o'clock. I have something very special planned tonight for my lady. I plan on popping the question to her, tonight," DeVonte said as he could hear the girls singing along to one of Beyoncé songs in the limo.

"Congratulations, young man! I'll make sure I get them back here on time, so we can arrive on time," Robert said as he admired DeVonte's white Maserati.

"Wow! Thanks, Robert. I'm going to call my girl at Major Souls and tell her to add another chair at our table if you care to celebrate along with us," DeVonte insisted after the nice jester Robert made. He even figured he would call upon the limo service to handle the transportation on his wedding day if Erica says yes to his proposal.

"I'll be a fool to turn down an offer like that. You kind of remind me of myself when I was younger. I'm glad to see you want to make that power move in getting married. Anyway, let me get on the road with the ladies, so you can handle what you have to do," Robert said as he shook DeVonte's hand and headed to the limo.

DeVonte watched the large limo drive off, down the driveway until it disappeared. He then walked over to his Escalade, and opened the driver's side door and hit the gate remote, attached to the sun visor. Once the gate was closed, he entered the house and walked towards the kitchen where the guys where still hanging out and announced that the women were gone. Mike and Rick started to make the phone calls that DeVonte asked them to do. DeVonte then asked Jason and Dennis to head out front, and await his return near the Escalade, as he headed upstairs and quickly returned with two large Gucci duffle bags. Dennis and Jason looked at the bags, but didn't even bother to ask what was in it, because they really didn't want to know.

DeVonte tossed Dennis the keys to the SUV, so he could drive and tossed the two duffle bags in the rear cargo space. He then climbed in the front passenger seat, while Jason sat behind him in the second row. Dennis slowly drove down the driveway towards the gate as DeVonte reached up to hit the remote to open the gate.

Once DeVonte and his two boys, made it out his front gate. He noticed the white van marked exterminator was nowhere in sight.

"Okay, ladies where to first?" Robert asked as he turned down the music and rolled down the divider that gave the passengers their privacy to hear instructions as he reached the main road.

"Wingate Mall please," Erica said as she poured herself a glass of Patron and Pineapple juice from the fully stocked bar.

"Anywhere you want to take us Mister Billy Dee," Doreen said as she giggled as the scent of Robert cologne traveled towards the back of the limo.

"Okay, Wingate's it is young ladies. Enjoy the bar, the music and the ride," Robert said as he cracked a smile to Doreen's comment and turned the stereo back up to party volume.

Everybody for a minute got silent as they looked at Doreen. She actually said what they all was thinking about Robert. He resembled the actor and damn near sounded like him too.

"Don't be starting no shit, Doreen! That man looks like he doesn't play," Stacy said.

"That man is fine! He could be my Sugar daddy anytime he wants to," Doreen said as she extended her glass for Erica to make her a drink.

"I, second that girl. There's nothing more better than an older man, who keeps himself looking dapper and smelling good. Plus, you see his hands all iced out with diamonds?" Stacey said as she looked at Erica whom just smiled and shook her head.

"Yeah he definitely has some swagger to him. And, I noticed that iced out wedding band on his ringer," Erica replied.

"Shit, a Sugar Daddy like him keeps a wife on the side, a pocket full of money and a bottle of blue power pills on deck," Doreen said as she put her glass up to make a toast.

"Shhh! Before he hear us and think he has a car load of freaks back here. For all we know, he could've put mickeys in these bottles and take us somewhere fuck and kill us once we pass out," Alexis said with a scared look on her face, because Robert looked like as if he was a pimp in his younger days.

Everyone got silent for a minute, until Erica burst out laughing as the others joined in.

"Damn Bitch, you almost fucked up my high," Doreen said as the limo continued to travel to their Mall. They continued to party until they reached the mall about forty-five minutes later. All the girls were a little tipsy as they were escorted out the limo by Robert.

Robert then handed each one of them his business card so they could call him for any reason as he waited on them.

After he escorted the young ladies to the entrance of the mall, he held the door as each one entered just before he returned to the limo and pulled into a parking spot nearby. Once he had the limo parked, he then exited the front of the limo and then climbed in the back of the limo to stretch out, make a few phone calls and watch some television via satellite.

Erica and the girls walked the entire mall as they explored and visited many high-end stores like Gucci Louis Vuitton, Chanel, etc. All eyes were on them as they walked through the mall looking like true divas to the fullest. Erica picked herself up a nice Fannie Pack and wallet from Gucci and purchased all her friends a nice size bottle of Flower bomb from Neiman Marcus as a small memento with the money DeVonte had given her. On the way to the spa after an hour of walking around, they bypassed the florist located on the ground level that was shipping out a large order at the time. The scent of the attractive fully bloomed purple and white roses perfumed the whole first level.

Wow! I could only wonder who the lucky lady is, that has her man loving her like that to send all of them pretty roses her way. I already know I'm very lucky to have DeVonte in my life, but if he ever sent me flowers like that, I'm gonna suck his dick all night. Erica thought to herself as she cracked a smile as she stood there and watched two delivery men load many dozens onto the truck, while her friends walked ahead of her.

Erica and her friends finally arrived at the entrance of TIA's. TIA's, a well-known spa, happened to be one of the biggest in the state of New Jersey. The spa practically takes up the whole lower level of the mall, and was located a few doors away from the florist. The spa was designed and decked with elaborate Asian artifacts and was very spacious inside to accommodate just about one hundred and fifty occupants. Once inside, Erica and her friends stopped at the front clerk's desk. Erica paid for a package deal that included: body scrub, facial, manicure, pedicure, and massage for her party of five courtesy of DeVonte.

After she paid for the package and received a discount for the party of five, they quickly strolled towards the locker rooms to secure their property and immediately hit the showers, just before they treated themselves to the sixty-minute body scrub. After the body scrub, they all went on to get an hour message from some muscular masseuse TIA's had assigned to the staff at the spa. Concluding their spa treatment, the girls had facials, manicures, and pedicures before venturing back to the locker rooms. The girls then went to the Jacuzzi for cheese, glasses of wine and assorted slices of fruit.

"Pull up, to that pizza shop right there!" DeVonte instructed Dennis as they road down Howard Boulevard out in Mount Arlington, New Jersey. Dennis pulled over and DeVonte quickly jumped out and retrieved the two duffel bags from the rear cargo space of the SUV.

"I need you two muscular black men to stand outside of the car, while I go inside and handle my business," he said as he observed two old school looking Italian mob wise guy types sitting out front of the parlor playing a game of cards.

"No problem Dee! We got you," Dennis said as both he and Jason stepped out the vehicle and leaned on the front grill as DeVonte closed the rear cargo space and bypassed them to head inside of the shop.

DeVonte walked up to the two guys sitting out front, just before walking inside the pizza parlor.

"Joey! Freddie! Como voi ragazzi facendo oggi(Joey! Freddie! How are you today?)?" DeVonte said as he switched over the duffle bags to his left hand, and gave them both a handshake.

"Good, Good" The two wise guys said as they waved DeVonte inside of the pizza parlor, while focusing on the two guys DeVonte had standing next to his big ole Cadillac. Once inside, DeVonte met up with his contract, who went by the name of Mikey Knuckles.

Before Dennis and Jason knew it, DeVonte was heading back towards them carrying the same two duffle bags, that he eventually tossed in the second-row passenger seat behind the driver's seat. He then instructed Dennis to get in the front passenger seat, because he was going to drive back himself and take a shortcut. Jason climbed back in the rear where he was sitting before as he stared at the two duffle bags as they rolled away.

DeVonte wasted no time in getting back home as he traveled a different route than he did to get there. Once he reached home, DeVonte jumped out of his SUV and grabbed his two bags and quickly entered the house. Dennis and Jason followed him in but got distracted by the sound of the basketball bouncing on the court, where Mike and Rick where playing game of one on one. They walked onto the court as they watched the two going at it like they were playing for the NBA title.

While DeVonte was upstairs in one of his rooms unloading his duffle bags that was filled with cash, he received a call from the delivery guy that worked at the florist, that he placed an order of purple and white long stem roses and petals with.

The caller informed him, that he was just outside his gate and needed to gain entry. DeVonte then stopped what he was doing and entered his bedroom and looked on his surveillance monitor. After he had confirmed it was the florist, he then hit the entry button for the gate and left the gate open. He pulled out his cell phone and called Dennis and asked him to open the front door to let the delivery guy in.

Dennis followed up on DeVonte request of him and instructed the delivery guy to leave everything in the foyer, Dennis tipped the guy as he brought in the last of the delivery.

"Damn! My boy is going all out! Look at all these muthafuckin roses," Dennis said to himself as he was also impressed with the delivery. DeVonte came downstairs after he finished with unloading his bags and the cash in a safe in one of his many rooms upstairs. He looked at his watch and started to head downstairs to see what everybody was up to.

"Where's everybody else at?" DeVonte asked as he only saw Dennis standing around looking at the roses.

"Rick and that fool Mike in there balling, while Jason just spectating," Dennis said as he picked up the large container containing purple rose peddles and handed it to DeVonte. He was glad to see that his delivery was there and on schedule. He took the large container with the rose petals in it from Dennis and asked him to help get the rest of the roses upstairs up to his bedroom. Dennis helped him get all the roses upstairs then went back downstairs to join the other guys on the Basketball court.

DeVonte left instructions for Nicole on his nightstand, in regard to where he wanted the roses and peddles placed. He figured the whole set-up, would blow her mind. Once he was done, he headed down to join the fellas on the basketball court.

"Yo, I got next," DeVonte said as he watched his boys playing a two on two half court.

"Man, you better save your energy for later brother. We don't want to see you get hurt, before your big night," Rick said as he played some tight defense on Mike.

"Yeah Dee, go get some rest! After you pop that question to Erica tonight, Yo old ass gonna need all the energy you could get, to make it through the night," Jason jokingly said while talking out of breath. DeVonte just laughed as he then pointed at Jason.

"Check this fool out; You call me an old ass? When Rick needs a fucking oxygen mask, to breathe right now," DeVonte said causing everyone to laugh. "Anyway, our limo will be here by seven, so finish up and wash your asses," DeVonte said as he put up his middle finger to his friends and headed out of the basketball court. He headed back to his bedroom and entered his walk-in closet to pick his outfit for the night. Once he selected what he wanted to wear, he laid it across the chaise he had in his sitting area. He then took a few photos of the layout he did for Erica with his iPhone to he could show the fellas later.

"Girl, what time are we heading to MAJOR SOULS tonight? Because these finger snacks, isn't doing anything for a big strong girl like myself," Doreen asked Erica as they chilled out next to the Jacuzzi.

"Oh shit! We got to be there at eight. Let me call Mister Robert and let him know we should be ready in a few," Erica said as she removed her cell phone from her robe she was wearing. "We need to be back at DeVonte's, at least by six, so we can get prepared," Erica continued.

Robert dozed off, while awaiting the girls. But was quickly awakened, by the ring of his cell phone.

"Hello, Mister Robert, this is Erica. One of the young ladies you dropped off at the mall," Erica said.

"Hello, young lady. How can I help you?" Robert said as he wiped his sleepy eyes.

"It's getting close to five o'clock, so me and the girls will be down in a few. Are you still nearby?" Erica asked.

"Yes, I'm in the parking lot. I'll be at the entrance, I dropped you off at, when you get there," Robert informed her as he exited the rear of the limo and started to straighten himself up.

"Okay, thank you Mister Robert. See you in a few," Erica said just before they ended the call.

DeVonte and his boys were all getting themselves right for the night, the aroma of different colognes filled the air. Everyone was looking extra dapper for the night of enjoyment at MAJOR SOULS, as they all met up in the entertainment room.

"Dee, don't forget to bring the ring player. Because if you don't, the surprise will be over," Rick said as he leaned on the pool table. DeVonte then stuck his hand into the pocket of his slacks and removed a small crystal case. As he opened it the glare from the diamond nearly blinded everyone.

"Damn, DeVonte! That's ring has enough karats, to feed a lot of rabbits my brother. The center piece alone gotta be at least ten carats," Mike shouted out as he moved closer to get a better look. Mike did a little security back in the days for a jeweler in the diamond district and knew a little something about them. The diamond center piece was a flawless 10 karats and it sat on 14 karat gold setting with two karats diamonds surrounding it. As a diamond of the finest quality, it reflected the overhead light resembling a disco ball.

"Man, if she ever thought about saying no to your proposal, just wait until she see that motherfucker right there! You will hear Yes from her for the rest of your life," Dennis said as he started to laugh as well as DeVonte and the rest of the fellas. Their laughter was interrupted by DeVonte's cell phone ringing. He didn't recognize the number, but answered it anyway.

"Hello, DeVonte, this is Robert the Chauffeur," The caller said as DeVonte could hear an engine starting.

"Hey, Robert! What's up?" DeVonte replied as he looked at his watch.

"I just got a call from one of the young ladies named Erica, that picked up from your house. She told me that they're ready to be picked up from the mall. I guess, we will be heading back to your house soon, so they could get themselves ready for tonight," Robert said as he reached into his glove compartment to retrieve some Visine for his red eyes.

"Okay, thanks for the heads up, Robert. Me and the fellas are already dressed and chilling out, waiting on them to arrive, "DeVonte replied. "I'll see you, when you get here," DeVonte said as he looked at his watch.

"No problem, I'll see you in a few," Robert replied, just before they both hung up.

Before DeVonte knew it, the girls we're back at his house, ringing the doorbell. Rick made his way to the door and let them in.

"Damn! You look good, Rick," Stacey said as she looked him up and down, while inhaling his cologne. Erica and the other girls, nodded with approval.

"Thank you, lady. The guys are hanging out in the entertainment room," Rick replied as he pointed in the direction of the room, where the guys were at. All the women quickly headed to the room to see the fellas. They were impressed, said hello, then quickly headed upstairs to prepare for the night. Robert waited outside in the driveway, until everyone was ready.

Once the women were ready, everyone headed outside to the limo and got in. After loading the limo with passengers, Robert got in and drove off.

Like every other Saturday night, Major Souls was packed to the max. Everyone was there to check out the live entertainment. Reservations was necessary to enter, no one without a reservation was allowed to enter. You would have to check for Major Souls venue months in advance if you wanted to catch a performance of your favorite artist.

DeVonte's reserved VIP booth directly faced the stage, and would give him and his guest perfect view of all that was going down on the stage. Most of Major Souls occupants requesting that booth paid top dollar for the best VIP booth in the building.

Many celebrities have previously occupied this booth as well as the ones right near it and the owner had the walls decorated with many photos of herself posing with them. Since DeVonte had a great connect with the owner, it meant nothing to her to lose a few dollars for her good friend.

The Deejay at Major Souls was assigned to keep the records spinning until it was time for the entertainers to hit the stage. He played a variety of music for everyone to enjoy. For everyone whom attended these special Saturdays, it was a red-carpet event. People came dressed to impress and posed for photos inside as well as on the red carpet located out front. Since celebrity sighting was very popular, it was no shocker to see the paparazzi photographers lingering in the vicinity snapping shots at any given chance at the front entrance. A few hip-hop superstars have mentioned Major Souls in their songs and the venue was featured in three music videos by a few R&B Artist.

DeVonte and his friends arrived at Major Souls. Robert pulled up to the front to the valet booth, and quickly let everyone out. DeVonte's friends made their way down the red carpet, while DeVonte exchanged a few words with Robert, instructing him to go park the car, then join them inside. He then caught up with the rest of his friends, who were lingering on the red carpet until he joined them. They all headed in, bypassing two very tall bulky security guards whom where dressed in black suits standing next to the entrance.

Once inside, they were greeted by a hostess, who escorted them towards their reserved VIP section. DeVonte and his crew were very impressed, by the whole setup of their VIP section.

Damn! Nicole did her thing DeVonte thought to himself, as he admired the who scenery. The roses and balloons, were the perfect touch to make Erica's night, a real special one.

DeVonte, escorted Erica to her seat, kissed her on the cheek, excused himself, and walked off in search of Kim to thank her for giving him the best seats in the house. He wanted also wanted to shoot the breeze with her for a little bit to catch up on the latest news. As he started to search for her and approached the kitchen area, He bumped into Kim's husband Joseph, is a high-ranking Lieutenant Colonel in the New Jersey State Police Department as he exited the kitchen.

Joseph was not only Kim's husband, he was also her head of her security staff at the club/lounge in New Jersey.

After, just two years of dating, Kim and Joseph were married in Hawaii a few years ago. DeVonte participated in their wedding as one of the groom's man, as an emergency replacement for one of Joseph's family members, who couldn't make it. Ever since then, DeVonte and Joseph have been in contact over the phone from time to time or when DeVonte stops by to dine at the restaurant. Joseph gave DeVonte a New Jersey State Police business card, that had his name, rank, and contact number on it. DeVonte kept this card in his wallet just in case he got pulled over by a New Jersey State Trooper.

"Hey, what's up DeVonte? Are you ready, to make that lady of yours, day very special tonight?" Joseph said as he greeted DeVonte with a smile, hand shake and then a hug.

"Yeah, man. I'm trying to be like you my brother," DeVonte replied after Joseph released him from his big bear hug he had him in. Joseph started to laugh.

"If you only knew, you're about to sell your soul!" Joseph jokingly replied while shaking his head.

"Anyway, my young brother, let me go check on my staff. Kim's is in her office if you're looking for her, "Joseph said as he pointed towards the office door.

"Damn! It's extra packed in here tonight man! Did Kim get R. Kelly or Maxwell to perform in here tonight or what?" DeVonte jokingly asked as he observed Joseph adjust an ear piece in his ear.

"Yeah Right, DeVonte!" Joseph said while laughing. "Man, if that ever happen, I would really have to increase the security. She didn't book those guys, but I could tell you this DeVonte, the lead singer in the band we got booked for tonight, could sing with the best of them. You're going to enjoy yourself tonight, these guys are very talented," Joseph said just before transmitting something over his hidden Microphone. Whatever the transmission was, changed his whole attitude.

"DeVonte! I'll like to chat with you all night, but I have a small situation I have to attend to. You can go in Kim's office, and check on her. You already know how she is, she'll catch an attitude that you didn't reach out to her as soon as you arrived," Joseph said, referring to Kim being aware DeVonte arrived, via the surveillance cameras, she monitors from her office. Before he walked off in a hurry. DeVonte then knocked on the door and was told to enter by a female voice. He walked in and a very large IMac computer monitor on top of a desk and heard the sound of someone typing. He began to walk toward the computer monitor and spotted Kim sitting behind her desk. She was dressed in a very elegant navy-blue sequin dress and four-inch navy blue sequin red bottom heels.

"Well! Well! Well! Is that what the chefs are wearing these days?" DeVonte asked with a smile on his face. Kim looked away from the computer screen and started to smile from the sound of a familiar voice.

"Wow, Baby Boy! Look at you, Looking extra dapper tonight! And you smell almost as good as you look," Kim said as she looked her friend up and down. She then stood up from her desk and gave DeVonte a big hug and kiss on the cheek.

"Damn! I always said you clean up nicely. I'm not saying you don't look good any other time. But, when you get all dressed up! Damn! Erica is a lucky girl," Kim said as she hugged and sniffed the cologne from DeVonte's chest.

"Thank You, lady! You look kind of hot yourself. Joseph better look out," DeVonte jokingly replied as he was still trapped in Kim's arms. Kim then unleashed her hug and sat back down at her desk.

"Damn, your gonna need glasses, after gazing into that big ass monitor, after a while. Does it hurt your eyes?" DeVonte asked. Kim started to laugh. "How many inches is that anyway?" DeVonte continued as he looked at the big monitor on her desk.

"It's fifty inches," Kim responded.

"Wow, I didn't know they made them that big, I should invest in one.

"Yes, you should. Now DeVonte, you know I always try to do it big, because I like big things," Kim said with a flirtish smirk on her face, before bursting into laughter.

"You know what? I'm gonna leave that one alone. That's way too much information for me right now," DeVonte said as he started to laugh. Kim began to look at her computer monitor and began to type.

"Anyway! What's Up? Baby Boy," Kim asked her buddy of many years. Are you ready to take your relationship to another level with Erica tonight?" She continued to ask as she typed. DeVonte without hesitation nodded yes as he walked towards the roses, he sent Kim and gave them a good sniff.

"Ahh! These smells so good," DeVonte said referring to the roses he ordered. "I see you got the roses I sent you. I hope you like them?" DeVonte continued to say as he already knew the answer.

"You know damn well, I love them fool! What woman in her right mind wouldn't appreciate roses?" Kim responded, expecting some type of response. DeVonte just shrugged his shoulders.

Just as I thought, the cat got his tongue Kim thought to herself, when she realized, DeVonte was at a loss for words.

"I've seen everyone's reaction, once you guys arrived at your VIP section, it was priceless," Kim said as she pointed to her surveillance monitor. DeVonte then took a glance at the screen, spotted his table and watched Erica and everyone else interact.

"Damn, you eye hustled, my whole arrival? DeVonte Jokingly asked?

"I sure did, I even snapped a picture. You want to see it?" Kim Jokingly replied.

"What?!" DeVonte asked, as if he was amazed.

"I'm just joking fool. You ain't all that," Kim responded with a smile.

"Man, I was about to say," Denzel said, as he jokingly whipped his forehead, and started to stare at Erica in the monitor.

The way DeVonte started to gazed at Erica in the monitor, Kim knew he was in love.

"Ahh, look at you. That's so cute. You can't keep your eyes of her, not even for a second. Get your ass out my office, and join your lady and friends. I got work to do, nigga," Kim told her love-sick buddy. DeVonte then snapped out of his trance, walked over to Kim as she continued to sit at her desk, and gave her a hug. "Thanks again, for everything," DeVonte gracefully thanked her.

"You're welcome, my love," Kim replied. DeVonte quickly walked out of Kim's office, and headed back to his VIP section. Once DeVonte returned. Erica immediately, jumped up, gave him a big hug and kiss. She thanked him for the lovely scenery, he had arraigned.

"Babes, you walked off so fast, before I could tell you," Erica said after giving DeVonte a kiss.

"Tell me what?" DeVonte asked.

"How beautiful this set is. These roses, are so, out of this world," Erica said, as she continued to give DeVonte another kiss. They both then sat down, and held hands.

By this time, everyone in the place were settled in, and at their prospective seating location. All eyes were on DeVonte and company. Other patrons, were naturally hating on DeVonte's whole set up on the low. Men patrons wishing they presented their dinner date with the same scenery, and women patrons, wishing they had a dinner date that set up such a nice scenery for them. Some of the women, even stared over their dates shoulder, just to get a glimpse of DeVonte;

Wishing, they had a man, just like him.

The purple and white roses and balloons stood out like a touch of royalty. Making it the best area in entire place.

Appetizers of Hawaiian style pineapple glazed beef ribs, honey wings, buttery lobster tails, buffalo shrimps, fresh made dinner rolls and toss salad were served to DeVonte's table. The food was washed down by top shelf liquor, wine, champagne by all present in DeVonte's VIP. Robert, who had to remain sober for the safety of the clients, only sipped on ice tea. The main course of ginger lamb chops, asparagus, and garlic mash potatoes were quickly served after the small group demolished the delicious appetizers. It didn't take too long before they tore through the main course and digested it, just before the Live Band took the stage.

The lights slowly dimmed to the sounds of a drumline and the spotlight suddenly hit the stage as Kim magically appeared holding a microphone. Kim took it upon herself to MC every live event on Saturdays, whether it was music or comedy, she always introduced herself as the owner and head chef of MAJOR SOULS and always thanked everyone for coming out to dine and enjoy the live entertainment. The sequin dress she was wearing sparkled from the glare of the light, as her smile brightened up the whole room. Since tonight was a special night, before introducing the band, she arranged for the spotlight to be directed to DeVonte's VIP Section.

"I will like to send out a special shout out tonight to a very good friend of mine, DeVonte. Over the years he has been mentally supportive of me from the start of my dream to open up my own business. He pointed me in the right direction to pursue that dream, and schooled me on the politics that came along with it. He's here tonight along with his friends sitting with him over there. They all came out to tonight to show me some love and support as usual and I am so very happy that they're here, As well as the rest of you are here to witness me live my dream," Kim said as she pointed in DeVonte's direction as the crowd started to applaud.

DeVonte had no idea, that Kim would put him on blast like that. He just started to smile and waved to the crowd whom he could barely see due to the spot light on his face, while he blew a kiss in Kim's direction. The applause died down and Kim introduced the band just before making her way off the stage and over to DeVonte's table. Once she arrived, she embraced DeVonte once again, along with everyone else sitting there with a hug and kiss before taking a seat reserved for her at the table.

The band immediately began to rock the house with a variety of songs, by mixing their act with dance tunes along with ballads. The occupants in MAJOR SOULS where practically rocking in their seats as the band put on a great performance. After a number of songs performed by the band, it was nearly show time for DeVonte himself.

The leader singer of the band suddenly signaled members of his band, to stop the music. The whole club became silent.

"Good evening, ladies and gentlemen. My name is Smooth and this is my band **Blackk Ice**. We will be performing a very special request, for a very special lady in here tonight. Erica! This one, is from DeVonte," The lead singer announced as the band was about to perform "LADY IN MY LIFE" by Michael Jackson.

Erica whom was already leaning her head on DeVonte's broad shoulders at the time of announcement, was so overwhelmed that she screamed out.

"OH, MY GOD! I LOVE YOU BABES!" And kissed DeVonte on the lips as he turned his head towards her.

Erica had no idea of what was to happen next as the lead singer was coming towards the end of the song. DeVonte skillfully eased out of her grip, just before the lights went completely out and the music stopped. Suddenly a spot-light beamed down at DeVonte's table and captured DeVonte down on one knee holding a small crystal case in his hand. Erica jumped to her feet, basically because DeVonte scared the shit out of her as he grabbed onto her left hand. She then nearly went into shock once she realized what was about to happen as she looked down into the eyes of the love of her life.

Oh My God! a female within the crowd shouted as everyone else eyes widen. Erica's female buddies were all taking by surprise as their eyes began to water with joy.

DeVonte began to say the following words as the whole place grew silent, while anticipating the reaction of the soon to be fiancée of the man kneeling.

Erica, I had no idea from the first day we met

That God had sent me, what my heart and life truly desired.

Your beauty, Your heart, Your soul

The love you give, is so genuine

It's way beyond, any man's dream

Our past, were mere experiences to prepare us both for the destiny of our souls to join together

I am willing to give you, my everything

My life, My body, My soul, and all of my heart

I will embrace all of you, and cherish you as long as, I live

May our families become one, as we become one.

May our hearts pump to the same beat, and we breathe the

same air of life.

You are truly, the lady in my life

And I want us, to hold each other forever

Only letting death, bring us apart

And when, the almighty decides to remove one of us from this earth

May he allow our souls meet again

And continue to stay together, into eternity

I love you Erica.

Will you be, my life?

Will you be, my wife?

Will you, marry me?"

DeVonte asked, as he opened the crystal case he was holding and revealing that large sparkling ten karat diamond ring.

Major Souls was at a complete silence as the tears of joy began to run down Erica's cheeks whom was mesmerized by the gorgeous ring her man just presented to her. Everyone awaited the words "YES" to escape Erica's shaking lips as she dazed into DeVonte's eyes. Erica then kneeled down and held DeVonte by the head and looked deeper into his eyes that were beginning to tear up. Their friends among the many other on-lookers could visualize all the loyalty, kindness, and love that this woman could have giving to this and that his action was a reflection of her dedication of her love for him.

"Yes! I will love to be your wife, and spend the rest of my life with you," Erica shouted with tears of joy streaming down her face as she hugged DeVonte tightly and kissed him all over his face. Flashes from cellular phone and mini digital cameras began to flash, while the sound of cheers and applause erupted as DeVonte slid the ring onto Erica's finger while her hand shook uncontrollably. Suddenly envy began to flow through the veins of every woman in the place that wasn't married or engaged yet, while they witnessed Erica take a trip to cloud nine. Some of the women even looked at their boyfriends with the expression of hope on their face, that maybe one day he would make the same jester towards full commitment. The fellas that stood victim to the looks by their women, knew after this they would have to step up their game.

Once Erica had that gorgeous diamond ring placed on her finger, both her and DeVonte raised up from their knees and kissed as they held each other tightly as if no one else was in the room. A waiter soon appeared out of the darkness and rolled over a large platter containing red velvet cupcakes covered in purple and white icing to their VIP table. The large cupcakes spelled out the words **ENGAGED**. Erica was overwhelmed on how DeVonte expressed his love for her, so much that she became nearly speechless. She was having an outer body experience as she mentally watched herself from across the room. It didn't feel real to her, she felt as if she was only dreaming, until the sound of Champaign bottles popping brought her back within herself and to reality.

The lights came back on, and the band began to perform "For the lover in you," by Shalamar, as the crowd started rocking and singing along with the band. Kim looked at her watch then congratulated DeVonte and Erica with a hug. She then posed in a few pictures with the newly engaged couple and their guests for the night. After all the hugging and kissing, Kim made her way back to her office. The waiter awaited Kim's departure, then began to serve DeVonte and his party of friends the cupcakes and was then instructed by DeVonte to serve the rest to the other occupants in MAJOR SOULS whom may want one. The band rocked on as the dance floor opened and was flooded with occupant's ready to get their boogie on.

Robert for his age was very smooth on the dance floor and had a crowd from around him while he danced with Doreen,

Alexis and Chantel. They cheered him on as he broke into **THE SLOP**, a famous dance that was said to have generated in Philadelphia and commonly seen performed by actor Sherman Hemsley as George Jefferson in the 1970's hit sitcom The Jefferson, Hemsley himself, was also a Philly native. DeVonte watched with amazement on how the old player still had the charisma to woo the ladies and only could wish he could be so smooth.

As the night, out at Major Souls was coming close to an end, DeVonte and his quest were feeling a buzz from whatever they were sipping on, and it showed. Robert, who remained sober, knowing it was his job and responsibility to get everyone home safely, escorted DeVonte and his guest to the limo and loaded them into it. After the last guest entered the limo, Robert quickly started up the car and turned on some sounds for the passengers to enjoy as he drove off headed to DeVonte's estate. The sounds of R. Kelly voice escaped the speakers and the party was just beginning as they made use of the bar inside of the limo.

DeVonte and Erica sat in the limo with their arms wrapped around one another, as they both looked at their friends enjoying themselves and having a good time. They both imagined to themselves on how the reception would be after their wedding. DeVonte began to smile, as he thought and was anticipating Erica's reaction in regard to the other surprise he had awaiting her in his bedroom.

Doreen could see the joy in Erica's eye as she continued to stare at the happy couple. Her eyes gazed at the nice rock DeVonte put on her friend finger with envy, as well as every other single woman in the room. She imagined herself being the one being proposed to by a man of her dreams. A prince charming dipped in chocolate vowing to give her the world was all she could think of as she looked on flowed through her bloodstream, and she felt she deserved what DeVonte had given Erica. She wasn't alone with that thought, due to half the women even the one's already married, at Major Souls whom witness the proposal felt the same way.

Where did Erica find this guy? What does he do for a living to spend money like it's no object? The big house! The Nice Cars! The clothes! The everything! Were The thought that ran through Doreen's mind as she just leaned back in her seat and sipped on her glass until the limo came to a stop.

Robert pulled up in DeVonte's driveway and parked the limo in front of the house. He then exited the vehicle and walked over to the passenger door and opened it to let all of his passengers out. As DeVonte exited the vehicle, he reached into his pocket with one hand in search of his home key chain and deactivated the home security alarm with the remote attached to it, as he held Erica's hand with his free hand. He leaned over and gave Erica a soft kiss on the lips, as the other guests started to head into his house.

"Babe, let me speak to Robert, and I will join you in the Master suite in a few minutes," DeVonte said while looking Erica in her beautiful eyes.

"Oh okay! I guess I will be impatiently waiting on you Babes. Please don't take too long my love," Erica replied as she gazed at him with passionate desire and spoke in a provocative manner, just before she walked away and towards the front door. DeVonte watched Erica as she slowly walked away and knew once she entered she would see the rose petals he had laid out for her leading to his bedroom, so he rushed the conversation with Robert as he walked towards the driver.

"Robert, I'm gonna call you so we could arrange some business together in regard to my wedding planning for limo service among other things," DeVonte said as he reached into his pocket to retrieve some cash and slipped Robert a tip during a handshake. Robert opened up his hand to find five hundred dollar bills rolled up.

"Thank you, for the very generous tip Young Blood. Make sure you contact me in regard to the wedding, but what do you mean among other things?" Robert asked as he placed his tip in his pocket.

"Connects, Robert. Connects," DeVonte Responded he winked his eye and smiled.

"Say no more; we will talk" Robert replied as he shook DeVonte's hand one more time before he headed back to the driver side of the limo and entered it. DeVonte remained out front as he watched the limo drive down his drive way and out the gate. He then hit the remote to close the gate located on his key chain and looked up into the sky and stared at the bright full moon.

Erica entered the house while DeVonte talked to Robert, observing DeVonte's buddies and her friends just standing in the foyer awaiting her to enter the house. She could see tears of joy and smiles on her girlfriends faces as she looked down onto the floor and spotted the rose petals covering it.

The petals trailed from the front entrance, to and up the staircase, until it reached DeVonte's bedroom. It was a beautiful sight, that temporarily paralyzed her with joy, as if she forward, until Doreen shouted out and brought here back to reality.

"Wake up girl! You better go see what's at the end of that rainbow, before I run up there ahead of you!" As all her friends burst into laughter. Erica then kicked off her heels and took off running so fast that she nearly slipped on the marble floor before reaching the staircase. Once at the staircase she darted up the staircase very quickly until she reached the top. She followed the trail of rose petals down the corridor that led her to DeVonte's bedroom.

Once inside she turned on the lights and observed red rose petals in the shape of a heart on DeVonte's bed. In the center of the heart shape of rose petals was a package wrapped in gold with a gold bow. Erica immediately dived onto the bed and proceeded to open the package.

Her eyes widened as she observed the gift package that

contained two velvet gifts cases inside of it. She opened up the long and narrow case first. The sparkles from the diamond on the bracelet mesmerized her. She wanted to scream, when she saw that the diamonds on the bracelet were similar in size to the ring on her finger. Her hands trembled as she placed it the bracelet on her wrist. Amazed to see her next package was labeled ROLEX, she slowly removed a gold Rolex watch and looked at the inscription under the time piece that read the following:

"Forever, Mr.& Mrs. Denzel DeVonte Major"

THE END

www.ingramcontent.com/pod-product-compliance
Lightning Source LLC
Chambersburg PA
CBHW051311250626
47155CB00007B/2282